Christmas Treasures

The Cape Light Titles

CAPE LIGHT

HOME SONG

A GATHERING PLACE

A NEW LEAF

A CHRISTMAS PROMISE

THE CHRISTMAS ANGEL

A CHRISTMAS TO REMEMBER

A CHRISTMAS VISITOR

A CHRISTMAS STAR

A WISH FOR CHRISTMAS

ON CHRISTMAS EVE

CHRISTMAS TREASURES

A SEASON OF ANGELS

The Angel Island Titles

THE INN AT ANGEL ISLAND

THE WEDDING PROMISE

A WANDERING HEART

Christmas Treasures

THOMAS KINKADE

& KATHERINE SPENCER

BERKLEY BOOKS, NEW YORK
A Parachute Press Book

THE BERKLEY PUBLISHING GROUP
Published by the Penguin Group
Penguin Group (USA) Inc.
375 Hudson Street, New York, New York 10014, USA
Penguin Group (Canada), 90 Eglinton Avenue East, Suite 700, Toronto, Ontario M4P 2Y3, Canada
(a division of Pearson Penguin Canada Inc.) • Penguin Books Ltd., 80 Strand, London WC2R 0RL,
England • Penguin Group Ireland, 25 St. Stephen's Green, Dublin 2, Ireland (a division of Penguin
Books Ltd.) • Penguin Group (Australia), 250 Camberwell Road, Camberwell, Victoria 3124, Australia
(a division of Pearson Australia Group Pty. Ltd.) • Penguin Books India Pvt. Ltd., 11 Community
Centre, Panchsheel Park, New Delhi—110 017, India • Penguin Group (NZ), 67 Apollo Drive,
Rosedale, Auckland 0632, New Zealand (a division of Pearson New Zealand Ltd.) • Penguin Books
(South Africa) (Pty.) Ltd., 24 Sturdee Avenue, Rosebank, Johannesburg 2196, South Africa

Penguin Books Ltd., Registered Offices: 80 Strand, London WC2R 0RL, England

This is a work of fiction. Names, characters, places, and incidents either are the product of the authors'
imaginations or are used fictitiously, and any resemblance to actual persons, living or dead, business
establishments, events, or locales is entirely coincidental. The publisher does not have any control over
and does not assume any responsibility for author or third-party websites or their content.

PUBLISHING HISTORY
Berkley hardcover edition / November 2011
Berkley trade paperback edition / November 2012

Berkley trade paperback ISBN: 978-0-425-25320-5

Library of Congress Cataloging-in-Publication Data

Kinkade, Thomas, (date)–
Christmas treasures / Thomas Kinkade and Katherine Spencer.—1st ed.
p. cm.
ISBN 978-0-425-24356-5
1. Clergy—Fiction. 2. Life change events—Fiction. 3. Intergenerational relations—Fiction.
4. Faith—Fiction. 5. Cape Light (Imaginary place)—Fiction. 6. New England—Fiction.
7. Christmas stories. I. Spencer, Katherine, (date)– II. Title.
PS3561.I534C484 2011
813'.54—dc22
2011016467

PRINTED IN THE UNITED STATES OF AMERICA

10 9 8 7 6 5 4 3 2 1

This book is dedicated with love and gratitude to my aunt,
Marion Giordano—
her beautiful, loving heart encourages
and inspires all who know her.

—Katherine Spencer

DEAR READERS

I am so pleased that we are again celebrating another Christmas together in Cape Light. But this year, Christmas may not feel like Christmas to many of our friends there. A crisis prevents Reverend Ben from presiding over the Christmas season as he has done for so many years. In his place is Isabel Lawrence, a young woman who seems so very different from their beloved minister. Meanwhile, Reverend Ben, who has always been the one to comfort and counsel others in their time of need, is finding that he may be the one in need of spiritual guidance.

And then there are the Rowans, who come to Cape Light looking for a chance to rebuild their broken lives. Richard and Regina have lost their home and their jobs. Now they're on the verge of losing each other. Can they find the time and peace necessary to celebrate the birth of the Lord—and give their children a joyous

Christmas? And can they heal old scars and rekindle the love that once drew them together?

We also meet the widower Jacob Ferguson and his teenage son, Max. Max is a good, smart kid but his mother's death has left him hollow and aching. Like many kids, he acts out, but Max makes the mistake of acting out in the church and damaging its beloved interior. It's up to Reverend Isabel to find a way to reach an angry teenager and soothe an outraged congregation.

Certainly we can all relate to those moments when troubles weigh us down and seem overwhelming, times when it is hard to look for the divine inspiration that is always there. Perhaps that's why the good Lord has given us the annual miracle of Christmas—a season filled with the spirit of hope and renewal.

The people of Cape Light will discover as we all do that, despite hardships, Christmas has the unique ability to open our hearts with its many treasures. We share them with you now, and hope that you, too, will be blessed by the joys of the holiday season.

Share the Light,
Thomas Kinkade

Christmas Treasures

CHAPTER ONE

❦

*B*EN PULLED BACK THE BEDROOM CURTAIN SUNDAY morning to find the world covered with snow, as if some unseen hand had lovingly draped a sleeping child with a soft white blanket. The lawn and garden behind the parsonage, the stone walls and the roof of the old barn, were all snugly tucked in.

He stared out at the veil of flakes that continued to fall, drifting through the bare branches. It was the first snow of the winter, just a few days after Thanksgiving. The forecast had predicted only a few inches, but it looked as though more than a foot had piled up out there already.

Winter had arrived, a New England winter, which was not for the fainthearted. He often wondered if he and Carolyn were getting too old for this merciless kind of cold.

But this morning, instead of fantasizing about tropical vacations or retiring in year-round sunshine, Ben was caught up in the

1

perennial thrill that always came with the first snowfall. It was the same wonder he had felt as a boy staring out his bedroom window down in Gloucester.

Sixty winters later, here I am, still amazed by the sight, the glory of God's handiwork. The flakes fell so slowly, such a long journey down from the clouds. How many millions or billions of tiny, intricately shaped flakes did it take to make those drifts? How long did it take them to travel all the way down here?

He was still awed by the deep quiet of the morning and the pearly light that reflected into the room, a special light that told him what he would find outside before he had even pulled back the curtain. He was still humbled in his heart by this ordinary, extra-ordinary miracle.

He glanced over at Carolyn, fast asleep, the quilt curled over her shoulder. He felt the urge to wake her. But they'd been on babysitting duty last night for their grandchildren—two well-behaved but active kids—and she deserved another hour or so of sleep before she followed him to church that morning. Sunday was a workday for him, the most important of the week, and he had to get to church early, well before the service started.

Ben trudged off to shower and dress, his thoughts turning to practical matters. He didn't look forward to shoveling out his driveway and cleaning off his and Carolyn's cars, then at church, clearing a path from the parking lot to the sanctuary. He didn't feel awed or humbled by that expectation.

Carl Tulley, the church sexton, was away for the weekend. The deacons would do most of the job, he knew, but there still had to be a clear path in case an older congregation member came to church early for the Bible study class or to help set up the coffee hour or flowers. Ben would never forgive himself if someone took a bad fall, so even the job of snow removal fell to the minister at times at so small a church.

Ben was used to serving at both the highest and lowest posts by now. As it should be, he often thought. He had never been the type of minister to put himself above the congregation. Though he sometimes wondered how long he would be able to keep up the pace, to have the stamina needed for this multifaceted job. He wasn't a young man or even a middle-aged one anymore.

Ben was reminded of that fact once again soon after arriving at church. Prepared with a snow shovel from the trunk of his car, he industriously began to dig his way from the parking lot to the big wooden sanctuary doors.

About halfway to his goal, he straightened up and rubbed his back, then took a deep breath. Or tried to. The ice-cold air pierced his lungs and he felt choked, as if he could hardly take in enough air. He was breathing so heavily from the exercise that he opened his overcoat and even loosened his scarf and tie. *Silly to get so winded after just a little shoveling,* he thought. *It's never bothered me before. Clearly, I need more exercise.*

Carolyn was so much better at that. She went for power walks every morning, rain or shine. He did admire her dedication—usually while seated comfortably in the kitchen, enjoying a second cup of coffee and scanning the newspaper headlines and sports pages.

Too much coffee this morning, he decided. It was catching up with him. His forehead felt clammy; he even felt light-headed. He took a wheezy breath and leaned heavily on the shovel.

"Morning, Reverend." Ben turned at the sound of heavy boots crunching on the path. Tucker Tulley, the church's head deacon, walked toward him. "You didn't have to do all that work. I called around. A few of us are coming early to shovel."

"I knew you'd have it covered, Tucker. I just wanted to clear a small path to the front doors. Just in case. There's that early Bible study class now. Sophie Potter and Digger Hegman both belong," he added, naming two of the church's senior members. "And it is the first Sunday of Advent. There should be a large attendance today."

"Usually," Tucker agreed, "though some people will stay home in this weather."

"Yes, that's true," Ben said. Not too many, he hoped. He had prepared a special sermon, the first of a new theme for the season of Advent. It was such a relief to move into the Christmas season. He got tired of preaching the long stretch of Sundays after Pentecost. Ordinary Time, it was called in the church calendar. Ordinary indeed. Not too much happening in the months from June to November, no holidays like Easter and Christmas to hang his preaching on.

He loved the Christmas season for many reasons, not the least of them being that it was an easy time to come up with meaningful, relevant themes for his sermons.

"You leave the rest of this to us." Tucker reached over and took the shovel out of his hands. "You ought to go inside now, Reverend. You look like the cold is getting to you."

Tucker stared at him curiously and Ben felt self-conscious. He took off his cap and mopped his forehead with his handkerchief, though the temperature was below freezing.

"Are you all right, Reverend?"

Ben pocketed his handkerchief. "I'm fine, thanks. Just overdid it a little. I have to get in better shape. It will be my New Year's resolution . . . as usual," he murmured.

"I know what you mean. Two steps forward, three steps back. Now that the holidays are coming—watch out, diet!" Tucker shook his head and patted his middle. He was impressively fit for a man in his fifties, Ben thought. As a police officer, he was obliged to keep in shape. Unlike a minister.

"Thanksgiving was the kickoff," Ben agreed. "Maybe that's it. That extra slice of pumpkin pie has slowed me down." Ben's tone was light, but the truth was, he hadn't felt quite right since the family's Thanksgiving Day feast, held at his daughter Rachel's home this year. He had gone to bed that night with a tight feeling that had persisted now for days. Almost as if a weight pressed down on his chest. It would abate for a while, then return—sometimes in the middle of the night, waking him from a sound sleep. He felt that way this morning, too. He must have taken half a bottle of antacids by now.

I'll eat very lightly today, he promised himself. *Just soup and crackers for lunch and dinner. That should set me right.*

"Good luck, Tucker. It's all yours."

Ben headed into the building, where he was greeted by a blast of warm air. He quickly made his way to his office, feeling as if he couldn't shed his coat and muffler fast enough. He hung both on the coatrack, then sat down heavily in the chair behind his desk. He did feel dizzy. The room was spinning.

Guess I overdid it out there. I was working too quickly, worrying about getting the job done.

What was it you were supposed to do if you felt faint? Put your head between your knees? Ben stared down at his knees for a moment. He would feel silly doing that. He took a few deep breaths and waited until the mild spell of vertigo passed.

Then he took out his reading glasses and opened the folder on his desk that held his sermon. He typed out his notes every week, though he usually didn't deliver the sermon exactly as it was written. He jumped around at times or embellished certain sections.

There was an art to delivering a sermon that moved your listeners both emotionally and spiritually. You needed to catch their attention using humor or drama, bringing in stories from real life, from history, and from the Bible, of course. But you needed to relate the Bible stories so that they seemed real and relevant, so that the audience could feel themselves standing in the place of Job or the Good Samaritan. Or even Jesus. Facing the challenges, making the hard decisions of conscience, suffering the consequences or reaping the rewards.

Sometimes events in the news helped bring the message home, or even statistics and surveys. Ben had learned to draw from many sources, weaving it all together into a cohesive design.

One would think that after all these years, writing a sermon would come automatically. But it was still a challenge, a moment of anxiety before he began, knowing what he wanted to say but not quite the best way to say it. Wondering if the idea was complex and meaningful enough—or too superficial or obscure.

Sometimes you struck a home run without even trying. Sometimes—not often, but there were still rare occasions—Ben could tell he'd totally struck out. The expressions on the faces of his congregation said it all.

Some ministers had changed the course of history with their sermons—sparked revolutions, overturned despots, and helped to free the oppressed. Ben felt honored to march in those ranks, even as a lowly foot soldier, bringing up the rear. But each week he tried earnestly to introduce some fresh new ideas to the little stone church on the green. It was a serious responsibility. And a privilege.

Delivering a sermon every Sunday was the most obvious and perhaps most important part of his job. Though there was much more to the job, for better or worse, ministers were often judged solely on that ten or twelve minutes in a Sunday service when they stood behind the pulpit.

He did enjoy hearing other preachers and had even gone to seminars to sharpen his style. He might be more emphatic, more dramatic. Tell more jokes or serious, true-life stories. Weave in more personal experiences, a confessional, soul-baring style. He might do a lot of things up there.

Finally, he just did the best he could, speaking to the congregation as he would a circle of friends: from his heart. He'd been preaching at this church for more than twenty-five years. Seminars or not, he wasn't going to change much at this stage of the game. Ben felt pretty sure that most of the congregation wouldn't want him to, either.

He settled himself again in his seat and took a deep breath, forcing himself to focus on the pages, practicing his delivery in his mind's eye. He usually rehearsed at least once in the sanctuary, but this morning he decided that reading it through silently would suffice. He felt too tired for a full-blown dress rehearsal. The service began at ten, and now it was just a few minutes before nine.

He could hear the Bible study class discussing the day's reading in the room next to his office. The sound was music to his ears. It told him that his church was thriving, the members intellectually and spiritually seeking to grow their relationships with God. A minister could lead them, even inspire them, but he couldn't do it all for them. Sometimes Ben felt as if that's what people did expect of him. It was a heavy burden, feeling responsible for the spiritual lives of so many.

Maybe that's why I feel this heaviness in my chest. It was the workload, which got even heavier during the holidays. His responsibilities as minister were catching up with him.

Or perhaps he had a chest cold coming on? He had to laugh at his own choices.

Then he did something he had rarely done in his entire tenure. He took off his suit jacket and stretched out on the couch in his office. He'd rested on this couch from time to time to let his mind wander while he wrote or sorted out some sticky problem. But never on a Sunday morning before a service.

He suddenly felt so depleted, his arms and legs weak, almost limp. There seemed to be no other choice but to rest. *Just a few minutes,* Ben told himself, *before I put on the cassock and get out there.*

He closed his eyes but felt unable to take a deep, calming breath. His chest felt tight again, that squeezing feeling. He was definitely coming down with something. What a bother. He didn't have time to get sick right now.

There was a meeting of the Christmas Fair committee after the coffee hour. The women who ran it, like Sophie Potter and Vera Plante, knew exactly what to do, but he was still obliged to sit in, at least at the start. After that, another short meeting with the parents and children involved in the annual Christmas pageant. An exercise much like herding cats. But somehow the children always learned their parts and songs on time, and everything came out just lovely.

After those obligations, he promised himself, he would go home, put his feet up, and watch a football game. He wouldn't even pick up the phone unless it was an emergency.

Ben closed his eyes and drifted off for a few minutes, but he was too uncomfortable to fall asleep completely. He still felt a bit short of breath, though he had finished shoveling nearly an hour ago.

He rose slowly and put on his white robes and scarf. The color of his scarf this Sunday was a blue-purple, marking the start of Advent. He checked his appearance in the full-length mirror on the back of his office door, then smoothed his beard and hair—what was left of it, he noted wryly—with a comb.

Out in the hallway, he heard the familiar sounds of Sunday morning activity: the choir rehearsing, children laughing and chasing one another, friends greeting each other as they entered the building, commenting on the snow, of course. Was that Carolyn's voice he heard? Possibly. She was going to play some special music during the offertory, part of a piano concerto by Mozart.

The voices on the other side of the door beckoned, tugging him into the flow of this sacred day, but he held himself back a moment. He took a deep breath and closed his eyes, sending up a silent prayer, the prayer he said every Sunday morning before he left his office.

"Lord, please bless all who gather to worship and hear your word this morning. I thank you for allowing me to be your instrument and humbly ask that you let your wisdom and love speak through me, so that I may bless and comfort the troubled, seeking hearts here today. Please help me to lift the spirits of the faithful and spread your message of peace and love. I ask this in the name of your son, Jesus Christ. Amen."

Then Ben opened his office door and stepped out into the hall. The snow had stopped and bright sunlight streamed through the corridor windows. He squinted and smiled at familiar faces.

"Some snow, huh, Reverend? They said two or three inches, not two feet." Sam Morgan was walking by with his family, his older son, Darrell, and younger son, Tyler, by his side. His wife, Jessica, was not far behind with their little girl, Lily Rose.

"A few people at our house were begging me to take them sledding," Sam reported, glancing at his two boys. "But I managed to hold them off until this afternoon."

"I was tempted myself," Ben replied with a smile.

"I was, too. The sleds are already in the trunk," Sam admitted.

Sam had grown up in the church and had raised his own family here as well. His wife Jessica's mother and sister were also longtime members of the congregation, though Jessica and Sam had spent their childhoods on very different sides of town. But all had turned out well, unlike the original Romeo and Juliet, Ben reflected as he watched Jessica gathering her Sunday school class.

A little girl, about six years old, Ben guessed, was seated on a bench, tugging off her large, red snow boots. She looked up as Ben approached and tugged on Jessica's sleeve. "Would you ask him, Mrs. Morgan? You said that you would," she whispered.

Jessica bent to help with the boots. "You can ask Reverend Ben, Christie. It's your question," she said gently.

Christie shook her head, the braids on either side flipping around like rotary blades.

"All right, I'll ask," Jessica said. "Christie has a question for you, Reverend. I didn't know the answer."

"Really?" Reverend Ben smiled and readied himself. Children came up with some very provocative theological queries. Some real stumpers had come his way through the years, ranging from "Does God eat and sleep?" to "Does He have any pets?"

"Some older kids were talking about making snow angels," Jessica explained. "Christie thought that meant that there are angels who fly around when it snows and help people. She says you can't see them because they're all white and glimmery and have lacy dresses. Like the snowflakes. She said we should ask you. You'd know."

Reverend Ben considered the theory. "Snow angels, huh?"

Christie nodded. She stared straight ahead, afraid to meet his eyes.

"I've never heard of those kind of snow angels, Christie. But that doesn't mean they don't exist," he hurried to add. "The Bible tells us that angels are messengers, sent to do God's work here on earth. God is watching over us all the time and sending helpers. You never know who they might be or how they might look. Old or young, rich or poor, some might be snow angels. I can't say that's impossible."

Christie looked pleased by his answer. Jessica did, too. "Thanks, Reverend. I'm sure she'll bring it up in class this morning. Now I have an answer for the other children."

"Sounds like the makings of a lively discussion. Let me know how it goes," Ben said lightly.

Maybe the snow angels will help me this morning, he thought as he headed for the sanctuary. He could use a little extra spirit to help him through the service. He just didn't feel like himself today.

But ministers couldn't call in sick. Especially not on Sunday. In all his years at this church, he had never once missed a service due to illness. Why, he'd stood up at the pulpit with toothaches and backaches and a fever of 103 degrees. One summer, covered with blackfly bites after a camping trip; another time with poison ivy. He'd even preached wearing a cast on one leg after a fall down the stairs, and with a patch over one eye after an unfortunate poke with the end of a fishing pole.

No, sir, this minister did not call in sick, and he was not about to start this morning.

Once I get up there and hit my stride, I'll be fine, Ben coached himself as he followed the choir down the main aisle of the sanctuary. They were singing "My Heart Sings Out with Joyful Praise," and he sang along, forcing a smile.

Carolyn was seated in her usual spot, in the second row on the right side of the pews, not far from the pulpit. He caught her eye and smiled. She smiled back, and he felt better. They would sit together in the family room this afternoon, reading the paper and watching a football game, and she would make a fuss over him. He looked forward to it.

But it was not too long after Ben stepped up to the pulpit and was delivering the day's reading from the New Testament that the symptoms returned. Full force this time.

"This morning's Scripture reading is from Mark 13, verses 35–37," he announced.

Then he began to read from the Bible, the words swimming in and out of focus. He read very slowly and carefully, hoping no one noticed how he faltered.

"'Therefore, keep watch because you do not know when the owner of the house will come back—whether in the evening, or at midnight, or when the rooster crows, or at dawn. If he comes suddenly, do not let him find you sleeping. What I say to you, I say to everyone: Watch . . .'"

Ben's words broke off. He swayed on his feet as a wave of nausea and dizziness washed over him. He clung to the pulpit, his chin dropping down to his chest.

But worst of all, a fierce, sharp pain pierced his chest, as if a spear had been driven straight through his heart.

Ben grimaced and gasped, unable to get his breath.

What was happening? He felt awful; he could barely hold himself upright. He couldn't breathe. The pain in his chest was horrific. He grabbed at his chest as he felt himself swaying. He made a fumbling grasp at the pulpit, but only succeeded in pulling down a microphone stand, a jagged edge of metal scraping against his face as he fell to the floor.

"Ben? Oh, dear God!" Carolyn was the first to stand. She shouted his name as Tucker, Sam, and Emily all ran toward the pulpit.

Tucker and Sam reached him first and gently rolled him over, so that he was staring up at them. "He cut his face. He's bleeding," he heard Emily say. She took a soft white handkerchief and pressed it to Ben's cheek. "Just stay still, Ben. You'll be okay," Emily whispered.

Ben met her glance. Emily—always calm and in control—looked very worried. Ben was about to reply but felt another sharp pain in his chest. He squeezed his eyes shut. The pain was so excruciating, he could barely breathe.

Tucker stood on his other side, speaking into his cell phone. "It's Tulley. We need an ambulance at the church. Right now. Looks like a heart attack . . ."

A heart attack? Ben heard the words and stared at Tucker. His old friend smiled back grimly. "An ambulance is on the way, Ben. Hang in there."

"Ben, can you hear me? Do you have pain in your chest? Is that what it is?" Carolyn crouched down next to him and gripped his hand. She stared at him, her expression pale and panicked.

He met her gaze, willing himself to answer. But he couldn't speak. His vision blurred, the stained-glass windows spinning in his sight like the colored bits of glass inside a kaleidoscope.

He heard his wife gasp and everything went black.

"HERE IT IS, TWENTY-THREE." RICHARD ROWAN POINTED TO the number on the snow-covered mailbox. It tilted on its post at an odd angle, Regina noticed. As if it were tired of standing and longed to fall down.

He parked the car and they both stared through the brush at the old house, set back from the road behind a gap-toothed picket fence. "Not much to look at, is it."

"No, but that's pretty much what I expected," Regina replied evenly. "And it's all ours," she reminded him. "No landlord, no mortgage. At least we have a roof over our heads."

"What's left of it. I'm surprised it hasn't caved in under all that snow," Richard said, squinting out at the house that was the very definition of disrepair. "How did you say this uncle was related to you again?"

"Not my uncle. My father's cousin. Or second cousin? Something like that."

She had told Richard about Francis Porter several times, but he never seemed to remember the details. He didn't listen to her that closely anymore, always distracted, his mind focused on something else. Distracted and impatient. Lately, anyway.

Regina had never met Francis Porter. The letter announcing that she had inherited this distant relation's property was the first she had ever heard of him. Warren Oakes, the lawyer handling the estate, had told her that Mr. Porter had been an old man who spent his last days studying his heritage. Obsessed, really, with his family tree, he had tracked down all of his ancestors using a website and discovered that Regina was his only living relation on the Porter side of the family. Which he obviously favored.

Porter was her maiden name. She and Richard had been married for nearly fifteen years, and she had grown used to the name Regina Rowan, especially after their children came and it was "Mrs. Rowan this," and "Mrs. Rowan that." Lately she wondered if she would be returning to the surname Porter soon. Perhaps sooner than she had ever imagined.

"He must have been some kind of nut, living alone out here in this falling-down wreck." Richard stared out at the house and shook his head.

"Maybe it's not so bad inside," Regina said, though she guessed the interior was even worse. The fresh snow hid a lot of the outside of the house and made it look a bit better. "We'll probably have to do some cleaning before we bring the kids over."

Their two children were waiting back at the motel, instructed not to open the door for anyone, not even housekeeping. Madeline was twelve, a little young for babysitting, but Regina had little choice at times but to rely on her to watch her brother, Brian, who was six.

Warren Oakes would be here any minute, she reminded herself, and he'd promised it wouldn't take long at all to sign the final papers and give her the keys.

"*If* we can bring the kids back here," Richard said, cutting into her thoughts. "What if it's not livable? Then what?"

Paying for even one more night in the motel would be a stretch. If it were just the two of them, they could sleep in the car. But they couldn't ask that of the children.

They couldn't go into a shelter, either, Regina thought. That would be too much. Richard would never recover. Not after that.

Dear God, please don't let it come to that. Please?

"Mr. Oakes said he thought we could move in today—if we didn't mind roughing it."

"'Roughing it'? Is that what he calls it? I'd call it being flat-out broke. He really thinks we can fix this place and sell it? He must be crazy, too." Richard turned away and gave a sad, defeated laugh. It was a characteristic he'd developed only recently. He'd never sounded like that when she first met him. She would never have married a man who laughed like that.

Regina didn't answer. She didn't answer him a lot lately.

It was the only way she could manage. It did little good to try to stay positive, to be encouraging and hope their situation would improve. Richard would manage to poke holes in those thin flags of hope as well. She was better off keeping those thoughts to herself.

But hopeful or not, the plain truth was that they had no other place to go. Besides, they had agreed to this plan. They'd been on the verge of splitting up. They were fighting all the time, arguing over every little thing. It was awful for them and even worse for the kids. Then, less than a month ago, she got the letter from Warren Oakes telling her that she had inherited the house. So they'd made a truce to stop fighting, come up to this house, and live here, just until it was fixed up. Then they would sell it, split the profits, and go their separate ways. At least they would stay together for one last Christmas as a family.

Regina stared at the small, snow-covered house. They had a place to rest for a while, rent-free. That was enough for her. She just wanted a place to catch her breath and get her bearings. To get the kids settled down a bit. Their lives had been so unsettled lately, a living nightmare.

Now the holidays were coming, and they would spend them here, in this house. Regina silently vowed she would make it as comfortable and cheerful as she could manage. She would give the children a good holiday. And after that, well . . . She wondered if she could manage to hold this family together much longer. She really wondered about that.

She heard the sound of a car approaching on the snowy road. A black Camry pulled up just behind their car, a mild-looking, middle-aged man at the wheel, bundled up against the cold in a coat, scarf, and flat cap. A woman sat next to him, just her eyes peering out from between her woolen hat and the high neck of her down coat.

"That must be the lawyer," Richard said. "Let's get this over with."

"Yes, that must be him." Regina unfastened her seat belt and pulled on her gloves.

She was surprised to see that Mr. Oakes brought his wife. Maybe they were on their way someplace. The attorney got out of his car and came toward them, moving slowly in the high snow. He carried a briefcase in one hand and waved with the other.

"Good morning. Mrs. Rowan, I presume?" He shook her hand and officially introduced himself and his wife. "I hope we didn't keep you waiting. These back roads are still full of snow. It was slow going."

"That's all right. We didn't wait long," Regina replied. Mrs. Oakes had gone back to their car and opened the trunk. Regina saw her pull out a large brown carton and start back toward them, her long down coat dragging in the snow.

"You'd better get the snow shovel from the backseat, Warren. There's a lot to carry."

Regina watched, puzzled. She had no idea what Mrs. Oakes was carrying, and there was more of it, besides. Had the attorney taken items out of the house for safekeeping? It was deserted out here, the houses long distances apart. Maybe he had been concerned about break-ins. As the executor, he was responsible for the property.

"Can I help you with that, Mrs. Oakes?" Regina offered.

"I'm fine, dear." Mrs. Oakes marched toward her with the carton. "And call me Marion, please."

Regina peered inside, expecting to see old lamps and perhaps some books or dishes. Instead, she saw that it was filled with groceries. Filled to the brim. She hadn't bought that much at the store at one time in months . . . years, maybe.

"There are a few more boxes. Just some staples we thought you might need to get going."

A few more boxes? Did they expect to be paid for all this food? Regina swallowed hard. She hoped not. They hardly had any cash left and needed every penny.

"It's a housewarming present," Mrs. Oakes added, as if guessing Regina's thoughts. Perhaps her expression had given her away, Regina realized. She could rarely hide her feelings.

"Thank you . . . That was very thoughtful."

"We know you have children, and the supermarket is a bit of a ride. You have a lot to organize today without running out to the store to shop, too, right?"

Regina nodded. "Yes, there's a lot to do. I really appreciate your help."

"It's nothing. We hope you feel welcome here," the older woman said. She turned and headed up to the house. Her husband had gone back to his car and taken out a snow shovel.

"I can do that," Richard said, offering to take the shovel.

"Why don't you help your wife with the boxes? I'd prefer the snow detail," he said honestly.

Regina headed for the Camry and Richard followed. He shot Regina a doubtful, suspicious look. As if this benign-looking couple was up to something.

Regina and Richard each took a box from the trunk. She noticed other items besides the groceries: a new mop, a broom, and a bucket. A carton with bed linens and towels, and another bag with pillows.

How amazingly thoughtful. Her heart was touched by their kindness. She had mentioned to Mr. Oakes on the phone last night that practically all their belongings, besides clothes and a few other essentials, had been put in storage in Pennsylvania.

"Oh, is that so?" he'd said, then went on to some other legal detail about the property and papers she would sign. She hadn't thought he'd even heard her, but obviously he had. A total stranger showing such concern.

The lawyer had cleared a thin path up to the house and stood on the porch, riffling through his briefcase. Regina set down the carton she was carrying, and Richard did the same.

"Here they are, your keys." Mr. Oakes pulled a key ring out of his briefcase and handed it to her. "The large silver one fits the front door. The others are for the side and back doors. And that little one is for the door under the porch that opens into the basement."

Regina nodded, distracted by a sudden, unexpected rush of excitement. The house wasn't much to look at, but she felt excited nonetheless, holding the keys in her hand for the first time.

She owned this. The land and house and everything inside, from the basement to the attic. It was a heady feeling, especially in light of the way they had lost their lovely new home to the bank back in Pennsylvania two years ago. So many of their possessions had been sold at garage sales for pennies on the dollar to cover bills, or simply given away when they had to move to smaller living spaces—a series of small, dingy apartments and, finally, a motel room.

She sensed the others waiting; the older couple, smiling patiently, and Richard, tense and impatient. She put the big silver key in the lock and opened the front door.

It made a creaking sound as she stepped into the foyer and looked around. She had expected a musty odor, but the air was fresh and smelled like furniture polish and floor cleaner.

"I had the place cleaned," Mr. Oakes said, following her inside.

"We left most of the furniture. A few pieces were broken and a few of the lamps looked like fire hazards. A lot of miscellaneous belongings were boxed up. I had someone put it all in the attic and out in the shed. You might want to go through it sometime. The rooms need a coat of paint, but we aired it out and turned on the utilities. I think you'll find it livable for now."

Regina wandered farther, staring into a large sitting room on her right and a dining room on the left. An oval-shaped wooden dining table with curved legs and matching chairs stood in the dining room. The seat cushions on the chairs were worn but easy to repair, she thought. The wood was still good and only needed a little polishing; a quality set, the kind hardly made anymore.

A long stairway with a wooden banister led to the next floor. The stairs were bare. She could see where some old carpeting had been torn off. "There are four bedrooms upstairs. And the attic space," Warren Oakes said.

"How many children do you have?" his wife asked curiously.

"Two, a girl who's twelve years old and a boy who's six," Regina answered.

"They can each have their own room with one to spare," Mrs. Oakes said. "There are some decent beds up there and a few dressers. I think you'll be fine until you can bring your own things here."

"Yes, it sounds like we will be." Regina was relieved. Beds and dressers were more than she had hoped for. The kids would be thrilled to have their own rooms again. They'd all been living on top of one another for the past few months. It had been very hard on them.

She was eager to go up and investigate, but then realized she hadn't even seen the entire downstairs yet.

She turned to the sitting room next. A big stone fireplace below a wooden mantel immediately drew her attention. There were bookcases built in on either side; many of the shelves still held books. Regina was glad to see that. She loved to read, and most of her books had either been given away or put into storage.

That was the high point of the room, she thought. The story got worse the longer you looked around. The wooden floors were bare and the finish dull and worn. A dusty oval rag rug sat in front of a caved-in sofa, and next to that an old armchair, its upholstery faded and torn. Regina felt a sneeze coming on just looking at the ensemble. They would have to get something to replace that soon, maybe in a secondhand store or a Goodwill shop.

"I think I put some slipcovers in that bag with the bed linen and quilts," Mrs. Oakes said. "I found them in a closet and thought they might fit that couch and chair. Just to start off."

"Slipcovers would be a good idea," Regina agreed.

Richard had been silent all this time. He had glanced around the front rooms quickly and then walked back to the kitchen. "That stove must be a hundred years old," he said to the lawyer. "Are you sure it works?"

"Good question, Mr. Rowan. It's in excellent working condition. I had it checked by the utility company before they turned on the gas. I didn't want any accidents with the house empty."

Richard cast him a doubtful look. "And the fireplace? Has that been checked, too?"

"Fireplace works fine. The chimney is clear. Tested it myself last week."

"A fireplace can be the heart of a home," Mrs. Oakes said. "I love the mantel. It's a wonderful focal point."

Regina agreed, but before she could reply, Warren Oakes cut in.

"Before we start decorating, ladies, we have some business to cover." He turned to Regina. "I have all the papers ready for you to sign. It won't take very long. Let's go into the dining room. We'll need the big table."

Regina followed him into the next room. Mr. Oakes sat at the head of the table, and Regina took a seat next to him. He took several folders from his briefcase, put on his reading glasses, and proceeded to go through the documents slowly, explaining to her exactly what she was signing and why.

Richard sat at the other end of the table and watched, his mouth set in a tight line. She was relieved that he didn't interrupt with a lot of questions. He had taken on a suspicious, challenging attitude lately, even about the simplest situations—with the mechanic or the kids' teachers, even with supermarket cashiers, as if everyone were trying to cheat him. He hadn't always been like that.

It was because they had lost so much, and Richard felt it was all his fault. As if he had been too trusting or too naive and had been tricked, played for a fool. First, by the county that he had worked for, and then by the people at the bank, and later by others who claimed they could help.

It had not been his fault. They were caught in a bad economy, and she had never once blamed him. But that's how he felt, and no amount of talking to him about it seemed to wash away the stain. Worse, it seemed he lost his trust in people. And in himself, Regina knew. Whether he could ever gain it back was the question.

Warren Oakes explained each document, and Regina signed and signed. Mrs. Oakes stood by and made neat stacks of the signed pages, then tucked the piles in different folders. "I help Warren at his office. I'm his assistant," she explained.

"Don't let her fool you. She's just being modest. She's the boss."

Mr. Oakes glanced up over his reading glasses for a moment and gave his wife a fond smile.

Marion Oakes just shook her head.

The older couple seemed in perfect harmony, exchanging looks and anticipating each other's needs with hardly a word. Regina couldn't imagine running a business with Richard. They would bicker so much, they wouldn't last a day.

"Last but not least, the deed to the property," Mr. Oakes announced. "You just sign the back, and it's transferred to your ownership."

Regina knew that. They had owned their home in Pennsylvania until the bank foreclosed on the mortgage.

"What about my husband? Doesn't he sign, too?"

Richard turned, suddenly alert. "It's your inheritance, Regina. I don't have to sign."

They had talked about this. Or at least she tried to. She couldn't really understand why Richard didn't want his name on the deed. Unless he planned on leaving her sooner than they had discussed and thought it would be less complicated that way. That was the only reason Regina could come up with, though she hadn't dared to say it straight out to him.

"Can we have my husband's name on the deed also?" she asked the lawyer.

"Yes, you can. That's no problem. It's safer for your family. In the event that anything were to happen to you, the property would go directly to your husband without any probate. I'm sorry, I thought I asked you about this during one of our phone conversations—"

"I'm sure you did," Regina quickly cut in. "I just didn't follow up with a clear answer." She turned to Richard, willing him with her eyes to comply. "This is safer for the family, Richard. For the kids, in case something happens. You never know," she reminded him.

He stared at her for a moment, then sighed. "Nothing's going to happen to you, Gina. But okay, I'll sign if you want me to. You know what this means, right? We own it together, fifty-fifty. You sure that's what you want?"

Regina was surprised he would be so blunt in front of Mr. and Mrs. Oakes. But the lawyer and his wife were apparently used to witnessing such private conversations; they immediately took on well-practiced blank stares.

"Of course, I'm sure. It's not much, but . . . what's mine is yours, Richard. We're married, aren't we?"

Still married, she could have said. For as long as it might last.

She saw a flicker in his gray eyes and knew that her husband had picked up on her unspoken meaning. And had the grace to look moved by it.

He just shook his head. "What a question." Then he moved down to her side of the table and sat in the seat next to her.

Warren Oakes cleared his throat, marked a few more *X*s on the pile of papers before him, and then passed them along.

"So you both print your names here"—he pointed out the lines—"then sign down there and on the back. Right there."

Regina signed first, then passed the documents to Richard. Then she sat back and rubbed her hand. She actually had a cramp between her thumb and index finger from all the signing.

"Well, that's that," Mr. Oakes said finally. "It's officially yours. Congratulations, Mrs. Rowan, Mr. Rowan." The attorney handed Regina one of the folders. "These are your copies. Put them in a safe place."

"I will. Thanks very much for all your help—and for all the

groceries and everything you gave us. We'd like to pay you back," she added. She knew they didn't have the money right now, but felt obliged to offer.

Richard nodded firmly, his jaw set. "It was very generous of you, Mr. Oakes, but we can't accept it. Not without giving you some repayment."

We won't accept charity. We're not that badly off yet, was what her husband was really saying.

"Nonsense," Mrs. Oakes said briskly. "We won't take a penny. This is just what neighbors do for one another, at least around here. We know that you've come a long way and have a lot to do, moving in here today," she added. "Really, it was no trouble at all."

"My wife is correct, as usual. I do receive adequate payment for the legal services. Anything further is totally unnecessary." Warren Oakes stood up and slipped a few more papers into his briefcase. "This is our gift to you and your family. To welcome you to Cape Light. We're happy to make this small gesture."

He shrugged into his heavy coat and picked up his hat and muffler. His wife already had her coat on and her purse in hand.

"We appreciate it. We'll make it up to you sometime," Richard added.

The lawyer reached out and patted his shoulder. "I'm sure if the opportunity arises, Mr. Rowan, you definitely will."

Regina walked the couple to the front door.

"Good-bye, dear. Good luck." Mrs. Oakes pulled her hat down over her forehead. "I know it doesn't look like much now, but this house has loads of potential. And you seem just the type of person to do things with it."

Regina wasn't sure how the older woman could know that after so brief a meeting, but she was touched by the compliment.

"I'm going to give it my best shot," Regina promised.

"Invite me back sometime to see your progress. I enjoy those before-and-after home improvement shows."

Regina had to smile at her reply. "Oh, I will."

"Good luck, Mrs. Rowan." Warren Oakes extended his hand and shook hers heartily. "If you have any further questions about the estate or the property transfer, or anything at all, please give me a call. I know your family has been through a lot the last few months. I hope this new home works out for you."

"So do I, Mr. Oakes," Regina said honestly. "So do I."

CHAPTER TWO

HE SURGEON TOLD CAROLYN THAT THE OPERATION
would take three to four hours. "Barring unforeseen complications," Dr. Chandler added.

Unforeseen complications? She didn't even want to think about what he meant by that. Four hours, even three, seemed an impossibly long time to wait in this anxious state. She didn't know how she could stand it without going stark raving mad.

Then she heard Ben's voice in her head, as clearly as if he stood right beside her. "Of course you'll get through it, dear. Just sit and pray. That's how you'll do it."

Yes, that was it. She had to give this over to God. She had to be strong for the both of them. She had to hold it together and put her trust in God. She couldn't let her faith falter now.

Though the only prayer that came to mind was, "Please, God, help Ben. Let him survive this operation. Please?"

Luckily, her daughter, Rachel, was with her. Rachel had dropped everything and driven up to the hospital as soon as Carolyn called.

Tucker and Sam had driven her to the hospital, following close behind the ambulance. They, too, were still waiting with her, but had gone down to the cafeteria to get a bite to eat.

Rachel sat with her in the surgical waiting room, which was quieter and more private than the general area. *Thank goodness for that,* Carolyn thought.

"Has Daddy felt sick very long?" Rachel asked.

Carolyn reached over and took her hand. Rachel rarely called her father *Daddy* anymore. The note of fear in her daughter's voice was wrenching.

"You know your father. He's not a complainer. The last few days, he was saying that he felt tired, but he thought that was just the cold weather. He did say he ate too much on Thanksgiving. He's been taking antacids for the past few days, complaining of heartburn. I guess that was the start of it. That's what the doctor said: a full feeling and pressure on the chest are two of the symptoms."

"Shoveling all that snow this morning must have pushed him over the edge," Rachel mused.

"It was too much. But this could have happened anyway, just sitting at home, watching TV. You heard what Dr. Chandler said. There's so much buildup in his arteries."

Just hours earlier, the surgeon showed them the results of Ben's tests, which included photographs of the inside of the arteries around his heart, taken soon after he was brought into the emergency room.

"The major arteries that carry blood to the heart are filled with plaque, cholesterol buildup," Dr. Chandler explained. "The blood flow is blocked, and the heart doesn't get enough oxygen. That's why your husband experienced shortness of breath and pain. Luckily, he survived the heart attack. Many men his age don't," he said bluntly. "But he needs a procedure."

Carolyn knew he meant an operation. *Procedure* was the word doctors used when they didn't want to alarm you.

"What type of procedure?" she asked.

"Sometimes we can perform an angioplasty; a tiny balloon is expanded inside the artery and opens the blocked passageway. But your husband's condition is more advanced. His arteries are more than seventy percent blocked."

"Seventy percent?" Carolyn had been shocked. That meant Ben was hardly getting any blood flowing through his heart at all. "How did he manage to even get up out of bed in the morning?"

"Sheer willpower, I'd have to say." Dr. Chandler shook his head. "His condition is so advanced, he needs bypass surgery. Right now, we think at least two arteries need attention. But it could be more. We'll take healthy veins from his legs or chest wall, and attach them to his heart, like this." He made a sketch on a sheet of paper. "These fresh veins take over from the diseased ones. If the surgery is successful, he'll feel better almost immediately. It's astounding that he's been able to carry on a full schedule with this level of deterioration."

"My husband is an astounding man," Carolyn had replied, still dazed by the news.

Rachel had asked the difficult question. "What are my father's chances?"

"Considering his age and other factors, like blood pressure or other medical conditions, I'd say he has a ninety-five percent chance of coming through the surgery without complications," Dr. Chandler answered. "The statistics show about three to four percent mortality."

Mortality. What a dark, heavy word that was. Carolyn hated to hear it, though she had silently thanked her daughter for asking the question. She had been working up the courage.

Back at the church, there had been a few awful moments when she thought they had lost him. Right before the ambulance came, when it seemed Ben was barely conscious and Tucker and Sam were taking turns at CPR, pumping Ben's heart with their hands and breathing into his lungs.

She was barely able to watch, but couldn't look away as she crouched beside Ben, holding his hand. Ben's eyes were closed and his skin looked gray. His hand felt limp in her own. He had no strength at all.

She watched Tucker and Sam exchange worried looks, but the two men didn't say a thing. That seemed the worst moment of all. She knew Ben was hanging on just by a thread.

Then the EMS crew rushed into the church. They took over the CPR and administered drugs to thin Ben's blood and stop the heart attack right away. Nitroglycerin, Carolyn heard them say. Then they bundled him up on a stretcher and took him away.

Carolyn wanted to ride in the ambulance, but Tucker drove her instead. "The paramedics need to work on Ben some more," Tucker had told her. "You might be in their way."

She wouldn't like to see it was what he really meant. It would only alarm her further.

Tucker's police cruiser kept them moving at top speed on the highway. Sam Morgan came, too, helping her stay hopeful with his calm, steady outlook.

By the time they found Ben in the ER, he was already getting tests and more treatment. A heart specialist, Dr. Chandler, soon told her what they all suspected: Ben had suffered a sudden, severe heart attack and needed immediate intervention. Nothing less would save him.

Of course, she told them to do whatever was necessary to save him.

Rachel had arrived just in time. "Mom, is Dad going to be all right?"

Carolyn didn't know how to answer. Then she fell back on her motherly instincts, honed after all these years. "He's going to be okay, honey. He needs an operation, but they say he's going to make it," she promised.

Though she wasn't sure at all.

After speaking with Dr. Chandler, Carolyn had signed some papers. Then she and Rachel were allowed to see Ben, just for a few minutes before he was prepared for the operation. He looked so weak and vulnerable. He was wearing a hospital gown with a thin blanket pulled to his chest, a plastic bracelet on his wrist, and lines for an IV in his arm. A big white bandage covered one cheek, where the emergency room doctor had closed his cut. They'd had to shave off his beard to take care of the wound, Carolyn noticed. She wasn't sure if Ben was aware of that and didn't have the heart to mention it. They had more important things to worry about right now, didn't they? A nurse had removed his eyeglasses, and now he squinted up at her, somehow managing to smile.

"Carolyn," he whispered. "The doctor says they're going to operate on my heart . . ."

"I know, Ben. We just talked to Dr. Chandler about it. It's going to be okay, dear."

He'd already been given a lot of drugs for the pain and tests, and he could hardly speak. But he fiercely gripped her hand and managed to kiss her back when she leaned over and kissed him.

She stroked the side of his head "You're going to be fine, Ben. We're all praying hard for you. I love you so much," she told him.

"I love you, too," he said.

It was so important to put positive thoughts in the mind of a person facing surgery. She had read that someplace and was glad she remembered.

"The doctors say you're doing very well, considering what you've been through, and this operation will repair your heart completely. You'll be better than new," she promised.

He wanted to speak, she could tell he did, but he could only nod. Then his blue eyes went all soft and watery at the sight of Rachel, who stood at the other side of the gurney.

"Hello, my girl," he managed.

"Hello, Daddy." Rachel leaned over her father and kissed his cheek, then whispered something in his ear that made him smile.

Later, Carolyn asked what she'd said, if it wasn't too private.

"I just told him that after all these years, we're finally getting to see what his face looks like. And I hope he doesn't scare his grand-children."

"Oh, Rachel—you didn't really say that, did you?" Carolyn had to laugh at the teasing. She was sure Ben had taken the joke in good spirits and would be telling everyone who visited while he recovered.

Yes, that was the way she had to think about this. He would survive this assault on his body, the cutting open and sewing up. He would be even better for it, she told herself. He would be sitting up in bed, talking and laughing, in no time at all.

She had to look ahead and picture that and beg God to come to the aid of her husband, who had always been such a good and faithful man.

Such a good and faithful servant.

* * *

THEY WAITED AND WAITED. CAROLYN HAD A PILE OF MAGAZINES
in her lap but couldn't read a word. A large, flat-screen TV hung
suspended from the wall a short distance away. She watched news-
casters talking, but had no idea what they were talking about.

"Are you all right, Mom? Can I get you anything?" Rachel's
soft voice jarred Carolyn from her wandering thoughts.

"I'm fine, dear. I think I'll make myself a cup of tea." Carolyn
wasn't hungry, and she didn't want to leave the waiting area while
Ben was still in surgery. "Isn't the nurse supposed to come in and
tell us what's going on?" she asked.

Rachel glanced at her watch. "Not for at least another hour."

Carolyn checked the time, too. It felt as if an hour had already
passed since the last report, but it had only been twenty minutes.
"Yes, I guess you're right. Has your brother called?"

"He sent a text. He just got on a flight and should be at Logan
in four hours. Dad should be out of surgery by then."

"Yes, he should be. God willing," Carolyn added quietly. "I
think this must be hard on your brother, too, being so far away."

Rachel nodded. "I could tell Mark was upset, though he was
trying to act very manly about it. He told me to tell Dad that he
loved him and he was on his way. At least Dad was awake and able
to hear that."

"Yes, I'm glad for that, at least." Carolyn knew the brief message from his son would mean the world to Ben.

Mark had left home when he was about eighteen, first for Brown
University and a major in philosophy. But he soon dropped out of
school, much to their dismay, then wandered the country for several
years, supporting himself with odd jobs and exploring various spiritual philosophies. He'd gone from ashrams in California to cattle

ranches in Montana. For several years, he'd been a stranger to their home, barely communicating. But when Carolyn had experienced her own medical emergency eight years ago, Mark had finally returned and worked out some peace with his family. Now he was a grown man, finishing his graduate work in child psychology and soon to be married to a lovely young woman.

"Carolyn . . . Rachel . . . How are you both holding up?" Emily Warwick and her husband, Dan Forbes, swept into the waiting area and hugged Carolyn and Rachel fiercely.

A long-standing member of the church, Emily was also Cape Light's mayor. She was a good friend of Ben's and had often turned to him for counsel during troubled moments in her life. It was no surprise that she would come to comfort and support his family now.

Rachel quickly updated the couple on her father's condition. "He's been in surgery a little over an hour. The last time the nurse came out, she said they were just getting started."

Emily took Carolyn's hand. "It's a long, hard wait. But we know he'll pull through. Ben is strong . . . and stubborn."

Carolyn had to smile at the reminder. "In his quiet, intractable way. That's for sure."

"You must be hungry," Dan said. "We brought some food. The food in the cafeteria is . . . well, it's hospital food."

"Don't worry, I didn't cook anything," Emily assured them with a grin. A notoriously bad cook, Emily did try. But it had become a joke around church: Whenever it was time for a potluck supper, Emily was assigned the bread and butter, or even the paper goods.

"Sophie Potter made you a care package. There's some hot soup, cheese, homemade bread, and apple crisp. And all the dishes and utensils, I see," Dan added, peering into the second bag.

"There's a little table by the window. Let's set up over there," Rachel suggested. "I could do with something to eat. I hardly had breakfast."

Even in the presence of Sophie's delectable food, Carolyn couldn't summon an appetite. She was too frightened and worried to be hungry. But she went to the table anyway and sat down while Emily and Dan set out the meal. She knew she ought to eat something, if only to keep up her strength. "This was so thoughtful of Sophie," she said.

"You know Sophie. She couldn't come up here, but she wanted to do something," Dan said.

"When we stopped at her house to pick this up, we found half the church there. She invited a group to go over and pray for Ben. They're praying right now, Carolyn," Emily assured her.

"And so is the rest of the congregation who couldn't make it to Potter's Orchard," Dan added. "Ben is blessed with an abundance of friends."

"You both are," Emily said.

Their words touched Carolyn's heart. She felt her eyes tearing and dabbed them with a napkin. She and Ben were greatly blessed in their lives in so many ways, especially in their relationships. With their children and grandchildren. With friends and family, near and far. With all the members of his congregation.

If it was God's will that her husband not survive, at least she knew he had lived a good life, a rich life. As Henry David Thoreau once said, "I've traveled widely in Concord." Her husband had traveled widely in the small country village of Cape Light. It was an entire world, and living in it, Ben had been truly blessed in so many ways. What more could one ask for?

She was the one who was asking for more now. Begging God for more time with her husband, the final years together they had worked so hard for, been waiting for, deserved after all they'd been through together. What would she ever do without him if—

She couldn't even think about that. She forced herself not to think at all and just closed her eyes and prayed.

SEVERAL HOURS LATER, THE NURSE LIAISON TO SURGERY CAME into the waiting room. "Mrs. Lewis?" she called, looking around.

Carolyn jumped up from her chair. "Right here!" Magazines slipped from her lap, but she stepped right over them to quickly meet the nurse.

"Your husband's surgery is almost finished. They're just closing him up. He's done very well," the nurse reported. "He should be wheeled out soon, and you can visit with him briefly in the intensive care unit."

Carolyn was speechless for a moment. She nearly felt her legs give way under her. Luckily, Rachel was holding her hand.

"Oh, thank you. Thank you so much," she said emphatically. The nurse touched her arm, then left to visit another family.

Carolyn took a breath and squeezed her eyes shut. "Thank you, God," she said out loud. "Thank you for taking care of Ben."

"Oh, Mom . . ." Rachel hugged her mother, hiding her face in Carolyn's shoulder.

"Yes, I know, dear," Carolyn replied. There were no words to express their relief, their complete and utter joy and gratitude.

BEN SENSED SOMEONE STANDING BY HIS BED. HE HEARD CAROLYN'S voice calling him. "Ben, are you awake? Can you open your eyes?" she whispered.

He tried, but he was tired. So very tired.

But he had to get up and get over to the church, get to work this morning. There wasn't much time left before Christmas, and there was so much to do. He had a meeting with the choir director to plan the special services. He had made notes in one of the hymnals. But where had he put it?

The snow angels would help him find it. All day, they'd come to help him. He'd seen them through the falling snow . . .

"Carolyn . . ." he said groggily.

"Yes, dear?" Her face was close to his; he could feel her breath on his cheek. "What is it, darling? What are you trying to say?"

"Have you seen my hymnal? The black one with the ripped cover? The snow angels must have moved it somewhere . . ."

"The snow angels took your hymnal, dear?"

"Just borrowed it," he mumbled. "They had some questions . . ."

As he finally managed to form the thought and open his eyes, he heard soft laughter. He looked up at her, and then at Rachel, who stood on the other side of the bed. And then at his son, Mark, who peered down over his mother's shoulder.

"What . . . what are you all doing here?"

"Ben, you're in the hospital. You had a heart attack. You needed an operation," Carolyn explained slowly. She was sitting on the edge of the bed now, her hand covering his. "Do you remember any of that?"

He met her concerned look and nodded. But in truth, he didn't quite remember. He felt groggy. His mind felt so fuzzy, as though his head were full of cotton.

Or snow.

He did remember the snow this morning, staring at it from his bedroom window, pausing to admire the pristine beauty of the scene.

Then shoveling it. And the pain in his chest. The shortness of breath . . .

"I collapsed . . . at the service," he told her. It was a struggle just to say those few words. His chest still hurt, but now he realized that was because of the surgery. His legs, too, hurt something awful.

"That's right. You'd just finished the Scripture reading."

"What Scripture was it, Dad? Can you remember that?" Mark challenged him.

Always pushing the envelope; that was his son, all right.

"Mark 13, verses 35–37," he murmured.

Appropriate, he thought. *The verse reminds us that we never know when the owner of the house will return, so we'd better not goof off.* Well, the owner of this particular house—his body and soul—had not come this time to find him. But He'd given him a good warning.

"Very good, Dad. I'm impressed," Mark said.

"Especially since the doctor said you might have some side effects from the anesthesia. Some disorientation," Rachel explained.

Ben tried his best to answer. "I had a dream. I was home. In my bed."

"If only you were, dear," Carolyn sympathized.

The post-surgery intensive care unit was an open area that did not offer any privacy. A nurse stopped by to check the many monitors and tubes that were connected to Ben's body.

"You'll have to go now," she told his family. "He really needs his rest. One person can visit again in about an hour, for a few more minutes."

Carolyn sighed and gazed down into his eyes. "We have to go, sweetheart. I'll be back soon. I bet you just want to sleep."

He nodded and tried to smile at her. His mouth felt funny. He wasn't sure why. Maybe he'd had one of those thick plastic breathing tubes down his throat during the surgery.

Everyone kissed him good-bye on the forehead, even Mark. Ben watched them go and closed his eyes. Despite the fog in his head and the fact that he felt as if he'd just been hit by a truck, he wasn't sure he could fall back to sleep that easily. So many sounds, so much activity all around him. The odd feeling of his body being connected to machines. He felt like a science experiment pinned on a display board.

He guessed that the stuff dripping down through the tubes into his veins was medication, some to block the pain from the incision in his chest and those in his legs where veins were removed. But he still hurt all over, his legs even more than his chest. *But I'm grateful for the pain,* he realized. *So grateful to feel anything, just to be alive. Thank you, God, for sparing my life. Thank you for allowing me to see my wife and children again.*

Ben felt his eyes fill with tears, realizing how close he had come to dying.

Perhaps as a man of faith I should be stronger and wiser, immune to the fear of death, he thought. *Wasn't a fear of death doubting God's promise of everlasting life? Wasn't it a lack of trust?*

But he was only human, just like any other man. Frail and imperfect, clinging desperately to this beautiful old world. His life, as fragile and temporal as a flake of snow, drifting down from heaven.

He had started the day awed by God's handiwork, Ben realized, and now ended it, overwhelmed by his maker's mercy.

Thank you, Lord. Thank you. Thank you . . .

The words sailed through his mind on a long white ribbon, floating against a blue sky. He closed his eyes and drifted into a deep sleep.

CHAPTER THREE

⌒

*T*HE FAMILY HAD MOVED SO MANY TIMES IN THE LAST
two years, Regina had all the necessary papers for school
registration in one large envelope, ready to go whenever needed.
When Monday morning rolled around, she needed them.

She kept the envelope in a plastic carton of important documents and always knew where that was at any time. Their messy,
spread-out lives had been condensed and condensed again, as
though boiling down a big pot of stew. Now the box contained not
only birth records, vaccination charts, Richard's college diploma,
and their marriage license, but favorite recipes, photographs, and
the children's special, scribbled drawings—valentines and Mother's
Day cards—made for her by hand.

Funny what you finally decide to keep and what to throw away,
she thought as she pulled out the school envelope.

Madeline wasn't eager to start over in a new school. "Can't I start tomorrow? I can help you and Dad today, unpacking and stuff." Her daughter gave her a hopeful look.

"There's not much to unpack right now, honey. Most of our things are back in Pennsylvania. You know that."

Madeline sat on the edge of her bed and stared at the bare floor. Regina could tell she was trying not to make a fuss, but she dreaded facing a school full of strangers. Regina's heart went out to her. It was hard to be the new girl over and over. Middle school was a fierce place, especially when you didn't have the right jeans or latest designer boots. Kids could be cruel.

Regina sat on the bed and stroked her daughter's hair. Maddy was so pretty and good-hearted. She always made friends easily.

"You'll be okay. I'll bet you have at least three friends by lunchtime, and you're invited to a sleepover by next weekend."

The last part of the bet made Madeline smile. "I don't know, Mom. I don't know what kids are like around here."

"Kids are pretty much the same all over. That's what I think. But there's only one way to find out. Come down and have breakfast. We'll leave in about an hour."

When Regina got downstairs, she found Richard and Brian at the kitchen table. Richard was dressed in jeans and an old sweatshirt. Brian was still in his pajamas, staring sleepily into his cereal bowl. He picked up his spoon, then sneezed so hard, Oat O's and milk flew across the table.

"His cold is worse. And he says his ear hurts." Richard glanced over at Regina.

"His ear hurts?" That was new. Regina hoped he didn't have an ear infection.

Brian's cold had started at least a week ago, but they were on the road and hadn't had time to stop and find a doctor. Regina had hoped that the usual regimen of extra rest, orange juice, and over-the-counter remedies would cure it. But now she noticed he looked pale and was barely eating.

She reached over and felt Brian's forehead. "He feels a little warm. I'll have to find the thermometer and take his temperature."

"Do I have to eat my cereal?"

"That's okay. Just drink the juice. If you get back in bed, someone will come in and read you a story."

"I'll put him back. Come on, pal." Richard watched his son finish his juice, then took him by the hand.

Richard's a good father, she thought. *He loves his children with all his heart. He just doesn't love me anymore.*

"Maybe there's a clinic we can take him to around here," Richard said as they left the room.

"Yes, I'll check the phone book," Regina answered.

They had lost their insurance when Richard lost his job. Buying private insurance was so expensive, it was out of the question right now. They had relied on a free health clinic back in Pennsylvania. The wait was always long and the doctors often harried, but at least it was medical attention. There was always the emergency room, she reminded herself, though Brian didn't seem sick enough for that.

Regina poured herself a cup of coffee and sat down at the table. It looked as though her day was planned. Register Madeline at school, then take Brian to the doctor. By the time they found a clinic, waited for an exam, and got home, it would be time to pick up Madeline again, Regina had no doubt.

And there was so much to do in this house.

No matter. First things first. Her children would always come first. At least that was one thing she and Richard still agreed on.

* * *

THE SCHOOL REGISTRATION WENT SMOOTHLY. REGINA DIDN'T have a utility bill, but when she showed her deed to the house and explained their situation, the woman in the school office—a Mrs. Anita Wilkes—was very understanding.

"Warren Oakes handled the estate?" Mrs. Wilkes asked, looking up from one of the documents Regina had offered.

"Yes, Mr. Oakes is the attorney."

"I see. Well, I'll give him a call later today to verify all this, Mrs. Rowan. Everything else seems in order. Madeline can start today."

Mrs. Wilkes smiled over at Madeline, but she barely smiled back. Regina guessed that she had hoped the missing utility bill would give her another day of freedom. No such luck.

Mrs. Wilkes offered to walk Madeline to her new classroom. Regina leaned over and kissed her daughter good-bye.

"Don't worry, it will be fine, Maddy. I'll be back at three to pick you up. Have a great day, okay?"

Madeline looked pale and anxious but tried to hide her panic. She took a step forward, then ran back and gave Regina a surprisingly tight hug. Regina hugged her back and quickly let go. Then she turned and walked out of the school.

BY THE TIME REGINA GOT BACK TO THE HOUSE, BRIAN WAS sleeping up in his room and Richard had started painting the kitchen, which they'd agreed yesterday was the priority.

Luckily, there were cans of white paint and some brushes and rollers in the basement, along with a ladder, and he didn't have to go out and buy any supplies. Not today, anyway. Regina would have preferred a cozier color in the kitchen—a soft shade of yellow, maybe—but at least the room would look clean and fresh.

She stood back, watching him work. "That looks better already," she said. "Maybe I can stencil a border up near the ceiling."

"How did it go at school?" Richard asked without turning.

"I couldn't show anything but the deed as proof of residence. Luckily, the woman in the office was very nice. She seems to know Mr. Oakes and said she'd call and take care of it."

"How was Madeline?"

"A little nervous. I hope she likes her new teachers and finds some friends. It will take time, I guess."

"Yes, it will. I hope it's worth the effort."

"What do you mean by that?"

Richard shrugged and dipped the brush into the paint can. "You know what we agreed, Regina. We'd fix this place up enough to sell it."

And then we separate, she added silently. Those had been the terms of their truce: to stay together long enough to flip the house and give the kids one last Christmas as a family.

"I remember," she said quickly. "But there's no predicting how long it will all take. I just hope Maddy finds some friends at school quickly. That's all I meant."

He glanced at her over his shoulder but didn't reply.

Regina had been the one to propose their plan. She'd grown tired of arguing with him. It was terrible for the children to be in that toxic atmosphere. Brian would cry and Madeline would try to hide in another room—until they were all living in one crowded, depressing motel room. That was rock bottom.

Regina had never imagined breaking up her family. But she felt worn out, as if there were no hope for them to ever get back on the right track with their relationship.

Richard agreed that he didn't want to stay together, either. It was too painful and difficult. So they would stay together until they could sell the house.

Richard had worked so hard while the kids were small; for years he supported them all. Regina felt she owed it to him to share the sale. They lost all the money they had invested in their house in Stover when the bank took it over. That had been a dark day. She knew Richard had never gotten over it.

But this house was in worse shape than she'd imagined. It was going to take time and effort to make it salable.

"I guess we'll just have to see how it works out," she said finally. "It's a roof over our heads and more comfortable than a motel; more comfortable than I expected."

He finally turned around to face her. "Yes, you can say that much for the place."

She heard Brian sneeze and then call out to her. "Mom? Are you home?"

"I'll be right there, honey."

She still had to find a doctor for Brian and, when she got home, tackle a mountain of laundry.

The mere sight of the washer and dryer down in the basement had made her heart sing. She had been dragging the family's clothes to Laundromats for over a year.

It was even more wonderful to have a real kitchen again, not being forced to make do with a hot plate and microwave in a motel.

As she hurried upstairs to check on her son, Regina wondered again about her husband. Wasn't he grateful for this second chance to give their family some stability?

All he seemed to see were the downsides. She just didn't understand him anymore. And that thought made her sad.

"BEN . . . I CAN'T BELIEVE IT. YOU'RE SITTING UP ALREADY? ARE you sure that's all right?"

Ben smiled proudly at his wife, though his chest and legs hurt something fierce. "The nurse helped me into the chair. She more or less insisted. They get you up here. No malingerers, that's for sure."

Carolyn turned to the nurse, who was checking his vital signs. "Is that safe? Just yesterday he had all that surgery. Isn't it too soon?"

"It's important for post-surgical patients to sit up and move around as soon as possible," the nurse explained. "We don't want him lying flat and risking pneumonia."

"Oh, right. I think the doctor mentioned that." Carolyn walked over to him and kissed his cheek. Her hand lingered on his shoulder.

"Gee, you look pretty today. That scarf matches your blue eyes," Ben said brightly. "I'm a lucky man, aren't I?" he asked the nurse, who smiled in reply.

"Oh, Ben, what a thing to say." His wife was surprised by his compliment but pleased, he thought. He could see her blushing as she turned to take off her hat and jacket.

Carolyn was such a pretty woman, even now in her sixties. They had grown so used to each other over the years, he didn't even see it anymore. Or tell her nearly enough.

This morning, he felt himself filled with joy at the mere sight of her . . . He'd come so close to . . . to losing everything.

I should give more compliments. Life is too short to be stingy with praise or a good word.

"More important, how do you feel?" Carolyn asked, turning back to him.

"I'm doing well. That's what the doctor says. Two of them already came by today. I'm getting plenty of attention."

"I wish I'd been here in time to talk to them." Carolyn seemed distressed.

"Oh, they'll be back. Don't worry."

She sat in a chair next to him and stroked his cheek. Except for the bandage covering the cut, his face was smooth, bare of his familiar beard.

"The doctor said that cut should heal quickly and shouldn't even leave a scar. Not much of one, anyway," she commented. "Do you miss your beard?" she added, curious.

"A little. I don't notice, really. Unless I look in the mirror," he admitted.

"I can't remember the last time I saw you without a beard. When Rachel was born?"

"That's right. I shaved it off because I was concerned it would scratch her skin. I really think it was because I didn't know what to do with myself. I was so nervous about being a father."

They both laughed a little. It was comforting to relive this memory, he realized, a great comfort after facing his own mortality.

"You look well, Ben. You have more color in your cheeks. You were looking a little pasty the last few days. I thought you were coming down with something."

"The doctor said I would feel improvement very quickly. I feel as if I have more energy already, honestly," he told her.

She stared at him with an assessing look. "That's good. But don't plan on running any marathons for a while, okay?"

"The nurse says that the next step is getting me up and

walking. Then laps around the corridor. I'm content to start with those modest goals for now," he promised.

"Fine with me. I have to take better care of you." Her expression changed, looking suddenly regretful. "I feel terrible. I haven't been a very good wife to let you get sick like this. I should have been watching you more closely, making sure you ate right and got more exercise."

She was close to tears, and Ben leaned over to give her a hug, though it hurt him to do so.

"Carolyn, how can you say such a thing? What about me? I think you did all you could to rein me in, sweetheart. You would broil fish for dinner, then I'd sneak a cheeseburger at the Clam Box the next day for lunch," he admitted. "How many times did you invite me to go out walking, or go to the gym? And I always put you off."

Carolyn tilted her head to one side. "That's true. But I should have tried harder. I should have been more insistent. I feel very guilty about this, Ben."

"You shouldn't. Nobody's blaming you, believe me. You did all you could, and you're just not the nagging type. For which I've always been grateful," he added with a smile.

She shook her head, attempting to look stern. "Things are going to be different around our house from now on. I've been reading up on heart-healthy cooking on the Internet, and—"

"No more cheeseburgers?"

"Or clam rolls," she added. "Or a lot of foods you like."

"Oh boy, I knew this was coming." He made a face, but wasn't really disappointed. "I have to change my evil ways. I'm ready to see the light. This was a wake-up call, Carolyn. I know that."

"Yes, it was. A really loud one," she replied pointedly.

She was angry at him for ignoring his health, but Ben knew her anger came from her concern, and he knew he deserved it.

"I will do better from here on in, Carolyn. I really mean it," he promised her, taking her hand in his.

"All right, then. That's all I ask. I'm sure the doctor will have some instructions about diet and exercise," she added.

"Oh yes, I'm sure he will, dear." It hurt a bit to laugh, but Ben couldn't help it.

Rachel, her husband, Jack, and Mark appeared in the doorway.

"I don't think we're all allowed in here at once," Mark said sheepishly. "But we all wanted to see you, Dad. And we couldn't choose who would come first."

"Just for a minute," Ben encouraged them. "You can stay until the nurse kicks you out."

The nurse who had helped him into the chair was gone. But she would be back soon, he was sure.

There were hugs all around. It was so good to see his family. The best medicine, he thought.

"Nora and Will made you these cards." Rachel took out a thick pile of handmade cards and drawings from her purse.

"They're worried about you, Ben," Jack added. "I promised to take a picture on the phone and show them that you're all right."

"Good idea." Ben sifted through the greetings from his grandchildren. The simple, heartfelt messages and so many Xs and Os to mark kisses and hugs nearly made him cry.

"I love my cards," he said quietly. "Let's hang them up on that bulletin board. We'll call the children later, and I'll thank them."

"They were afraid that you wouldn't be home from the hospital in time for Christmas," Rachel reported with a smile. "I told them you'd be home in plenty of time, and that by Christmas, you would almost be back to your old self again."

As a physical therapist, his daughter knew the course of the recovery for this type of operation. Ben was sure that she would be a great help to him in the days to come.

"The doctor told me this morning it will be about six weeks," he said. "I'm just worried about the church. Why couldn't this have happened practically any other time of the year—when there's nothing that important going on?"

"Now, Ben, don't get yourself excited. That can't be good for you." Carolyn's voice was firm, her new tough-love policy kicking in, he realized. "There's always something going on at the church. There's never a good time to get sick, is there?"

"Mom is right, Dad," Mark said. "The church will survive without you for a few weeks. You do so much there, it might even be good for the congregation to miss you a little. They'll appreciate you more when you come back."

"The congregation appreciates me," Ben replied. *Most of the time,* he added silently. "Has anyone told Reverend Boland that I'm in the hospital?"

Reverend Boland was Ben's superior and the minister at a church in nearby Princeton.

"Yes, dear. I believe Sam Morgan called Reverend Boland at least twice yesterday, and Reverend Boland called me at home last night. He's very concerned about you. He said not to worry, he'll put out a call for a temporary minister right away. He promised to call and speak to you later, if you're up to it."

"As long as the wheels are in motion. I hope he can find someone soon." Ben knew he wasn't supposed to worry about the church right now, but it was second nature. He couldn't help it.

"I'll try him at his church later. We have a lot to figure out." He took a breath and suddenly realized he was very tired again.

"Dad, are you all right?" Rachel leaned toward him with concern.

"I'm fine, sweetie. Just tired from sitting in this chair. Isn't that something?" He tried to laugh at himself, but couldn't quite.

"I'll get a nurse to help you back to bed," Mark said, and quickly left the room.

"I'd better go back to the waiting room before she catches me in here," his son-in-law said. "Take care, Ben. See you soon."

His guests dispersed in all directions, like a flock of birds taking wing. Ben was suddenly alone with Carolyn again.

"Are you all right, Ben?" she asked quietly.

"I'm fine. Don't worry. This is all par for the course. The doctor said I would feel very tired. And I'd have some pain." Which he did indeed, though he didn't want to worry Carolyn about it. "It's only the first day."

"Yes, and you've overdone it. Too much visiting and talking."

"Yes, dear," he said contritely. He was a talker, a trait that seemed to be part of his job.

But neither of them was willing to acknowledge out loud the plain truth of the matter, he realized. He'd had a near-fatal heart attack and a complicated surgery.

He had to respect what he'd gone through. He had to let go and let God take over the church and all his other responsibilities. For a while, at least. He'd take another nap and call Reverend Boland when he was able.

REGINA WASN'T ABLE TO FIND A LISTING FOR A MEDICAL CLINIC, except for one that seemed to be located on a nearby island. She didn't know any of the roads and decided this wouldn't be a good time to explore, especially when she found a listing for a family practice in town, a Dr. Harding. The office was located right on Main Street, so little chance of getting lost, she thought.

She dialed the number on her cell phone. It rang a few times before someone finally picked up. "Doctor's office," a woman said.

Regina introduced herself, then added, "My son is sick. He's had a cold for a few days, and now I think he has an ear infection. We're not regular patients of the doctor; we just moved here. But I wondered if I could bring him in today."

"I can fit you in this afternoon. We just had a cancellation. Can you come over around one?"

"Yes, of course." Regina had found her way to the middle school this morning using a map, so she knew the way to the village. It was pretty simple. They weren't quite as far out of town as she had first thought.

"Great. I'll put you in the appointment list. Rowan, right?" the woman asked.

"That's right. I did want to mention—"

Before Regina could finish, the woman interrupted. "Thanks. Come fifteen minutes early for the paperwork, okay? See you soon, Mrs. Rowan." Then she hung up.

Regina sighed. She wanted to tell the receptionist that she didn't have insurance. What kind of a medical receptionist didn't ask that question?

Regina thought of calling back, but realized that she had no other alternative. She had to get Brian looked at by a doctor. She would simply have to be prepared to pay for the office visit. She just hoped it wasn't too expensive.

At promptly twelve forty-five, Regina and Brian entered the doctor's office. A few patients sat in the waiting room, but the receptionist was nowhere to be seen. Regina sat Brian down and found a picture book for him, then returned to the front desk.

After a few minutes, a woman with dark curly hair and brilliant blue eyes bustled out to the desk. She seemed harried and

THOMAS KINKADE AND KATHERINE SPENCER

distracted. A man who appeared to be a doctor followed. He wore a white lab coat and a stethoscope around his neck.

"I told you this morning, I can't come back tomorrow," the woman was saying. "I'm sorry, honey. I'll call another agency. I'll let you know what they say."

"All right, let's hope for the best." The doctor picked up some files from the desk and disappeared into the back of the office again.

The familiar tone of the conversation told Regina that these two were more than just boss and employee. She felt pretty certain that they were husband and wife.

The reluctant receptionist finally noticed Regina standing by the desk and looked at her with a charming, contrite smile.

"I'm so sorry to have kept you waiting. Can I help you?"

"I'm Mrs. Rowan. We spoke over the phone this morning?"

"Yes, of course. You made an appointment for your son."

"That's right." Regina took a breath. "I wanted to tell you over the phone, we don't have any insurance right now."

The receptionist seemed unfazed, and Regina felt instantly relieved. At some doctors' offices, they made a big fuss and embarrassed you. Or turned you away.

"Just fill out the information on this sheet, medical history and so forth. On the back, also . . . and this one, too." The woman handed her a second sheet. "The office has a fee for service. It's a sliding scale," she said simply. "Or we can bill you and you can pay us when you're able."

Regina was surprised at that offer. The receptionist seemed to read her thoughts. "Dr. Harding is most concerned about patients getting the care they need."

"That's a generous policy," Regina replied.

"My husband is a very generous man," the receptionist said. "He's a good doctor, too."

Regina smiled and returned to the seat next to Brian. As she filled out the forms, another part of her mind was piecing together the situation here. Obviously Mrs. Harding was not the regular receptionist and was only helping her husband for the day.

That meant they needed someone. Even temporarily. Regina had never worked in a medical office, but thought she could do it. She had worked in plenty of offices and knew general procedure and most of the computer programs that were usually used.

She finished the paperwork quickly, then walked back to the desk, working up the courage to ask if there was a job here. Even a day's pay would help her family.

She handed back the clipboard and papers. "Thanks," the receptionist said, looking it over. But before Regina could ask about the possible job opening, a nurse came through the door to the inner office. "The doctor can see your son now, Mrs. Rowan. I'll take you back."

Regina took Brian by the hand and followed the nurse down the narrow corridor to an exam room.

Dr. Harding was waiting for them, washing his hands at the sink. "Hello there. I'm Dr. Harding," he said, introducing himself. He helped Brian up onto the exam table. "Not feeling very well today, are you?"

Brian shook his head. He was unusually quiet today.

Dr. Harding gave him a sympathetic smile. "All right, let's see what's going on and how we can fix it for you."

The doctor asked questions about Brian's symptoms, noting them on a chart. Then he took Brian's temperature with an electronic thermometer. "One hundred and two," he said. He examined Brian, listening to his heart and chest and looking down his throat and in his ears.

Brian was uncomfortable with that part, but didn't fuss too much. "It's almost over, honey," Regina soothed him.

"You're doing great, Brian," Dr. Harding told him. "When we're all done, you can pick out a few toys from the treasure chest. Would you like that?"

Brian nodded eagerly, distracted from his woes by the offer.

New toys, even inexpensive small ones, would be very welcome, Regina thought. When they left Pennsylvania, they hadn't been able to take a lot of the children's belongings, only their very favorite toys that could fit in the car. Brian was definitely getting bored with those choices.

When the exam was over, Regina helped Brian put his sweatshirt back on while Dr. Harding brought a test for strep out to the nurse. When he came back, he showed Brian a cardboard treasure chest in the far corner of the room, and left him to figure out his reward for surviving the ordeal.

"We took a test for strep, just in case. Right now, it looks as if he has an ear infection. I'm going to give you a prescription for an antibiotic and another for ear drops, and there are some other instructions for care. Motrin for the fever, plenty of fluids . . ." The doctor reviewed the usual care for colds and flu. "If you have any questions, or if his symptoms don't improve in a day or so, just call the office."

Regina was soon zipping up Brian's jacket, putting the prescription slips in her purse, and thanking Dr. Harding for his kind attention. Then she was out in the waiting area again, which had become much busier. Dr. Harding followed.

Dr. Harding's wife now looked quite overwhelmed, trying to answer several calls on the multiline phone at once while checking patients out and checking patients in and giving the doctor the proper charts for his appointments.

"How's it going out here, Molly?" he asked his wife.

"How does it look like it's going? I'd have more luck sitting in for the day as an air-traffic controller. Did everyone in town get sick overnight? Is this some sort of plague?"

Dr. Harding grinned. "Calm down, honey. It can't be that bad. Cynthia seemed to manage just fine."

"Really? Then why did she quit without any notice?"

So they did need help. And not just temporarily.

"Do you need some office help?" Regina cut in with a burst of boldness. "I have some experience," she added.

Molly looked at her as if she'd just dropped down from heaven. "Are you looking for a job?"

Regina nodded. "Yes, I am. We just moved here. My husband and I are both looking," she added.

"Have you ever worked in a medical office before?" Dr. Harding asked with interest.

"No," Regina said honestly, "but I do have a lot of office experience." Regina briefly reviewed her relevant job experience and the computer programs she knew. She'd had so many jobs since she married Richard. Off again, on again, in and out of the workforce as their income and circumstances demanded.

"And I can give you references," she added. "We just moved up from Stover, Pennsylvania. If you'd like, I can come back for an interview . . ."

"Wait here a minute, would you?" Molly cast her a quick smile, then tugged her husband into the back office.

Regina checked on Brian, who was totally entranced by his new toys, a plastic car and a neon-green Slinky. He didn't even notice the delay.

The doctor's wife soon swept out to the reception area again. "We can offer you a temporary position for now. Would that be all right?"

"Absolutely."

Molly looked pleased—and greatly relieved. "Can you be here tomorrow at eight forty-five?"

Regina's heart nearly broke out into a tap dance. "Yes, I can. No problem." It would be problematic, getting out of the house that early and into town, but she couldn't risk being anything but positive.

"Okay, then you're hired. You can give us your references tomorrow and all the other information we'll need to put you on the payroll." Molly told Regina what the hourly wage was for the job. "Would that be all right with you? To start, I mean?"

The salary was very generous, Regina thought. She hadn't made nearly that much in her last job.

"It's fine. Thank you very much, Mrs. Harding."

"My last name is Willoughby, but call me Molly, please." Molly shook her head and grinned. "We're not formal around here."

"Please call me Regina. I look forward to seeing you tomorrow."

"I'll be here. At least for a few minutes to show you around. Then I have to get back to my own job," she added.

"What type of work do you do?" Regina asked, curious.

"I own a catering company, Willoughby Fine Foods. We also have a food shop on Water Street. Come by some night when you don't have time to cook dinner."

"I will," Regina promised, though she guessed that the store was expensive.

Regina left the office and bundled Brian into the backseat of her car. She stopped at a drugstore to get his medicine and then headed over to the middle school to pick up Madeline.

Tomorrow, Madeline could take the bus. Mrs. Oakes had told them where the stop was. A lucky thing, Regina realized, because with her new job, she wouldn't be able to drive her daughter both ways to school each day.

Regina reached the school just as the bell rang. She parked on the curb and watched for Madeline. Her daughter was one of the first to leave the building. She was walking with two other girls who both waved good-bye as they headed for the school buses. Regina thought that was a good sign.

Madeline climbed into the front seat and fastened her seat belt. Regina didn't want to pounce on her, but couldn't help it. "How did it go? Do you like your new teachers?"

"My teacher for my core subjects, Mrs. Finch, is pretty nice. And today we had a double period of science and gym. We played basketball. Almost no one got rebounds, but it was fun. The gym teacher asked me to practice with the girls' team."

Madeline seemed quietly proud of that compliment. She was very athletic and had played guard for the girls' team back in Stover.

"Nice. Are you going to?" Regina asked, trying not to sound overly eager. *Do it, do it. Please? That would be a great way to make new friends,* she wanted to say. But she practically bit her tongue. Regina already knew that Madeline was liable to do just the opposite of anything she said. Not because she was a bad kid, but because she was a tween, and it was her job and sworn duty to be contrary.

"Maybe," Madeline replied. "Did you see those girls I walked out with?"

"Are they in your class?"

Madeline nodded. "Jen sits next to me and Alyssa is in my math group. I sat at Jen's table during lunch. She called me over."

"That was very thoughtful of her," Regina said, feeling overwhelmed with relief that some nice girl had taken pity on her daughter.

"Jen has a horse. She said I could come over and ride it sometime. Could I?"

"I don't see why not," her mother replied. "I told you you'd make friends easily."

"It's not a sleepover invitation, so you didn't win," Madeline replied.

"I didn't win *yet*. The week isn't over." Regina smiled and Madeline had to smile back.

Madeline grew quiet again; she watched out her window as they drove back to the house. Just beyond town, the scenery became rural, with hardly a house in sight. The road was edged by brush and trees, the boughs heavy with snow. Every few minutes, the landscape would open and a wide snowy field would come into view, or a pond edged with trees and brush.

Regina had been back and forth on this road all day, but only now noticed how serene and scenic it was. Maybe because her heart felt a bit lighter, certainly lighter than yesterday morning when she and Richard had driven this same route, coming over to meet Warren Oakes.

All in all, their first day in the new house had been a good one, Regina reflected. Madeline liked her school and was starting to make friends. Brian had gotten medical attention, and some new toys, from a very caring doctor. Most amazing of all, she had a job, at least for a while.

Even Richard would have to admit they'd taken a few steps in the right direction. Well, he probably wouldn't actually say it out loud, Regina knew. But he would have to admit it to himself. Cape Light might be a brief stop. But not an unpleasant one.

"BEN? CAN YOU WAKE UP?"

Carolyn sat on the edge of his bed, her hand resting on his shoulder. He thought he was at home, in his own bed, but as his eyes slowly opened and he felt the tug of tubes and the pain in his legs and chest, he remembered.

The room was cast in the shadows of late-afternoon light. "Are you all right?" she asked with concern. "Do you need anything?"

"Some water would be nice." His mouth felt dry as cotton. It must be from all the medications. Carolyn handed him a plastic cup with a straw sticking out the top, and Ben sipped. "How long was I asleep?"

"About two hours, give or take."

"And you sat here the whole time? How boring for you," he said sympathetically.

"I came prepared with my knitting. Did you think I was going to let you out of my sight for one minute today? No chance of that," she said firmly. "I would have let you sleep longer, but Reverend Boland just called. He said you're not to worry about a thing. He's found a temporary minister who can start at church this week. He wants to come and visit, but I told him that you'll be home in a few days, and it would probably be best to come then. Was that all right?"

"Yes, dear. That was fine. As long as he's found someone to step in at church." Ben took a breath, then shifted under the sheets. He suddenly felt restless and confined. It was so annoying to get sick like this, so undermining. "Did he say who's coming? Maybe it's someone I know."

"He did tell me the name. I wrote it down somewhere . . ."
Carolyn got up and went to the chair where she had been reading.
She found a slip of paper stuck in her book. "Here it is. Reverend
Isabel Lawrence. Does that name ring a bell?"

"Isabel Lawrence? A woman?"

"I guess so, dear. I've never heard of a man named Isabel,
though you never know these days."

Carolyn was clearly amused by his reaction. He could have
been more politically correct about it, he realized. He was all for
women's rights and female equality in the workplace and every
place. This choice had just taken him by surprise, that's all. He had
nothing at all against female ministers. The truth was, he didn't
know many.

"Did he say how old she is?"

"No, dear. He didn't really say much at all, except that she
should get to town by Thursday, and he would find someplace for
her to live before then. And he said he would talk to the deacons
and make sure that a few members of the congregation would welcome her and give her some orientation."

"Oh, of course. That goes without saying. I'll put in a word,
too." Ben's mind jumped to the church leaders he would call. Isabel
Lawrence would be warmly welcomed, he had no doubt.

"There's a lot I need to tell her," he said. "Maybe she should
come here first, before she goes over to the church."

Carolyn gave him a thoughtful look. "The doctor said you
could be released in a few days, Friday or Saturday. Maybe you
should wait until you're back home to talk to her."

He knew that look. It meant he was acting as if the old stone
church were going to tumble down to the ground without him.
"All right. If you think the church won't fall down by then, I suppose I can wait to see Reverend Lawrence."

"It might tremble a bit, but I don't think it will cave in completely," Carolyn told him. "I'm sure your very responsible trustees and deacons will spot any warning signs and prop it up in time."

"I'm sure they will. I have to take care of myself now, I guess. That's the priority. The sooner I get well, the faster I can return. The doctor said that I'll be able to return to all of my usual activities with a lot more energy than I've felt lately," he reminded her.

He had been glad to hear that, though he found it hard to believe. He couldn't imagine being back to work in six weeks . . . or even six months. His mood seemed to swing between happiness at being alive and fear because he felt so weak. Like an old man.

This, too, shall pass, he reminded himself. *It will take time to get back on an even footing again.*

"Dr. Chandler did say you could go right back to the church when you recovered. If that's what you want to do."

He knew what his wife was hinting at, but didn't know how to respond.

"Even ministers retire, Ben," she added, before he could answer. "I know you've had a great shock and this isn't the time to make any big decisions. But have you thought about that possibility at all?" she asked gently.

"I have thought about it," he admitted. But each time he did, his mind automatically rejected that path. It felt too much like giving up. Even when he felt so weak that merely sitting upright wore him out. "I'll tell you honestly, Carolyn: To retire now, because of the heart trouble, makes me feel as if the decision has been taken out of my hands somehow."

"Well, maybe it has," she said quietly. "Maybe someone else is making the decision for you. You're the minister," she teased him. "You would know better about that than me."

Ben smiled but didn't say more about it. He'd thought of that possibility, too. He had been plucked by the hand of God and set on the sidelines. Given a good scare, to boot. Practically forced to pause and reflect, to reconsider what he'd done with his life so far and what he was going to do with the rest of it.

It had all been a shock, and he hadn't had a chance to process any of it. Except to feel grateful that he was still alive.

It would be wise, as his wife had suggested, not to make any rash decisions.

Still, sitting in this hospital bed, attached to tubes and wires, Ben knew he'd arrived at a crossroads, one he couldn't and shouldn't ignore. Very soon, he would have to decide which way to go.

CHAPTER FOUR

⌒

*R*EGINA HAD BEEN WARY ABOUT WORKING FOR A
doctor. She'd heard that doctors could be demanding
and arrogant. Dr. Harding was nothing like that. He treated her
respectfully, as an equal, unlike most of the managers she had
worked for. Sally Heller, a nurse who had been with the practice
many years, was also very friendly and happy to answer Regina's
many questions.

On Tuesday morning, Molly had met her in the office to show
her the ropes. The orientation was a little daunting. There were a lot
of plates to spin at her small desk—answering calls, scheduling
appointments, pulling files and record keeping, billing and dealing
with insurance companies. But it was only temporary, Regina kept
reminding herself. If she didn't like the work, or they didn't like
her, she didn't have to stay.

She had always been a people person and liked talking to the patients and feeling she was helping them in some small way. She also liked earning money again. That was enough of an inducement to stick with it.

"Looks like you made it a whole three days in this nuthouse, Regina. This is a good sign."

Regina had been answering two calls at once and hadn't even noticed Molly standing at her desk. It was Thursday afternoon, almost lunchtime. Molly had dropped by the office a few times since Regina had started, to talk to Dr. Harding and sometimes bring him lunch. She even brought Regina lunch, too, which was both thoughtful and delicious—a cold beet salad with blue cheese and walnuts.

"I'm hanging in," Regina answered brightly.

"Matt says you're doing a great job. Thank goodness," Molly added. "He's such a nice man at home. I don't know why he just flies through receptionists."

"I don't know why, either. He's a very easy person to work for," Regina answered honestly.

"Maybe he just needs someone who can get things in order around here. That's not his strong point."

It was true. The office was not efficiently organized, but it was nothing a few new systems and set routines couldn't fix.

"I noticed that," Regina replied. "I have a few ideas about reorganizing the patient files to make them easier to find," she added. "I could work on that while I'm here if it's okay."

"By all means, please do," Molly said enthusiastically. "Matt never has ideas like that," she added with a grin.

"He's a doctor. He needs to focus on his patients, not paperwork," Regina reasoned.

Molly smiled. "No wonder he likes you. How are your children doing? Do they like school so far?"

While Molly had been showing Regina the ropes on Tuesday morning, the two women had gotten to know each other a bit. Molly was the type of person who wanted to know your entire life story the first five minutes you spent together. Not in a nosy way, Regina thought; she just liked people and was curious.

"Madeline is making friends and likes most of her teachers. She's going to join the girls' basketball team, too. Brian started at the elementary school this morning," she added. "Richard brought him over. I hope he likes it."

"I hope so, too. How's Richard? Did he find anything yet?"

Regina knew Molly meant work. "He's been watching Brian the last few days and painting some rooms downstairs. He hasn't had time to look."

"Right. It's only been a few days. What does he do again?"

"He's a civil engineer. Back in Stover, he mainly worked for the county."

"Right, I think you told me that the other day."

They both knew jobs for engineers were scarce in this economy. That went without saying.

"Is he handy at all? He's an engineer—he must be, right?" Molly laughed, answering her own question.

"He is, actually," Regina agreed. "He's one of those guys who can fix pretty much anything."

"My brother, Sam, may be looking for help," Molly told her. "He renovates old houses and does all kinds of construction and renovation work. I think he's taking on some big job and is looking to hire more help."

Richard could do that, Regina thought. It would be great if he could earn some money while he was looking for a permanent job. And sooner or later, he was going to need a real job. Once the holidays were over, they were going to have to negotiate a way for him to continue to help support the kids. Living separately would be a bigger drain on their incomes than if they kept their household together. It pained her to think about these things, but she had to face facts.

"So, do you think he'd be interested?" Molly's question drew Regina from her wandering thoughts.

"Oh . . . sure. I think he would be. Richard knows a lot about construction, and he used to have a shop in the basement of our Pennsylvania house and did some carpentry." That's why they thought they could fix up the old house and turn it over for a profit. Richard knew he could do most of the renovation himself.

"Great, I'll tell my brother. I'm going to stop by his shop later. It's just down the street, in the barn behind the Bramble," Molly added. Regina nodded. She had noticed the antique store a few doors down in a small Victorian house with a barn in back. "Here's his phone number." Molly grabbed a pen and a piece of scrap paper. "Tell Richard to call if he's interested."

"Thank you so much, Molly. I appreciate all your help. You're a one-woman employment agency," she added with a grateful smile.

"It's nothing." Molly brushed off the compliment with a grin. "I know what you're going through, Regina. I really struggled myself for a while, raising my two girls. Just hang in there. Hope for the best," she encouraged her. "It will all work out. You'll see."

Dr. Harding came out of the inner office. Regina could tell he was there, even before he spoke, just from the expression on Molly's face and the way her eyes lit up. It was so sweet to see a married couple who had such a strong, loving connection.

She and Richard were like that once. But they'd lost that bond somehow. When their eyes met, more often than not Regina felt uneasy, trying to sense if Richard was upset about something.

Regina had a feeling that if she ever confided the entire story to

Molly, her new friend would advise her to "hang in there and think positively." That formula might not solve every problem, but it could go a long way, Regina thought.

Sometimes it felt as if you were meant to meet certain people. Molly was one of them. Regina didn't think of herself as religious, though she did believe in God. The last two years, she and God had certainly been carrying on regular conversations, as she asked for His help and direction more and more.

She had once heard that, instead of answering our prayers directly, God often sends other people to answer them. It seemed to Regina that Molly's kindness and help was just that—an answer to some of her most heartfelt concerns. If she and Richard were both earning decent paychecks without the burden of a mortgage or even rent, they might actually start to catch up.

Maybe they couldn't keep their marriage together, but they could give the children a good Christmas. Regina had been dreading the holidays. They had been forced to celebrate Thanksgiving on the road, stopping at a fast-food restaurant. At least the kids thought it was fun. Or maybe they just acted that way because they could see that she and Richard were so upset and humiliated, even fighting about the situation in front of them.

Regina regretted acting that way. She knew it wasn't right, but sometimes the tension was too much.

Their pathetic Thanksgiving meal was probably the low point, Regina thought. The last two holiday seasons had been very difficult to navigate. So much forced happiness all around and everyone buying and buying. It put their own situation in stark contrast, with little to celebrate and unable to buy gifts for the children. Too proud for handouts, they had just tried to ignore the whole season. Which didn't work, either.

This year, it could be different. They could decorate the house and have a few gifts for the kids. Nothing lavish, but there would be presents to open.

Regina didn't want to get too carried away. Richard had to find some work first. If Sam Morgan couldn't hire him, Sam might know of some other jobs in the area.

One thing leads to another. Regina felt a spark of hope. Molly was right: She had to hang on and hope for the best.

CAROLYN HAD SPENT THURSDAY AT BEN'S BEDSIDE, MAINLY IN the armchair near the window, knitting. Ben had been up and about, doing laps around the hospital corridor with her help. But he was tired out, back in bed, just about dozing off when she got a call on her cell phone from Vera Plante.

The church wasn't sure where to house the temporary minister, Vera explained, especially on such short notice. She certainly couldn't stay at the parsonage. But Vera Plante had a large old house and often rented rooms, providing meals and other necessities. The church council had decided to house Reverend Lawrence with Vera, at least to start off. Vera was clearly in a flurry, getting the room and house ready. She didn't have any other boarders at this time.

She had called Carolyn to tell her that she was bringing Reverend Lawrence to church that evening, so that the congregation could meet her.

"Tucker thought I should bring her to the Peace & Plenty meeting," Vera said, mentioning the weekly gathering in Fellowship Hall where church members met to make sandwiches for those in need throughout the community. "I just wanted you to know that we'll all be there, in case you're home from the hospital."

"Thanks, Vera. I'd love to meet her. But I might stay here with

Ben tonight," Carolyn replied. She glanced at her husband, who had perked up with curiosity.

"I thought you might. I hope he's improving. Please give him my best."

"I will," Carolyn promised. They hung up, and she turned to Ben. "That was Vera. Reverend Lawrence is going to board with her. She's quite excited."

"I'm sure she is. What's Reverend Lawrence like? Did Vera say?"

"She hasn't arrived yet. Vera expects her any minute. They're going over to the church tonight, to the food outreach meeting. Tucker thought it would be a good opportunity for Reverend Lawrence to meet some church members," Carolyn reported.

"I'm sure everyone is eager to meet her," Ben said.

Carolyn gave him a sympathetic smile. The one person who was the most curious, Ben, was unable to attend.

"I think you have to go, Carolyn," he added. "The minister's wife should welcome her. That's the polite thing to do."

"Of course I want to welcome her, Ben. We'll have her over this weekend, once you're home."

Ben's doctors had told them that Ben could go home as soon as Friday, news that pleased everyone. As much as Carolyn wanted him home, she hoped he didn't try to do too much too soon. She could tell he was already getting restless in this unusual role—someone who was getting care, not giving it. He was the one usually stationed at the bedside, comforting and ministering. He didn't know how to be the one in the bed, she noticed.

"We'll invite her over for coffee," Carolyn continued. "The two of you can settle in front of the fire and have a long talk about what's going on at church. That would be very welcoming, don't you think?"

"Of course it will be." He sighed and avoided her gaze. "It's just that . . . well . . ."

"It's just that you can't wait that long to find out what she's like. So you want me to go and spy for you. Is that it?" Carolyn was amused. She continued with her knitting and peered at him over the edge of her reading glasses.

Ben sat back against his pillows and took a breath. She could tell he was trying not to smile, but couldn't help it.

"I can't get anything past you, can I?"

"Very little," Carolyn agreed.

Though you did a good job hiding your heart condition, she silently added.

She felt her own heart clutch at the reminder—how they had almost lost him. After the sheer elation of Ben's survival, they had both been hit by the enormous, sobering truth of the situation, wondering how they should carry on from here. Did they need to worry every minute if Ben was going to have another heart attack, and this time not survive?

Their lives were forever changed. But they weren't sure yet *how* they had changed.

Being sidelined from church at the holidays was going to be tough. Ben had so many concerns about a minister stepping into his place. As Carolyn looked over at him, he sighed and picked up a newspaper he had already read twice that day.

"Okay, I'll go. I'm curious to meet her, too," she admitted.

"Good, I'm glad," Ben said without looking up from the newspaper. "I think it's the polite thing to do . . . And don't get home too late; I'll be waiting up for a full report."

He finally looked up at her and met her glance. They both laughed at the same time.

* * *

THE PARKING LOT WAS FULL OF CARS WHEN CAROLYN REACHED the church. The word had spread; Vera was good at that, Carolyn knew. Obviously, many people had turned out to meet Ben's replacement.

It was a boost for the Peace & Plenty committee, Carolyn reflected. They usually struggled along with a skeleton crew of volunteers in the winter. No one liked to come out on cold nights. But there would be a pile of sandwiches made tonight, thanks to Reverend Lawrence's debut.

Sophie Potter stood in the hallway, just inside the glass doors, and greeted Carolyn with a hug. "Carolyn, so sweet of you to come. How are you holding up? How's Ben?"

"I'm fine, just a little tired. Ben is doing very well. He might come home tomorrow, or Saturday. He's getting restless."

"That's a good sign. He's not the type to linger in bed a minute longer than he needs to. He'll be back to his old self very soon," Sophie predicted.

Carolyn hung up her coat on a hook in the hallway, and they walked toward Fellowship Hall. They first passed the church kitchen, which was bustling with activity. Wearing an apron and plastic gloves, Molly Willoughby was slicing a large ham with a stainless steel slicing machine, while her sister-in-law, Jessica, arranged the food on platters. There were others in the kitchen as well, making hard-boiled eggs and slicing loaves of bakery bread. Carolyn wasn't sure where all the supplies came from, though the whole program was run on donations.

As she walked into Fellowship Hall, she saw a few of the deacons setting up folding tables in a long row that nearly went the length of the room. Other volunteers were covering the tables with plastic and setting out other supplies.

Carolyn heard a few friends call out to her. Tucker Tulley and his wife, Fran, paused in their work to greet her. Emily and Dan waved from across the room, and even Lillian Warwick deigned to acknowledge her with a tilt of her head.

Carolyn was surprised to see Lillian. Though she was a church trustee who contributed generously to their funding, she rarely came out of her house at night and never volunteered for anything. Obviously, she was eager to interview Reverend Lawrence and decide if she was worthy or not.

But where was Reverend Lawrence? Carolyn looked around and finally spotted the new minister.

Tall and thin, she had short red hair with long bangs that emphasized her large brown eyes. Her face was bare of makeup, but she didn't need any, Carolyn thought. She had a few freckles across her nose and high cheekbones that made her look young, even tomboyish. But she had to be in her mid- to late thirties, Carolyn thought, noticing the little laugh lines around her eyes and mouth.

Reverend Lawrence stood with Digger Hegman and his daughter, Grace, her head tilted to one side, listening with complete attention.

Grace Hegman was best known as the quiet proprietor of the antique store in town, the famous Bramble. But she was quite active at church and sat on the council and other committees. Her father, Digger, a retired fisherman, had been famous in his clamming days. Grace was devoted to him. They lived together over the shop, which had been a challenge the last few years, since Digger's mind was no longer very clear. Grace was quite stoic. She never complained, but she often went to Ben for counsel. Carolyn knew Grace would miss that support, even though it wouldn't be for long.

Sophie suddenly reappeared and took Carolyn's arm. "I think

it's time we rescued the new minister," she said in a quiet voice. "I love Digger, but he's probably bending her ear with some story from fifty years ago."

Sophie wasn't being snide; it was true. Most of Digger's conversation now involved the distant past, which seemed more vivid to him than his everyday life.

"Oh yes. That was a blizzard," Carolyn heard Grace saying. "But we usually don't get snowstorms quite that bad here. The snowfall is always a little lighter here on the coast."

Carolyn suspected that Grace was afraid her father was going to scare poor Reverend Lawrence away with his stories of blizzards and hurricanes—and giant, man-eating clams.

"I grew up in Minnesota, so I know a little about snow," Reverend Lawrence replied. She had a nice smile, Carolyn thought.

She had a nice voice, too, even and low, but not too soft. A nice speaking voice was important for a minister.

Her outfit was simple: a blue-gray cardigan with a white top underneath, worn over dark jeans. A single piece of jewelry, a cross that hung from a thin leather strip around her neck, was the only suggestion of her profession. It appeared to have been made by hand, a folk or native design. The piece had an exotic, primitive beauty, Carolyn thought. The choice seemed to say a lot about the woman who wore it.

"Excuse me, Grace. Carolyn would like to meet Reverend Lawrence." Sophie edged her way into the little group and pulled Carolyn along, like a little tugboat.

"Reverend Lawrence, this is Mrs. Lewis," Sophie said in her most social tone. "Reverend Ben's wife."

"Yes, of course. How nice to meet you. Please, call me Isabel. I'm not the formal type." She put out her hand and shook Carolyn's hand firmly.

"You can call me Carolyn. I'm not the formal type, either."

"How is Reverend Lewis? Reverend Boland said he might be out of the hospital soon."

"He should be out tomorrow or Saturday," Carolyn reported. "He wants to meet you very soon. We'd like to have you over sometime this weekend. Maybe for coffee?"

"That's very kind of you, but I don't want to cause you any extra work or trouble. He might not be up to visitors."

"It's no trouble. Ben is eager to meet you and talk about the church. It's hard for him to be forced to stay away like this," Carolyn confided. "Especially during Christmas."

"I understand," Reverend Isabel answered with a serious expression. "I can stop by whenever it's convenient. Reverend Boland has told me such wonderful things about this church and your husband's work here. I'm very eager to meet him."

It wasn't so much what she said, but the way she said it. The warmth and compassion in her eyes and her tone of voice. *I like her,* Carolyn decided. *Ben will, too.*

Before they could talk further, Tucker Tulley came out of the kitchen and drew everyone's attention.

"I just want to thank you all for coming out on such a cold night. We're going to bring the supplies out in a minute and get started. We'll be making two hundred bagged lunches tonight, and also sending out lots of fruit and hard-boiled eggs.

"If you haven't done it already, please wash your hands and put on gloves. We need people making sandwiches at this end of the table and baggers down at that end." He pointed to the different stations at the folding tables that had been set up along the length of the room.

"And last but not least, I need a few people in the kitchen, washing apples and watching the eggs."

"I'm going to go wash up and get my gloves on," Carolyn told Sophie and Isabel. "Be right back."

"Where do I get gloves?" Isabel asked.

"In the kitchen. Just follow me," Carolyn said.

Isabel followed Carolyn into the church kitchen, where pots of eggs covered every burner on the big stove. The kitchen was large but crowded. Isabel dodged a woman carrying a platter of sliced cheese and another carrying a case of apples.

"This is quite an operation, isn't it?" she said to Carolyn when they met again at the sink.

"Oh, it is. I haven't volunteered here for a while," Carolyn admitted. "They've really expanded lately. It's wonderful to see."

"Where does the food go?" Isabel asked.

"It's given out to children mostly. They take it over to two or three youth centers not far from here. Most of these kids get free breakfast and lunch at school, but there's not enough food at home and they're always hungry," Carolyn added. "You'd be surprised. Even the nicest-looking neighborhoods, never mind the poorer ones, have kids in need."

Isabel knew that child hunger was a hidden problem and could be found anywhere. But she had come here from a place where need was so obvious. She never expected that her first interaction with this church would involve this kind of ministry.

"Volunteers do this every week?" she asked Carolyn as they each snapped on gloves.

"Every Thursday night," Carolyn confirmed. Then she glanced back with a little smile. "Though they rarely get this large a turn-out. I think a certain new volunteer is a big attraction tonight."

Isabel laughed. "Since everyone is watching me, I'd better get to work. You might decide you got stuck with a lazy minister."

As they walked back out together, Isabel noticed that the noise level in the room had risen considerably, with everyone talking and laughing as they worked on the sandwiches. It was all a bit overwhelming, but heartening to see that energy and goodwill in motion.

"Jump in anywhere," Carolyn advised. "I like the far end, the brown-bagging post. It's less crowded."

"I'll join you then," Isabel said.

She followed Carolyn to the end of the table, where a group was focused on a platter piled high with ham and cheese sandwiches in plastic bags. The sandwiches were put into brown bags and passed to another station, where an apple and a bag of cookies were added to each one.

"Here's a spot for you, Reverend." Isabel's new landlady, Vera Plante, stepped aside and made room for her. Isabel squeezed in between Vera and another woman she had met earlier, Emily Warwick, the town's mayor.

"Just dump a sandwich in and pass it on," Emily advised, handing her some brown bags.

"It's all so well organized," Isabel said, starting in. "How long has the church been doing this?"

"A few years," Vera answered. "We started off slowly. Some church members were visiting after-school centers to help the kids with reading and homework. They started bringing sandwiches and fruit because the kids were so hungry, they could barely concentrate. You can imagine the sort of junk food those places give out, like chips and candy."

"Pretty soon, a few of us got together and began meeting once a week," Emily continued, "making food and bringing it to different places where we knew there was need."

"I'm impressed," Isabel said honestly. "A lot of congregations donate money to those in need, but too few have real hands-on ministries."

"Oh, we do a lot of that here," Vera said. "Reverend Ben is very big on hands-on outreach and involving the community. He's been here so long, he has a big network in town. We could never do all this work without finding volunteers outside the church."

"Reverend Ben lights a fire under us," Sophie said plainly. "He makes us go out and practice what we preach."

"Practice what *he* preaches," Emily corrected her with a laugh.

Isabel laughed, but she was also impressed. The congregation seemed to have an unusually close relationship with their minister. They clearly admired and even loved him. She was glad that she was only a temporary fill-in. Reverend Lewis would be a hard act to follow, she thought.

"Reverend Isabel," Vera said, "tell us about yourself. Did I hear you say that you grew up in the Midwest?"

"In Minnesota, a town called Minnetonka. It's not too far from Minneapolis. But it was a pretty rural place when I was young—a lot of open land, farms, and horses. A lot of snow in the winter," she added with a short laugh.

"Sounds lovely." Sophie Potter stood nearby, adding apples and cookies to the bags.

"Sounds a lot like right here," Digger added. "You'll fit right in."

"I hope so," Isabel replied. She was a country girl at heart, and no amount of travel or living in distant places could take that out of her.

"Where did you serve before coming here? Did you have your own church out in . . . Minnesota?" An older woman down at the end of the table addressed her now. She named the state as if she were talking about deep outer space.

Tucker Tulley had introduced the woman earlier. Lillian Warwick, the mayor's mother, Isabel recalled.

The Warwick matriarch pinned her with a cool gray stare. Isabel was reluctant to make assumptions about people, but she had read somewhere that the first three seconds of a meeting were the most important, that people gathered information quickly on an unconscious, even intuitive basis. Isabel had a feeling that this woman had already judged her, and the judgment was not flattering.

Would she win over Lillian during her tenure here? Isabel had no idea. She did know that she wouldn't make any special efforts to do so. Lillian Warwick was a certain type—and so was Isabel.

"I've never had my own church," Isabel replied calmly. "After being ordained, I served as a youth minister and then an assistant pastor at a small church in Minnesota. For the past four years, I've been part of a ministry down in Haiti. We rebuilt houses and schools that were lost in the hurricanes of 2008 and after the 2010 earthquake."

Her reply was enough to give even Lillian pause for thoughtful reflection.

"It's hard to believe that one tiny island has suffered so many natural disasters," Sophie said. "It doesn't seem fair."

"It's the poorest country in the western hemisphere," noted Dr. Ezra Elliot, Lillian's husband. "It's amazing to me how those people carry on and have any hope at all."

"It is amazing," Isabel answered quietly. "But they have hope and faith."

Jessica Morgan turned to her. "What demanding work that must be."

"Very impressive," Dr. Elliot agreed. "We can all write a check and send a donation, but it takes a certain kind of person to work hands-on in a place like that. My hat is off to you."

He glanced at his wife a moment. She didn't look up at him, focused on counting the brown bags that were going into a larger one.

"Were you there when the earthquake struck?" Carolyn asked.

"Yes, I was, but not near the epicenter," Isabel explained. "Still, it was terrifying."

"Oh, it must have been," Vera agreed, looking afraid to even imagine it.

"How brave of you to stick with it so long," Emily said. "Four years is a long time in such a challenging environment. Was there some term of service you fulfilled there?"

"I never planned to stay that long," Reverend Isabel admitted. "I went down for a two-week visit with some members of our church, a service trip with a youth group. We were there to help build houses and restore clean water systems. But when I saw all the need, I felt a real calling. I went back to Minnesota briefly to resign my position, then returned to Haiti."

Isabel paused and took a breath. She picked up a paper bag but didn't open it. "The year before that, I had a great personal loss . . . My husband died of lung cancer. It spread very rapidly. We didn't have much time together after the diagnosis," she said simply. "My family and friends, even the minister at our church, all thought I was still in shock and acting impulsively. But I knew it was the right thing for me to do. I needed work that would totally consume me."

A certain hush fell over the group, and Isabel wondered if she had said too much. They wanted to know about her; they'd asked so many questions. But maybe this disclosure had been too personal?

Then she felt Emily's light touch on her arm. "I'm so sorry for your loss," she said sincerely. "I lost my first husband when I was twenty. It's hard to pick up the pieces and keep going."

Isabel smiled gratefully at her. She could see that Emily understood, and she appreciated her words. She still missed Steven every day. She always would, no matter where she went, what she did, or who she met.

"That takes a lot of character, to take your grief and channel it into something good," Sophie said. "A lot of people just curl up and give up after a loss like that."

"I'm not sure it was a question of character," Isabel said truthfully. "I felt lost, overwhelmed. As if I were drowning in my sorrow. I asked God to help me, and that was the rope He tossed down."

"Maybe so, but a lot of folks wouldn't have seen it that way. A lot of folks wouldn't have grabbed that rope," Digger replied. "They would have prayed for another one."

The old fisherman's observation broke the somber mood and made everyone laugh.

"Maybe so," Isabel agreed. "But it didn't seem like I had a choice, which was a blessing. I felt an irresistible need to go back there and work."

"You were filled with spirit," Grace said quietly. "That's what happened."

"I hope our church doesn't seem boring after all you've been through, Reverend Isabel," Vera said, stuffing another sandwich in a paper bag. "Reverend Boland only told us that you were coming off a medical leave and weren't currently attached to any particular church. We had no idea that you have such an interesting background."

"If you don't mind my asking, what made you return?" Emily asked curiously. "Did you need a break from that environment?"

"I took a fall . . . and then a break," Isabel said with a small smile. "I fell off a ladder and fractured my right leg. I needed an operation and decided to come home for the surgery and rehab. My family was happy to see me," she added.

"I'll bet," Sophie said. "I'll bet your folks are bursting with pride to have you as a daughter."

"And we are, too, to have you as our minister. Even temporarily," Tucker said.

"Very true," Emily agreed, "but I think we have to let poor Reverend Isabel out of the hot seat for a little while so we can get these sandwiches done. It's getting late."

A teenage volunteer had just put down another large platter of bagged sandwiches and cleared away the empty one. Isabel wasn't sure how many they had packed so far, but on the next table, large clear plastic bags stood filled with lunches.

It still amazed her, the sheer abundance that surrounded her in this country. In this room and kitchen alone, so much meat and cheese and eggs—enough to feed an entire village in Haiti for a year, she thought. Well, maybe not that long. But she wondered if these good people realized how scarce such stockpiles of food were in some places.

It had been jarring to return to this land of plenty after what she'd seen and the way she'd lived in Haiti. Isabel still wasn't entirely used to it and often missed the way of life she'd left in the Caribbean. Though it had been low on creature comforts, there had been certain freedoms and benefits that were hard to explain. Despite the many hardships, she wanted to return to Haiti, or some other area of the world, to continue relief work. While her leg was healing, she had applied to ministries in the Caribbean and Central America. She hoped that by the time Reverend Ben was ready to return to his post here, she would have a post in some distant land.

Now she glanced at the four huge bags filled with sandwiches. "Tucker said we were making two hundred sandwiches tonight," she recalled. "It looks like we're almost done."

"Yes, we are," Sophie said. "Many hands make light work."

"That's true," Isabel agreed. It was true in Cape Light or Haiti or Minnetonka. Wherever people came together to do good work.

She was not sure what she had expected of this congregation. But Isabel decided that, so far, she liked them. Perhaps she assumed that these people would be spoiled or, at the very least, insensitive and unaware . . . unintentionally, of course. But they were none of that. In fact, they were just the opposite.

God has sent you here for a reason. You may never know entirely why. But so far, it seems to have something to do with you being such a reverse snob, she chided herself.

I won't be here very long, but I'll definitely learn something, she decided.

CHAPTER FIVE

~~~

"THE SHOP IS JUST UP THE STREET. YOU SEE WHERE THAT little house is? The one with the sign that says 'The Bramble'?" Regina pointed down Main Street, a few doors down from the doctor's office. It was Friday morning; Richard had driven her to work and was keeping the car. He had some things to do. The first on his list was meeting Sam Morgan to talk about a job.

"There's an old barn in the back," Regina continued. "Sam Morgan's shop is on the left side."

"I'll find it. Don't worry." Richard forced a smile, trying to act more positive about this job quest than he felt.

"Well, good luck. Let me know how it goes." She stared at him a moment, and he thought she might kiss him good-bye. Just on the cheek, but that would be something.

Instead, she reached over and patted his arm. Awkwardly.

"Have a good day at work," he said. She nodded and slipped out of the car.

He watched her walk up the path to the doctor's office. She looked very pretty today, he thought. He wished now he had told her. But it wasn't the sort of thing he said easily anymore. He felt as if he weren't allowed to say things like that to her anymore.

She looked pretty . . . and happy. She had seemed that way ever since she started her new job. Regina loved to work and loved to be productive. That was something he had always admired in her, even though it put a bigger load on her at home, with taking care of the kids and everything else. She rarely complained. He tried to help with the housework since he was there all day— picking up the house, doing laundry, cleaning the kitchen. But the kids still missed her and didn't like his cooking.

Regina is not a quitter. She never gives up, no matter what, he thought as he pulled away from the curb. He needed to take a page from her book today. Even if it was too late to keep the family together, he had to do his best to support them. There was never any question about that.

He didn't really want day work for some carpenter he had never met. It felt . . . humiliating, considering his experience and education. It sounded to Richard as if Sam Morgan was just doing his sister, Molly Willoughby, a favor by seeing him. Richard didn't want to beg some guy for a day's wages painting houses or sanding kitchen cabinets. He could stay at the house and paint or sand. They would be able to put it up for sale a lot faster then.

Not that anyone was likely to buy it soon. The real estate market was weak almost everywhere. Then again, the longer it took to flip the place, the longer he and Regina would be living under one roof. They couldn't go their separate ways until the house was sold.

So in that way, Richard had been secretly happy that the house was in such bad shape and would take a while to renovate.

It surprised him to find that he was hoping it would take longer. He was sorry now for all the harsh words, the arguments and recriminations. How he wished he could take it all back, wipe the slate clean. But that was impossible. Some things could never be undone.

He knew that what he had to do now was try his best and savor the short time he had left with Gina, store up the memories to last the rest of his lifetime. Still, he couldn't help having a glimmer of hope. Maybe, if they just had a little more time together, they could find their way across this chasm.

Regina was so eager for his interview with Sam Morgan to work out. He just hoped he didn't disappoint her.

Richard parked on the street in front of the Bramble, then walked down the gravel drive to the woodworking shop. He knocked on the door, hearing the sound of power tools whirring. When nobody answered, he pushed open the door and peered inside.

The place was dim, with a few bright shop lights hanging from open beams and rafters, the original barn interior. Sawdust filled the air, and the scent of freshly cut wood lured him. A tall man wearing a shop apron worked at the lathe. He paused and looked over at Richard, then pulled off his work glasses. His hair was dark, flecked with gray, and his eyes a startling shade of blue.

"You must be Richard Rowan," he said in a friendly tone.

"That's me," Richard answered.

"Come on in. I'm just fooling around with this cabinet. I also repair and refinish antiques, in between the bigger jobs. Ever work on furniture?"

Richard shook his head. "Just our own stuff. If a drawer breaks or something. They're not antiques, believe me."

"That's all right. There's not too much of that. I do it mostly as a break. I design furniture, too. But I don't have much time for that."

Sam showed him a small table with gracefully curved legs. The top was inlaid with redwood, maple, and something that might have been mahogany. The design was both traditional and original at the same time. Richard ran his hand over the tabletop. It was a fine piece of furniture.

"That's very good work," he said simply.

"Thanks." Sam walked over to a battered old coffeemaker. The plastic had more than a few paint and varnish stains. "Want some coffee?"

Richard could not imagine what the coffee from that machine tasted like. "No, thanks. I'm good," he said politely.

Sam poured himself a mug. "My sister told me that you just moved to town. From Pennsylvania?"

"That's right; Stover. It's about a hundred miles outside Pittsburgh. My wife inherited a house up here from a distant relative and"—*we had nowhere else to live* was the flat-out honest rest of the sentence—"we thought we could fix it up and flip it," he said instead.

"Molly mentioned that. Good idea. The market is slow now, but houses still sell if the price is right," Sam added optimistically. "Maybe you'll be lucky and just the right person will come along. There's a market lately for summer homes, selling to people from Boston mainly. Maybe you could sell it that way."

"Maybe we could. I never thought of that," Richard replied. It did make sense. Cape Light was only a couple of hours from Boston, but still very rural and close to the water. He doubted the market for summer homes was booming, but it gave them more opportunity.

"The town is quiet now, but it's a great spot in the summer. A lot to do, a lot more people around—sailing and fishing, going to the beach," Sam said. "Your kids are going to love it."

Richard wasn't sure they would be here that long but didn't want to seem disagreeable. "I'm sure they will," he said. "We hardly ever got to the shore, living in Pennsylvania."

Richard thought Sam must be busy with his work, but he was acting as if he had all day to shoot the breeze with a perfect stranger. He was so friendly and relaxed. Richard had been in a lot of job interviews over the last year or so, and this was certainly unlike any other.

Sam sipped his coffee. "Molly told me you're a civil engineer."

"I worked for the county, but with budget cuts I was laid off. The job market is terrible in my field right now. Nobody seems to be hiring."

"Yeah, I hear it's pretty rough out there. I don't have any real engineering work, but if you have some experience with construction, I'm starting a new project and can definitely use someone with your skills and knowledge base."

"I've got lots of experience with construction. I worked on building sites all through high school and college, and I supervised construction when I worked for the county."

"Sounds good. I just won a big bid, the Silas Basset House. It's a fine old mansion in Newburyport that's going to be turned into a museum. It's been closed to the public for the last two or three years, but the village just got a grant from the state and I got the job to work on it."

Richard liked working on old houses. That's why he didn't mind working on the place Regina inherited.

Sam walked over to a cluttered desk and pulled out a photograph. "Here, this is the house. It's set on a large piece of land near the harbor. A merchant built it. He used to go up to this turret with a spyglass and watch for his ships to come in."

Richard gazed down at the photo. It was a magnificent old place, though even in the small photo he could make out crumbling masonry and boarded-up windows. There was clearly a lot of work there.

"Maybe that's what I need, a turret and a spyglass, so I can see when my ship comes in," Richard said dryly.

Sam laughed. "Well, you can watch from there on your lunch breaks if you want to join my crew. I have about three or four other guys, most of them master carpenters, who work on the older houses around here. But we don't have an engineer or anyone who's done heavy construction. Sounds like you would bring some extra skills to the table. I'm pretty much offering every man the same wage, though with your degree, I'm sure you usually earn more."

Sam named the figure, and he was right: It was less than Richard usually earned, at least in his former position. But it was much more than he was earning right now, which was zero. Richard knew he wasn't in any position to bicker, especially since the wage was generous, more than he expected from such a small operation.

"That sounds fair," Richard replied. "Thanks for the offer. I accept. When would I start?"

"How about today? I was just going to take a ride up there to meet with the rest of the crew." Sam took off his shop apron and left it on a hook near the workbench. "Are you free?"

"That's fine. I'd like to see the place and meet the other guys before we start working together," Richard said.

"Okay, we're on. Welcome to my world, Richard." Sam offered

his hand and Richard shook it. "I'm glad you came by. That was lucky for the both of us."

"I hope so," Richard said.

Was Sam Morgan always this positive and sunny? Richard had never worked for anyone with this much energy and enthusiasm. As he followed Sam outside, Richard thought about how he would describe Sam to Regina. She would be happy to hear he got the job. He could hardly wait to tell her.

A SHORT TIME LATER, RICHARD SAT IN THE PASSENGER'S SEAT OF Sam's truck as they headed up to Newburyport. Sam had been raised in Cape Light and was a perfect self-appointed guide to the area, pointing out places of interest and entertaining Richard with bits of local history.

"These are the famous marsh flats. Photographers come from all over to take pictures out there. There are even a few famous paintings of this place hanging in museums. It's a real magnet for birders and kayakers, too. Every year a few people get lost out there. But we usually find them," he added with a grin.

Richard looked out the window at the marshland, the tall, gently waving grass that was a golden color this time of year. He could see why the setting was so inspiring. He could also see how a person could get lost out there. The view was serene and calming. A flock of birds with long wings rose from a distant shore and flew across the sky. Richard watched them, mesmerized. They looked so graceful and free.

"What kind of birds are those?" he asked Sam.

"Oh, those must have been kites. If you plan on staying up here, you ought to get yourself a book. They have some good ones in town showing all the local wildlife."

Richard just smiled in reply. He wasn't sure he would be here long enough to make the book purchase worthwhile. But that wasn't the sort of thing you confided to a new employer.

They turned off the main road, then drove down streets with grand old Victorians built side by side. Then the village center of Newburyport came into view.

It was set on a hillside that swept down to a long, busy harbor. The entire town was visible from a distance, looking a lot like a folk-art painting, Richard thought. Sam told him that the town had been founded in the colonial period, which was obvious as the truck bounced down narrow, cobblestone streets with gabled brick townhouses set close to the sidewalk.

A large white church with a tall steeple was the town's centerpiece. It stood on a hilltop, and Richard could not help but admire it and wonder what it looked like at night with the steeple lit. "That's quite a church," he said as they drove by. "A real classic."

"It's the jewel in the crown of this town," Sam agreed. "But there are many jewels in this particular crown," he added, "and we've been entrusted to restore a very valuable one."

They drove down toward the harbor and soon arrived at the Silas Basset House, where the rest of Sam's crew was waiting. Sam introduced the men: Frank and Wendell, who were both in their late twenties, and Johnny, who was about his own age. Richard felt nervous meeting so many new faces at once, but Sam's upbeat manner as they toured the property and all his ideas and plans captured everyone's attention.

Sam spoke to them as if they were a team, each with a valuable talent to lend. Sam, Richard noticed, had a good eye for architecture and design. He wondered if Sam had ever wanted to be an architect. What mattered, though, was that he already respected Sam's ideas and opinions. That was important to Richard. In the last year, he'd had to work under people who were either inexperienced or incompetent, and he found it incredibly frustrating.

When the meeting was over, Sam talked a little more about the hours and responsibilities everyone would have and their deadline to finish the project. "This building is over six thousand square feet. That's a lot of ground to cover in the next few months."

"Yeah, but at least we all have work for the winter," Frank said happily.

The other men laughed, and Richard could tell they had all been thinking the same thing.

"Yeah, we do. And it starts on Monday. You're all good with that, right?" Sam asked, gazing around.

Everyone agreed they could start. Richard was relieved. That meant he would see a paycheck very soon. He'd be happy to tell Regina that, too.

After a few questions, the other men left and Richard and Sam headed for Sam's truck.

"How about some lunch back in town?" Sam asked.

Richard shrugged. "Fine with me." It was after one. He was hungry and hadn't packed a lunch. Which he would start doing on Monday.

"I know just the place." Sam was looking out at the road, but Richard saw him smile. "The Clam Box. Have you tried it yet?"

Richard didn't even know what Sam was talking about. "No, not yet."

The truth was, they didn't eat out unless it was an emergency. Certainly not just for fun. They still hadn't finished the load of groceries Warren and Marion Oakes had brought with them on Sunday. Regina had become a very resourceful cook and rarely wasted a crumb.

"You have to eat at the Clam Box at least once, or you can't really say you're a Cape Lighter. The place is low on atmosphere, but most people like the food."

"I'm not fussy. Sounds fine." *As long as it's cheap,* Richard thought.

They soon arrived at the village where Sam drove down Main Street and parked his truck in front of the Clam Box. It was a classic old-fashioned diner, silver with red trim, the kind that had been very common when he was growing up but was now rare. A sign above the big plateglass window said THE CLAM BOX, and one in the window read BOXED LUNCHES TO GO. TRY OUR FAMOUS CLAM ROLLS.

The eatery was crowded, though it was almost two o'clock. There were booths near the window and along the far wall, and tables, too. A long white counter with old-fashioned stools stretched back from the doorway.

As they walked in, a little bell over the door sounded. A teenage waitress with dark eyes and a long ponytail met them with menus. "Hey, Sam. Table up front okay?"

"Sounds perfect. We can watch the world go by."

She led them to a booth next to the window. Richard took a seat and opened his menu but was distracted by the view. Beyond a block or so of shops and offices, he saw the snow-covered village green and harbor. A large Christmas tree stood at the end of the green, and off to one side, a stone church.

Regina had told him that she walked down to the harbor on her lunch hour and went into some of the shops. He could tell she liked the town. It was a pretty spot, he had to agree. They could have done worse than landing in a place like this by accident.

"Can I get you something to drink?" the waitress asked, setting silverware on the table.

"I'll have some of Charlie's wicked coffee, Zoey," Sam said.

"Some coffee here, too," Richard replied, though he hoped that by *wicked* Sam meant good and strong, not wicked on his stomach.

When she left, Sam watched her for a moment. "That's Charlie Bates's daughter. She goes to school part-time and works here. She was a runaway, and he and his wife took her in last winter."

Richard was impressed. "Lots of people want to help someone in trouble, but they rarely go to those lengths."

"Charlie's wife, Lucy, is a sweetheart," Sam explained. "I think she had to persuade him. But you have to give the guy credit, right? Our oldest son, Darrell, is adopted," Sam added. "My wife and I were having problems starting a family and Darrell came along. He was only nine. It just seemed the right thing to do. As soon as it was all decided, Jessica got pregnant with Tyler," he added with a laugh. "You never know, right?"

"No, you never do," Richard agreed. He wasn't used to such personal conversation with a guy he didn't really know, but maybe that's just the way people were around here. He had heard New Englanders were not very friendly, even snobby. Sam Morgan was exactly the opposite. Richard, though, wasn't built that way. It took him a while to open up, even to a good friend.

"How many children do you have, Richard?"

"We have two: Madeline, who's twelve, and Brian. He's six."

"Nice. Our youngest, Lily, is two. It's a sweet age. I'm try-ing to enjoy it with this last one. They sure grow up fast. Darrell is already sixteen and starting to think about college. I'm going to need a few more of these big renovation jobs to foot that bill," he added.

Richard forced a smile and nodded in agreement. College tuition . . . He couldn't even think about that. He and Regina were in survival mode now. Every dollar they had once saved for the kids' tuition had already been spent on necessities. He felt guilty about it, as if he had somehow cheated his children. But what choice did he have? You couldn't not feed your kids.

Zoey returned and took their orders. Sam ordered a turkey club, and Richard decided to try the clam roll.

"He's new in town," Sam told her. "He's never been here before."

"I'll tell Charlie not to screw up," she promised. "The clam roll can be pretty good if he does it right."

Richard thanked her and handed back the menu. He wondered what he was getting into here and if he should have stuck with a plain hamburger.

"What sort of projects did you work at your last job, Richard? Roads and all that?"

"Mostly roads and bridges. I drew up plans for a lot of the new construction and renovation work, and supervised what we built. Then there were budget cuts, and the construction stopped and I was dropped back to part-time, then laid off altogether."

"Too bad. A lot of people have had it rough in this economy. They say it's coming back, though."

"Yeah, maybe. But too late for some of us." Richard didn't mean to sound bitter. He might get another job someday, but he would never get his old job back. He missed it. He missed the people there and his sense of belonging.

"How long did you work there?" Sam asked.

"Over ten years."

"That's a long time. But maybe you'll get something else up here that you like as much. Maybe even more."

"Maybe," Richard said, agreeing for the sake of it. He didn't actually believe it.

"I've had a dip in my workload, too," Sam admitted in a more serious tone. "I've had to branch out, diversify, take jobs I don't normally do. I guess being a small operation, you have more flexibility. So it's easier in some ways to weather these things."

"That's true." Richard liked Sam. It was hard not to. But he couldn't help thinking that Sam Morgan didn't have a clue about the bad breaks he'd been through. Losing his job and then his house. The setbacks and disappointments he faced trying to find work. Losing the respect of his wife . . . and even her love. It was easy for Sam to be so upbeat and cheerful. It looked like life had treated him pretty well.

Zoey brought the food to the table. "Bon appétit, fellas." Her tone was a bit sarcastic and typically teenage. "Can I get you anything else?"

"Just some water to wash down this fine cuisine," Sam answered in an equally wry tone.

Richard felt himself smiling as he took the first bite of his clam roll. He noticed Sam waiting for the verdict.

"Not bad," Richard said as he swallowed. "I like the sauce."

"Charlie's *Secret Sauce*, you mean," Sam said with a grin. "Listen, if he comes over, please don't tell him you like it. He'll go into this long rant about how he tried to have the recipe copyrighted or patented or something and sell it in supermarkets and it didn't work out. He thinks he's going to be the next Paul Newman and make a million dollars with that stuff."

"Paul Newman didn't make millions from his products. He gave all the profits to charity," Richard said, taking another bite. It really was good. He had to bring Regina here or take one home for her one night.

"That's what we all tell him. But he doesn't want to believe it. The man's incredibly stubborn." Sam shook his head, then took a bite of the turkey club. "But he's a good cook, you have to hand him that."

The bell above the entrance jangled, and a uniformed police officer walked in. Sam waved and the man smiled and strolled over.

"Hey, Tucker. This is Richard Rowan. He started working for me this morning."

The officer extended his hand and Richard shook it. "Tucker Tulley. Nice to meet you."

"Likewise," Richard said.

"Richard's wife inherited the Porter place on Old Field Road. They just moved up from Pennsylvania to take it over."

"I know that house. I knew Mr. Porter, too. I didn't know he had any family."

"We didn't know about him, either," Richard confessed. "Until my wife got a letter from a lawyer about the will."

"Wow, just like in a movie," Tucker said.

"Almost," Richard agreed. But in the movies, the person usually inherits a fortune or something of real worth. Not a broken-down old house in the middle of the woods.

"I know that house doesn't look like much," Sam said, seeming to read his thoughts, "but it has real possibilities."

"He would know," Tucker cut in. "Sam picked up an old house on the Beach Road about ten or twelve years ago and renovated it from top to bottom. It was a showpiece."

"It was," Sam agreed. "People would leave notes in our mailbox, asking if we wanted to sell."

"Really?" Here was a subject that keenly interested Richard. "So what happened? Did you flip it and buy your dream house?"

Sam looked down for a moment and shook his head. "No, sir. That *was* my dream house. I bought it at an auction before I even met Jessica. I knew I was fixing it up for the perfect woman and the kids we would have someday. That's just what happened, and we were happy there for years." He looked back up at Richard. "But the house caught fire in the middle of the night about three years ago. Burned down to the ground, right before our eyes."

Richard felt his heart clutch at the answer. "Really?"

Sam nodded. "Faulty wiring in an old lamp. We were all asleep, but we all got out fine. Me and Jessica and the two boys, thank God. Lily wasn't even born yet. We lost everything," he added. "It was either burnt to ash or the firefighters' chemicals ruined it."

"It was a real nightmare," Tucker agreed. "Your very worst."

Richard didn't know what to say at first. "That's too bad," he said finally. He felt embarrassed now for judging Sam harshly. The man had seen his share of trouble and setbacks, that was for sure.

"It was tough on the family," Sam went on. "Especially on my wife. The fire was an accident, could have happened to anyone. But we didn't have good insurance. That was my fault. And it hurt us, in more ways than one." He looked grim for a moment. "But we hung in there and got through it. That's all you can do, right?"

"I guess," Richard agreed. He glanced at Sam, then looked away. That was all you could do. Though most people would add to that simple formula some anger and frustration and a lot of self-pity.

Maybe Sam Morgan had gone through all that, too. Richard didn't see how a person could escape those reactions, under the circumstances. But Sam obviously hadn't gotten stuck there, and Richard wondered why not. For months now, Richard had felt stuck in his own life. As if he were trying to walk through a muddy swamp in high boots, the mud and muck pulling him back every step of the way. It was exhausting—and starting to feel like a useless effort.

How did Sam, or anyone, get out of the muck? That's what he wanted to know. Richard had an impulse to ask him, but he felt too embarrassed. Still, Sam had given him something to think about.

"So, what do you think of Reverend Lawrence?" Tucker asked Sam, changing the subject.

"I was impressed. When Jess told me Reverend Ben's replacement was a woman, I didn't know what to expect. But I liked her."

"I did, too," Tucker agreed. "I'll miss Reverend Ben, but it's only for a few weeks, thank goodness. I heard that he's coming out of the hospital this afternoon. I'm going to swing by the parsonage later and see how he's doing."

"That's good news. I'll give him a call tonight." Sam glanced at Richard. "The minister at our church just had bypass surgery. He's going to be recuperating for about two months, and we just met the temporary minister last night."

So they were churchgoing, as well. Richard's mother had taken him to church when he was a child, but he hadn't felt the need as an adult. It was the same story for Regina. She was a little better about it and took the kids to services on Christmas and Easter. But they'd never belonged to any church in particular, and he hardly knew what these guys were talking about. He didn't want to know, either. Before you knew it, these churchy types tried to pull you in.

But before the two men could go any further with their minister update, a short, wiry man came out from behind the counter. He wore an apron and a pugnacious expression. Richard guessed it had to be the infamous Charlie Bates, the diner's owner and head chef.

"Hey, Tucker. Hey, Sam," Charlie greeted the others. "What's up? Are you going to eat your lunch standing up today, Tucker? Is that some new diet tip your wife gave you?"

If Tucker was fazed by the taunt, his expression didn't show it.

"Fran gave me a real good diet tip the other day, Charlie. She told me not to eat here. There's nothing healthy on the menu."

"So you're just here for the socializing," Charlie muttered, then turned his attention to Richard. "How'd you like the clam roll?"

"It was good," Richard said evenly. He saw Charlie's brow knit with concern at the tepid review. "Very good. I've never had clams like that before." *I really liked the sauce,* he almost added, then remembered Sam's warning.

"How'd you like the sauce?" Charlie asked.

Richard looked up at him. "It was . . . tasty."

"Just *tasty*? Most people really like it. Most people ask me how I make it," Charlie insisted.

"But you'll never tell," Tucker finished for him.

"That's right."

Richard nearly asked, *Why not?* But Sam and Tucker were now silently signaling him not to encourage the conversation. Though Charlie couldn't see him, Tucker was shaking his head. Sam also shook his head very slowly.

Richard thought he was going to burst out laughing. He noticed the waitress nearby and waved his hand. "A little more coffee here, miss? Please?"

"I'll have some, too," Sam said, finding the idea of coffee very amusing.

Tucker was laughing, but disguised it by coughing into his hand. Zoey gave them all a curious look, then quickly poured the coffee. "Anything else?"

Richard shook his head. "No, thanks. I'm good."

"I guess that's all. Just the check, please," Sam managed. He glanced at Tucker, and Richard thought, *This is it.*

"What's so funny?" Charlie looked around at all of them. He clearly sensed he'd been left out of a joke.

Tucker and Sam shrugged. "Nothing's funny, Charlie. We take your cooking very seriously. Especially the clam rolls," Sam promised him.

"Especially the sauce," Tucker chimed in.

Charlie looked about to start an argument, but Zoey scooted between them and dropped the check on the table. "Here you go, guys. Thanks."

"Thank you," Sam said, and picked it up.

"What's my share?" Richard reached into his pocket for his wallet, wondering how much money he had with him.

"I've got it. You buy next time," Sam said lightly.

"Thanks, but you don't have to do that. I can split it with you," Richard insisted.

"It's my party. Your first day and all," Sam argued back. "Besides, it's a law in this town: New residents must eat a clam roll within five days of moving here. And somebody has to buy it for them. Right, Tucker?" Sam asked the officer.

Tucker tugged on the edge of his blue uniform jacket. "That's right. I could write a ticket right now if he didn't pay," he told Richard in a very serious tone.

Richard finally had to smile. "You've got some strange laws in this town. Thanks anyway."

"Don't mention it." Sam put down a few bills. Then he rose and grabbed his jacket. Richard did the same.

"Well, nice to meet you . . . even though no one introduced me," Charlie pointed out.

"Richard Rowan." Richard offered Charlie his hand. "I just started working for Sam."

"Nice to meet you. Come back and try my chowder, an old family recipe. I could bottle the stuff and make millions."

Richard followed Sam to the door. "Sounds good. I'll be back soon."

Tucker waved without saying anything. Richard liked him. He was a quiet man, but watchful. Richard had a feeling that there was a lot more going on inside of Tucker than was immediately apparent.

Once outside, they got into Sam's truck, and Sam turned to Richard. "Charlie's chowder isn't bad, but never, ever, under any circumstance, order the lobster roll. Charlie is stingy as a spinster with the meat. I think he just waves a lobster claw over the bun, like giving it a blessing. All you get is celery and mayonnaise."

"I'll try to remember that." Richard glanced over at Sam curiously as they drove back down Main Street. Was the guy joking again? No, he was perfectly serious. More serious than he'd seen Sam so far today. Except when he'd told that story about his house burning down.

These men were particular about their seafood, weren't they? He had heard that New Englanders were obsessed with chowder and fish dishes, but now he was seeing it firsthand. Richard felt he had finally arrived in this strange new territory.

Chapter Six

"Are you sure you're comfortable in that chair, Ben? It might be better if you sit on the couch. That way, if you feel tired and want to lie down, you can just stretch out. You don't have to get up again."

"I'm not going to lie down in the middle of talking to her, Carolyn. That wouldn't be polite, for one thing." Did she really think that in the middle of giving the new minister instructions on how to run his church he would just lie down and take a nap?

"You just came home from the hospital yesterday. I'm sure Reverend Isabel will understand if you want to rest a minute."

Ben glanced up at Carolyn. She was hovering over him like a little blond helicopter. A helicopter that delivered soup and the newspaper. And kept telling him what to do. He took a breath and reached for his patience, wondering if some of that deep, natural store had somehow been removed during the operation.

"I'm supposed to get up and down and move around a bit. I'm not supposed to lie down very much. You heard what the doctor said," he reminded her.

He knew she meant well and was only concerned for him, but all this hovering . . . It was getting on his nerves. Still, he knew he had to be patient. He'd given Carolyn the scare of her life. She was afraid now that any twinge, any deep breath, any discomfort at all was the sign of another imminent heart attack.

The truth be told, he felt the same. He knew it wasn't rational; it wasn't even true. The doctors had told him that this state of mind was normal after his experience, but Ben couldn't help his feelings.

You can only help what you do about them, he reminded himself. *Don't give in to the fear, the knee-jerk reaction. Don't give in to the anger, either.*

He did feel angry, another post-operative syndrome. This pathetic "Why Me, Lord?" song stuck in his brain. Especially when the simple things, like reaching for a book or his glasses, resulted in a sudden twinge of real agony. A few minutes of conversation or just walking from one room to the other could tire him out completely.

It will take time to heal, he reminded himself. *It hasn't even been a full week.* He hadn't even missed one service at church yet. Remarkable, when his entire life had changed, done a giant one-hundred-and-eighty-degree spin. Like a car on black ice, spinning out of control.

"I think that's her now." Carolyn was over by the window, where she had pulled back the curtain to peer outside. "Are you ready?"

"If you help me with this sweater, I will be."

It had been a struggle to dress that morning. He had to take a long break after getting his shirt on. The wound on his chest hurt from moving his arms so much. Now Carolyn helped him slip on the sweater. She was about to button it for him, too, but he gently took over.

"I can manage the buttons fine, dear. Maybe you should go get the door."

Reverend Lawrence hadn't rung the bell yet, but Ben needed a moment alone to collect himself. Handing over his church, even for a few weeks, was harder than he expected. Was he that much of a control freak? He didn't think so. But he had become an organic part of the place, like a crusty old barnacle clinging to a gray whale, dependent on it for its existence.

He closed his eyes a moment and said a prayer. "Please, God, help me say and do the right things in this meeting. Help us have a good understanding and work together to keep my church running smoothly while I'm away."

When he opened his eyes, Isabel Lawrence was standing in the living room doorway next to Carolyn.

"Ben? Reverend Lawrence is here. He's been very tired," he heard Carolyn add. "He's still getting his strength back."

"Reverend Lawrence, how good to meet you. Please excuse me if I don't get up." Ben smiled and awkwardly extended his hand.

She stepped over and shook his hand heartily. "Reverend Lewis, so good to meet you. Finally. And please, call me Isabel."

"Please call me Ben."

She had a surprisingly strong grip for a woman. Carolyn had described her to him a little, but he hadn't expected this air of vitality, the red hair and bright eyes. She looked healthy, as if she liked the outdoors and hard work, he thought. She wasn't all that young; in her late thirties, he guessed. But something about her seemed younger. She took a seat right next to him and smiled.

"Would anyone like some coffee or tea?" Carolyn asked.

"No, thank you. I'm fine," Isabel said.

Ben declined, too. "Maybe later, dear," he told his wife.

"All right, I'll leave you. I know you have a lot to discuss. If you need anything, just give a shout," Carolyn said to Ben.

"I will, dear, thank you." When his wife had gone, Ben turned back to Reverend Lawrence. "She's taking very good care of me. I've never had such service."

"I can see that," Isabel replied. "You're very fortunate. Home care is sometimes the hardest part to figure out when people are recovering from something like this. That's a big part of the reason I came back to the States. I knew my folks would take care of me while I recuperated after my operation."

"Yes, you really count your blessings after this type of crisis. You count them and double-count them," he agreed.

Isabel asked about his operation and how he was feeling. Ben answered as succinctly as he could. He was tired of talking about himself and eager to talk about his church.

"So you met some of the members at the lunch-making meeting, I heard. And had the grand tour."

"Yes, I did." Reverend Lawrence nodded. "It's a beautiful church, and everyone I met was very welcoming."

"I don't doubt it. Sorry you're getting thrown right into the deep end. Your first service is tomorrow," he pointed out. "But everything is planned: the hymns, the prayers, and any special music. It's the first Sunday that we light the Advent candles. We choose a family every week of Advent to say the prayer and light the candles. Did Tucker mention that to you?"

"He explained everything. I'm going to meet with all the deacons Monday night to plan the rest of the month's services."

"Yes, of course." Ben nodded. "Are you prepared with a sermon?

I made some notes for this week, working with the Scripture; just a draft, really. I'd be happy to give them to you," he offered.

"I'm all set. But thank you," she said sincerely. "I think it would be hard to deliver someone else's sermon, even if it was just notes."

She was frank and straightforward, but her manner didn't offend. She had a certain way of speaking her mind that was sincere and actually refreshing.

"Well, that's good then. Sounds as if you're all set." *Set to take over my church,* he thought to himself.

She sat smiling at him calmly, but didn't answer. Then she said, "Do you think the congregation will find it difficult to have a female minister?"

A good question, he thought, and an honest one. He liked this woman. She cut straight to the chase.

"There will always be a few holdouts, but most will be fine with it," he predicted. "Though it will be a big change for them. I have no problems with women in the ministry," he assured her, "but I don't have much experience with female ministers. Working with them, I mean," he clarified. *Gee, I sound like a grumpy old man. If not grumpy, at least horribly out of date.*

"Let's see, how can I help you?" Isabel asked, her tone calm. "Women ministers are a lot like male ministers," she began slowly. "But there are a few differences in how we lead a congregation."

"For instance?" He tried to sound just mildly curious, but was, in fact, a little nervous.

"Well, suppose a female minister were leading her congregation through the wilderness, to the Promised Land—"

"Like Moses," he cut in.

"Exactly. It wouldn't take her forty years. She would definitely stop to ask for directions long before that." She delivered this punch line with a small, playful smile.

Ben had to laugh, even though it hurt a little. "Very good; I never heard that one." He sighed. "I guess I deserved that."

"Not at all." She waved her hand at him. "That's my standard joke."

"Well, it brings up a valid point. Women have a different temperament than men, a different perspective on the world. It's not about one sex being superior to the other. They're just different."

"Exactly," she agreed. "You get it, Ben."

"So I've been told," he said with a smile. It was easy to catch on with such a charming teacher, he thought. She wouldn't have much trouble winning them over. Even Lillian Warwick would eventually melt.

"I hear you've been at this church for a long time," she said. "It must be hard to stay away, especially at Christmas."

"It is hard. But I'm also relieved," he admitted. "I've been feeling . . . overburdened lately."

Ben paused. He wasn't sure how much he wanted or even needed to reveal to Reverend Isabel. They had just met. But the truth was that he had not been facing Christmas in his usual, enthusiastic frame of mind. He could see that clearly now.

Was that because of my health, the undetected heart condition? Or was it simply minister burnout? Which happens to the best of us.

"It was probably my heart condition getting worse," he concluded aloud. "That's what the doctor said."

"Probably," she agreed. "It's a busy time for a minister, the busiest of the year."

"Yes, it is. But it's also the heart of the church calendar, don't you think?" He heard the wistful note in his own voice and was surprised. Though he was truly relieved to pass on these responsibilities, it was hard to hand the reins to someone else, especially after all these years.

Isabel smiled gently. "I agree. I think Christmas is the heart and soul of the church year. The story of the birth in the manger is so unimaginably deep and rich and full of meaning. I can't think of anything else that speaks so beautifully of kindness and love and hope, and recognizing the divine in the most humble places. It would take a lifetime to talk about every layer and dimension. It's so simple and apparent, yet also so mysterious."

"Exactly," he agreed heartily. "That's exactly it."

She would do fine. She could see the subtleties. That was so important. There were so many good, well-meaning ministers, he knew, who weren't as sensitive or intellectually astute.

"Are there any topics in particular that you'd like me to touch on during the next few weeks? Or at least think about?"

He could think of many to suggest. He always planned his sermons well ahead, though he didn't write them out that far in advance. But he tried to connect them, week to week, in each liturgical season, with an ongoing theme or lesson. His sermons for this Advent season and Christmas Day were already drafted. He could have easily asked Carolyn to bring in the folder from his study and hand it right over. He would know then that his flock would be well cared for, at least in that way.

But Ben held his tongue.

It wouldn't be right to try to influence Reverend Isabel Lawrence's sermons that way. It would be disrespectful for one thing, though it was kind of her to ask. She was an ordained minister, the same as he, and he'd found that the gifts of ministry were not necessarily richer according to a preacher's age. Lately, he secretly worried about his own gifts. Was he getting stale and lackluster? Losing his spiritual and intellectual vigor?

It was only natural to feel that way in his condition. He was physically weak right now and wasn't as mentally sharp as he could be. He would recover in body and mind . . . and in spirit, he reminded himself. But would he recover enough to lead the church again? The jury was still out on that question.

Ben turned his attention back to Isabel. "I don't have any suggestions for you, but I'll be looking forward to hearing your sermons. We record each service for the church archives. Even though I can't attend for a few weeks, I'll be there in spirit. And I'm going to listen, if you don't mind."

"I don't mind at all. I hope you do. I'll be interested to hear your reviews," she gently teased him.

He thought she was sincere, not just saying that to be respectful. Ben had a feeling she wouldn't be touchy if he disagreed with something she said. She seemed to welcome intellectual give-and-take. Isabel Lawrence didn't seem even a tiny bit nervous to be dropped into this spot, facing a new congregation for the first time. He imagined himself in the same situation and knew that he wouldn't be half as calm, at least not for the first service.

"So you're not nervous at all about facing the congregation?" he had to ask.

"I'm looking forward to it. To me, a large part of being a minister is trying to bring my message to new people. Your congregation has enjoyed the benefit of your wisdom all these years, Ben. But they'll be new to me," she pointed out.

"That's true. I didn't think of it that way," he said honestly. "I understand you've been doing service in a mission down in Haiti," he said. "That must be very challenging work."

"In some ways," she agreed. "But in others it may be easier than ministering in a church like this one. It's very hands-on," she tried to explain. "Very action- and results-oriented."

"Not as many committees and boards?" he prompted her.

"None at all," she said wistfully. "Though I've served in a church like that as well," she assured him, "as an associate minister back in Minnesota."

"That's good. Here, we have a board of trustees and a church council, who guide many of our decisions. But all the big questions must be decided by the entire congregation. Then, of course, there are the deacons," he continued. "You'll be working very closely with them, especially at this time of year. You've already met our head deacon, Tucker Tulley."

"Yes, at the food outreach meeting. And his wife, Fran. They gave me a full tour of the church."

"Tucker is very committed to our church. He's been a member since . . . well, he was a babe in arms. Though I'm sure that's hard to picture," Ben admitted with a smile. "He'll be a big help to you. If you have any questions or problems, he's your go-to guy. And you can always call me. I'm not going anywhere for a while," he added with a laugh.

"Thank you, Ben. I'm sure I will need your advice at some point. But the time will pass quickly," she promised him. "You'll be back in your pulpit before you know it. Think of me as just . . . just a bookmark, holding your place. You'll step back in and go on with your story whenever you're ready."

Ben was touched by her kindness. Did he seem threatened by her taking over this way? He certainly hoped not. But he must have been projecting some concern. He did feel a certain sense of loss, now that they were face-to-face. At the same time, he felt so utterly relieved, handing over his responsibilities.

He was very conflicted. Maybe that's what she sensed.

"So how's it going?" Carolyn peeked into the living room.

"Fine, it's going fine," Ben replied, almost too heartily.

THOMAS KINKADE AND KATHERINE SPENCER

"Would anyone like coffee or tea? I can bring it in a minute," Carolyn promised. "And some of Sophie Potter's delicious meringue cookies."

"Sophie heard I was permitted only low-cholesterol treats, but she was not daunted," Ben told Isabel.

"They sound good, though I think I'll pass today. I have to get going. We can meet again and talk more some other time, Ben. I don't want you to overdo it."

"Good point," Carolyn said before Ben could reply.

His wife stood by his chair and rested her hand on his shoulder. She had been doing that a lot lately, needing to reassure herself that he was still there.

"Oh, I'm fine. But you must have things to do to prepare for tomorrow's service," Ben said, giving himself a graceful way out. The talking had tired him, but he was embarrassed to admit it. They had barely been visiting for half an hour. Was he that weak and frail?

Reverend Isabel rose and picked up her purse. "Yes, I'm still unpacking and settling in. Mrs. Potter has invited me over for supper tonight, and I have some errands to do this afternoon, before it gets too late."

"Are you still at Vera Plante's place?" Carolyn asked.

"Yes, I am. It's very comfortable. I don't think I'll look for an apartment or anything like that. I'll be here such a short time, it doesn't make sense. Besides, it's nice to have some company and learn about the town. Vera is very helpful."

Vera was undoubtedly helpful. But her talkative nature had driven away more than one boarder, Ben knew. In addition to her other fine qualities, Isabel was clearly blessed with an abundance of patience.

"So long, Ben. We'll talk again soon." Isabel leaned over and shook his hand again. Ben wanted to get up to say good-bye like a gentleman, but he couldn't quite manage it unassisted and decided not to try.

"I hope so. Thanks for coming to see me, Reverend," he said sincerely.

"Don't even mention it. And don't worry, I'll take good care of your congregation."

"I know you will."

While Carolyn showed her to the door and thanked her for coming, Ben sat alone in the living room and sent up a prayer of thanks.

Thank you, Lord, for sending such a wonderful minister to stand in my place. I couldn't have imagined someone like her. Yet I feel as if she'll bring some very special gifts to the church. Please bless her and help her in the weeks to come. And please help me heal, so that I can soon return, he added quickly.

But do I really want to return?

Whoa. He shook his head in amazement. Where did *that* come from?

He had been pondering retirement ever since the heart attack. Even before that, if the truth be told. He and Carolyn had even touched upon the subject again this morning.

He hadn't made any decision yet. It was still too soon. But every time he did think of leaving his church, he had always worried about the minister who would follow and fill his place.

He didn't consider himself irreplaceable. He knew that no one was, in any job, anywhere. But he had been at this church for such a long time. It was hard to picture someone good enough for these fine people, the members of his congregation who were such dear friends, some like family.

Then along came Reverend Lawrence. Not that she was staying

for the long haul, mind you. But maybe God was trying to tell him something. To show him that there were many excellent young ministers out there who could take his place, all with unique gifts and talents. Talents different from his own.

I can handle this, Ben. Cast your cares, God was telling him. *I can send someone who will work out perfectly.*

God's solution always surpasses anything we can bring about, or even imagine, in our limited minds, Ben knew.

So that worry, that obstacle to retiring . . . well, that one had been blown right out of the water by Reverend Isabel. And by the One above who sent her.

Now Ben sat and wondered if there might be other important reasons for him to return to the pulpit. As he leaned back in his armchair and closed his eyes for a short nap, none came to mind.

REGINA HAD NEVER MET SAM MORGAN, BUT SHE KNEW WHO HE was right away. He was a masculine version of his younger sister Molly—the same dark hair and blue eyes. The same sunny smile making her smile when she answered the door on Saturday after-noon.

"You must be Sam," she said. She pulled open the door and stepped back so he could come in.

"You must be Regina. Nice to meet you." He was a tall man, and she had to lean back a bit to look him in the eye.

"Nice to meet you, too. Richard's out in the back. I'll go get him."

"That's all right. I can find him. I'll help him load the truck. It looks like we might need to make two trips."

Richard had been working hard in his spare time to clean out the basement and the large freestanding garage, which was more like an old barn. He had collected a huge pile of unusable furniture and other unwanted old items. It would definitely be more than one load going to the dump.

Richard had asked Sam if he could borrow an old pickup truck they used at work to bring the stuff to the dump, and Sam had offered to help him cart it over. Regina hoped he wasn't sorry now, seeing the size of the load. "My cousin was a bit of a pack rat," she explained. "So now at least I know where it comes from."

Regina had been tempted to go through the items just to check if there was anything worth saving. Her idea of "worth saving" and Richard's were radically different. She often rescued broken things that needed a little glue or paint or a few stitches—then never got around to fixing them. Richard was decisive. He liked to get rid of clutter and half-broken objects. He threw out first, asked questions later.

It was best if she didn't go near the stuff, Regina decided. She would probably try to save half of it.

"When you have a sentimental attachment to things, it's hard to throw them out," Sam agreed. "But it's easy to throw out someone else's old stuff. No memories, right?"

"Exactly," Regina agreed. "It's still a lot of work, though. Thanks for helping."

"No problem," Sam said. "I had to bring the truck over, anyway." He headed for the door, and Regina closed it behind him.

Sam seemed like such a nice guy. She wondered if he and Richard might one day be friends. Once upon a time, she and Richard had a lively social life. But when their financial troubles started, their friendships seemed to dry up along with their bank account. They were embarrassed about their circumstances. It was easier to hide themselves away. It was hard to keep up relationships with people who were doing well when you were sliding further and further down a slippery slope of problems, problems that nobody wanted to know about. It was almost as if people thought they were contagious or something and didn't want to catch this awful bug.

Richard said that was when they learned who their real friends were. The deeper relationships lasted. But there weren't many, that was for sure.

Regina was cleaning the kitchen when Richard came in through the back door. She had seen from the window that the men hadn't left yet, though the truck was packed and ready to go.

"Brian wants to come with me," he said. "We won't be gone long."

"That's all right. He's getting bored around the house. Are you sure he fits?"

"There's a small backseat in the cab with a seat belt," he promised. "Madeline is out in the barn. She found a box of old clothes. It's a real mess, but she won't let me throw it out. Maybe you can persuade her and I'll take it on the next trip."

"Okay. I'll go out and talk to her."

"See you later." Richard gave her one last long look, then left. Regina noticed that he didn't try to kiss her good-bye, even on the cheek. There was a time when they wouldn't leave each other for a few minutes without some sort of embrace or affectionate gesture. Now they were so distant from each other in every way. It made Regina feel sad and empty.

But she tried not to dwell on the problems in their marriage. She had to look on the bright side. They had this house, which was looking better every day. They both had jobs now, too. Maybe not their ideal jobs, especially for Richard. But there was more money coming in than they had seen in a while. Most of all, Regina thought, they had two wonderful children who were both healthy and settling down in their new schools.

I'm a lucky person, Regina told herself. *Even if Richard and I do separate, I have a lot to be thankful for.*

When Regina went outside, she found Madeline in the garage. She was pulling clothes out of a wooden crate, looking over the objects, and flinging them aside.

"Hey, what's up? Are you helping Dad or making a bigger mess?" Regina asked in a mostly amused tone.

"I'm making sure he doesn't throw away any good stuff," her daughter insisted.

"Oh no, you've got the pack-rat gene."

"Like Mr. Porter?" Madeline asked.

"And your mother," Regina added. "What did you find?" She couldn't help herself. She had to ask.

"Some really cool stuff. I found this shawl. It just has a little stain there, and the fringe needs to be sewed up a bit. But isn't it pretty? I can hang it up in my room, on the wall."

The shawl was pretty, Regina thought, fingering the silky fabric. It had a finely knotted fringe and a beautiful flowery pattern of cabbage roses on dark blue silk. "It's beautiful, Maddy. Good find. I do see the stain . . . a watermark or something," she added, pulling the fabric taut. "I'll try some stain remover. We need to wash it, anyway. It smells really musty."

"Yeah, it smells like a raccoon must have tried it on."

Regina laughed at the image while Madeline kept rummaging. "What else did you find?"

"Some ice skates. They fit me, too. They just need the blades sharpened."

"Really? That's worth saving. Let's make a pile for the good stuff."

Madeline put the skates with the shawl on top of an old wooden table. Then she ran to another box, obviously encouraged.

"Look at this, Mom. Isn't it pretty? I could use this to hold my jewelry—unless you want it for downstairs?"

Regina couldn't even tell what Madeline was holding up, but from the tone of her voice, she didn't want to part with it.

"That's all right. Finders keepers." Regina stepped closer to see that Madeline had discovered an old, carved wooden box. It was painted mustard yellow, with an old metal latch on the lid. "It looks intriguing. Keep it if you like it," Regina said.

"I'm going to put it on my dresser. Hey, I wonder if there's anything inside." Madeline set the box on the table and opened the latch. Regina could tell from her disappointed expression that the box didn't contain anything exciting.

"Just an old book." Madeline took it out and set it on the table. "I'm going to clean out the box. It smells musty."

"Don't get the wood too wet. You don't want to ruin it," Regina warned.

Regina picked up the book. It was wrapped in yellowed plastic and fastened around with string. She peered through the plastic to read the title, gold-stamped on a brown leather cover.

It was a Bible. That made sense. A very small one, no more than six inches long and four inches wide. It fit right in the palm of her hand. Many old books were small, Regina knew, because resources like paper had been expensive and precious.

Most old books were not worth much; she knew that, too. Especially something as common as the Bible. But it had been special to someone, to be preserved so carefully. Someone who had lived long ago, maybe even in this house.

Maybe the lady who owned the shawl? Regina imagined the woman carrying the little Bible to church and back every Sunday, or keeping it close by her bedside and reading it by candlelight or an old oil-wick lamp.

It was easy to picture the woman praying with the little Bible, and Regina wondered if her prayers had helped her. She didn't pray much herself, though she did talk directly to God at times. More than ever lately, since their lives had gotten tough.

Sometimes, she thought He even answered. Not directly. It wasn't as if she heard a voice in her head or anything like that. But now and again, she would ask for help and help would appear, out of the blue, coming in a way she never imagined. In the form of some extra money, or advice from someone who knew how to fix her problems. Or the way she brought Brian to the doctor for an earache and Molly Willoughby had offered her a job. Those gentle little nudges kept her going.

Regina held the little brown Bible in her hand and looked it over. She didn't want Richard to throw it away. That didn't seem right. Though it was so old, she guessed that if she ever opened the plastic and turned the pages, the book might crumble in her hand.

She tucked it into her jacket pocket. If only for the sake of the lady who may have lived in this house, who ate, slept, and prayed under the very same roof. If only to respect her memory, Regina thought.

RICHARD AND SAM RETURNED AND TOOK THE REST OF THE stuff away. When Richard came back again with the empty truck, it was already dark and Regina had supper ready. He had dropped off Brian after the first trip, and the kids were both in the living room, playing a board game they had found in one of the closets. The ancient TV set was on, too. It didn't get any cable stations and the reception was snowy, but they still found a program or two they wanted to see.

Richard came in the back door and quickly closed it against

the cold air. He looked tired, Regina thought, but had a strange expression on his face. Not exactly happy, but almost. Happiness mixed with confusion or surprise, she'd have to say.

"How did it go? Were you able to drop off everything?"

"The bulk of it. There's more in the basement, but we'll leave that for another day." He took off his jacket and hung it on a hook in the mudroom, then poured himself a cold beer.

"It was nice of Sam to help you," Regina said.

She had made roast chicken and potatoes and now took the pan out of the oven to check. She didn't want the food to get too dry.

"Very nice. He's got to be the nicest boss I've ever had." Richard sat down at the table, the confusion on his face reflected in his voice. "I just don't get it."

"Maybe there's nothing to get. Maybe he just likes to help people."

Richard sighed. "I never met anyone who liked to help people as much as he does. You know what else he did today—I mean, besides coming over here on his day off and doing all that work with me?"

"What did he do?" Regina turned to look at him.

"After we brought over the second load, he told me to drop him off at his house and said I could borrow the truck for a while. As long as I bring it to work and we can use it to haul things to the job site. He has another truck," Richard added. "A big, new one. So he said this one was just sitting in front of the shop most of the time and we might as well get some use out of it. This way, he knows I'll be at work on time."

Regina knew her husband would be at work on time, no matter what. Even if he had to walk all the way. That was the way Richard was. Sam probably knew that, too, but was just coming up with some rationale for his generosity.

Now Regina understood why her husband came in looking so mystified.

"He gave it to you? Really?" Regina looked out the window. She saw the old red truck parked in front of the garage, right behind their car. "Wow . . . that was very generous. What a guy."

She didn't know what else to say. She could sense that the gesture had disturbed—or maybe just shocked—her husband. He'd had so many bad breaks lately and had been let down by so many people he'd trusted, he didn't understand how anyone could be so nice to him.

"I didn't want to take it. But he insisted." Richard's face flushed. "I think he knows we need another car, but we don't have the money."

"Well, we don't. This truck will be a huge help. It won't be forever," she reminded him.

Richard glanced over at her but didn't say anything. He finally offered a small smile, but she could see that he had mixed feelings about accepting Sam's charity. For that's what it really was, and it was hard for Richard. It hurt his pride to admit need. Regina understood that, too.

She decided not to talk about it anymore right now. Richard needed time to process this unexpected good turn. She knew it hurt a little to take the truck, but she was also relieved. She had been worried that whatever extra money they earned at their new jobs would be eaten up buying a necessary second car, which would undoubtedly be used and needing a repair every other week. But they'd been saved from that pitfall. At least, for now.

Richard called Madeline and Brian in for dinner as Regina

finished setting the table. The kids seemed happy, Regina thought. They didn't seem to notice that the house was shabby. They seemed to like their new rooms, especially Madeline, who had spent a lot of time today fixing up hers.

"Dad, you'll never guess what I found today in the junk pile," Madeline said.

Richard smiled in spite of himself. "Did you finally come up with something good, Maddy? You sure took a long time poking around in all that stuff."

"I found this beautiful shawl. I'm going to hang it in my room, on the wall. After Mom washes it," Madeline added. "I left it downstairs on the machine," she added, glancing at her mother.

It couldn't be washed in the machine; it would shred to pieces. But Regina didn't bother telling her that. "Okay, I'll get to it soon. She also found a very pretty wooden box. It looks handmade. She's going to use it on her dresser. Oh, there was an old Bible inside, wrapped in plastic. Someone must have saved it; a family memento, I guess."

"A Bible? Maybe it belonged to one of your ancestors, Gina. Sometimes people write a family tree in the front pages. Did you check?" Richard asked between bites of food.

"I thought of that, too. But it's so old, it looks like it might fall apart if I even opened it. I'll show you later."

"Sounds interesting," he said. "Maybe there are a few useful things in all that junk. Maybe we shouldn't toss it all without at least looking through it."

Had her husband just agreed that being a "saver" wasn't entirely a bad trait? Regina nearly laughed out loud but decided not to point that out to him.

It was moments like this, when things felt relaxed and easy between them, that she wondered why they were going to separate.

She felt warm and affectionate toward him, noticing how handsome he looked tonight in a dark blue pullover and worn jeans, his hair mussed from working outdoors all day.

But it wasn't always like this. Most of the time, it was just the opposite, she reminded herself. This was only a truce, for the sake of the children. Otherwise, they'd be right at each other, fighting and arguing over every little thing.

"Okay, close your eyes, everyone," Regina said when the dinner was cleared away. "I have a surprise."

She quickly started off toward the mudroom, where she had hidden the chocolate cake she baked that day when everyone was out of the house. Then she glanced over her shoulder and noticed Brian peeking. "Hey, cover those eyes, buddy, or you won't get any."

"Won't get any of what?" he asked, sounding perfectly frustrated and making everyone else laugh.

"You'll see," Regina called back from the next room.

"Okay, now you can look." Regina placed the cake in the middle of the table, and smiled as Brian's eyes widened.

"Wow! Thanks, Mom! It's not even my birthday!" Brian got so excited, he slipped off his chair.

Richard grabbed him just in time. "Steady, pal. It's just dessert."

"Can I have a slice with a lot of icing?" Madeline leaned over, watching Regina cut the cake.

"Me, too?" Richard asked in a quieter voice.

"Coming right up." Regina carefully cut the slices and dished them out. Everyone was silent for a long time—even Brian—as they savored the delicious cake.

"This is the best cake you ever made, Mom," her son said finally. "Really."

"It is," Madeline agreed. "But I still don't understand what we're celebrating."

"Oh . . . I don't know. We'll be living here one whole week tomorrow. Let's celebrate that," Regina suggested.

Richard glanced at her with a doubtful look. Regina pretended she didn't understand him.

"Okay," Madeline said. "That's a good thing to celebrate."

"Let's have a big cake every week we live here," Brian suggested.

"There's an idea," Regina answered, not agreeing or disagreeing, which was a tactic she often used with her children. She did wonder how many cakes she would end up making if Brian had his way.

"Can you make a cake like this on Christmas?" Brian was picking up the last crumbs on his plate with his fingers.

"Sure thing," Regina promised. That, she figured, was one thing she could safely guarantee them.

Soon it was time for the kids to get ready for bed. Richard took Brian upstairs to give him a bath and read him a bedtime story while Regina cleaned the kitchen.

By the time Richard came down again, she was sitting in the living room with a cup of tea and a novel that Sally Heller, the nurse at Dr. Harding's office, had loaned her. Richard sat down on the couch but didn't turn on the TV.

Regina put her book down and looked over at him. "Did the kids go to sleep already?"

"Brian went out like a light. I didn't even finish the picture book I started. Maddy put her pajamas on, but she's doing something to her hair."

Madeline liked to try new hairstyles at night, when there was little risk of anyone she knew besides the family seeing her.

"Cute." Regina paused. "They're excited about Christmas."

Christmas Treasures

"No kidding. I bet they already know all the gifts they want." Richard sounded worried.

"Well, they are children. The last two years have been very hard on them, especially the holidays. But this year, we have this house and we're both working. It's definitely getting better, don't you think?"

Richard gazed at her, then rubbed his hand over the back of his neck. "We have jobs, that's true. And we have a roof over our heads. But it's nothing like our old life, Regina."

Nothing like the salary I used to earn and the house I bought for you and the kids, he wanted to say. To compare the past and present made him feel even more of a failure somehow, more ashamed of the way he had let her down. Didn't she see that?

"No, it's not. But it's better than it was a few months ago. That's all I'm trying to say." Regina sighed. "I hope we can stick to our agreement and hold it together a little longer to give the kids a good Christmas. As good as we can manage. After that . . . well, we can figure things out. If you don't want to stay together, I guess I'll understand. I told you before, I don't want to fight with you anymore. And I can't change your feelings. I can't talk you into being happy," she told him. "I don't even want to try."

"What do you want me to say?" he asked wearily. "Let's just get through the holiday."

"All right, I understand." Regina's voice was calm. "We've already gone over this a million times. There's no need to talk about it anymore."

She stared at him a minute, her mouth set in a tight line. When she looked at him that way, he felt like his heart was going to burst. Sometimes he thought they had a chance to work things out. He would see a spark in her eye or she would smile at him or laugh a certain way. But he must be imagining all that, he thought. Just wishful thinking. She didn't love him anymore. How could she, if she could say that to him, so plain and matter-of-fact?

"Right." He managed to keep his voice steady. "There's no need. You're right about the kids. They come first. They ought to have a nice Christmas this year. I agree with that, too. They've had enough problems to deal with. They need a break."

Regina nodded, feeling her heart crack in a few places, though it didn't quite break.

"All right. That's what we'll do then." She got to her feet, picked up her book, and headed for the stairs. "I'm going up. Good night."

"Good night, Gina," Richard said quietly.

She thought he sounded sad, but she didn't turn around to look at him and maybe go back and talk it out and try to make things better. She felt too tired for that. She was tired of doing all the work in their relationship. She felt a lot of hope about her life lately, Regina realized. But not about her marriage.

CHAPTER SEVEN

THE MEETING OF THE DEACONATE ON MONDAY NIGHT
had taken much longer than Isabel expected. She didn't
have much patience for meetings. That was just the way she was;
she couldn't help it. It did seem at times as if God sent you certain
situations to build up the weak places. As if the universe were some
big spiritual fitness room. Patience with meetings and committees
was definitely her weakest muscle group.

But the deacons were a great group of men and women, and
there had been a lot to discuss, mainly all of the special services and
events leading up to Christmas and the Christmas Day service
itself.

Isabel's first service on Sunday had been reviewed as well. She
had been given high marks. She'd done well coming in and out
with her parts of the liturgy, taking her cues. She had not given a
long Sunday service in a while, so it had been a challenge. Her

sermon, which she based on the day's Scripture, had been well received, too.

Now it was on to Christmas, full speed ahead. She was new here and so much had to be explained. It would take her a while to process all the information coming at her. She might not even get it all straight before it was time to go, she realized.

Isabel went into her office right after the meeting to get her coat and briefcase. Tucker stuck his head in the door a few moments later, startling her.

"You're the last to leave the church tonight, Reverend. I can wait and lock up if you like."

"Oh, that's all right, Tucker. You go ahead. I can lock the doors. I remember how to do it," she assured him.

She had heard Tucker say that he had to be at work tonight for a late shift, as a favor for a friend. She didn't want to keep him.

"I'll just leave the glass door near the office open. I'll lock up the rest," he replied. "Good night now. You should go home and get some rest. Tomorrow is another day."

"Yes, it is. Good advice," she agreed. But tomorrow would be filled with its own demands. Every day here so far had been filled to the brim. She had forgotten how much work there was running a church, even a church this size.

Tucker said good night again and she heard him walking down the hall, closing up the church. She started to shut down her computer, but a few important e-mails caught her eye. Isabel sat down and started to write quick answers, hoping to save herself some time in the morning.

Before she realized it, she had been sitting there another hour. With her coat on. She leaned her head back and tried to stretch out her shoulders. It was time to go back to her cozy room at Vera Plante's house. Maybe she could sneak into the kitchen and make herself some hot cocoa. She needed some downtime, all alone. That would be a treat, Isabel thought.

She finally shut down the computer and turned off the light on her desk. Then she headed out to the hallway to let herself out of the church. The long hall was dark, with only the light from outside streaming in through the windows.

As she walked to the glass door, she heard strange sounds. Was she imagining it? No, she heard them clearly. Voices, coming from the sanctuary. Along with an odd noise she couldn't identify. It sounded like bowling balls, rolling down wooden lanes . . . so peculiar.

Without giving a thought to what she might find—or even to her own safety—Isabel headed through the wooden doors and into the church sanctuary.

Nothing could have prepared her for the sight she saw in the dim shadows.

Three teenage boys were skateboarding around the front of the church, doing rings around the altar table and down the long aisles between the pews, whooping and laughing and egging one another on.

Isabel flung the doors open wide, then turned on the lights. "What in the world is going on here? Stop that this instant!" she demanded.

Amazingly, they all obeyed her. For a split second. As if she'd hit a pause button on a remote control.

Then she saw them exchange looks and heard shouted expletives. Two of the boys grabbed their skateboards, flipping them up with a quick foot movement, then scuttled out the side door. But one boy was much closer to her. He was the most daring of all. He jumped on his board and raced down the center aisle, determined to brazenly escape by charging right past her. She saw him speed up the board with a foot maneuver just as he came her way.

Riding the board fairly low, his hands out for balance, he came straight at her. He must have been expecting her to be too shocked to do anything except jump out of the way. That's what most people would have done.

But Isabel was not most people.

Instead of leaping clear, she stepped directly out into his path. In a split second she watched confusion and fear flash across his face. He tried to swerve around her at the last minute, but she reached out and grabbed the hood of his sweatshirt and held on tight. The speeding board flew out from under his feet and his long, lanky body stumbled backward onto the floor.

Isabel kept her hold. She didn't want him to fall and hit his head. She quickly managed to grab his arm and fold it behind his back, a martial arts move she once learned for self-defense.

"Not so fast," she said quietly.

"Hey, let go! What are you, nuts, lady? You're hurting me."

The boy tried to squirm free, but she wouldn't let go. She knew he would take off the second she released her grip. She was stumped. What should she do now?

"Hey . . . what's going on?"

Isabel spun around at the sound of Tucker's voice. He was running into the sanctuary, dressed in his uniform.

"Are you all right, Reverend?" he called out.

"I'm fine, but . . . where did you come from?"

God had sent him, of course. What a question.

Once the boy saw the police officer, his body went slack. There wasn't any need to hold on to him. He sat down heavily in a pew, and Isabel rubbed her wrist where she'd been holding him so tightly.

Tucker came closer and looked down at her captive.

"I was driving around on patrol, and I noticed the lights on in here. Then I saw two kids run across the green. They looked like they'd been up to trouble. I thought maybe you forgot to lock up when you left."

"I stayed to answer e-mails and lost track of time. They must have found the open door and snuck in."

The boy she was holding on to peered up at her, and she knew she had guessed correctly.

"They were skateboarding in here. This boy and two others."

Tucker stared down at the boy. "Do I know you?"

The boy shook his head. "I don't think so."

"Well, we'll soon fix that," Tucker promised. "Let's start with your name . . . and don't lie."

"Max Ferguson."

"How old are you?" Tucker asked.

"Fifteen."

"Do you have some ID? A student card or something? Get it out," Tucker told him.

The boy looked annoyed but reached into his pocket and took out a plastic identification card. Tucker looked it over.

Fifteen. Isabel felt bad for him. What was ahead for this boy if this was what he was up to right now?

"Why did you come in here tonight?" Isabel asked. "Don't you know that this is a church, a sacred place?"

Max Ferguson met her gaze a minute, then looked away. He had thick blond hair cut close to his head on the sides and back, and long and spiky on top. A few silver studs glittered on his earlobe, and a tiny silver ring pierced his eyebrow.

"Yeah, I know it's a church." He laughed to himself. "That was the whole point."

Tucker asked the next question. "Those kids running across the green, they were with you, weren't they?"

"I want a lawyer," he replied sullenly. "Are you going to arrest me?"

"I would it if were up to me," Tucker said. He looked at Isabel. "What do you say, Reverend? I have to make out a report either way. You want to file a complaint against this kid?"

The boy turned and stared at her. She was dressed in her everyday clothes, so he probably hadn't realized she was a minister. He looked surprised for a moment, then hid his reaction behind a blank expression.

Isabel paused and took a deep breath. She was a minister. She didn't want to decide this question out of anger or even righteous indignation. She wanted to come from a place of peace, even love.

Though it was hard right now to get there.

"Where are your parents, Max?" she asked.

"My father is home, hanging out, I guess."

"Where does he think you are?" Tucker asked pointedly.

"At a friend's house, studying."

"Do you have a cell phone?" Isabel asked. "I want you to call him. Tell him where you are and ask him to pick you up."

The boy stared at her, looking suddenly scared and pale. "What if I don't want to do that?"

"Then you can come with me, and we'll call him from the police station," Tucker told him.

The boy made a horrible face at both of them. Isabel wondered if she should let him take his chances with Tucker at the station.

Then he pulled a cell phone out of his sweatshirt pocket and hit an automatic dial number. It rang once or twice, and he started talking.

"Yeah, it's me. Can you pick me up?" He paused, waiting for an answer. He fidgeted and chewed on a fingernail. "No, I'm not at his house anymore. We came into town . . . We just did, that's all. No big deal."

He waited again and Isabel wondered what his father was saying. "I'm in the village. At that old stone church on the green. Yeah, that's the one . . . No, I'm inside. No, I'm not alone in here . . ."

Tucker stuck out his hand. "Let me talk now. This isn't Twenty Questions."

Max looked reluctant but finally gave over his phone. Tucker quickly introduced himself and explained to the boy's father that his son had been caught trespassing in a church and had damaged property. And was in plenty of trouble.

"I could bring him down to the station right now. Yes, sir, even though he's a minor," Tucker said firmly. "But Reverend Lawrence doesn't want me to handle it that way. We'd like you to come to the church and pick him up. We'll wait ten minutes. Can you make it by then?" Tucker asked, looking at his watch.

Isabel saw Max swallow hard. It was bitter cold outside, but he wore only a black T-shirt with a ragged collar and a thin black hoodie. His baggy jeans hung loosely on his hips and covered his big orange sneakers. Not the best outfit for December, Isabel thought. She wondered if his parents looked after him at all.

Tucker finished the call and handed the boy his phone. "Your father is on his way."

Max met Tucker's stern gaze, then turned away and stared at the floor. He was scared, Isabel realized. Well, that took a while, didn't it?

"I hope he shows," Tucker said.

"You think the boy's father might not come?"

Tucker shrugged. "You never know with kids like this. I mean, there's a reason a boy his age isn't home doing his homework."

Isabel knew that was true. Many children in Haiti, where she had been working, lacked consistent, reliable parenting. But that was usually for different reasons. She just didn't expect it in such a stable, middle-class community.

"Let's figure out the damage," Tucker said. He turned to the boy. "You just sit here a minute. Don't get yourself into any more trouble," he warned.

Max looked up but didn't say anything. Isabel didn't think he would try to run away from them. It was too late for that.

Tucker walked around the sanctuary, following the deep scratches in the wooden floor made by the skateboards.

"Can those scratches come out?" Isabel asked.

"With some sanding and elbow grease. But it won't be easy. Carl's going to love working on this floor," he added, talking about the church sexton who was also his brother. "And right before Christmas."

"That is bad timing," Isabel agreed. Though was there a good time for vandalism?

"And this vase and candleholder are broken," Tucker added, kneeling down near the altar table. "This vase was an antique. We've had it since the church was founded."

The boys had also knocked over a pedestal table in the altar area that held a flower arrangement and some candles.

"Good thing the candles weren't lit," Isabel said.

"I guess so." Tucker sounded upset. He had started picking up the bits of broken vase, carefully collecting them in a small box he found under the altar table.

"Can it be glued together again?" Isabel asked.

Tucker didn't answer, just glared at the boy. "Was it worth it? Did you have a good time, wrecking other people's things? You kids could have set this place on fire. Is that your idea of a good time?"

Isabel understood his anger, but there was nothing to be solved by it. She could see the boy withdrawing, curling into himself. It was just what he had expected, maybe even wanted, someone getting angry at him. Did he feel he'd somehow won?

She moved toward Tucker and gently touched his shoulder.

"I know you're upset, Tucker. But let's remember where we are. And who we are."

Tucker let out a long breath. "I know. I just don't understand why people . . . even kids . . . do stuff like this. This is someone else's property. Not just property . . . it's a church, for goodness' sake."

Isabel nodded but couldn't answer. The question was complicated. There could be a million reasons why this boy and his friends snuck in here and broke whatever they could get their hands on.

She looked at Max; she could tell he was scared and confused. Riding a skateboard through the sanctuary didn't seem shocking to him the way it did to her and Tucker. To Max, it was just a building filled with stuff, not a sacred space where people came together to build community and open their hearts to God. He had no idea of how precious the church and its contents were to the congregation. She wondered if she could possibly make him understand, and then, if that was even her job.

A knock sounded on the sanctuary doors, and Tucker went to answer it. "That must be your father," Isabel said to Max.

"Either him or God. Coming to ground me and take away my cell phone for the rest of my life. And the hereafter."

The image was amusing. Isabel had to smile. It sounded as if the boy's parents at least tried to rein him in.

Tucker soon entered the sanctuary followed by a tall man with fair hair, like his son. He wore a dark blue down jacket and jeans and an irritated expression.

"I'm Jacob Ferguson, Max's father."

"I'm Reverend Lawrence," Isabel said easily. He looked surprised but quickly covered his reaction. "I found your son in the sanctuary tonight with two other boys. They got away, but I got hold of Max and then Officer Tulley arrived," she explained. "The boys did a lot of damage. You can see for yourself."

"Here, let me show you, sir," Tucker said. He took Max's father for a quick tour of the mess the boys had made.

When they returned, Jacob Ferguson stared down at his son. "I can't believe this. Why did you do this?"

The boy shrugged. "It wasn't my idea. We just thought it would be cool to ride our boards in here."

"Who were you with? The officer said there were two other kids. Was it Zack? Was this his idea? I told you I didn't want you hanging out with that kid anymore."

Max shook his head. "It wasn't Zack. I'm not saying who, either. You can ask me all night."

Isabel shook her head wearily. She'd seen this before. Max was being loyal, even though he was stuck taking the entire blame. But desecrating a religious sanctuary was a serious offense, and the other boys should be found and punished, too. Not just this one, she reflected. She hoped that Tucker could pursue this somehow. She would talk to him about it later.

Max's father looked frustrated and even angrier. Isabel didn't think they were getting anywhere.

"It's very late," she said. "You and Max need to talk more at home. I'm very interested to know why he did this. I'd like to meet with both of you sometime to discuss it."

"Who knows why he did it. He doesn't even know himself," Jacob said angrily.

"I asked you here because we need to figure out a way for Max to fully understand that what he did was wrong—and figure out a way for him to make up for it."

"Pay for the damage, you mean? I guess I should have brought my checkbook," Jacob said.

"I didn't mean that exactly," Isabel replied. "The church may ask you to cover some damages, Mr. Ferguson. But writing a check doesn't help your son. I'm talking about real consequences for his actions."

"What kind of consequences?" Jacob asked. "He's going to be grounded. No computer, no cell phone, no TV—"

Before he could go further, Isabel cut in. "All that sounds severe, but I have a sense you've done it before . . . and here he is. I think it would be more meaningful to him if he had to come here after school and fix the damage."

"Fix the damage? How could he do that?"

"Right, like I'm a carpenter or something," the boy said, making a goofy face.

"He can work a piece of sandpaper and a broom. You don't have to be a carpenter to do that much," Tucker cut in.

Jacob didn't answer. He looked over at his son. Had he ever performed any real work? Isabel doubted it.

"You mean, come here and clean up the mess, is that it?" Jacob asked.

"Yes, and I think this week would be a good time to start. I'm sure our church sexton will get right on this. It's a big job. The sanctuary has to be spotless for Christmas."

Jacob nodded, suddenly looking grim. Somehow the mention of Christmas annoyed him. "All right. He can come on Wednesday after school."

"Good. I'll be here and I'll introduce him to the sexton," Isabel said patiently. "And I'd like Max to come a few days a week after school for the next few weeks. Until all the repairs are done. They certainly won't be completed in one afternoon."

"A few days a week in a church? No way. Are you crazy or something? I'd rather go to jail," the boy complained.

"Max, close your mouth and keep it closed. You've already said enough tonight." Jacob Ferguson's voice was low, but he sounded as if he were about to explode. "Go to the car and wait for me. I'll be out in a minute."

"I'll walk him out," Tucker offered. "You seem to be done here, Reverend. If you need me, just give me a call."

"I'll be fine, Tucker. I'm leaving, too, as soon as I finish talking with Mr. Ferguson."

Isabel sensed that Max's father wanted to talk without his son present. At least he seemed concerned about the boy and upset by Max's bad behavior. Isabel had actually expected someone who did not seem nearly as responsible.

Once Max and Tucker were gone, Jacob turned to her. "I know my son's behavior is inexcusable, and he's very lucky that you didn't file a complaint and cause a lot of legal trouble for him. I realize that and I'm grateful," he said sincerely.

"I'm handling this as I think best. I don't think Max would have gotten much out of going down to the police station for a few hours. You might wind up paying some sort of fine or going to court a few months from now. And that would be that—except for bills from a lawyer."

"That, too," Jacob agreed, rubbing the side of his jaw. He needed a shave, Isabel noticed. Though something about his manner suggested he was a businessman or some type of white-collar professional.

"The thing is, believe it or not, my son has not always been like this. Yeah, he's a bit unconventional and can get a little wild at times. But he's always been a good kid. Until recently."

He paused, and Isabel waited for him to continue, but he didn't.

"All right, I believe you. Is there some reason for that?" she asked quietly.

"His mother died about six months ago. She had breast cancer. It moved to her lungs before anyone caught it. It's been very hard for Max. Hard for both of us," he admitted.

"Oh, I see. I'm very sorry for your loss," Isabel said sincerely. "He's so young."

"Yes, he is," Jacob added. "He thinks he's old enough to understand what happened. But he really doesn't."

"Has he had any grief counseling?"

"Yes, he's been to counselors. But it hasn't helped much, has it? I think it's just going to take time, a lot of time. Until then, I have to figure out how to get better control over him. But that's hard, too." Jacob Ferguson ran a hand through his hair. "I'm not trying to excuse what he did here. I just wanted you to know that there are other issues. He's not as horrible as he seems."

"I don't think he's horrible. I think he's hurting. I could see that even before you told me about your wife, Mr. Ferguson. I do understand," she added. "But I still think having him come here and help repair what he damaged, and get to know the place and the people in it, would be good for him."

He didn't answer right away. She could see him thinking over her reply. "All right. I'll tell him he has to come. I just want to warn you, it might not go very well. He can be a tough customer. Are you going to supervise him?" He sounded skeptical.

"We have a church sexton, Carl Tulley. He's Officer Tulley's brother," she added. "Carl will work with Max." She paused. "I think Carl will know how to handle him."

"Really? Maybe he can give me some pointers." Jacob sounded skeptical of that possibility as well. He pulled out his wallet and gave Isabel a business card. "I'll call the church Wednesday morning and let you know what time I can drop him off. If you need to get in touch, here's my number."

"Thank you. Then I'll see Max on Wednesday."

"You will. Thank you, Reverend." Then he turned and left Isabel alone in the sanctuary.

Isabel looked down at the card imprinted with the insignia of a local college. Jacob Ferguson was a full professor of mathematics. Interesting, she thought.

Tomorrow morning first thing, she would have to tell the trustees and church council what had happened here. If Tucker didn't beat her to it. She hoped they would approve of the way she handled it.

I didn't even think of that. Isabel smiled to herself. She wasn't used to working in a church where there was a hierarchy and governing boards. She wasn't used to taking orders or checking in with supervisors.

She wondered now what they would say.

ISABEL DID NOT HAVE TO WAIT LONG TO FIND OUT. ON TUESDAY morning, she arrived at the church a few minutes past nine and found several messages on the answering machine.

"This is a call for Reverend Lawrence. It's Lillian Warwick, one of the trustees. I've just heard that the church has been vandalized. Please call me immediately."

A long beep sounded, then the next call played back. "This is

Grace Hegman, Reverend Lawrence. I've heard some disturbing news this morning that somebody broke into the church last night. I'm not even sure if it's true. Please call me back when you have a chance. I'll be in my shop until six. Thanks so much."

"Good morning, Reverend Lawrence. This is Warren Oakes. I've heard there was a disturbance at the church last night. I'd like to discuss it with you. If you'd call me back at my office, I'd appreciate it."

Isabel let out a long breath and sat down heavily in the desk chair. She knew that news traveled fast in a small town, but this had to be a record breaker. She decided to answer the calls in order and took out the church directory, searching for Lillian Warwick's number. She also opened her coffee mug and took a few fortifying sips while she punched in the number.

She had so far only spoken to Lillian Warwick two or three times, and very briefly. Lillian had not been very warm or welcoming. Isabel was guessing it had nothing to do with loyalty to Reverend Ben. The aloof attitude seemed to be Lillian's basic personality, and Isabel braced herself for a conversation that would likely be difficult.

The phone at the Warwick house was answered on the second ring. "Good morning, this is Reverend Lawrence. I'm returning a call from Lillian Warwick."

"This is Lillian Warwick. Thank you for getting back to me so promptly. I've been quite distressed ever since I heard about last night's episode. I had to take an extra pill for my blood pressure this morning."

"I'm sorry to hear that," Isabel said sincerely. "Are you all right? Do you need to visit a doctor?"

"I'm married to a doctor. He believes there's no danger. At the present time."

"Yes, well, I'm glad to hear that."

"Tell me, Reverend, what exactly happened? How did these barbarians crash the gate? And what sort of damage did they do? I heard that the vase from the founders was broken."

It was a bit worse than that, Isabel nearly said aloud.

She cringed, knowing that she had to be as honest as she could. Then again, she did have to consider the woman's medical situation. She decided she could be a bit vague on the details. Not lie, of course, but she did need to consider Lillian's blood pressure. "I was in my office late after the deaconate meeting and heard sounds in the sanctuary. I found three boys there—"

"Boys? How old were they?" Lillian interrupted.

"Teenagers. High school age," Isabel said.

"Delinquents, you mean. Hooligans! I heard they were on skateboards. Could that possibly be true?"

"Yes, they were. I managed to stop one of the boys, but the other two got away. Luckily, Tucker saw the lights on and came in to help me."

"That was very lucky indeed," Lillian said. "You could have been hurt."

"Oh, I don't think so. I wasn't in any danger," Isabel assured her.

Lillian made a sound that seemed to be a wordless disagreement. "And the vase from the church founders was smashed to bits?"

"Well, not bits," Isabel clarified. "We might be able to repair it."

"Oh, you might glue such a thing together. But it's lost all its value," Lillian insisted.

"If you mean as an antique, I suppose that's true. But it's still valuable to the church for its historic significance, isn't it?"

Lillian ignored her rebuttal. "What else was damaged? This will cost the congregation a small fortune. I hope the boy's parents will foot that bill."

"I believe Mr. Ferguson is willing to cover the cost of the damage. It's mainly the floor."

"The floor? What on earth did they do to the floor?"

Isabel paused. She had to tell her. There was no way around it. Lillian Warwick was sure to hear it anyway.

"Well, as you already know, they were riding skateboards in the sanctuary."

"Skateboards in the sanctuary," Lillian repeated. "These children have no respect for anything, not one single shred of respect."

Isabel tried to calm her down. "Tucker said that Carl could refinish the damaged spots."

Lillian let out another long, tortured sigh. "I would be in favor of professional repair. However, this is a matter for the trustees to decide. It's a shame that people these days don't know how to raise children. Parents take no responsibility. They don't know how to be firm, how to say no. They spoil their children, rotten to the core, and then the rest of us are left to suffer the consequences. That boy's parents should be ashamed. They should write the church a formal letter of apology."

Isabel considered telling Lillian that the boy's mother had recently died and he was dealing with grief, anger, and the many stages of loss. Along with a heavy dose of adolescent angst. Perhaps she was being unfair, but Isabel guessed that explaining all that wouldn't change Lillian's opinion.

Lillian paused, and Isabel wondered if the conversation might be over. Were all of her phone calls this morning going to be this difficult? She certainly hoped not.

Dear Lord, please give me patience with these reactions. I know that Lillian is just trying to express her shock and distress and her sense of violation, because she loves this church. Please help me to deal with her empathetically, she silently prayed.

"So I suppose Tucker brought the boy down to the police station. That must have scared some sense into him. Though they probably didn't keep him overnight, his being a minor and all that—"

"Actually," Isabel cut in, "we decided not to handle it that way. I thought it would be best if the young man came back to the church after school, a few times a week, and helped repair the damages."

There was a long, tense silence.

"You mean to say no legal action was taken against this boy at all? Tucker didn't want to take him to the police station?"

"Tucker would have. But I didn't think that was the best way to handle it. Don't you think he will learn a valuable lesson by fixing what he's damaged?"

"He might," Lillian granted. "But that doesn't mean he should be absolved of facing legal consequences, as well. I'm surprised that you didn't consult one of us—one of the trustees or the church council—before you let this little hoodlum off the hook completely."

"Frankly, I didn't think of it," Isabel said honestly. "It was very late, and I did what I thought best."

She was also not accustomed to reviewing her decisions with boards and councils. She was used to thinking and acting on her feet and trusting her own judgment. Without the need for a rubber stamp from anyone.

She would have explained why she thought it was the best way to handle the situation, but Lillian didn't pause to hear more.

"Yes, well, you did as you thought best, I suppose. But you are new to the church, and this is clearly a matter for the trustees to decide. We will have to meet as soon as possible. Then you can explain your rationale to all of us at the same time, Reverend. I'll be interested to hear what the others say."

"I will, too," Isabel said honestly.

Lillian soon said good-bye and ended the call. Isabel was sure that she was speed-dialing the other church trustees without taking a breath.

Isabel checked the time, wondering how long it would take before she was ordered to appear before them. Would they all be so severe and judgmental? She doubted it. But she did realize now that not everyone would agree that she had taken the right course in letting Max Ferguson bypass the legal system.

She glanced at the other two names and numbers that she had jotted down on the message pad. Grace Hegman and Warren Oakes. She decided to call them right away and get the chore over with. Those conversations couldn't be any worse than the one she'd just had with Lillian.

Isabel reached Grace just before ten. Fortunately, the conversation was much easier than the one she had endured with Lillian. Grace was concerned about the damage, but she listened carefully to Isabel, not nearly so eager to assert her opinion before hearing the facts.

Isabel didn't speak to Warren Oakes until the afternoon. He had been out of his office at a court hearing. He was reasonable, too, though concerned about the law. As an attorney, that was only natural, Isabel thought.

A time had been set for the trustee meeting, he told her finally. "As our minister, you are already part of the board. However, in this situation we definitely need you there to explain the events."

And defend my unilateral decision, Isabel silently finished for him.

"We've also asked Tucker Tulley to stop by," he added. "He's not a trustee, but we think he can help sort this out."

Isabel was relieved to hear that. Tucker was clearly respected by the congregation, and she felt sure he had seen the wisdom in her decision and would support her.

"I'd be happy to meet with you," she said politely. "Just tell me when and where."

"Seven o'clock tonight at the church. Does that work with your schedule?"

"Absolutely. See you then."

Isabel hung up the phone, feeling a heavy weight in her stomach. It was just nerves, she knew. She had never imagined that this situation would evolve in this way. It suddenly felt as if she were in the line of fire alongside Max Ferguson.

The thought suddenly sprang to mind: Would she be asked to leave this post? This congregation, kind as most of them were, might decide she was not a good fit and ask her to go. She could easily imagine Lillian Warwick arguing for a new minister.

Isabel took a deep breath and centered herself. She still believed she had done the right thing. That was all she could tell them. Stay or go, it was finally God's decision. Not her own. Not Grace Hegman's or Warren Oakes's . . . or even Lillian Warwick's. Isabel knew that she could only speak from her heart tonight and pray that the trustees of this church would be guided to consider the situation in a fair and spiritual manner.

FOR THE REST OF THE DAY, ISABEL TURNED HER ATTENTION TO the other tasks of running the church, though many other church members called or e-mailed, inquiring about the vandalism. She filled them in, as succinctly and politely as she could, explaining that the trustees were meeting to discuss the matter that night. That seemed to satisfy most people.

The meeting hung over her like a heavy cloud. It was late afternoon, almost five and already growing dark outside, when the phone console lit up with one more call.

She glanced at the caller ID, bracing herself. The sight of Reverend Ben's name and number made her sigh with relief.

"Hello, Isabel. Sorry to have taken so long to get in touch today. I heard about the vandalism at the church this morning, but I had to start my physical therapy," he explained. "So I wasn't able to call until now. How is it going? Have you been bombarded with calls all day?"

"*Bombarded* is just the word for it. I'm practically ducking under my desk," she managed to joke.

"I can just imagine it. I've had a few days like that at the church myself. More than a few in my long tenure . . . Though not in the first week I arrived there," he added sympathetically.

Isabel had to smile at that observation. It was her first genuine smile of the day.

"I don't know that it would have been any easier if I had been here twenty years like you, Ben," she said. "The damage to the sanctuary is upsetting enough. But it seems that the real problem now is how I handled it," she admitted. "Some people think I should have dealt with the boy more severely—sent him off with Tucker to the police station to be fined, or face whatever legal charges there were to be leveled at him."

"Tucker was the one who called me. He told me about that part, too."

Ben had obviously heard this story, or some of it, already, but was patiently listening to her version.

"I just didn't think it would serve any good purpose, Ben. This boy has recently lost his mother and he's hurting. His father said he's not normally so callous and disrespectful. I was upset to see the damage the boys did, too. Very upset. But I wanted to deal with him in a compassionate and hopefully instructive way, not strike back in a punitive, angry way. Does that make any sense to you?"

"It makes all the sense in the world, Isabel. I would have done the same myself . . . or at least aspired to that attitude. It's not easy to take the spiritual high road in such an emotionally charged situation. Those boys violated something that we all hold dear and revere so deeply. But the congregation must see this as a test, and an opportunity to exercise all the values we preach and teach: compassion, understanding, patience, forbearance. Turning the other cheek," he quoted. "Most of all, love. I think that you tried to do that. Though you didn't consult the trustees or council, you did consult a higher authority—the lessons of the Scripture that have been ingrained in your heart and mind."

Isabel didn't know what to say at first. Ben's eloquent explanation of her actions overwhelmed her. She had liked him from the first, but now could truly see why his congregation respected and admired him so much. He was a truly wise and thoughtful man.

"Thank you, Ben," Isabel said sincerely. "I have to say, after talking on the phone all day to the church members, who have been very upset, I was starting to doubt I'd done the right thing."

"Yes, it can be lonely at the top. I know just how you feel," he quipped. "You will second-guess yourself at times, but I am with you on this, Isabel, one hundred and ten percent. I will talk to the trustees myself, if you'd like. It's possible that, in my absence, they're also a bit . . . insecure. That could be part of it, too."

"Yes, of course. They don't know me yet or trust my judgment. That's only natural," she agreed.

"If it's any comfort, I'm sure that I, too, would have taken some heat on this from a few church members . . . who will remain nameless," he added with a small laugh. "There are always a few to keep us on our toes."

Isabel was sure she knew who he meant and smiled again.

"It is a comfort," she replied. "I'm used to flying solo, more or less. Not leading an entire flock. That's part of it, too," she admitted. "But I thank you from the bottom of my heart for calling, Ben, and giving me this reality—*spirituality*—check. Though I'm tempted to have you plead my case, I don't want to bother you. Still, it's good to know you're there for backup."

Ben laughed. "Yes, you have a spare in the trunk, so to speak. Bald, partially deflated, and just been in the shop for a retreading. But I'm here for you," he joked with her.

Isabel laughed at his self-deprecating description.

"I'm sure you'll do fine, Isabel. They're all reasonable people. Just tell them what you've told me."

"I will," she said, realizing it wasn't so much what she had told him but what he'd told her that was worth remembering. "How did your physical therapy go?" she asked.

"Oh, it was an experience. I was more tired than I expected," he admitted. "The first time is the hardest, that's what the therapist told me. No pain, no gain, and all that. This healing business is as much about healthier habits as it is about learning more patience. Progress on both fronts is going to take time."

"I hope the next time is easier for you, and I hope to see you again soon, too."

"Same here, dear. I'll say a prayer for you. Let me know how it goes."

Isabel thanked Ben again for his counsel and said good-bye.

She leaned back in her chair, feeling much better. Her spirits were lifted and her mind clear again. She felt reconnected with her rationale for treating Max Ferguson the way she had. A decision that had come from the right place, she'd thought at the time. And now did so again, thanks to Reverend Ben.

CHAPTER EIGHT

⌁

*B*EN HEARD THE PIECE—BEETHOVEN'S PIANO CON-
certo no. 5, he thought—end in a flourish and was not
surprised when Carolyn appeared in the bedroom doorway a few
moments later. She'd been downstairs practicing while he took a
nap. His round of physical therapy and then the phone call with
Reverend Isabel had worn him out.

Carolyn seemed full of energy today. She had gone for her
morning power walk, cleaned the house, and done the laundry. She
had also given lessons that afternoon, started dinner, and then
practiced the piano . . . all while he was resting.

"Did you sleep at all?" she asked, sitting on the side of the bed.
"I'm sorry if I was playing too loudly. I should practice later, after
dinner."

"I love hearing you. Beethoven is one of my favorites; a wonderful way to wake up."

That was true, not just a pleasing compliment. Waking up to her playing, Ben realized how he had taken Carolyn's music for granted so much of the time. Now he appreciated every note.

"I did sleep, for nearly two hours," he said, looking at the clock. "I really didn't do very much in that rehab place this morning— just walked around a tiny indoor track. I don't know why I should feel so tired. I thought the doctor said I was going to feel a lot more energetic now."

"Don't you feel any better at all?" she asked with concern.

Ben caught himself. He shouldn't have worried Carolyn. He was just venting. "I do, honestly. I'm not short of breath anymore or light-headed—"

"Oh, Ben, did you really have all those symptoms and never say anything about it? That's what scares me most," she confessed.

"I know. I was an idiot. I was so lucky that . . . Well, we've covered that ground. Let's not go back there again. I'm resolved now to do better," he promised her. "I've learned my lesson. As for feeling tired now, it's a different kind of tired. It will just take time, and I'm impatient," he admitted.

"Yes, you can be," she agreed with a smile. "Are you worried about the church? That call this morning was troublesome. I hope you aren't worried."

"No, not at all. Of course, it was disturbing. The sanctuary has never been vandalized in all these years. We just started locking up the church recently," he reminded her. "But it sounds as if it's all reparable and under control." He sighed. "To tell you the truth, Carolyn, after I spoke to Reverend Isabel this afternoon, I felt relieved that I wasn't there and didn't have to deal with it. Maybe it's just the post-op fatigue, but I've been thinking more and more—and praying about it, too. I'm wondering if I'm really up to returning to the church, even after I've recovered."

Carolyn didn't answer him. Her blue eyes grew very wide. "What do you mean, Ben? Are you saying that you're thinking of retiring?"

He let out a long, slow breath. As much as he'd mulled this over in his head, it was hard to finally say the words out loud. Even to Carolyn.

"Well . . . yes. I guess that's what I'm saying. I'm thinking of retiring. It's starting to look as if that would be the right thing for me to do. As much as I never expected to be knocked out of the saddle this way and thought I'd just brush myself off and jump back on . . . Well, I'm starting to think that's not what I should do."

"Oh . . . well . . . my goodness." Carolyn was shocked. Though they had talked this question over several times since his heart attack, he always maintained that he would go back to the church once he felt better. There was no reason to think he couldn't do it. "I'm just surprised," she said at last. "You kept saying you would at least try to go back and decide from there."

"I know I did. But maybe there's no reason to test myself that way. Maybe it's best to just step aside and let someone younger, stronger, and fresher take over. Maybe that's best for me . . . and best for the church, too."

"Maybe," she agreed. "But I hope you're not saying that just because you think I want you to."

"Not at all. I know how you feel about it. But you've hardly said a word," he said honestly. "Which I appreciate."

He did know how much Carolyn wanted him to start a new stage of their life together, a stage that she had perhaps started already without him. But she'd been very good about keeping her opinion to herself and not lobbying for that decision.

"I've tried not to nag," she said. "But now that you've gotten sick and I've been worried about you, I'm not sure I've been all that patient and quiet about it."

"This is my own decision entirely," he promised her. "And I haven't really made up my mind yet. Though I think I'm getting there. I know it seems very soon after the heart attack, but I've really been thinking about it for a while. I just haven't talked about it," he admitted. "This heart business has been a good thing in a way. It's made me face this question squarely. Am I even fit enough to go back to the church? If someone asked me that right now, I'd have to say no, I am not."

"But Ben, you will get stronger. You've seen it yourself," she reminded him. "I wish you would try to remember that."

He had seen many people in his situation, recovering from heart surgery, bypassed arteries, valve replacements, even an entire heart transplant. He had visited them before operations, after surgeries, and during recuperations, and practically all of them had survived and gone on to lead full lives, and yes, some had become even stronger. He didn't know why he couldn't remember that and hold on to that idea when he was feeling low or tired—or felt a painful, ominous twinge in his chest.

"I have to remember that. I know it's true. I've seen it with my own eyes, many, many times. But I don't think that should really be the deciding factor here. In a few months, I'll be fit and full of energy. Better than new," he added in a snappy tone. "But does that mean I should buzz right back to the church, like some bumblebee that's been away from the hive on sick leave?"

"Oh, Ben, you're far more than a sick bumblebee," Carolyn said with a laugh. "You're the very heart of the church. You're the spiritual leader, the moral compass. You're the head cook and bottle washer and—"

"I am all that . . . and more. But no one person is the church,

Carolyn. Even the building is not the church, or all the committees and structures that keep it going. The congregation is the church. I know they depend on me. But they will go on and find a new minister, who will bring new talents and a fresh perspective. Someone like Reverend Isabel," he offered. He paused and took a breath. "I think it might be time for that to happen," he added somberly. "Not so I can hide away, reading the sports pages, or spend my days on the beach, surf casting. There are other ways I can serve. So many possibilities, including all those trips we want to take and classes at the university. And spending more time with the kids."

"We always talk about doing those things someday," Carolyn agreed. "When you fell to the floor at the altar, and Tucker and Sam were struggling to keep you alive, I thought that day was never going to come."

"For a minute there, so did I." He met her glance and sighed. "'To everything there is a season, and a time to every purpose under heaven,'" he reminded her, quoting one of their favorite passages of Scripture. "The secret of life seems to be to accept change, gracefully and gratefully. Change is the only thing we can depend on. We can't avoid it or fight it. We have to face it head-on and try our best to make something positive of it."

As she listened to his words, her expression was relaxed, full of acceptance and even admiration. Ben felt good inside, as if he had just jumped a hurdle. One he didn't even realize had sprung up in his path.

"How did I ever marry such an intelligent, wise man?"

Ben smiled and shrugged. "You forgot dashing and handsome, dear . . . or I will be, once my beard grows back."

Carolyn laughed and touched his stubbly cheek. Then he opened his arms and hugged her as well as he could without hurting the incision in his chest.

"It's a big, big step. But I'm starting to think it's the right time to make it. Are you with me on this? I can't get through it without you."

"Absolutely," she agreed.

It was Ben's ministry and his decision alone when to end it. Still, she couldn't deny that she'd hoped he would decide to retire. She had made some sacrifices as a minister's wife, not the least of which was sharing him with everyone for his round-the-clock duties. But now that he had finally said the words aloud and seemed close to making the decision, Carolyn felt a little shocked. Was it really going to end? Ben's life in the church was her life, too, with so many responsibilities as the minister's wife.

"Are you all right? You seem a little sad," he said, holding her hand on his chest.

"I'm relieved," she said slowly, "but also a little sad. It's a milestone for me, too, Ben. Your leaving the church—with me along with you—will leave a great gap in my life."

"It will. I would never minimize that," he agreed, watching her expression. "But we won't be leaving the church entirely. We'll still be members . . . private citizens, though."

"That's right. Though we won't be at the center anymore, we'll still be there on the sidelines. There will be a gap in our lives, but we'll fill it easily." She smiled at him. "We won't have enough time to do all the things we've put off. We need to get out and see the world a bit while we're still able, don't you think?"

"Hey, I've just had a complete tune-up, bumper to bumper. I'm ready to hit the road," he teased her.

Carolyn laughed but soon looked serious again. "When will you decide for sure? Do you know?"

"The sooner, the better. Don't you think?"

"You sound as if you're afraid you might change your mind. Maybe you should sleep on it a day or so."

"I will, dear. Don't worry." He patted her hand. "This is the right thing to do. I'm starting to feel very sure of it."

Carolyn nodded and smiled. He didn't seem one hundred percent positive, but of course it was only natural to have some doubts about leaving a position that he held for so long, one that had been the center of their lives. Ben loved the church, and the congregation loved him. It was never going to be easy, she realized. She needed time to get used to the idea, too.

THE TRUSTEES MEETING WAS NOT NEARLY AS DIFFICULT AS ISABEL had imagined it would be. But few things in life were, she reminded herself, thinking of one of Mark Twain's lines: "Some of the worst things in my life never even happened."

She knew very well that the Scripture implores us not to worry, that it's a useless waste of time and undermines real faith. But being only human, Isabel knew that sometimes it was hard not to give in to worrying.

She said a silent little prayer before she entered the church meeting room. *God, I know that whatever happens here will be all for the best. Just help me say what I believe is right.*

Tucker was a friendly face at the table, though not the only one. Warren Oakes, Grace Hegman, Julie Sawyer, and some other members she didn't know all greeted her in a friendly and respectful manner. The sole exception was Lillian Warwick, who acknowledged her with a cool, regal nod.

All of them, however, were concerned about what had happened and wanted to understand her reasoning—and Tucker's—in not prosecuting Max Ferguson. After the basic facts were recounted by both Isabel and Tucker, Lillian Warwick began the discussion.

"Despite the boy's age and other circumstances, I still find it surprising that no legal action was taken. I mean, to desecrate a house of worship—"

"I wouldn't say he desecrated it, Lillian," Tucker cut in, his voice calm. "It wasn't that malicious. It was just some kids with attitude acting out, egging one another on."

The group debated, back and forth, whether the act was malicious or merely foolish. Finally, Grace cleared her throat. She was a shy woman, Isabel could see. She barely looked up at the group and kept touching the buttons on her cardigan as she spoke.

"Whether it was malicious or just a teenage prank that got out of control, what happened in the sanctuary is done. The question now is, how will we react to it? You can't end violence with more violence. You can't end hate with hate. You can only end hate with love," she said quietly. "I think Martin Luther King, Jr., said that. And it's in the Bible, too. Jesus said to turn the other cheek," she reminded them.

Good work, Grace, Isabel thought. Grace caught her eye and smiled shyly.

"So you're saying Reverend Lawrence did the right thing?" Lillian challenged her. "Is that what you mean?"

"Yes, that's what I'm saying. I think she made the right decision," Grace said, standing up to Lillian.

"I do, too," Julie Sawyer said. "He's a boy who recently lost his mother. He's just grieving and acting out."

"Yes, I heard that part of the story," Lillian replied tartly. "So now the church offers therapy to troubled children? Is that it?"

"Oh, Lillian . . ." Tucker was frustrated, Isabel could tell, but didn't know how to answer her.

"I think the church should offer counsel and comfort to anyone who's hurting," Julie Sawyer said.

"Even if they hurt us? Even if breaking in at night and damaging our property is their calling card?" Lillian demanded. She stared around the room. "Am I the only one here who still believes people should follow the law and pay the consequences when they don't?"

Her steely gaze finally settled on Tucker. "I wasn't sure at first if we were doing the right thing, letting the boy off the legal hook," he admitted. "But I've changed my mind. There was nothing to be accomplished by dragging him down to the police station. It might have put some fear into him. Chances are, though, it would have made him feel cool in front of his friends, and made him want to go further the next time. The legal system doesn't make most people better citizens. It makes a lot of them worse, I'll tell you that much."

Lillian looked about to challenge Tucker on that statement when Warren Oakes spoke up. "It seems to me, what we're debating here is the difference between civil law and spiritual law. And as a church, we have the opportunity in this case to follow spiritual law."

"That's exactly it, Warren," Tucker jumped in. "When I saw the damage those kids did, I was so angry, I almost lost it. Reverend Isabel was upset, too. But she looked at me and said, 'Tucker, let's remember where we are. And who we are.' I think we all have to remember that right now."

"I was upset," Isabel told them, "very shocked and angry at those kids. I've never seen anything like that. But I had to get hold of myself and not let some knee-jerk reaction take over. How can I preach about love, patience, understanding, and charity my whole life and not put those words into action when the opportunity arises? These are the lessons our Scripture teaches us. This is what we're told to do. To turn the other cheek. To practice compassion and understanding. To forgive easily and love unconditionally. That is who we are. Or who we should strive to be."

Isabel gazed around the room. Everyone was quiet. Even Lillian seemed mollified.

"Well said, Reverend," Grace said quietly.

"Yes, that's the right way to look at this situation," Julie agreed. "That's what I've been thinking all along. We're a church. If we can't forgive this boy and try to help him, who will?"

"That's what I think, too," Tucker agreed.

There was little left to say. Warren Oakes soon adjourned the meeting.

As Isabel walked to her car, she paused on the green to look at the harbor. The meeting had been tense and she needed to unwind. She gazed out at the dark water and the sky above, nearly the same color and studded with stars tonight. It was certainly pretty here. Her descriptions in notes to her family and friends didn't quite do it justice.

Now she had another chapter to relate. She didn't feel as if she had won an argument or a debate. More as if they'd been heading in the wrong direction and she'd had to work hard to turn them onto the right path. As if she were a little border collie, barking and nipping at their heels.

She felt as if she finally knew what it was like to be the minister of a congregation. It wasn't all meetings and sermons and pleasant talk at coffee hours. Sometimes you had to bark and nip at the flock to help them onto the right path.

Though I don't think I want to do that again any time soon, Isabel thought with a small smile. *This job is hard work. Harder than I ever expected.*

CHAPTER NINE

~⌒~

*I*SABEL WAS WORKING ON THE CHURCH NEWSLETTER Wednesday afternoon when Max Ferguson walked into her office. Her gaze was fixed on her computer screen, but she glanced at him a moment and smiled. "I'll be right with you. I just need to finish this."

It was close to four o'clock, she noticed. He had not come straight after school, which his father had said ended at three. But at least he kept his promise and was here. She should be thankful for that much.

Max lingered in the doorway a moment, then finally walked in, a belligerent expression fixed on his face, his chin jutting up at a sharp angle. He sat on the edge of a chair in front of her desk, as if ready to take flight again at any moment. A ragged green army pack was slung over one shoulder, and his skateboard dangled from one hand.

Once again, he wasn't wearing a coat, just a thin gray hoodie and a black T-shirt, though it was frosty outside and the forecast called for more snow.

He huffed and sighed, but Isabel kept typing. She wasn't being deliberately rude. She really did need to finish what she was working on before she lost track of her thoughts. Besides, Max needed to learn some patience and respect for the needs of others.

A few moments later, she hit "save," then sat back and studied him. "Thank you for waiting. I was just getting to the end and didn't want to forget what I needed to say." She rose from her desk and walked over to a table near the window. "Would you like something to eat? There's some fruit here and cookies. I could get you something to drink—some milk or hot cocoa?" She couldn't help it. The boy looked cold and hungry.

He seemed interested in her offer, shifting in his seat to get a better look at the food. Then he sat back and shook his head, as if remembering his principles. "I'm good."

"You can just come over and help yourself if you want something," she encouraged him. She picked out a crisp apple and bit into it, savoring the tart taste. "Good apple. Braeburn, my favorite."

She smiled at him, but he showed no reaction. He crossed his arms over his chest and sighed again.

Isabel walked back to her desk and sat down. "How was school today?"

"It was just . . . school. No big deal."

Isabel took another bite of the apple. She could tell he was losing patience with her, but she had to try. "What subjects are you taking?"

"Math, history . . . the usual, useless pile of boring stuff. What's the difference?" He somehow seemed angry, weary, and tense all at the same time. Quite a feat, she thought.

This boy had not always been like this. She tried to remember that. He was in pain, hurting badly. She could see it in his eyes, hear it in his voice. Her heart went out to him.

"So tell me something. What did your friends say today in school? The two other guys who trashed the sanctuary with you? Were they at least grateful that you didn't turn them in?"

He shrugged. "I don't know what you're talking about. What guys?"

Isabel shook her head. "I wouldn't mind having a friend like you. I hope they appreciate your loyalty."

He leaned back and stared at her. "Are you a shrink or something? I thought you were a minister—and I was here to work."

She had a degree in counseling. Many ministers did. But she didn't want to get into that now.

"You are here to do a job," she assured him. "We need to find the church sexton, Carl Tulley. You're going to be working with him."

But before they could leave the office to look for Carl, the sexton appeared in the doorway. "Carl, we were just on our way to look for you," Isabel greeted him.

In his usual laconic style, Carl didn't answer. He glanced at her, then walked in and stood near Max's chair, staring down at him. Carl was not that tall, but had wide shoulders and a barrel chest. And there was something in his bearing that made it clear that there wasn't much on this earth that scared him.

"This is Max," Isabel said. "Max, this is Carl Tulley, our church sexton."

Carl squinted down at Max. "You're the kid who trashed the sanctuary? Get your things. Follow me."

Max stood up and grabbed his pack, then glanced back at Isabel. His defiant expression had melted into one that was uneasy, even panicky. *You're leaving me alone with this guy?* he seemed to say.

"Go along with Carl. I'll be around in a while to see how you're doing."

"Come on, kid. I don't bite. If you don't give me any trouble," Carl clarified.

"Right." Max hefted the pack to his shoulder, trying to sound cool again.

The boy followed the sexton down the long hallway, purposely keeping a step or two behind the older man. He was bent over and walked as if his legs hurt, but he still looked incredibly strong. The sleeves of his gray utility shirt were rolled to the elbow, and Max saw a full gallery of tattoos. Awesome tattoos, he thought. He wanted to ask about them, but the guy didn't seem very interested in conversation. Not like the woman minister, asking all kinds of questions and trying to give him cookies and milk. He wasn't sure which was worse.

They came to the sanctuary, and Carl pulled open the heavy doors. He ran his big calloused hand lovingly over the wood, which was shiny and smooth, the brass fittings polished bright as gold.

"This here door is almost two hundred years old. It was made out of wood from the ship that the settlers who founded this village came over the ocean in. And all those big gray stones in the foundation, outside? They were carried on wagons up from the shore and laid by hand. Did you know that?"

Max shook his head. "Nope."

"Nope, huh?" Carl mimicked the sound of the boy's voice. "Do you even care?"

Carl opened the door all the way and walked into the darkened sanctuary. It seemed different from the other night, even darker and more mysterious. The big stained-glass windows glowed from the late afternoon light; Max hadn't really noticed them the night before. The air was damp and cold and smelled like burning candles. A simple wooden cross hung over the offering table.

Carl turned to him, his battered face looking fierce. "Do you understand what I'm trying to say? A long time ago, people built this place by hand. And every generation since, other people take care of and preserve it. It's like . . . like a museum or something. Ever been in a museum?"

Max nodded and shrugged. "Sure I have."

"Well, would you race around on your board in a museum, wrecking the place? No, I don't think you would," Carl answered for him. "This place," he added, waving his hand around the darkened sanctuary. "It's even more special than a museum. It's a church, a sacred place. God is here. Get what I'm saying?"

Max just nodded. He felt a tightness in his throat and wasn't sure if it was just nerves or feeling angry at this old man's scolding. Or maybe feeling guilty for what he had done with Zack and Leo. He didn't think people cared this much. He really hadn't been thinking much at all the other night when they broke in. It just seemed like a fun thing to do. He wasn't trying to hurt anybody.

Carl went to the back wall and flipped a row of switches. It was suddenly very bright, and the sanctuary looked different, not quite as mysterious and holy, Max thought.

"Let there be light, the Good Book says." Carl's deep voice echoed in the emptiness. "So we can see the infernal mess you made Monday night," he added. "I started in here yesterday but didn't get too far. There's a broom over there. You know how to work one of those, right?"

Max nodded and took hold of the broomstick. "Yeah, I do."

"Then start on this side and sweep this whole floor—in between the pews, the aisles, up and down—everything. All the pieces of things you kids tore down and tore up, you put that in this bag, see? Some of the women in church are going to try to put these banners and such back together again. The rest of the stuff, you throw in that barrel. Got it?"

Max nodded. *It wasn't just me,* he wanted to say. *I wasn't the only one.*

But the grizzled old guy was giving him such a hard, angry look, he wasn't going to get into it with him.

"Hey! You . . . kid."

"My name is Max."

"You got to look at what you're doing. Pay attention. You're pushing it along without even looking." Carl took the broom and demonstrated the way he wanted the floor swept. "See, these wooden tiles have rows. You go up and down, short quick strokes. Press the broom down, and watch what you're doing so you don't miss any dirt. You understand?"

Max nodded. "I get it. Don't worry."

Carl handed him the broom, then stood there and watched Max sweep, making sure he did it exactly as instructed. His surveillance made Max even more annoyed. He wanted to just drop the broom and stalk out.

But he knew that would only make things worse with his father. His dad said the church was being very nice about the situation and that he had better just do what they said—or he would be in even more trouble. Max knew that if he got in any more trouble, he was going to have problems getting into college. And that's what his father worried about the most lately.

"Eyes on the floor, son. What are you, daydreaming again already?" Carl scolded.

"I'm watching, don't worry." Max finally focused, moving the broom up and down the rows the way he'd been told.

Finally, after Max demonstrated that he could also use a dustpan properly, Carl stalked over to the center aisle and knelt down on the floor near a spot where the wooden tiles had been badly damaged by the skateboards.

"Okay, I'm going to run the sander now. This will make some noise and plenty of dust. You'll need to sweep and mop," Carl warned him. "Then I have to varnish these spots all over again, and then we have to buff the entire floor."

"All right. Whatever."

Carl didn't look that pleased by Max's answer, but he turned on his machine and started to work on the floor. For crying out loud, it was just a scratch in some wood. The guy was making a world crisis out of it. Though Max had to admit, he had no idea how complicated it was to fix the scratches. It really was a pain.

" Max returned to his assignment, trying hard to focus on the task. Zack and Leo didn't know what they were missing. Max wasn't sure why he hadn't turned them in and let them share the good times around here. Right now, he was thinking maybe he ought to. But he wouldn't snitch on his friends. They had made fun of him for getting caught, but he could tell they sort of respected him, too, for keeping his mouth shut. That part was cool. He wasn't proud of what they'd done Monday night. But he wasn't completely sorry, either.

NEARLY TWO HOURS LATER, AS ISABEL APPROACHED THE SANCtuary, she heard Max and Carl talking. She didn't approve of eavesdropping, but couldn't help wondering what they were discussing and how they were getting along. Max's voice seemed genuinely interested and totally without its sardonic edge.

She peered inside and saw them working together, polishing the wooden pews. They didn't even notice her standing there.

"You were really in prison? What did you do?" she heard Max ask.

"Killed a man. By accident. We were fighting in a bar. I was just trying to defend myself. I broke a chair over his head. I wasn't thinking . . . but I paid the price. I took a man's life, accident or not." Carl sounded as somber as Isabel had ever heard him. "I ruined my own life, too, that night, but here I am. By the grace of God," he added.

"How many years were you in jail?"

"Fifteen. They let me out a few years short of the term for good behavior. So that's where these tattoos come from. While I was inside, I did this to myself. I wish now I didn't have them, but I'll wear them to the grave."

Isabel stepped into the sanctuary just in time to see Max's thoughtful expression. It always amazed her, the way God worked things out just right, though as a person of faith, she shouldn't be surprised.

She had insisted that Max return to the church in order to teach him a lesson. She had hoped to talk with him, to get to know him and help him. But she had never factored in Carl's influence, which might have the most impact of all.

"We're almost done for the day, Reverend." Carl stepped out of the pew carrying the big buffing cloth in one hand and a can of wax in the other.

"Everything looks great. You're doing a good job," Isabel said to Max. He met her gaze for a moment then looked away, seeming not sullen but shy.

"We have a ways to go before we're ready for Christmas." Carl's tone was friendlier but still stern as he glanced at the boy. "Give me your cloth. I'll put this stuff away." He took Max's buffing cloth and added it to his own in a plastic bucket. "You stow that broom and dustpan in the closet I showed you."

Isabel watched Max obediently head for the choir room. Carl went in another direction to put away his sander and tools.

"Reverend? Is my son ready to go? It's six o'clock."

Isabel turned to face Jacob Ferguson, Max's father. He looked very different today, wearing a tweed sports jacket, a blue shirt, and a tie. He also wore an impatient expression that matched his tone of voice perfectly.

"I sent him a text and he never answered. I got a little worried," he explained.

"He'll be right back. He's just putting away supplies. Why don't we wait outside? I'm sure he'll find us."

As they walked out to the narthex, Carl followed carrying some of his equipment. The two men eyed each other as they passed through the big wooden doors.

"You the boy's father?" Carl asked abruptly.

"Yes, I am. And you are?"

"Doesn't matter. I'll probably never see you again, mister. I just want you to know your boy is all right. He's not a bad kid. I thought he might be when I saw what he did in there Monday night," Carl said bluntly.

Isabel tried to interrupt the sexton before he could go any further. "Carl, I'm not sure Mr. Ferguson—"

"That's okay. Let him speak." Jacob studied Carl, his expression curious. "I want to hear what he has to say. Go on. He's not a bad kid, but . . . what?"

"Don't let him get no tattoos, for one thing."

Jacob's eyes widened, then narrowed. "He told you he wanted a tattoo?"

"Yes, sir, he did. But don't let him. Just put your foot down. Don't coddle him. Put him to work. He's got a lot of energy. You can't let a kid like that glide around on his skateboard all over town, doing anything he pleases. No wonder he got into trouble. It could have been worse, believe me."

Isabel waited to see how Max's father would take this advice. She wondered if he would be angry, but if he was, he didn't show it. "I get your point," he said finally.

Max walked out of the choir room and came toward them, his backpack in one hand and skateboard in the other. "Hey, Dad. I missed your text. Sorry. I didn't even know what time it was."

"You were working so hard, you lost track?" his father asked dryly.

"Yeah, I guess. There aren't any clocks in there. It's sort of like being in this timeless place."

Jacob nodded, an amused expression on his face, then turned to Isabel. "He'll be back next week. Any particular days?"

"I already worked it out with Carl. I know when he needs me to come," Max cut in.

Jacob exchanged another look with Isabel. "That man with the wood sander, that was Carl, I assume?"

"Yes, Carl Tulley, our sexton. He's in charge of cleaning and repairs around here."

"I see."

"Don't worry, Dad. He's cool. He was in jail, like, for killing somebody," Max informed him.

Jacob's eyes widened and he turned to Isabel. "Is that true? You left a former convict alone with my son?"

"Carl went to jail for manslaughter more than twenty years ago. He's held this job for the last five years, ever since his release. I don't believe anyone at church has had any reason to doubt his integrity or to fear him. There are children in this church, Mr. Ferguson. We certainly wouldn't employ anyone who posed a threat to them. Your son is perfectly safe around Carl."

"I know he's scary, Dad. But it's, like, a cool scary once you get him talking a little."

Jacob sighed. "Let's go. It's getting late." He turned to Isabel. "I'll be speaking to you, Reverend."

Isabel didn't answer. She wasn't sure what he meant. He wanted to talk more about Carl? Or about their agreement to have Max work here? She could handle that. She wouldn't mind talking to Jacob some more. He was intelligent and clearly cared about his son. He did seem conservative and a bit of a rigid thinker, which were not qualities she admired. But something about him caught her interest. She noticed that today even more than Monday night. Or maybe it was just the sports jacket and tie. He was very good-looking. She hadn't noticed that Monday night, either.

CAROLYN WAS ALREADY IN THE KITCHEN FIXING BREAKFAST when Ben came downstairs on Thursday morning. Though he was still moving slowly, he had showered and dressed and was ready for the day. He kissed her on the cheek and poured himself a cup of coffee. He had to drink decaf now and still wasn't quite used to it, but he decided to keep his usual grumble to himself today. He would get used to decaf in time. A small burden to bear, considering the alternatives.

"What's for breakfast? Smells good." He sat down at the table and glanced at the newspaper.

"Egg-white omelet with low-fat cheese. Whole-wheat toast, no butter," she added in a stern voice, glancing over her shoulder at him.

"All right. No butter." He put his hands up in a gesture of surrender, then mimicked a police officer's voice. "Drop the butter tub and come out with your hands up."

"Oh, Ben, you make me laugh. You're certainly in a good mood today," Carolyn commented. "You must be feeling good."

"I feel very good. And I've finally decided," he added.

"Oh . . . decided about what?" She glanced at him over her shoulder, then looked back at her cooking.

"About retiring, dear. You know."

"I thought that's what you were talking about. I just wanted to make sure," she admitted. She separated the eggs into two portions, put a slice of dry toast and orange sections on each plate, and brought them to the table. Then she sat down facing him. "Well, what's the verdict?"

He could see the anticipation in her eyes but could tell she was trying to hide it from him.

"I think I should do it. I think *we* should do it," he corrected himself. "I think it's time."

Carolyn let out a long, loud breath. "Well, I'm glad to hear you say that. I hope you're sure and have given yourself enough time to make this decision."

"I've had plenty of time. I'm very sure," he promised her.

She took a bite of her eggs. He could tell her thoughts were spinning. "It's very exciting, Ben. It really is. What's the first step?"

"I need to call Reverend Boland, but I don't think he'll be surprised."

"No, I don't think he will be," Carolyn agreed.

"Then all the church members. That will be the hardest part," he said quietly. "I think I should tell the trustees and church council all at once, rather than make a dozen calls and say the same thing . . . and answer the same questions over and over again. That way no one will feel left out or as if they were the last to be told."

"Why don't you ask them to come over here?" Carolyn suggested. "I'll serve some coffee and cake."

"Good idea. The sooner, the better. Maybe tomorrow night? Would that be all right with you?"

"Oh, it's fine with me. I have no plans. Even if I did, this is important enough to cancel most anything, don't you think?" she asked with a small laugh.

"Yes, come to think of it, it is," he agreed. He reached over and squeezed her hand. "It's finally happening, dear. Are you excited?"

Carolyn smiled at him and returned the pressure of his touch. "Yes, very. And happy, too," she added. "Are you, Ben?"

"Yes, I am." He did feel happy—and even more, relieved. If he felt a quiver of regret or ambivalence saying the words out loud, well, that was only natural. It was going to take time to get used to the idea.

WHILE DR. HARDING FINISHED WITH HIS LAST PATIENT ON Friday afternoon, Regina went out to the empty waiting room and straightened up the magazines and chairs. People always forgot things, mostly gloves and scarves; children left behind toys. Tonight she found one black waterproof mitten and a well-worn copy of *The Little Engine That Could*. Regina knew the story well. She stared at the cover a moment and smiled. *That's me,* she thought, paging through the book.

"That one is hard to resist, isn't it? I keep a copy in my office and still read it from time to time."

Regina looked up to find Molly standing in the office doorway. She smiled and closed the book. "It is a good one," she agreed.

"If you're done with it, give me a turn. I could use a pep talk from the Little Engine right now." Molly dropped onto one of the fabric-covered chairs and let out a long sigh.

She looks tired, Regina thought. *Not her usual high-energy self.* "Bad day?" Regina asked. She sat down on a chair nearby with the book in her lap.

"Real bad. I am in over my eyeballs with work. As I should be, since this is the busiest time of the year. But my staff is dwindling down to a skeleton crew. I just got a call on my cell—another server is down with the flu and can't make it tomorrow. And I had her scheduled to do two events: a birthday brunch and a cocktail party at night. Betty and I are both willing to get out there and serve," she added, mentioning her partner, Betty Bowman. "But we're only two people. We can't be four places at once."

Regina had never seen Molly like this. She always seemed so confident and in control, a master at juggling so many responsibilities at once.

"Can I help you somehow? The office closes tomorrow at one. Maybe I can come and serve at a party for you?"

Molly looked over at her. "Regina, that's so sweet of you to offer, but I couldn't ask you to do that."

"No, really. I don't have plans. Richard is working so hard on the house. I offer to help paint or clean out the basement with him, but I feel like I'm just in the way. He gets so . . . serious."

"Please, send him over to my house, would you? Matt is all thumbs. We have to hire a guy to hang a picture on the wall."

Her exaggeration made Regina smile. "He couldn't be *that* bad."

Molly answered with one of her classic expressions. "No comment."

"Really, I'd like to try the work," Regina said. "I've had

waitressing jobs. It can't be much different. I was going to look for something extra around town," she added. "To make a little more money before Christmas."

Molly tilted her head to one side. "If you really want to, Regina, I'd love to have you try it. We have a party tomorrow from two until six. If you come to the shop around half past one, I'll give you a uniform and all that. There are a lot more events coming up in the next few weeks. I can go over the schedule with you tomorrow, too." Then she told Regina the wage. "And the host or hostess usually gives the servers a good tip. Does that sound all right with you?"

"It sounds great. I'll be at your shop right after we close here."

"Great." Molly leaned over and squeezed her arm. "You're a lifesaver, Regina. Honestly."

Regina just smiled. It was nice of Molly to say that, but Molly had really been the one to swoop in and change her life by giving her this job, on the spot, no questions asked.

The last patient came out with Dr. Harding. Regina took their fee and gave them a receipt. Meanwhile, the doctor and Molly walked back to his office to talk. Regina could already hear Molly launch into an animated story about how she was just at her wit's end and Regina had totally saved the day.

She knew how Dr. Harding would react. He would patiently listen to his wife's dramatic tales and then approve of her conclusions and solutions, offering advice only when asked. He was definitely Molly's biggest fan.

Regina wondered what Richard would say. Would he mind if she was out of the house a lot more? She would be earning more money; he couldn't object to that. He wasn't the type of guy who loved cooking, but he managed all right if she wasn't home. He never minded taking care of the kids, either, and enjoyed having them to himself from time to time.

She did wonder if he would miss her, especially if she had to work evenings. But they hardly talked at all anymore, even after the kids went to sleep. Mostly, they just sat together in front of the TV, with Regina reading a book.

Regina straightened out her desk and shut down her computer. Then she found her coat and bag and headed home. As she passed the Bramble antique store, she noticed the red truck parked on the street. Richard was still working with Sam. *Just as well,* she thought. *It gives me some time to get dinner ready and straighten up the house a little before he gets home.*

As she drove through the village and down the winding, tree-lined roads to their new home, she felt very lonely. As empty and cold inside as the big swath of dark blue sky that floated above the frozen fields.

When she was busy, working at the medical office, taking care of the children, working on the house, doing all the things she had to do, she rarely felt this way. But it was always there inside her lately, lurking just below the surface. When she was alone in the car like this, at night especially, a certain sadness snuck up and pounced—a hollow feeling that made her heart ache. She yearned to be close to someone, and even now, after all they had been through, that someone was Richard.

She used to feel so close and connected to Richard, even when they hadn't seen each other for days. But she didn't feel that way anymore. She doubted he did, either.

She turned down Old Field Road and pulled up in front of the house. The lights were on in the kitchen and living room, and the place looked warm and cozy. This was their house. They owned it. Nobody could take it away. She had to remind herself of that from time to time. She almost had to pinch herself.

She wished that Richard felt happier about the house. But she knew he was struggling with so many things right now. She had a feeling that by working on the place, he was starting to like it more, though he didn't quite admit it.

Regina knew she couldn't blame him for what had happened to their relationship. She had played a part, too. She had to try harder to reach out to him, especially now that things were getting a little bit better, day by day. That had to help smooth things over between them. She hoped it wasn't too late.

THE SURETY AND EXCITEMENT BEN HAD FELT ABOUT HIS DE-cision on Thursday morning had waned a bit by the time Friday evening rolled around. He didn't intend to make a formal speech to the church leaders, most of whom were his close friends. But he did take a few minutes in his study to jot down his thoughts and rehearse what he wanted to say in his mind.

It was a big announcement and he wanted to get it right. Although he didn't expect it, as the time drew closer, he found himself feeling nervous, though he was almost never uneasy or anxious about speaking at this sort of meeting.

He heard the doorbell and then heard Carolyn greeting Tucker Tulley and Sam and Jessica Morgan. By the time he came out to the living room, others had arrived—Emily Warwick, her mother, Lillian, and Ezra Elliot. Grace Hegman and Sophie Potter fol-lowed, along with Warren Oakes and Charlie Bates.

Everyone walked in, milled about, and helped themselves to the coffee and cake Carolyn had set out in the dining room. There was some social conversation about the weather and Christmas getting closer, along with many questions about how Ben felt and how he was progressing, of course. For a few minutes, Ben felt as if they were meeting for a book discussion or to plan some annual church event, like the rummage sale or Christmas Fair.

Was he really going to tell these good people that he wanted to stop being their minister?

As he took a seat in his wingback armchair and the others settled on the couch and other comfortable spots around the room, Ben struggled to rekindle the surety and resolve he had felt about his decision only hours ago. He took a deep breath and exhaled, silently reviewing his talking points in his head.

"Thank you all for coming out on such a cold night," he began. "I'm sure you must be wondering why I've called this meeting. I've only told you that it has to do with church business, and I'm sure you assumed I meant running the church in my absence.

"It does have to do with that. During the past two weeks, I've been forced to slow down and cease all productive activity. Which, as you all know, is probably a first for me," he added, drawing a laugh. "I've had time to think. To see the big picture," he clarified. He paused again and took a steadying breath. "I believe that it's time for me to retire."

He didn't mean for his voice to sound anything less than resolute, but he knew that there had been a slight tremor in his words. He looked around, gauging the reactions.

Shock and surprise registered on practically all the faces. A few people looked as if they had guessed what he would say but were not happy to have their intuition confirmed.

Lillian Warwick looked as if she had just bitten into a lemon. Then again, she often looked like that.

She was the first to speak. "I expected as much. After your heart attack, I'm only surprised it didn't come sooner."

Before Ben could react, Lillian's daughter Emily leaned forward in her chair. "I suppose we all wondered if you were considering retirement now," Emily said, her tone far more conciliatory than her mother's. "I, for one, did hope that even if you considered it, you would decide not to retire, Reverend Ben. Or at least put off any final decision until you recovered."

As usual, Emily was putting forth her suggestion in a diplomatic way. She was, after all, the town's mayor and well versed in political negotiations. But Ben knew his position was nonnegotiable.

"I did consider waiting, Emily. But I feel very certain this is the right thing to do. I don't believe that a few weeks will make any difference at all. I could have held back from announcing it, but I felt you all had a right to know, to go forward and make your plans."

"Find a new minister, that's what you mean," Grace Hegman piped up in her abrupt way. "We'll never find a minister like you, Reverend Ben. How can we ever replace you?"

She looked about to cry. Ben was shocked. Grace was so stalwart and stoic and reserved. The only time he had ever seen her shed a tear was when her daughter died, almost twenty years ago now, and when her aged father had wandered off and was lost for almost two days. Now here she was, sitting in his living room, sniffing and dabbing her eyes with an embroidered, lace-edged handkerchief—a rare sight these days, but abundantly available in her antique store.

"How will I tell my father? He won't believe it," Grace murmured.

Oh, Digger might be surprised at first, but Ben knew that he would quickly accept the situation. Having always lived close to nature, the old seaman knew change was a natural part of living and didn't fear it.

"I'll tell him if you'd like, Grace. I'll have a word with him personally," Ben offered.

"Oh, would you? That would be so kind. It would mean a lot to him, too, to hear it from you firsthand, Reverend," Grace said.

"I'll do that then. I want to make this as easy as I can for everyone. A smooth and orderly transition," he added, remembering some well-worded phrases from his notes. Funny how, so far, most of those fine, thoughtful words had escaped him.

"I did wonder if you might think about retiring now, after all you've been through, Reverend," Tucker admitted in his slow, thoughtful manner. "But I must admit, I am surprised to hear you say it. It's hard to get my head around it."

"Are you sure it's not just some reaction from your illness?" Sam asked. "You've been through a lot, Reverend, a life-threatening crisis. You're bound to have some emotional reactions."

"That's true, Sam. I've had emotional upheaval of all kinds and I expect more. But this . . . this is coming from a different place. Please believe me. I'm not just reacting to my heart attack. I've been thinking about this for some time."

"How will we ever survive without you?" Jessica asked. "I knew the day had to come sooner or later. But now that it's here, I can't quite believe it."

"Oh . . . you will. I'm not that important. I'm not the church. The church is never just one person, or even one committee or board. The church is all of us, together. We'll go forward together and find a new minister. Someone different from me, I expect. Doubtlessly younger, for one thing," he noted, bringing back a few smiles. "Someone with fresh energy and fresh spirit. Different ideas and plans . . ."

He paused and searched their faces. It was suddenly too hard to go on with this pep talk, no matter how well he had thought it out. It was too soon perhaps for them to hear it. Too soon for him to say it, too.

"Oh . . . you all know what I mean. Most ministers stay at a church about five to ten years. Rarely as long as I have stayed here."

"I have been in this church all my life, so I remember them all. But I'm probably the only person in this room who does," Sophie said.

"My point exactly. Ministers have their day, just like everyone else. There comes a time when the old must step aside and make way for the young, the new blood and new energy," Ben added.

Tucker nodded but did not look totally convinced. He exchanged a serious look with Sam, and Ben felt a twinge in his heart. They were good men, committed to the church. The church could and would go on without him, but not without men like Sam and Tucker. Or women like Emily, Sophie, Grace, and Jessica . . . even Lillian.

"All right, enough violins. I think you can put them away now," Lillian suggested in her tart tone. "What are the practical matters we need to address at this point, Reverend? What are the steps of transition in this situation?"

"Excellent questions, Lillian," Ben said. "There is a process we must follow. The first thing I need to do is speak to my superior, Reverend Boland. You all are the first to know. I haven't consulted with him yet."

"What if he says he doesn't want you to retire? What then?" Sam asked.

He and Tucker were still holding out some hope, Ben realized.

"I doubt he would say that, especially under the circumstances. He might encourage me to wait, to think about and pray on it a bit more." Ben paused. "I don't believe I'm making this decision impulsively. Though it may well look that way," he acknowledged.

No one answered for a long moment. Emily rose and brought her empty coffee cup to the dining table. "I believe that you have searched your soul, Reverend, and you feel sure that this is not only the best decision for you and Carolyn, but for our church, too. As for the process and next steps . . . well, we have time to discuss those details. You probably better let Reverend Boland know your plans before we do anything more."

"Yes, I guess that's the next order of business. I'll call him tonight," Ben said. "Oh, and I will call Reverend Isabel—if not tonight, then first thing tomorrow. She should know, too."

"Before she hears it through the ubiquitous grapevine," Lillian agreed. "In that case, you had better call her before we leave the premises."

Ben heard some muffled laughter. As usual, Lillian had made a good point with her sharp tongue. This news would spread like wildfire. He wondered if anyone in the church would be unaware of his plans by tomorrow morning.

"This has been big news. I don't know that I can really focus on very much more tonight." Sophie looked around at the others. "I think we ought to let Reverend Ben rest now. This couldn't have been easy for you," she added, turning back to gaze at him with sympathy and affection.

Ben felt another twinge in his heart. Oh, he would miss these good people. It would never be quite the same once he gave up his post as their minister.

"I do feel a little tired, Sophie," he admitted. "This was a very difficult conversation for me. Thank you all, from the bottom of my heart, for your understanding and support."

"We'll miss you, Reverend, but we'll do all we can to make this a smooth transition," Sam answered. "If this is what you really want."

Ben let out a long breath. Was he about to cry? Oh, he hoped not. He met Sam's gaze and nodded.

"Thank you, Sam. This is what I want. I'm certain of it."

CHAPTER TEN

⌒◟

"*T*HEY MUST HAVE BEEN WORKING IN HERE FOR A FEW hours. It looks a lot better." Tucker gazed around the sanctuary on Saturday morning, surveying the work Carl and Max had completed so far.

"They're making good progress. Your brother is very good with Max. I think Carl gets through to him somehow. I know I didn't get very far," Isabel admitted.

Tucker was carrying a box holding a Christmas tree stand and now knelt down to put it together. The deacons were going to put up the Christmas decorations and Isabel wanted to help. She also wanted to be there to talk to church members about the vandalism and about Max.

"Just goes to show, you never know." Tucker shrugged, but Isabel guessed he was pleased to hear her compliment his brother.

Though opposites in many ways, the two were still family. Isabel had heard from others that Tucker had helped Carl a great deal when he was released from prison. Tucker must have taken some criticism then for standing by Carl. No matter how friendly this town was, Isabel couldn't imagine that they had welcomed Carl back from prison with open arms.

"Carl was very good with Max, but he didn't make that good an impression on Max's father." Isabel sighed. "The man is uneasy about Carl's background."

"You mean because he's done time in prison?" Tucker asked. "You don't have to mince words, Reverend. It's the first thing that comes into everyone's mind. Do you want me to talk to Mr. Ferguson?"

"Would you? I told him that the church trusted Carl completely, but I suspect he has some questions that you could answer better than I."

"No problem. I'd be happy to," Tucker said easily. "Have you had any more calls from the congregation?"

"A few," she confided. "Some of the church members still think we should have been much tougher on Max, even though they know the trustees discussed the matter."

"People have said the same to me. I guess they don't think I'm a very tough policeman," he added, making her laugh. "But I tell them just what you said in the meeting. We preach forgiveness and forbearance at our church. It can't just be all talk, no action. We need to set that example for this boy—and for the rest of the world, for that matter.

"The boy is lucky that Reverend Ben decided to announce his retirement this week," Tucker added. "I figure most of the church has been so distracted by that news, they haven't had time to think too much about Max Ferguson."

"That's probably true." Isabel had considered that, too. Reverend

Ben's announcement had been a surprise to her as well. "You know, I never expected there would be so much action at a church like this," she confided with a smile. "I thought it would be much . . . quieter."

Tucker laughed. He had assembled the tree stand and now stood up and brushed off his hands. "This town is like a little anthill, Reverend. It doesn't seem like much is going on at all, but if you just sit still and keep watching for a while, you'll see it's a very busy place. There's a lot going on, above and below the surface."

How true, Isabel thought.

OTHER CHURCH MEMBERS BEGAN TO ARRIVE. MOST OF THE deacons came, and many of their spouses and some children, as well. The decorations were stashed in different parts of the church. Isabel soon realized that you had to be a longtime member to know where to find these Christmas treasures.

People ran down to the basement and into the choir room, to a storeroom near the church school classrooms, and in the sacristy, the special closet behind the altar.

Ladders came out, and along with the decorations, boxes of tacks and rolls of duct tape. Isabel didn't know if Reverend Ben took part in this annual ritual, but she jumped in, happy to dust off boxes and untangle strands of lights.

This was the first time in a long while that she was going to have a white Christmas, with snow on the ground. It made her a bit homesick for the family gatherings in Minnesota, which she would be missing again this year.

But Isabel put aside homesick thoughts of the Midwest and even nostalgia for holidays in tropical places like Haiti. She threw herself into the task of decorating the church; it was a good chance to get to know the members of the congregation better.

Sam Morgan had been outside, putting up a crèche in the front of the building; he poked his head in the door for a quick announcement. "Jack's here with the trees. I'll go help him." Isabel knew who he meant—Jack Sawyer, who ran a nursery and tree farm with his wife, Julie. Tucker had told Isabel that every year Jack donated trees, wreaths, and pine garlands to the church.

Quite a few others went outside to help, and Isabel realized the delivery was bigger than she'd expected.

Sophie stood by the door, directing traffic and telling people where to put the greenery. "What do you do with all these trees?" Isabel asked Sophie.

Sophie laughed. "Oh, we put them places. You'll see. One in the sanctuary, another in Fellowship Hall. That one the kids decorate at the Advent Supper. Then we put a small one downstairs for the church school. We usually have several left over, too. Those are given out to families who need a tree but can't afford it. Good trees are so darned expensive these days," she added, shaking her head.

"Yes, they are," Isabel agreed. Which made the Sawyers' generosity that much more impressive.

As the truckload of greenery came in, Isabel found herself carrying a large black bag of pine boughs and other scraps into Fellowship Hall, where several women were working together, making a giant wreath for the sanctuary doors. It was a tricky feat of engineering, Isabel noticed, since the wreath was actually split in half, so that the big doors could open and close. The greens were being fitted onto two wooden frames, each a half circle, which would be completely covered and fit together to appear as a whole.

"Wow, who figured this out?" Isabel said, joining the wreath workers.

"Sam Morgan built it. We used to put two small wreaths on the doors, but that didn't look like much. The big wreath looks prettier and we make it together, so it has more meaning," Emily explained.

"Reverend Ben loves this wreath," Grace added. "He would be very upset if we ever stopped making it. I hope he gets to church before Christmas."

"Oh, I think he will," Sophie said. "It's hard to hear he's finally retiring, but he's not leaving the church. He'll still be with us, out in the pews."

"Yes, but it won't be the same," Grace said with a sigh.

"Everything changes, Grace," Sophie replied in a tone of wise resignation. "That's just life. God closes a door and opens a window. But you have to stop staring at the closed door in order to notice it."

Isabel didn't even realize she was standing on the sidelines until Emily reached out and pulled her into the circle. "Here's a spot for you, Reverend. I'll show you what to do."

Isabel was soon donning gloves and sharing the shears that were passed around. She worked to fill up her spot on the big wreath while watching what the others did, so that it would all blend. An apt metaphor for this church, or any group effort, she thought, the blending of so many individual visions and talents.

While the women worked, they shared conversation. Isabel mostly listened and was not surprised when the talk soon turned back to Reverend Ben.

"I know what you say is true, Sophie. But it's hard to believe Reverend Ben's retiring," Vera Plante said. "I just can't get used to the idea. Any chance he'll change his mind?"

Since Isabel boarded at Vera's house, she already knew how her landlady felt about this situation. Vera's reaction was typical of many in the congregation, Isabel thought, especially the older members. They loved Reverend Ben, and his departure felt like a great, unimaginable loss.

Sophie was the lone senior who seemed to hold a different position. "Oh, I don't think he'll change his mind now," she answered. "Why should he—because we'll miss him? We can't be selfish about this. We've had him for over twenty years. He wants to enjoy his remaining days and do all the things he's put on the back burner because of this church. That's hardly too much to ask. I don't think we should even try to persuade him to stay on any longer."

"Sophie has a good point," Emily said. "As much as we might wish Reverend Ben would change his mind, we really have to respect his decision and show him that we understand."

"I think we do understand," Jessica Morgan spoke up. "We're all just worried about how we go about finding a new minister even half as wonderful. It's not just his sermons, but the way he always manages to say exactly the right thing when you need it most. I'm sure that at one time or another, he's helped almost everyone here."

"That goes without saying," Sophie agreed. "He's the spiritual rudder of this church, steering us in the right direction. But there are plenty of good ministers out there, I'm sure. Different from our reverend, but talented and capable."

Isabel suddenly felt self-conscious and hoped her cheeks weren't turning red. That was a drawback of being a fair-skinned redhead, one she had never outgrown.

She sensed Sophie glancing at her and looked up to meet the gaze of the older woman. Was Sophie's smile sending a message, Isabel wondered, or did she always smile that way?

Isabel managed to smile back, then grabbed a hunk of greenery and tried to focus on her handiwork. But she felt as if everyone was looking at her.

"Everyone has their own unique talents, and newcomers bring something different to the table," Emily said. "Take Reverend Isabel, for example. As much as we all love Reverend Ben, he never helped us put this wreath together."

Some of the women laughed, and most of them nodded.

"Very true, Emily," Sophie said. "There are a lot of things a new minister might do differently around here. There's a lot that a woman minister could bring to our congregation."

Isabel didn't mean to call attention to herself, but she suddenly dropped the garden shears and they clattered to the floor, the sound echoing in the big room. "Oh, dear . . . I can get clumsy. Sorry."

She leaned over quickly and picked them up, taking just a moment to get a breath and compose herself. She should have expected this. There was an opening at the church now, and they all assumed she would be interested. It was actually very flattering, considering she had been here such a short while.

"Well, Reverend, what do you think?" When Isabel stood up and took her spot again, she found Emily staring at her.

Was Emily already asking if she was interested in taking over from Reverend Ben?

"It's hard to say . . ." Isabel began.

"About the wreath," Sophie clarified. "It looks like it's just about done. We don't want to overdo it. Sometimes less is more, you know."

"Oh, the wreath . . . It's magnificent," Isabel said sincerely. She still held a bunch of greens but could see that there were no empty places to stick it. The wreath was round and full now, multilayered with a variety of evergreens and holly. "You could never find one like this in any shop or nursery," Isabel added. "I understand now why you need to make it here."

"It's one of a kind, different every year, but with its own special charms," Sophie explained. "Just like the folks who make it."

"We always put a big red bow on it. That never changes," Vera said. One of the other women had been working on the bow, and now Vera took it off a different table.

"The crowning touch. Here goes," Emily said.

A brief but animated discussion followed before the perfect spot was found and the bow was fastened on with wire. Then the women carefully carried the two halves of the wreath to the sanctuary doors where Sam and Dan Forbes, Emily Warwick's husband, aligned it just right and fastened it up with hooks and more wire.

Then it seemed that everyone working in different parts of the church came outside to see how the wreath looked, standing a little distance from the front doors, huddled together in the snow like a choir. Sam and Dan stood back to check that the two sides hung evenly and to give the rest a clear view.

"That's a fine-looking wreath. Wow, it's a whopper," Digger Hegman said. "I once trapped a lobster that big . . . but he was about to tip over my boat, so I threw him back."

"Oh, Dad." Grace nearly groaned, shaking her head.

Everyone else laughed at the fish story. Isabel wondered if Digger was joking or telling the truth.

"It's beautiful; best one we've ever made," Sophie pronounced.

"You say that every year, Sophie. But this time I think it's true," Vera replied.

"I'm going to take a picture. We'll put it in the church newsletter." Jessica pulled her phone out of her pocket and checked the settings.

"I'll take it," Sam said. "All you ladies who worked on the wreath, you get in there and line up under it."

The women hesitated but were soon persuaded to take some credit for their lovely work.

"You, too, Reverend Isabel," Emily insisted. "You have to be in the picture with us." She gently took Isabel by the hand and led her to the wreath. Isabel found a place, wedged between Emily and Sophie. She felt a little awkward, but was touched by their efforts to include her.

"All right, everyone smile now." Sam took the photo and then another just in case.

"Thank you for helping us, Reverend. That made it special," Sophie said as the women filed back into the building.

"Thank you for asking me," Isabel said honestly.

It seemed such a simple thing, making a wreath with the women of the church. But the experience had touched her. She was not used to serving in this type of easygoing, mostly middle-class environment. Her work in mission situations took her to places where people struggled each day just to survive. In Haiti, she would not be making a Christmas wreath, but digging a well so that villagers would not need to walk several miles every day, carrying buckets of freshwater up and down steep hillsides.

But there had been happier, easier times there, too. It was all important and all part of God's great mosaic. Making a wreath to honor this church, the spiritual life here, and the celebration of Christmas—that was important, too.

Could she ever adjust to life in this sleepy village? Did she really want to?

Maybe the congregation would not invite her to stay. She was jumping to conclusions on that question, wasn't she? Especially in light of the situation with Max Ferguson.

As for returning to mission work once she left here, Isabel wasn't sure about that, either. Now that she'd been away from it a few months, she wondered if she had only needed that intense experience after losing Steven. She had needed to immerse herself in something to feel productive and distracted back then.

She still missed her husband, especially at this time of year. That was an ache deep in her heart that would never truly fade. She had learned to live with it. Whether she was stationed in a seaside village in Haiti, on a mountaintop in Guatemala, or in the heart of New England, there was no outrunning those feelings—anywhere on God's green earth.

And didn't these folks need spiritual guidance and support just as much as anybody, anywhere? The answer to that question was yes, of course they do. Everyone confronted difficulty and pain in their lives, and all the comforts in the world could not bring peace to a restless soul.

REGINA WAS NERVOUS ABOUT WORKING THE COCKTAIL PARTY ON Saturday afternoon, but she tried not to show it. It had been a while since she'd done this type of work, and even then only at diners and family restaurants where it didn't matter much if you were the most polite or elegant waitress. You just had to get the job done. But once she donned the uniform at Molly's shop and listened to the many instructions from Molly and her partner, Betty Bowman, Regina realized the standards were quite a bit higher at these private parties in the town's fanciest houses.

She worked in a crew with three other employees. Molly helped them set up, then ran off to run another party. Regina felt a bit overwhelmed at first, but managed to carry on and do her part pretty easily. She was feeling quite comfortable with the work as the day wore on. The two women she worked with, Eva and Carley, were both very helpful and told her she was doing great for a newbie.

Regina was pleased, though her feet hurt terribly. Later, though, the pay she received back at the shop and her share of the tip more than compensated for those aches. When Molly reported that another employee had called in sick for an evening party and neither Eva nor Carley could step in, Regina quickly volunteered to work at that event, too.

"Jumping right in the deep end, are you, Regina?" Molly teased her.

"I guess so," Regina agreed. She called Richard and explained that she would be home late. He didn't seem upset and said everything was under control with the children and not to worry.

Regina was relieved. She had half expected him to be annoyed at her staying out longer, especially on a Saturday. But she wouldn't be doing this all the time. Just until Christmas.

When she finally arrived home, a few minutes past midnight, she felt tired but happy. A few more parties and they would have enough to buy the kids all the necessities they needed and some fun stuff, too. Maybe they could even get the kids cell phones, which were becoming a necessity with both herself and Richard working and the kids left alone after school for a few hours every day, especially since they didn't have a landline.

The house was dark, except for a light at the front door and the small Tiffany-style lamp in the living room window. Regina kicked off her shoes and climbed the steps quietly. Then she washed up and fell into bed beside Richard, who was sound asleep and snoring so loudly, she could have dropped a tray of dishes in the middle of the bedroom and he wouldn't have missed a beat.

Not that she had even come close to dropping a tray tonight, she reminded herself. She smiled at the image and fell asleep the moment her head hit the pillow.

REGINA WAS THE LAST ONE UP THE NEXT MORNING. SHE DIDN'T even realize how late it was. She finally opened her eyes and heard sounds downstairs. She smelled coffee and another aroma that she could positively identify as burned pancakes.

She slipped on her robe and slippers and soon found her family in the kitchen. Brian was sitting at the table playing with a small plastic truck, a sticky, burnt pancake in his dish. Madeline was standing at the stove alongside Richard, peering around his arm as he poked at the skillet.

"Good morning, everyone. How's it going? Are you guys making pancakes?" she asked casually.

"Mom . . . thank goodness. Daddy tries, but cooking just isn't his thing." Madeline flounced back to the table and poured herself a glass of juice. She had delivered her greeting in that grown-up tone she used lately; middle school going on middle-aged, Regina called it.

Richard looked over his shoulder at Regina and offered a small smile. "They're not so bad . . . if you like your pancakes a little chewy."

She walked over to the stove to investigate, and he quickly surrendered the spatula. "Here you go, though I think most of those are beyond repair."

"I'll see what I can do," Regina said.

He was right; the whole batch had to be tossed. But the batter didn't look too bad. She stirred it, then added a little milk and another egg.

"Okay, let's try this again," she said, wiping the burnt crumbs out of the skillet. "Thanks for trying," she added, glancing up at him. "It was nice of you to let me sleep."

He smiled back at her, looking pleased that she noticed this small gesture.

A short time later, they all sat together at the table eating Regina's pancakes, which were done just right.

"Worth the wait," Richard said, helping himself to another from the stack on the platter.

"It's nearly eleven o'clock," Regina noticed. "You shouldn't have let me sleep *this* late."

"You needed the rest. What time did you get home?"

"About midnight. You were all asleep . . . but I tucked you guys in anyway," she said to Madeline and Brian.

"I saw you. I was only pretending to be asleep," Brian said, though Regina knew that was not true. "Let's stay in our pajamas all day and watch TV," Brian suggested. "That would be cool."

"Yes, very cool." Madeline rolled her eyes.

"Very lazy, I'd say," Richard added, though Regina could tell he was amused by his son's suggestion. "I guess we have to call you Mr. Lazybones now. I thought you were going to help me paint your room. You can't do that in your pajamas."

Brian looked excited by that idea. "Oh, right. I'll get dressed. I can paint, too, Dad."

"Yes, I know you can," Richard agreed. "And I need a good helper."

Regina had to smile at Brian's happy expression. Richard was so good with the children. He'd never had a good relationship with his own father, and his mother had been a very quiet, distant woman. He always said he wanted to be different with his own kids, and he kept his word.

After breakfast, everyone helped clear the table, then Brian dashed upstairs to get dressed, and Richard headed down to the basement to gather the painting supplies. Regina was loading the dishwasher when she heard a knock on the back door. Madeline glanced out the window. "It's Sam Morgan. I see his truck."

"Oh, he must want your father. Go call Dad, Maddy. I'll get the door."

Regina wiped her hands on a towel, then headed for the front door. She was still in her bathrobe, but the big flannel robe covered her from her chin to her toes. It wasn't an ideal outfit for greeting guests, but it was decent.

"Hello, Sam. Come on in. We all got up late today. We just finished breakfast."

"I don't want to bother you," Sam said, remaining outside. "I was just over at church, and we have all these Christmas trees left over. Jack Sawyer always brings way too many. I wondered if you'd gotten your tree yet?"

"A Christmas tree? No, we haven't gotten to that yet." Regina wasn't even sure they were going to buy a real tree this year. She and Richard hadn't discussed it, but money was so tight and trees were so expensive, she had been thinking the cost should be put toward something more necessary.

"Well, I have a really nice one right here." Sam reached beside the door and pulled out a tree. The fresh pine smell was so strong, it instantly filled her senses. It was a large tree, too, full and nicely shaped. Not a bargain tree at all.

"Oh my, that's beautiful," she said.

Sam took that as a yes and quickly stepped through the door with the tree. "Great. Where do you want it?"

Before she could answer, Richard appeared. "Hey, Sam . . . What's going on?"

"Sam has a bunch of Christmas trees he needs to give away—or return to the tree farm. He wants to know if we'd like one."

Regina could tell by the way Richard's mouth set in a tight, straight line that he wasn't pleased by the offer.

"That's very thoughtful of you, Sam. But I'm sure there's some other family that really needs it more. We were thinking of getting just a small tree this year, especially since all our ornaments are still in storage in Pennsylvania."

Sam nodded, as if he totally understood Richard's reasons for refusing the tree. He understood that Richard felt uncomfortable accepting charity, Regina thought.

She did, too. But what a beautiful tree. She hated to see it go to waste. Still, she didn't want to contradict her husband.

"Wow, a Christmas tree! Is that ours? Can we decorate it today?" Madeline had dressed and come down the back stairs into the kitchen. Her entire face had lit up at the sight of the tree, and now she was practically dancing around the kitchen.

"It's not ours, honey. Sam just—"

Before Richard could finish his sentence, Brian came into the room, exclaiming, "A Christmas tree? Cool! I want to put the star on top this year, okay?" He gazed straight up at his father. When Richard didn't answer right away, Brian tugged on his father's flannel shirtsleeve. "Can I, Dad? Remember how you lifted me up last year?"

"Yes, Brian. I remember." Richard let out a long breath. He knew when he was beaten, Regina realized, and finally smiled. "We can do it just like that again," he promised Brian. Then he looked over at Sam. "I guess you made a sale here, after all. Why don't you leave it outside for now until we figure out where we should put it."

Regina felt relieved. Their children's excitement had melted

Richard's reserve. Maybe he had recalled the promise he and Regina had made to try their best to give the children a good holiday after all they'd been through.

"No problem. I'll leave it right here by the door. You can keep it outside a few days if you're not ready. Just stick it in a bucket of water."

"Good idea. We might do that," Richard said, following Sam out the door.

"Thank you, Sam," Regina called as he headed back to his truck.

"That was very thoughtful, Sam. Thank you," Richard added.

"Don't mention it. You're actually doing me a favor, saving me a ride back to Sawyer's place. Here . . . I'll throw in a wreath for free." He reached back into the bed of the truck and set a large, undecorated door wreath near the tree.

A few moments later, he backed out of the drive and was gone. Richard came back into the house and joined the rest of the family in the kitchen.

"I'll make the star," Madeline offered. "I already have an idea how I can do it."

"That's a start. But we don't have anything else to put on it. Maybe we can hang some of those burnt pancakes," Richard joked. "Did you throw them all away yet, Gina? Maybe we can put some sparkly stuff on them."

"Oh, Dad, don't be so silly," Madeline scolded him.

Gina had to laugh at the idea, though Brian looked as if he was taking his father seriously.

"We'll get some ornaments at the variety store in town," Richard assured them. "They don't have to be fancy. Or we can make some ourselves, right, Maddy?"

"There are some in the basement. I saw a box the other day," Madeline reported.

"I think I saw a box that said 'Christmas' down there, too," Regina said. "We might find a tree stand at least."

"Okay, I'll go down and look," Richard offered.

"I'll help you," Brian offered. "Wait, let me get my flashlight and stuff. I don't want to get attacked by the giant spiders."

Richard watched with amusement as his son geared up for the expedition.

Regina hoped they would find a few things to use downstairs. Now that they had the tree, she was as eager as the kids to put it up and decorate. It might really start to feel like Christmas here, she thought.

She suddenly realized how much she'd been dreading the holiday. Now she felt a little better about it, more in the spirit. It wasn't just the surprise gift of the tree, but something in Richard's mood and attitude this morning, something softer and sweeter. Was she just imagining that, just hoping it was true? She wasn't sure but resolved to be nicer to him.

Regina hated to admit it, but sometimes acting distant and treating him coldly felt like a habit, or self-protection. Too many times she had put up a cool, impregnable wall before he could hurt her.

That wasn't right. They had agreed to treat each other respectfully, at the very least. He was doing that and more. So she should, too, she thought.

Who knows? I might even bake some cookies. Peanut butter to start, Richard's favorite.

IT TURNED OUT THAT THERE WERE A FEW BOXES OF CHRISTMAS decorations in the basement. Richard brought them upstairs, setting them on the porch because they were so dusty. Regina wiped them off with a rag, then opened them carefully. She took out wads of crumbling newspaper used for padding and showed Madeline the date. "Look at that, honey. Your father and I hadn't even met yet when these were wrapped and put away."

"Let's see what's in there." Brian was impatient, bouncing from foot to foot.

Regina felt around for solid objects and carefully unwrapped the first one she found. It was a glass ornament in the shape of an ice-skater, complete with a bit of fabric glued on for a scarf. "Wow, look at that. Be very, very careful with this, kids. It feels so fragile. We better put it someplace safe."

"Let me take it, Mom. I'll bring it inside."

For a second, Regina wondered if she could trust Madeline with the fragile piece. Madeline was acting more and more mature since they had moved here. She had a lot of responsibility in the afternoons, watching her brother before Regina and Richard got home from work.

"Good idea. Take a dish towel or two and put them down on the table for a cushion."

"Don't worry. I'll be careful. This is fun," Maddy said as she headed inside. "It's like a treasure hunt or something."

It was like a treasure hunt, Regina thought as she set about unwrapping the rest of the ornaments. She gave Brian permission to open another box, where he found other kinds of decorations that were less fragile—a music box, a snow globe with very cloudy liquid inside, and three nutcrackers, all different sizes and wearing different uniforms.

"Look, Mom. Remember that story you read to us last year?" He held up the largest nutcracker for her to see. "He looks just like the one in the book. Can I put him in my room?"

"Sure, why not?" She was pleased that Brian and Madeline

were so engaged and happy. She hadn't seen them this cheerful in a long time.

When the box was empty, Regina brought the last ornament into the kitchen. Madeline had carefully wiped each one off with a damp paper towel, and now they lay gleaming on a patchwork of dish towels.

"Nice work," Regina praised her. "Where's Dad? Is he still downstairs?"

"I think he went up to start painting Brian's room," Maddy reported. "He just passed by with some painting stuff a few minutes ago."

"Oh." Regina was surprised, and not surprised. She had been hoping that Richard would take part in decorating the tree, the way they all used to do it together, not leave it to her and the kids. But she had also wondered if he would bow out.

Brian came in carrying his new nutcracker. "The last box had some strings of lights and a stand for the Christmas tree. I think we need some tools," he added in a manly voice. "I'm going up to show Dad my nutcracker and tell him."

"Okay. Ask him to come down to put the tree in the stand, will you?" Regina called after her son. If Brian asked him, Richard would do it right away. It was hard for him to refuse his kids any little favor like that.

Brian soon came downstairs with his father, who was wiping his hands on a rag.

"Sorry to interrupt the painting, but we need some help," Regina said.

"You're going to decorate the tree with us, aren't you, Dad? Look what we found in those boxes," Madeline said, showing her father the rows of ornaments on the table.

"Wow, those are old ones. I remember Christmas ornaments

like this from when I was a kid." Richard picked up one shaped like a polar bear and turned it around in his hands to study it. "Let's see what shape the tree stand is in. We might have to buy a new one. I wouldn't even go near the lights. We'd better toss those out."

"Good idea," Regina said, relieved to see her husband was going to take part.

A short time later, the tree was secure in the old stand, set in a corner of the living room, to the left of the fireplace. Regina had found an old red blanket to put underneath, and it looked very pretty, she thought, even bare of any decorations.

Not all the ornaments she found were usable. Some were chipped or broken. Most of them had hooks on top, and she was able to salvage a few more hooks from the discards, so that they didn't have to worry about that niggling detail.

They each took turns picking ornaments to hang. Richard went first and picked a helicopter and a sailboat. Madeline chose a ballerina and an ice-skater. Regina chose Santa Claus and an angel, and Brian chose an elf, a leaping reindeer, and a candy cane. There were many plain, round ornaments, and some icicle shapes, too, which filled out the branches nicely. Regina and Madeline worked on those while Richard made a fire. As for lights, it would be no trouble to buy a pack or two in town and add them later.

By the time the tree was done, it was time for lunch. Regina made some sandwiches and cocoa and brought it all into the living room, where they had a living room picnic, enjoying the fire and admiring their Christmas tree.

"I found a box with trains inside. Did you see that, Dad?" Brian asked.

"Really?" Richard looked interested. "You mean those old toy trains with tracks?"

"Yeah, they had tracks. And little trees and crossing bars and all that stuff," Brian explained through a mouthful of sandwich.

"Don't talk while you're chewing, honey," Regina reminded him.

Brian didn't seem to hear her. "Can we put them together and make the trains drive around?"

"If the transformer is still good and we can get the trains to run," Richard said. "But that stuff is probably pretty old, Brian. I used to have a set like that when I was your age. Setting it up every year was my favorite part of Christmas. I played with those trains for hours."

The news of the train set had definitely brightened her husband's mood, Regina observed. She hoped the set would work. If it didn't, she resolved to find one secondhand and have Santa leave it for Brian and Richard.

Richard squinted at the Christmas tree. "We can lay the track under the tree," he suggested.

Brian suddenly looked worried. "What about all the presents? Won't the trains get in the way?"

Regina laughed. "There will be room for presents, don't worry."

Richard glanced at her, and she hoped the mention of gift buying wouldn't spoil the mood. They were having such a good day together.

"What do you want for Christmas this year, Brian?" Richard asked. He didn't seem annoyed or even nervous, Regina thought, just interested in his son's answer.

Brian quickly named the top three items on his wish list: a basketball hoop and ball, a certain kind of transforming robot toy, and a handheld video game.

"What about you, Maddy?" Richard asked.

Madeline grinned at her brother. "Maybe Brian will let me practice jump shots on his hoop."

"Maybe," Brian said, not looking happy about the idea.

"You must want something for yourself," Regina pressed.

Madeline shrugged. "Just some clothes, jeans and stuff. You know, Mom." Regina sensed that she knew her parents were having hard times financially and was trying to be considerate.

"How about a pair of Snugs? I thought you wanted those, too," Regina said, mentioning the brand of trendy boots all the girls were wearing.

Madeline shrugged again. "The stores have boots that look just like them but cost half as much. You can get me a pair of the no-name kind, Mom. I don't care. Kids who need to wear all this stuff with special labels, they really need to get a life. My new friends at this school aren't into that."

Regina was pleasantly surprised to hear that. Madeline's friends at her old school definitely were into Snugs and all kinds of status fashions.

"Listen, kids," Richard said. "We know it's been hard for you to move up here and leave all your friends in Stover, and your school and all that. You've both been really good about it. We're very proud of you. We love you both a lot and we want you to have a good Christmas."

"In our new house," Brian said proudly.

"Yes, in our new house," Richard agreed. "I think it's coming along, too," he said, glancing around. "If we can get more of the painting done, it will make a big difference. Maybe I'll have it done by Christmas. I'm going to try."

"That would be good, Dad," Madeline said. "But even if you don't, I hope we have a good Christmas, no matter what, adults included. Can I be excused?" she said abruptly.

"Sure, I guess we're done," Regina replied.

Madeline got up and took her dirty plate into the kitchen. She had been moody lately. Her days of being a cuddly little girl were clearly over. Regina sensed she knew something was going on between her parents, but she hadn't asked any questions yet.

Brian was still a happy camper. "I'm done, too," he announced. "Want to see the trains, Dad?"

"Sure, let's see what's out there." Richard wiped his hands on a paper napkin and stood up.

"What about painting my room?" Regina heard Brian ask as he followed his father out the front door. "Don't you have to do that first?"

"Oh, I'll get it done. Maybe I can do that another day. Let's find out if this stuff works."

Regina was glad to hear that the trains would come first. Richard needed time off to relax and do something that was actually fun. She knew that if there was any way at all for that old train set to chug along a track again, Richard would get it going.

Was it possible to repair the damage in her marriage like that train set? To get it up and running again? Regina hoped so. But right now, she had no idea if that was what Richard wanted, too.

CHAPTER ELEVEN

SABEL WAS SURPRISED TO SEE MAX STANDING IN THE doorway of her office on Wednesday morning. It was a little past nine o'clock, and she had just walked in. "Good morning," she greeted him.

"Hey, Reverend." He walked in and sat in the chair in front of her desk, setting down his skateboard and hungrily eyeing the muffin she'd bought at the Beanery, a café just across the village green.

"Would you like some of this? It's much too big for me. It's banana-bran crunch, I think." She held it out to him so he could get a better look.

"Okay, if you really don't want it. It smells sort of good."

"Lots of cinnamon," she agreed. She cut it in half and handed him half on a napkin. "Shouldn't you be in school today?" she added, trying for a casual tone.

"Finals week. We don't have classes. I don't have any tests until tomorrow, and my dad said it was better if I came over here for a while than if I hung out with my friends. Which was my original plan. He's going to pick me up at lunchtime. He knew I wouldn't stay inside studying all day."

"What kind of test do you have tomorrow?"

"Just trig. I'm okay with math. It's, like, a family thing. My dad's got the math gene, just like his father, and I have it, too. My dad's a supernerd mathematician at a college."

"I'm impressed," she said honestly. "I'm not good at math at all."

"No big deal. It's just what I do," Max said with a shrug. "There are, like, nine kinds of intelligence, not just one kind, like they used to think."

"I've heard that," Isabel replied.

"Well, everybody's got to have something going on for them with that many chances," he reasoned. "Maybe you stink at math, but you have musical intelligence. Or you're a good writer, or have, like, social intelligence."

"Being good with people, you mean?"

"Yeah, that's right. That counts, too, you know," he said very seriously.

"I believe it does. At least in my line of work," she agreed, trying not to smile. "How do you know all this about these different types of intelligence?"

"My parents had me tested in grade school. They thought I was some kind of baby genius or something."

"Were you?" Isabel could almost see that. Her guess was that Max was highly intelligent but a classic underachiever.

"Maybe," he said. "Luckily, I grew out of it."

"I see," she said, sipping her coffee. "But a person could be good at math and good with people, too. Don't you think?"

He shrugged, licking some muffin crumbs off his fingers. "Yeah, sure you could. You don't have to be a professional geek, like my father."

Isabel thought Jacob Ferguson was far from a geek. But she didn't share that impression with his son.

"I think your father is very intelligent, but I don't think he lacks social skills. Just because a person is smart, does that mean they can't be cool?"

Max laughed. "I guess you could be really smart and cool . . . but I don't know many kids who are."

"You are, Max. I can see that you're highly intelligent and have many other fine qualities, too. And you're very cool."

He looked embarrassed by her compliments. "Even though I broke in and messed up the church?"

"That wasn't cool, no. Maybe in spite of that," she added. "Everyone makes mistakes, even really smart people. The important thing is to try to learn from them, to use a misstep as a stepping-stone to become a better version of yourself."

He didn't answer, just sighed and stared down at his sneakers. She was losing him. And it had been going so well for a while there. *Some progress, that's what counts,* she reminded herself.

"Do you want me to help you look for Carl? I think he's down in the basement checking the furnace. Something's off with the heating system today," she told him.

"I can find him," Max answered. "Thanks for breakfast."

That was your breakfast? A growing boy needs much more than half a muffin to start the day, she wanted to rail at him. But she heroically held her tongue.

Meanwhile, he brushed off his hands on his napkin, wadded it up, and tossed it at the wastebasket as if it were a midcourt shot. They both watched it arc up in the air and drop in.

"Three points," Isabel observed. "No net."

Max laughed.

"I have three older brothers," she explained. "If it bounced, rolled, or skid on ice, we played with it."

He stared at her a moment. "Cool," he said shortly.

"Yeah, it was." She smiled and sighed, remembering for a moment. She missed her brothers, especially Danny, who was a year older. They had the same coloring and had often been mistaken for twins growing up. "I got an e-mail from one of my brothers this morning. If you think it's cold and snowy here, he's got thirty-nine inches of snow already, and it's only ten degrees."

"Whoa, that's gruesome. Sounds like he lives in Siberia or something."

"No, just North Dakota," Isabel answered.

"Is that where you're from?" Max asked.

"I grew up in Minnesota. But it's not that far away."

"I know where it is. One of those big square states in the middle of the map," Max said.

Isabel smiled at his description. "Yup, that's right. One of the big square ones."

As he left her office with a lanky, loping stride, she suddenly realized that so far, he had not apologized. He did seem to understand better now what he had done, the way he'd violated and disrespected the congregation at this church. But he had never said he was sorry—and Isabel had never asked. She knew that if she did, he might say he was sorry just to placate her. She wanted it to come from him, from his heart, if he was to learn anything from working here.

* * *

A FEW HOURS LATER, ISABEL WAS JUST LEAVING THE CHURCH TO walk into town for lunch when she found Max standing out in front of the church with his backpack and skateboard. The weather had taken a sudden warm turn; the temperature had to be near the forties, she guessed.

"Done for the day?" she asked.

"Yeah, I've been dismissed. Carl's got to work on the furnace and said he didn't need me anymore."

"It's such a nice day, I hope you get out and enjoy the weather a little before you have to study."

"Tell me about it. My friends want me to hang with them." He looked across the green, and Isabel noticed two boys with skateboards sitting on a park bench. "But I have to wait for my dad. Oh . . . here he comes. In his mean, green driving machine," he added in an extra-sardonic voice. "Professor Ferguson, one man saving the environment. I swear, that car is tragic."

Before Isabel could respond, Jacob pulled up to the curb in a white Prius. To her surprise, Jacob parked the car and got out, smiling as he walked toward them.

"Hello, Professor Ferguson. How are you today?"

"I'm fine. Please, call me Jacob. Max and I are going to grab some lunch before he hits the books today. Would you like to join us?"

Isabel was surprised by the invitation, but didn't see any reason to refuse.

"Thanks, I'd like that," she said. "Would you like to walk into town? This weather is a real treat after all the cold and snow."

"Fine with me. I like to walk whenever I'm able—"

"It's better for your health and for the planet," Max cut in, clearly having heard that before.

"It definitely is," Isabel agreed. "And it's better for your mind and spirit, too."

"That's exactly how I feel about riding my board," Max said. "Can I hang out with my friends while you guys have lunch, Dad?" Max glanced at the boys who were still on the bench. "They've, like, texted me a million times."

Jacob looked concerned at the question. Isabel noticed him squint as he checked out the two waiting teenagers.

"Who is that? I see Chris, but who's that other boy?"

"It's Tom Dooley. From my old soccer team, remember?"

"Oh, sure. I remember him. All right, you can go. But don't go far, and keep your phone on. Meet me back here in an hour. Got it?"

Max nodded. "Totally. See you later."

"And wear your helmet. Or I'll take you home to study right now."

"All right . . ." Max looked annoyed but took his helmet out of his backpack and stuck it on his head. "But I'd really like a turkey BLT—or two. And some fries?" he called over his shoulder.

"All right, I'll get it for you," his father said. "One hour, okay?"

Max nodded and waved as he jumped on his board and scooted away. Isabel stood alongside Jacob a moment and watched. Then they turned and began walking down a path in the opposite direction.

"He has finals this week. I hope he remembers that he has to study," Jacob said.

"He told me he has a test tomorrow. He did seem aware that he has to do some work later," Isabel said on Max's behalf. "He might concentrate better after he gets some air and exercise," she pointed out.

"Like a golden retriever, you mean?" he joked, turning to her with a grin.

"Exactly," she agreed. Jacob looked much different when he smiled. It lit up his whole face.

"Well, where would you like to eat?" he asked once they were headed toward the village.

"I'm new here; I don't have any preferences. I'll leave it up to you," she said.

"Oh, big decision . . . let's see. Have you tried the Clam Box yet?"

"Not yet. Though people tell me it's an important Cape Light experience."

"It definitely is. You can't really say you've visited this place unless you've eaten there at least once."

"Sounds like I'm falling behind. I'd better give it a try."

"Yes, you'd better. How long have you been here, Reverend? How do you like the town so far?"

"Let's see . . . only two weeks, but it feels like longer. In a good way, I mean," she added quickly. "A lot has happened at the church."

"Max told me that Reverend Lewis has decided to retire."

"He told you that?" Isabel was surprised. She didn't think Max paid any attention to what was happening at the church, though he did hear a lot of news. Carl probably mentioned Reverend Lewis. He was still upset about the minister's retirement.

"Oh yes. He's brimming with stories when he gets home. He finds it all very interesting. He likes you," Jacob added. "He likes talking to you."

Isabel smiled ruefully. "You'd hardly know it if you overheard our conversations. I feel as if I'm doing all the talking most of the time."

"He can be pretty spare with his words," his father agreed with a sly smile. "But he's listening. And I think he likes that you care so much and try so hard. He can see that. It makes a difference." He paused and glanced at her. "I like that, too."

"I do care. That's why I didn't want to go the usual route with this situation."

"I appreciate that. I know I thanked you before, but I wanted to tell you that again," he said. "When you first suggested that Max work at the church instead of going through the police, I was so relieved, I didn't think to question it. But later, I doubted it would do any good. I didn't think it would make any difference to him. In fact, I expected to have a lot of trouble getting him over here. But it just goes to show I don't know everything, do I?"

"Nobody does," she replied. "We just think we do."

He laughed. "Very true."

She liked people who could so easily admit they were wrong and even laugh at themselves. Especially a man who could. "I'm glad you were wrong, if you don't mind my saying so," she added.

"No, I don't mind. Not about this."

They reached the Clam Box. Isabel tilted her head to look up at the old-fashioned neon sign. A hand-printed sign in the window read BOXED LUNCHES TO GO. TRY OUR FAMOUS CLAM ROLLS.

"Are the clam rolls really famous?" she asked.

"Absolutely . . . for at least a half-mile radius from where we stand," he joked.

They went inside and a teenage waitress showed them to a table and gave them menus. Isabel glanced around and recognized a few faces. Tucker Tulley, Sam Morgan, and another man were eating at the counter, and she knew the diner owner, Charlie Bates, who was also a member of the church.

"Something the matter?" Jacob asked.

"Nothing at all. This is such a small town, I see church members everywhere I go. I guess I didn't expect that."

"Were you at another church in New England before you came here?"

"I was doing mission work in the Caribbean. I came back for a few reasons. I'm here in Cape Light temporarily, because of Reverend Lewis's illness. Now that he's announced he's retiring, it changes things."

"How do you mean?" he asked curiously.

"Well, I only came here to have something to do while I was waiting to find a new position in another mission, in Central America probably. I've applied to a few places down there. Now it seems as if the church members are looking at me differently, as if I'm auditioning for the job of their full-time pastor."

"Maybe people know a good thing when they see it."

"That's nice of you to say. I guess I find their attention flattering, to a point," Isabel admitted. "But even if the congregation decided that they want me as their new pastor, I'm not sure I'd accept."

He seemed surprised. "Any particular reason why not? Is the winter too rough for you already? We aren't even done with December."

"Snow doesn't bother me. I grew up in Minnesota," she told him. "I'm just not sure my talents as a minister are best suited to this congregation. Though there is need everywhere," she acknowledged. "Sometimes the places that seem so pleasant on the surface need good pastors the most."

"What was it like working at a church in the Caribbean?"

"I was in Haiti. We worked with the community to put up houses and schools and freshwater systems, medical clinics, too. To improve the standard of living where we were able. It was very hands-on service."

"That sounds like difficult work. This must be a huge change for you."

"It is. But I'm starting to see that in some ways, the mission work was easier. Oh, life was hard and you had to give up every possible convenience. But the work you needed to do was very . . . obvious. Up here, back in civilization, well, situations aren't so obvious, and it gets more complicated."

He was listening with interest, but she wasn't sure he really understood what she was trying to say.

"I think it's all complicated," he said finally. "I'm not religious. I wasn't raised that way. I can see that people like you often do a lot of good in the world, and I admire that. Like helping my son, for instance, when you really didn't have to. But let's just say I see you as someone with good values, making an ethical choice. I don't believe in anything beyond that."

Isabel smiled. "You're telling me that people can essentially do what I do without any need for God to come into the picture?"

"I suppose I am," Jacob admitted.

"And I'd suggest," she said gently, "that it's a matter of perspective. Perhaps they make similar ethical choices and don't see God being part of it, but that doesn't mean He isn't there."

The waitress brought their order, clam rolls for both of them. The interruption was welcome, Isabel realized, since she was suddenly sitting in the theological hot seat. How did this happen?

"I'm sorry . . . I didn't mean to start a philosophical debate, Reverend," Jacob said, once the waitress had left. "Why are you smiling? Did I just say something funny?"

"Not really. I was just thinking that when God said, 'There's no such thing as free lunch,' He really meant it. That's not in the Bible, by the way." Isabel surveyed her plate. She dabbed at a bit of the sauce that had come on the side of the roll and tried to figure out how to politely attack it. "And you can call me Isabel. *Reverend* sounds so formal."

"Well, I may be a nonbelieving mathematician, Isabel, but I do know that God didn't have much to say about free lunches." He was smiling in spite of himself now. "But I didn't realize true believers could be so—"

"Flip? Irreverent? That's something most nonbelievers don't realize. God has a terrific sense of humor. I thought we were just going to talk about Max, and maybe the clam rolls. Now here we are, in the thick of it. But let me ask you this," she continued, diving in with both feet now. "Do you believe in some power greater than yourself—in something going on in the universe beyond what's apparent to our senses?"

His expression was thoughtful. He was taking this conversation seriously. "Something . . . or someone?" he asked finally.

"I'm not talking about an old man in the sky with a long beard, if that's what you mean. I think our minds are too limited to truly understand or imagine God. But I see God everywhere, in a blade of grass, a baby's smile, in your son's expression when he's riding his skateboard. As Whitman said, 'In the faces of men and women I see God.' I know you're a mathematician," she added, "but even Einstein believed."

"Yes, he did, in his way," Jacob acknowledged. "And I respect his right to hold that opinion. The same as I respect yours, or anyone's. My wife belonged to a church and was a great believer. She was the sweetest, finest person I ever knew. But what I can't figure out is: If there is a God, why did He have to make her die? It doesn't seem fair, and it doesn't make sense if you want to believe in some all-powerful source of goodness, watching over us."

It didn't make sense if you put it that way, Isabel had to agree. Jacob had put her in a difficult spot. As she gathered her thoughts to reply, he suddenly continued.

"Don't worry. You don't have to try to explain anything to me. I'm asking a purely rhetorical question. You don't have to say, 'It's not our place to understand. God is mysterious, beyond our understanding.' Or 'She's gone to a better place. We should be happy for her. It's harder for the ones left behind' and all that claptrap. My wife believed that," he added quickly. "I guess it was some comfort to her at the end."

"But not to you," Isabel guessed.

"Not one bit." Jacob shook his head, seeming annoyed with himself. "I'm sorry for speaking out. I know you can't answer all these heavy questions, especially not over a few bites of lunch. How did we get on this subject, anyway?"

"I don't know . . . but I do understand, in my own way," Isabel replied. "I lost my husband five years ago. He had lung cancer and died very quickly. Despite my faith, there was pain. Great pain. There is no escape from that. Even for believers."

He looked surprised by her reply, and a little embarrassed. "I'm truly sorry for your loss . . . and I apologize for my assumptions," he said. "I feel very foolish now. Please forgive me for being so . . . so blundering."

Isabel met his gaze a moment. He had very warm brown eyes, and when he smiled, his mouth turned down at the corners, she noticed. He had a sharp, quick mind. She enjoyed talking to him, especially the intellectual sparring. But she thought for now it was best to change the subject, which had touched raw nerves on both sides of the table, it seemed.

If she ever spent more time with him, they would probably get around to this topic again. It did seem to be something he wondered about, though he claimed his mind was made up on the question.

"I know you're a mathematician and teach at the community college. But what does that mean exactly?" Isabel asked. "Do you work on math problems all day long?"

"Not quite . . . but almost. I do when I'm working on my research papers. It sounds pretty dull when you put it that way," he said with a laugh. "There are certain mathematical theories or equations that have yet to be proven. Somebody like me—when I'm not teaching, that is—works on those questions or proofs. Sometimes, only small parts of them. I might study a single equation my whole life and never get close to the answer."

"You must be very dedicated," she said, genuinely impressed. "And fascinated by the subject. How do you know the problems even have a solution?"

He smiled. "You don't. I guess you might say, you have to take it on faith." His smile widened as he bit into his clam roll. "You're pretty good, Reverend. Now you've got me admitting I might be religious in a way, after all."

"It's a start," she conceded, feeling she had won a round without really intending to.

When their lunch was over, Jacob and Isabel walked back down Main Street and through the village green toward the church.

The harbor was half-frozen, covered with choppy white and blue-gray sheets of ice. A few valiant old fishing boats were still tied to their moorings but locked in the ice at odd angles, and would remain that way until the spring thaw.

"This is a very pretty place," Isabel remarked. "I've been in New England once or twice, but only to Boston. How long have you and Max lived here?"

"About ten years. Max was about to start first grade when I

took the teaching position at the college. We were living in Guilford, a small town near New Haven, before that. Guilford is very nice, a lot like this place, in fact. I was just finishing my doctorate down there."

"New Haven . . . as in Yale?"

"Yes, as in Yale." He looked a little embarrassed. He was modest, she thought. She liked that, too. Most people would brag about that résumé. "I guess I could have found a position at a bigger university, but my wife's family is from this area and she wanted to come back. It's been good for Max to have family ties after she passed away. His grandparents and all my in-laws have been wonderful to us. I'm thankful for that, especially since he's an only child."

"It sounds like you've made some sacrifices for him."

"Oh, I don't know, maybe. I was much more ambitious when I was younger. It doesn't seem so important to me now to be at some big-name college. This place has been very good for him. He needed the stability. When you have children, you have to put them first. That's just what parents do."

What some parents do, she thought. He was a good father and had good values.

"Do you have any children, Isabel?" he asked.

"No, I don't. My husband and I put off starting a family, and I regret that now," she said honestly. "Though I know that if I did have children, I wouldn't be able to move from place to place so easily."

"No, you wouldn't," he agreed. "But there are great benefits."

"I'm sure of that," she agreed. "Speaking of benefits . . . there's one waiting for you right now. I think he might even be early," she said, seeing Max gliding toward them on his board.

"Now there's a first. I think he's just hungry. He wants his turkey BLT," Jacob said, waving the take-out order. "He actually wanted me to get two of these. Can you believe that?"

"Yes, I can. I've seen him eat. Though I don't know where he puts it." Isabel paused, wondering if she should tell Jacob something Max had mentioned to her. It might spark another intellectual debate, and they were having such a nice time. But she decided she had to at least mention it. She didn't want Jacob to think she was trying to hide something from him.

"Max told me that he'd like to come to a church service sometime," she said finally. "Did you know that?"

Jacob turned and looked at her. They were walking side by side. She was tall, but he was taller. Just the right amount, she thought. The light wind lifted his thick hair, and his expression seemed confused. Was he angry at her? She thought for a moment he might be.

"I didn't know that. He hasn't said a word to me about it. When did he mention it? In what context, I mean?"

Now he sounded lawyerly—or suspicious. Perhaps he thought she was trying to brainwash his son, lure him into church as if it were some type of cult. Many people thought that way. She was used to it. She didn't take it personally.

"Please don't worry. No one has tried to persuade him to come or even mentioned it to him. I was as surprised as you are," she said honestly. "I think he's just curious about what goes on in the sanctuary. He's been cleaning it and working on it all this time."

"That's possible." Jacob looked calmer, but still sounded suspicious. "Max's mother took him to church when he was younger. But he hasn't gone since she died and never expressed any interest in going," he said pointedly.

Isabel shrugged. "I don't even know if he will come. He just said he might. I guess you should ask him how this came about."

"I will."

Isabel smiled gently. She had a feeling this would be the very first topic they covered during the trip home. She wondered what Max would say. She hoped he wouldn't be mad at her for telling his father that he wanted to come to church. But now she wondered if she'd betrayed a confidence of some kind. She hoped not.

"What took you guys so long? I'm starving." Max grabbed the bag of food and opened it, foraging for his sandwich.

"You could have come with us and eaten sooner," his father reminded him.

"Yeah, yeah. Choices and consequences. It's the same old story," Max replied in a singsong voice as he pulled some fries from the bag and stuffed them in his mouth. He grinned at Isabel and she grinned back. He already had some ketchup on his chin, but he looked cute, she thought.

Though Isabel felt bad that Max had been waiting here with hunger pangs, she'd enjoyed her time alone with Jacob. It would have been fun to go out with both of them, but she doubted that Jacob would have spoken so openly. Or that she would have, either.

"Thanks so much for lunch," she said to Jacob. "I enjoyed the clam roll and our talk very much."

"I did, too, Isabel. I hope I wasn't too . . . argumentative."

"Not at all. I liked our debate most of all."

"To be continued then," he said, smiling at her.

"Anytime," she replied.

When they finally parted and Isabel went back inside the church, she wondered what he'd meant. That they would resume their discussion about the existence of God sometime? Or he would ask to see her?

As committed as you are to spreading the good news and defending your faith, I think that you're actually hoping for the latter, she told herself.

Yes . . . I am. I actually . . . like him.

The realization took her by surprise. She had been alone now for nearly five years, and in that time had met only a few men she enjoyed spending time with, mostly as friends. But for some reason, Jacob reminded her of what it was like to feel real chemistry, the kind she hadn't felt for a very long time.

Wasn't that ironic? Isabel almost laughed out loud at herself. How awkward . . . and how unlikely a match they would be.

But as she'd just told Jacob, God has a great sense of humor. Here was even more proof.

ON WEDNESDAY NIGHT, REGINA WORKED AT ANOTHER ONE OF Molly's parties. When she got home, everyone else in the house was asleep. The only light came from a small lamp in the living room and the Christmas tree. She dropped into a chair, not even bothering to take off her jacket. It had been quite a day.

The weather had started off on the warm side, so she'd skipped her heavy wool coat, but now it was cold out again and she felt chilled and tired.

She leaned back and slipped off her shoes. She was relieved that no one was awake. She was actually too tired to talk. She needed some downtime, alone. But part of her wished that Richard was up. She wanted to tell him that Dr. Harding had offered her the receptionist job in his office full-time. "You've been such a great help here, Regina. We'd be crazy to hire anyone else," he'd said.

Regina had been thrilled at the news, which came with a small raise. But not large enough for her to skip the catering. Besides, she had promised Molly that she would work through Christmas. It would be a tough schedule. After working at the doctor's office all day and then the party all night, she was flat-out exhausted. Still, it had been worth it. At the end of the party, the hostess had given everyone small white envelopes that contained huge tips. Regina had checked the amount in the car and couldn't quite believe it. She had tucked the envelope in her jacket pocket. Now she patted the spot to make sure it was still there.

It was still there . . . along with something else. She reached in and pulled out the little Bible wrapped in plastic that she and Madeline had found in the garage. She hadn't worn this jacket in a while and had forgotten all about it.

Curious, she took it out, carefully unwrapped it, and opened the brown leather cover. The paper was dry and fragile, but it had been well preserved. On the first pages she saw a family tree, written in an old-fashioned hand, the letters elaborate and swirling: *Jonas Porter* and *Elizabeth Fairchild*. They had five children—two boys and three girls, but one of the boys had died as an infant and one of the girls as a teenager.

Of the other children, marriages and births had been recorded. Regina peered at the book in the dim light to make out the many names. The writing was small in order to fit on the page.

Fascinating, she thought. She had never really read the Bible, but like most people was familiar with a few passages. She carefully turned the pages, stopping at random. The book opened to the New Testament, Corinthians. She glanced at the page. The language was so formal, she could barely understand it. "Charity suffereth long, and is kind . . . is not easily provoked . . . Beareth all things, believeth all things, hopeth all things, endureth all things."

Charity. That meant love. Regina knew those verses, though not in that sort of language: "Love is patient, love is kind. Love bears all things, believes all things, hopes all things, endures all things."

She sighed and closed the little Bible, clasping it in her hands.

That's what love is, she thought. Did she still love Richard? She knew that deep inside, she did. Had she been patient with and kind to him? Had she shown him all those other qualities?

Well, some of the time. She had tried at first. But not lately. She had to admit that, even to herself. But she did love him. There was no question. Maybe if she had been kinder, more patient, more hopeful, their marriage would not have unraveled this way, she thought.

Sometimes she blamed it all on him. Not their financial problems, but the problems in their relationship. That wasn't fair, she knew. It took two. She wasn't blameless, not in the least. Was it too late to change, to be any of those wonderful things—patient, kind, someone who hopes and believes? She felt so tired, she just didn't know.

All of a sudden, Richard was standing next to her, gently shaking her shoulder. "Gina?"

She opened her eyes with a start. "Richard . . . you scared me."

"I'm sorry." He stepped back. "I didn't even know you were home. How long have you been down here?"

She blinked. "I don't know. What time is it?"

"A little past one," he said, looking at his watch.

"I thought I was just sitting here a minute, unwinding. Guess I fell asleep."

"I guess you did. What's that? Were you reading?"

"Not really. It's just that little Bible I found in the garage." She showed him the book. "I told you about it, remember?"

Richard gave it a quick glance. "There are a ton of old books around this place. I threw out a few boxes that were full of dust and mold. I hope reading that one doesn't give you a headache."

"The printing is a little blurred, but it's in good condition. Someone wrapped it up in plastic. I found all these names in the front. I think they must be my ancestors." She put the little Bible on the side table and looked back up at him. "How were the kids? Were they good for you?"

"No problems. They did all their homework and went to bed without a fuss. I made their lunches for tomorrow, too."

The lunches . . . Good thing. She had totally forgotten.

"How was the party?" he asked curiously.

"Big. About a hundred people. In one of those big Victorians on Providence Street; a mansion, really. I got a big tip. That part was fun."

"I'm sure you deserved it. But I'm not so sure about this extra work, Regina. I can handle the kids all right—it's not that," he said quickly. "I just think it's too much for you. You're working so hard. I don't want you to get overtired and sick."

Regina was surprised. Lately, she didn't think he thought that much about her. But he did seem concerned and caring, which was touching. She had the impulse to reach out and take his hand. But at the last minute, she held herself back.

"Don't worry. I'm okay. It won't be forever. I told Molly just until Christmas, and that's only a week away," she reminded him.

He still looked concerned, but didn't argue.

"I'm excited to go shopping for the kids' gifts now. I was sort of dreading it before," she confessed.

"So was I," he admitted. "But they don't seem to want very much."

"No, I think they were afraid to ask for too much," she said honestly. "Especially Madeline. I think we should give her some nice surprises if we can."

"She's a good kid. She's been a trooper. She's had it the worst, I think, because of her age. Brian really doesn't understand or have the sort of social pressure that Madeline goes through," he said quietly.

"Exactly," Regina agreed, glad that Richard understood.

"When should we do the shopping?" he asked. "It's getting a little close, don't you think?"

Regina was surprised to hear him say that. Most men she knew thought nothing of starting on Christmas Eve.

"I thought we could go Sunday afternoon. I'm scheduled to work at a brunch. It's over at three," Regina said.

"That sounds fine. What about the kids? Can they stay alone all that time?"

"They've been staying on their own after school," Regina pointed out, "though they're rarely alone for that long. Still, Madeline's very responsible. I think she can watch Brian for a few hours. Let's just see how it goes."

That was one of Regina's favorite sayings, and it sometimes drove Richard crazy, since he was the exact opposite. He wanted to know specifics, not wing it. But tonight he just stared down at her and shook his head, a small smile on his face that was hard to decipher.

"Okay, Regina. We'll see how it goes," he teased her. "Now come on upstairs, before you fall asleep in that chair again."

Regina laughed. "Okay . . . just help me up. I'm so tired, I can't move." Regina extended her hand, and he gently tugged her out of the chair. When she finally stood up, she kept going and put her arms around him. She gave him a hug, and she could tell he was startled. He hugged her back, gently at first, then all of a sudden tighter and closer. He held her in a sweet, tender way, dipping his head down to touch his cheek to her hair.

Regina was so surprised, she couldn't even respond for a

moment. Before she could say or do anything, he seemed to feel self-conscious or awkward about his sudden expression of emotion, and he slipped from her arms.

"I'd better unplug the lights and check the doors again. You go up."

Regina nodded and headed for the stairs. She wished he hadn't pulled away so quickly. But she felt things were getting better between them, little by little. Maybe, though, it was just the Christmas spirit making them feel more tender toward each other.

Christmas would soon come and go. Then they would know what the future held for their family.

CHAPTER TWELVE

O N SUNDAY MORNING, CAROLYN WAS THE FIRST TO WAKE
and get out of bed. Ben saw her standing by the window,
looking out at the backyard.

"Snow again," she said quietly.

"I heard there might be some flurries overnight. How much
is it?"

"An inch or two."

Just like the morning you had the heart attack, he could tell she
wanted to say. He was thinking the same thing. They were so often
of the same mind now, it was uncanny.

She turned to him. "Still want to go to church?"

"Yes, I do." He sat up and pushed the covers aside in one swift,
decisive move. Sudden movements still caused an ache here and
there, but he was healing and the physical therapy had led him into
a whole new world . . . or maybe a world that he had left behind in

his thirties or forties. He was walking and even jogging a little on a treadmill, working out with weights, too. Growing muscles again, like a young man. The body was amazingly regenerative. What a divine invention.

"Do you know what today is?" she asked as he put on his robe and slippers.

"The fourth Sunday of Advent?"

"Besides that. It's been three weeks since the heart attack."

"Oh, right. But who's counting?" He glanced at her, and they both smiled. "It seems like it was a long time ago, but in a way, it could have been yesterday. Do you know what I mean?"

"I do. It's changed our whole lives." She paused. "It's going to be . . . different for you at church today. I'm sure you've already thought about that, Ben. It's just that . . . don't you think it might be hard?"

"It will be, in some ways. In other ways, it will be a re-lief, I think, to just relax and enjoy the service." He reached out and patted her shoulder. "I know you're concerned about me, honey, but you can't anticipate all my worries and fix everything. You can't be a little airbag between me and the world, Carolyn, puffing up at the first sign of possible impact. I am recovering, nearly completely healed. I'm not fragile or in any danger at all," he promised her.

"Yes, I know." She nodded. They had talked about this before. "I do worry about you, though. I just can't help it."

She had always been a caring partner. But since he'd fallen ill, she had been extra vigilant and extra anxious, anticipating his every interaction and possible reaction. It wasn't good for her, he knew. Or for him. Or for their relationship.

"I know you do. And I know I'm very blessed to be married to someone who loves me so much. Very blessed," he repeated. He put his arms around her and held her tight. "See how strong I am now? This PT is turning me into a regular muscleman," he teased. "Almost fifteen pounds thinner, too," he added, reminding her of the weight he had lost over the last three weeks. "I'm better than ever. So cast your cares, my dear."

"Oh, Ben . . . I will try. What would I ever do without you?" she asked him. Then she squeezed him back and kissed him. "Let's get ready. It's getting late."

"Yes, we'd better hustle. This time, they can start without me."

BEN WASN'T SURE IF RACHEL AND HER HUSBAND WERE JUST being considerate or if Carolyn had engineered things, but when he went downstairs for coffee and a quick breakfast, Carolyn reported that Rachel would be coming by soon to pick them up and drive them to church.

"This way, we won't have to bother cleaning off the car and shoveling the driveway. Jack said he'll do that later."

"Oh, that's good, very kind of them." Ben had always done it automatically, without thinking. He had totally forgotten he wasn't really up to that task today.

A short time later, he followed his wife into the church. *We're late,* he realized. The doors to the sanctuary were closed, and he heard the choir singing the opening hymn.

He had always frowned on folks who walked in during the announcements or even later, interrupting everything as they tried to find a seat and settle down, inevitably dropping their programs so that all the inserts flew out and fluttered around the pew. *Judge not, and ye shall not be judged, Ben. Now you're one of them,* he realized with chagrin.

Tucker was standing by the sanctuary doors with a handful of programs. "Reverend Ben!" His voice was hushed but elated. "So good to see you. You look great."

"Thank you, Tucker." Ben smiled and shook his hand.

"Let me find some seats." Tucker opened the heavy wooden doors for them, then followed them into the sanctuary.

"Somewhere in the back, please?" Carolyn whispered. She had confessed a fear that Ben might not be able to sit in church for the entire service and wanted to be able to slip out quietly if necessary.

Ben preferred the back rows, too. He didn't want to make a big entrance and draw too much attention to himself. This was Reverend Isabel's service. He was just a private citizen now, just a regular member of the congregation.

Tucker found Carolyn and Ben two seats on an aisle, and seats in the next row for Rachel and her family. Heads turned and many smiled and even quietly waved at him. "Look, Reverend Ben is here," he heard them murmur.

Ben smiled back but tried his best to keep his gaze forward, fixed on Reverend Isabel who was just delivering the weekly announcements.

"And many thanks to everyone who took part in this year's Christmas Fair. I want to thank the committee for putting together a wonderful event and all the volunteers who worked so hard this weekend. And everyone who donated supplies and services. We raised over two thousand dollars, which will be used to buy Christmas gifts and food for families in need. It's wonderful to see this church reaching out and sharing the true meaning of Christmas."

Well said, Ben thought. He was very proud of the congregation for the work they put into that project. It helped many families every year. He had, in fact, started it, his first or second year at the church. Not that he wanted any credit, he reminded himself. It was gratifying to see the tradition carried on. It would be, too, after he was gone, he realized.

"And one last announcement." Reverend Isabel looked up from her notes, a wide smile on her lovely face. "I know we're all happy to see Reverend Ben and his family joining us for worship this morning. Welcome back, Reverend. I hope you enjoy the service," she said, smiling straight at him.

The congregation broke out in applause, and Ben waved from his seat, feeling a little like a celebrity.

"I'm so glad to be here. You can't imagine," he said honestly.

Many in the congregation laughed at his frankness. It was true. All morning he had sent up silent prayers of thanks that he was simply alive and well enough to return to his beloved church. And he did love it, he realized, gazing around as the service continued. He loved it, but like any long-term relationship, after so many years together, he had taken it for granted.

I didn't appreciate all I had as a minister here, he realized. *Not for the last year or so. I let the routine and the church traditions and the same problems that we never seem to solve—fund-raising, finding new members, keeping this old building in some sort of repair—I let all that bog me down, drain me of energy, optimism, and inspiration. My heart condition didn't help, either.*

For the first time since his decision to retire, he felt a deep pang of loss and regret. He closed his eyes and took a breath.

Carolyn touched his hand. "Ben, are you all right?" she whispered.

He turned to her, trying to compose himself. "I'm fine, dear," he whispered back.

But he wasn't fine. He felt confused. He stilled his mind and sent up a silent prayer. *Dear God, please help me. I thought I had this all figured out . . . Am I doing the right thing?*

* * *

AFTER THE SERVICE, RACHEL AND HER FAMILY CAME TO THE parsonage for lunch. After the meal, they helped Ben and Carolyn put up their Christmas tree.

They usually put their tree up much earlier, but Ben's illness had thrown them off schedule this year. Carolyn had barely done any shopping yet, and he kept reminding her that everyone would understand if her gifts weren't perfect this year.

"Yes, I know. I'm thinking of just sticking a big bow on your head and plopping you under the tree. You could really let me off the hook if you would just cooperate," she teased him.

"I'll think about it," he'd replied.

The subject was so serious, joking about it helped them. His health—*his life*—was the gift this year. He didn't want or need anything more. Neither did Carolyn, he knew. Still, he had already arranged with Rachel to surprise his wife with a bottle of her favorite perfume and a day of relaxation at a local spa. She certainly deserved some pampering after waiting on him hand and foot all these weeks.

The full house and all the activity were a great distraction. Ben enjoyed watching his grandchildren decorate. He sat back on the couch, more like the cheering section this year and the chief hook-fastener. But that was all right, even more fun in a way.

Carolyn made some hot cocoa and popcorn—no salt or butter on his—which was pretty dry and boring, he thought. But he resisted complaining. *I'm alive and chewing,* he reminded himself, *and very thankful.*

While Ben amused his grandchildren, Jack and Rachel helped Carolyn put away all the boxes and clean up. By the time they left, it was late afternoon. The winter sun was just about to set. The children had homework, and the adults had to get ready for the last full work-week before the holidays.

Ben walked them all to the foyer and cheerfully waved good-bye from the door. Watching their car pull away, he felt very tired. It had been a full day. He wasn't used to all this activity.

When Carolyn came back into the living room, he was already stretched out on the couch with his feet up. He had the newspaper open, spread across his chest, but he wasn't actually reading it.

"Are you tired, Ben? Maybe you should go up and have a real nap, on the bed." She sat in the armchair near him and took a pile of Christmas cards off the side table. She was intent on getting a few out, though not her usual long list.

"I'm okay right here. I like to look at the tree. It smells so good," he said. "It finally feels like Christmas."

"It does," she agreed. "Being in church this morning and singing some carols got me more in the mood, too."

"Me, too. It made me feel a lot of things," he admitted. "It was hard, in a way, to sit there. Maybe just because it was the first time after I decided to retire. But it was difficult to face the fact that I won't be running the service or the church anymore. It all happened so suddenly," he added, lifting his head to look at her.

"It did happen suddenly," she agreed. "You pretty much had the rug pulled out from under you."

"Exactly." Ben sighed and sat up. "It's like anything else, Carolyn. We don't appreciate what we have when we have it. Just human nature, I guess. But if I had realized four weeks ago that it was going to be my last month, or my last week, or my last Sunday serving as a minister, I would have done a lot of things differently."

"Like what, for instance?" Carolyn stopped writing and gazed at him, curious.

"The sermons, for one thing. I would have prepared better," he admitted.

"I'm sure once you're fully recovered Isabel, or whoever the new minister turns out to be, will step aside one Sunday and let you give a final sermon."

"I know that," Ben replied. "Maybe I mean more than the sermons. More of the big picture. You know, the more I heal, the better I start to feel, the more I realize how this heart problem must have been going on for a long time, Carolyn. It was draining me, making me feel tired, physically and emotionally. And spiritually, too," he added. "You must have noticed it."

"I did," she admitted. "I thought the church was becoming too much for you, a sign that it was time to retire. I didn't suspect you were sick."

"Neither did I. I thought I was just getting too old to be a good preacher. It's some comfort to know there was a physical reason and I wasn't just getting stale, like an old cracker left at the bottom of the box."

"Oh, Ben, don't be so hard on yourself. You were never like a stale old cracker. Not one bit. You were always very . . . very crisp," she told him with a little laugh.

"I know . . . but inside, I felt like the tank was on empty, or getting perilously close. Now that I'm getting my energy back, I feel capable of all kinds of things."

"Continuing at church, you mean?" Carolyn asked.

"I don't mean that. Not exactly." He heard a distinct note of alarm in her voice and automatically rushed to assure her. She would not like to hear that he didn't want to retire after all. Not that she would argue with him or pressure him to change his mind.

Carolyn was not like that. But he knew her well enough by now to know when she was unhappy and disapproved of his decisions. He didn't want to make her unhappy. That was a big consideration.

Today in church, his doubts about retiring had been distressing. But maybe it was just going back the first time and facing the fact that a long, fulfilling phase of his life had come to an end. Right now, he couldn't see around the bend in the road to the milk-and-honeyed land of retirement.

But it would come, he told himself. *Just keep putting one foot ahead of the other—even on that monotonous treadmill—and you'll get there. You shouldn't even consider reversing this decision,* he told himself. *You're just having some sort of buyer's remorse. It probably happens to most people who genuinely enjoy their work.*

As an ordained minister, his calling would never really end. He would just practice service in a different way.

Ben comforted himself with that thought. There was so much to look forward to—more time with Carolyn and the kids, waking up in the morning with no pressures, no obligations, no meetings to attend. Time to read, write, just sit and think if that's all he wanted to do. Time to travel to places in this country, or other countries, where he could put a lifetime of experience to good use and help those in need.

He had to keep his eye on the prize, he reminded himself. He had so much ahead of him.

THE SHOPPING EXPEDITION DID NOT TAKE NEARLY AS LONG AS Regina had expected, mostly because they found practically everything in a big discount store that sold everything from snowblowers to lingerie. Regina found all the necessities for both Madeline and Brian there—jackets, boots, and pajamas, a few sweaters and jeans for Madeline, and all of the new clothes Brian needed, plus new sneakers.

While Regina shopped for the practical items, Richard cruised the toy department. He found a snowboard, helmet, and a basketball hoop and ball for Brian. He placed them in the cart, and they headed for the register.

"He won't be able to shoot any hoops until the snow melts," Richard said, "but he should have fun with the snowboard. There's something else I really want to get him, but we won't find it here."

"What's that?" Regina asked.

"A new transformer for that old train set—and a few more cars and bits of scenery, if I can find them. It was running fine for a few days, but something burned out. I can't fix it anymore."

"Oh, that's too bad. I wondered why he wasn't using it lately. He seemed fascinated with it at first."

"He loves it. I never realized he would be so intrigued. He hasn't mentioned that video game thing at all lately."

"No, he hasn't," Regina agreed. "Where would we find old trains like that, though? Doesn't the part have to match?"

"It does. But I checked the phone book, and there's a place in Hamilton that might have one. It's not far from here. Sam and I have done some work in that town."

Regina glanced at her watch. "It's not too late. Maybe they're still open."

Driving over to Hamilton from the discount store, Regina realized that she and Richard had not spent time alone like this in months. If they had, they would have been snapping and bickering with each other, or in some tense, silently reproachful standoff. But today she actually felt relaxed, and maybe even . . . happy. She glanced over at Richard and suddenly realized that the tense, watchful feeling that made their relationship so strained had practically disappeared today.

They weren't arguing about what to buy, or how much to spend, and easily came to agreement on just about all of their purchases. It felt good to do something together for their kids. Did that mean Richard felt happier with her? Happier in their marriage? She wasn't sure she could go that far. She was just thankful for an easy day, wondering how long it would last.

She felt happier with him. Happier and grateful.

Hamilton was an old, distinguished village, famous for horse breeding and equestrian shows. It looked a bit wealthier than Cape Light, Regina thought as they parked in the small village center. She liked Cape Light better, she quickly decided. There were more shops and the harbor, and it had a bustling, comfortable feeling. This town seemed a little too sedate for her taste.

She had lived in Cape Light less than a month, but she already knew that if something were to happen between her and Richard, she would stay in the village. Aside from owning the house, she had made friends there and had a decent job. It seemed like a good place to raise children, too. They had landed there by accident, but it had been a fortunate accident, the first bit of good luck her family had known in years.

"Here's the place." Richard led her a short distance down a tree-lined street to a narrow shop that looked like an antique store. When she looked inside she could see it was filled mainly with toys and books. The place was dark, and a card in the window read BACK IN TWO SHAKES.

"How long is a shake, do you think?" He turned to Regina, looking amused.

Her husband was still quite good-looking, she realized. Somehow, he'd even gotten better-looking as they'd grown older. If they parted, Richard would have no trouble finding someone new. No question about that.

"I think they mean two shakes of a lamb's tail. That old expression?" she reminded him. "It shouldn't be too long."

"Depends on the lamb, I guess," Richard said. He stuck his hands in his front pockets and looked up and down the street. "I'm hungry. Want to grab a bite and come back? Maybe they'll be open by then."

"Good idea. I'm hungry, too."

They walked down the street and soon found a café. Regina read the menu in the window while Richard peeked through the window. "This looks okay to me," she said, mainly meaning that it didn't look expensive.

"Well, it's not the Clam Box," he joked, "but I guess we can try it."

The menu actually was a lot like the Clam Box, including their own version of a clam roll. While Richard gave the waitress their orders, Regina called home and checked on the kids.

"They're fine," she reported. "Madeline's doing homework, and Brian's watching a video. I told them we won't be much longer. I'm just not sure how we're going to keep them from seeing all the presents. Where should we hide them?"

"Good point. I didn't even think of that. There's no place around the house that's safe. They'll hunt every day when they get home from school."

"Definitely. Even if we tell them not to."

"*Especially* if we tell them not to," he agreed with a grin. "I've got it. I'll take all the packages over to Sam's shop and leave them there until Christmas. He won't mind."

Sam wouldn't mind that at all, Regina thought.

"Can you show me how to take a picture with the cell phone?"

she asked. "I want a shot of their faces when we come home empty-handed."

Richard's smile grew wider. "That would be priceless. I can't wait."

They were still laughing when the waitress brought their orders. Regina could hardly believe it. They hadn't relaxed like this together for a long time. Or laughed. Or gone out for a bite to eat alone. It was almost like a little date, she thought, the way it used to be. They would always manage to carve out some time to spend together, even doing something ordinary, like grocery shopping or going out to breakfast. The day had given her hope . . . though she tried not to hope for too much.

When they were finished with lunch, they found the little antique shop open again. Richard went straight to the back, where Regina saw a large collection of train sets. The shopkeeper was an old man with a large round stomach and a handlebar mustache. He wore a black vest and glasses balanced on the end of his nose, fitting in perfectly with the decor.

While the two men hunted around for the transformer and other items Richard wanted, Regina browsed, though she wasn't interested in buying anything.

I have so much dusty old stuff in my own house, I could open a store like this, she thought.

Old books, for instance. There were shelves of them in the store and some in a glass barrister case. A title behind the glass, embossed in gold type, caught her eye: *Little House on the Prairie,* one of her favorite novels when she was a little girl. She had read it aloud to Madeline years ago. She wanted to take a peek at it again, and she began to lift the glass door.

"Please, ma'am, don't touch those. I need to help you with any items in the case."

"Oh, sorry. I was just curious. You don't have to bother."

"I'm sorry if I startled you, but some of those are first editions. Quite valuable. Feel free to handle any of the copies on the open shelves, though. I can give you a good price if you find something you like."

"No, thanks, we have plenty of old books at home," Regina said honestly.

She glanced at Richard and he smiled in reply, raising his eyebrows at the shopkeeper before the man could see.

A short time later, Richard met her at the door, holding a large cardboard carton filled with pieces for the train set. "Eureka," he said.

"You couldn't look happier if those trains were for you," she observed.

"Brian will go wild when he sees what I found. That's even better, don't you think?"

"Yeah, I do," she said quietly. He looked so pleased, she nearly kissed him. But the moment passed and it just seemed too difficult to bridge that gap. Even after such a good day together.

They drove back to Cape Light and parked in front of Sam's shop. Richard had his own key, and they had soon stored all their packages and headed back to their house.

"Now we need something special for Madeline," Richard said as they drove home. "What can we get her?"

"I'm not sure. Molly says there are some good shops up in Newburyport. She buys her girls a lot of clothes up there. And I can look in town on my lunch break. Maybe I can find her a piece of jewelry in the Bramble? Though something nice probably won't be cheap," she admitted, wondering if Richard would object.

"That's a good idea," he said after a few moments. "She's getting old enough to have nice things. She deserves something special, too."

Regina agreed. She stared out the window on her side of the truck. She was sure she could find something special for Maddy. Maybe a pretty ring with her birthstone?

She allowed herself to feel a little thrill of anticipation. For the first time in years, they were going to have a really good Christmas. Then her heart sank as she realized it might be their last Christmas together. Everything between them was still so . . . uncertain. Everything still put on hold until the holidays were over. Despite the way they'd managed to get along so well today, she had no idea of what was to come.

Chapter Thirteen

~~

*I*SABEL KNEW THAT THE TRUSTEES OF THE CHURCH NOR-
mally met on the first Monday of each month. As the
acting minister, she was part of that board. She had not been at
the church long enough to attend a regular meeting—only the one
they had called to talk about Max.

So she was surprised when she got to church on Monday morning, the final week before Christmas, and heard from her secretary
that the trustees were coming to church that night for another special meeting. One that she had not been invited to attend. Nor had
she been invited to the special meeting called by the church council
for Tuesday.

Something was up. Isabel wasn't quite sure what it could be
and felt a little silly and self-conscious trying to ferret it out.

Maybe it was just about the church's old furnace, which seemed
to be chugging along, continuing to spew heat due only to the

persistent prayers on the part of the congregation and fear of Carl Tulley.

The temperature had dipped below freezing again, and Isabel practically felt a cool breeze sifting through her office. She wore a fleece vest over her cotton turtleneck and jeans, but was hunting around for an extra sweater in the closet when she heard a knock on the door.

She was pleased to see Max. He hadn't stopped by yet today to say hello. He had come a couple of hours ago, and Carl had put him straight to work.

"Is Carl working on the heat?" she asked. "It seems especially frigid in here today."

She had some bagels and fruit for him, set up on the small table near the window. He went right to it and took a seat at the table, fixing his paper plate.

"He's working on it. He's a regular furnace therapist." Max spread some cream cheese on a bagel, smashed it together, then cut it in half. "But you guys need to get a new one. It's getting ugly down there."

"The trustees might be figuring that out tonight," she said, still wondering why they hadn't included her.

"That's not what they're talking about," Max said decisively. "Don't you know?"

"Know what?" Now she was utterly stumped. And how did he know—and she didn't?

"I thought someone would have told you," he said. "I didn't think it was such a big secret."

"Is it a secret? How do you know then?" she asked curiously.

"Carl told me. We had to clean up the meeting room and set up chairs and stuff. He said there was going to be a special meeting tonight to decide if they want you to be the real minister."

Christmas Treasures

Isabel was surprised—shocked, actually—but she tried not to show it. "I am a real minister. How much realer can I get?"

"You know what I mean. They want to hire you. Do ministers get hired? You get paid, don't you?"

"I get a salary, a small one. But I get called, not hired. It's just a term that's used. The congregation has to take a vote and decide if they want to offer me the position," she tried to explain.

"Like an election or something?"

"Exactly. Majority rules. This church is run as a democracy. The congregation hires and fires. Ministers aren't assigned. We don't have much hierarchy. We're descended from the Pilgrims."

"I get it. Religious freedom and all that stuff."

"Right, all that stuff," she agreed. "Speaking of history, how did your tests go last week?"

"I did all right. In most of the classes," he clarified "My dad said if I didn't get a B+ average, I couldn't come here after school anymore."

Isabel was surprised to hear that, mostly because it set up Max's visits to the church as some sort of reward instead of a punishment. Did his father object to his coming here? Isabel wondered about that now, in light of their lively theological discussion.

She had expected to hear from Jacob and even to make plans to see him again, but there had been only one or two e-mails about when Max would come to work and when he would be picked up. She had thought Jacob might ask to see her again, but it hadn't even been a full week since their lunch, and he may have been busy with the end of the term at the college. She tried not to think about it too much. Though she had to admit, even if only to herself, that she did wonder.

She decided not to ask about his father's new rule, feeling it was none of her business and would only make the boy defensive.

"Your work in the sanctuary is just about finished," she pointed out. "Do you still want to come work here once the repairs are done?"

"Yeah . . . I guess so," he answered casually. "I like hanging out with Carl. He can fix anything."

"Just about," she agreed. "Perhaps in the new year you should be paid for your time. Like a real job."

"Nice. I could use some change."

"I'll look into it for you. And you'd better ask your dad if that would be okay with him."

"Yeah, I will. I don't see how he could complain about it, though. He's been saying I have to get a job this summer so I won't be hanging out all the time." He stood up and took an extra handful of grapes and an apple. "I did mean to come to church this Sunday, but I didn't get up on time."

"Oh, that's all right," Isabel said as if she hadn't even noticed. "We're here every Sunday. Maybe another time. It's up to you, Max. You can come and visit me and work here as long as you like without ever coming to a service."

She kept her tone light. She didn't want him to feel pressured or coerced. She was not that type of minister and never would be.

"Yeah, I know." He was standing in the doorway now and bouncing on the balls of his feet. He looked restless and distracted. Down in the basement, they could hear Carl banging on the pipes.

"That's Carl's signal. He needs me."

Isabel thought it was only a signal of the sexton's persistence— or utter frustration—with his task. But she nodded anyway. "You'd better get down there and help him."

Isabel was soon left to sit and wonder about this news. The church leaders were trying to decide if she should be called. Perhaps they hadn't told her just in case they decided not to for some reason. But, of course, she would find out anyway through the grapevine. Apparently, everyone except her knew. Even Max.

Though Isabel had more or less expected this, it was still a shock. She thought the congregation would wait until the holidays had passed to deal with replacing Reverend Ben. But the truth was that many congregations invited ministers with far less knowledge and familiarity than this congregation had with her. She had been part of the church for nearly a month now, she had worked with them on projects and Christmas preparations, and they had heard several of her sermons. They had even disagreed with her on an important issue and worked it out.

So the audition was over.

She suddenly realized that if they didn't extend an invitation now, she would probably feel hurt and insulted. But did she really want to stay here? Or did she just like the idea of being asked, which was a balm to her ego?

That was the question. One that had been hovering in the background ever since Reverend Ben announced his retirement. But now the question had come swooping down with surprising speed, like a seabird diving for a bite to eat.

She sat at her desk and stared out at the snow-covered village green. She always thought of this room as Reverend Ben's office, even his desk and his chair. His name was still on the door and on the church letterhead.

But it could soon be my name, my desk, my chair. My church, she realized. *Would that be so bad?*

Not at all, her inner voice answered. There were many benefits to being a minister here . . . and many challenges, too. Enough to keep life interesting. More than she ever imagined when she first arrived.

But did she really want to stay? Was that the right path for her at this time in her life? Isabel couldn't say.

Well, they hadn't asked her yet. All this soul-searching was a bit premature. But now that she knew what was going on with all these special meetings, it was impossible not to think about it.

By WEDNESDAY MORNING, BOTH THE TRUSTEES AND THE CHURCH council had met. They had most likely come to their decision, Isabel guessed as she headed over to the church to start her day. But she was no closer to knowing what her answer would be.

As she headed down the long hallway to her office, she saw Tucker waiting on the bench near her door.

"Reverend, may I speak to you a minute?" Tucker said politely.

"Yes, of course. Come on in, Tucker." Isabel unlocked the door and led him inside. She sat behind her desk and flipped open her coffee. Tucker sat in a chair facing her, the cap from his uniform balanced on his knee.

"You probably already know why the trustees and council have called special meetings this week. There aren't many secrets in this church. It's not really a secret, anyway," he explained. "We've been talking about replacing Reverend Ben. The boards have decided that, instead of conducting a big search, we will recommend to the congregation that they vote to call you as our new minister."

Isabel felt a lump the size of a marshmallow in her throat.

"I'm honored, Tucker," she said sincerely. "Thank you very much for that news." She didn't know what else to add. Did he expect her to give him her answer on the spot? She hoped not.

"You don't need to say anything right now. We won't be able to call a meeting of the congregation until after Christmas. But we've set the day: Sunday, January eighth." He shook his head. "Too bad we couldn't figure it all out before the holidays."

He seemed to assume that she would automatically say yes. Isabel smiled politely in reply.

"This is an important question for the church. I don't think it's wise to rush," she said finally.

Tucker stood up and put on his hat, preparing to go. "That's exactly why we want to call you, Reverend. Answers like that. We aren't likely to find another minister of your caliber. That's what I told them, anyway."

His compliment was sincere and touching. All Isabel could do was thank him.

Once Tucker had left and she was alone again, her mind was flooded with the pros and cons of the question.

Tucker had been a great help and support since the day she arrived, and Isabel was very grateful to him. She also knew that if she ended up turning down this invitation, she would disappoint him—along with many other church members she had come to respect and appreciate.

But was this the right place for her? She had looked into returning to mission work. Before coming to Cape Light, she had applied to several ministries to continue the type of work she had done in Haiti. She didn't have to look very far to find need. She applied to ministries as close as Louisiana and Kentucky and farther away in Nicaragua, Guatemala, and even Cambodia. After serving here for what she expected to be a short time, a kind of spiritual rest stop, she had fully intended to move on.

But now she was faced with a choice. A real crossroads. *I must find a ministry at this church appealing in some way,* she realized, *or this choice wouldn't be so hard for me.*

She had to think about this carefully and pray. God would direct her. He always did. If she listened.

But she still wondered if there was anyone at all she could talk to, to help her sort it out. She considered her family and friends, even a few friends in the ministry. But they were all so far away, and it would be hard to describe this place and this congregation. It would be hard to really do it justice, hard for someone who had never been here to understand the pros and cons she was weighing.

One face came to mind. Reverend Ben, of course. She would ask his advice. He was the only one who could really understand. The one who could help her now.

WHEN REGINA CAME HOME ON WEDNESDAY NIGHT, SHE FOUND Richard waiting for her. He was in the kitchen with parts of the old train set spread out on the table.

"You're still up? It's past midnight." She slipped off her coat and hung it on a hook by the door.

"I want these trains to be running around under the tree on Christmas morning. My deadline on this project is getting close."

"It is. I can't believe it. Only two days until Christmas Eve. I have one more party tomorrow night. That's it."

"I bet you're happy about that," he said.

"Oh, the work isn't that bad. I sort of enjoy it. But I am glad it'll be over soon." She filled the kettle with water and set it on the stove. "Do you want some tea?"

"If you're making it. The kids and I baked gingerbread. They wanted to make a house, but it fell down," he admitted with a little laugh. "So we ate it. They saved you a few pieces on that plate near the stove."

Regina was surprised. This was a first. For one thing, Richard was laughing at himself for a failed construction project, even if it had just been a gingerbread house. For another, he'd actually baked with the kids. Richard never took part in Christmas cookie–making. The lure of building must have persuaded him.

"I think I will try a bite," she said. She found the foil-covered plate and nibbled on a crisp fragment. It tasted good, if a little overcooked. "This isn't bad. Maybe I'll try again with the kids on Friday night. It would be a good project for Christmas Eve."

"What can I say? Gingerbread was not covered in my engineering courses. But I'll loan you my hard hat."

Intent on his project, he didn't look up as he spoke. He wore reading glasses and worked with a tiny screwdriver that just about disappeared in his big hands. His hair was messy, and he had a heavy shadow of beard on his cheeks. But something about the way he looked tonight, working so hard on the trains despite being tired, endeared her to him in a way she hadn't felt in a long time.

She turned and finished fixing their tea, wondering at her feelings.

"I got home a little early today, so I tested out this stuff I bought for Brian," he said as he worked. "It wasn't working well and I called that man in Hamilton. Luckily, Brian went over to his friend's house after school. This Mr. Cyrus, who owns the store, came right over with some different pieces and showed me a few tricks to get it running. Can you beat that?"

"That was nice of him." Regina took their tea over to the table and set out milk and sugar.

"He said he was coming this way for an estate sale. But still. I didn't think people had that kind of concern for their customers anymore. Especially in a store like that. These trains are so old, it's hit-or-miss once you put 'em together."

"A lot of people that you meet around here are like that. They go out of their way to help you," she remarked.

"It's an out-of-the-way place. I guess they've learned to help one another, just to survive. It's the kind of small-town life we aren't used to."

That was true, Regina thought, though she felt it was something more. A certain attitude of concern for other people, whether you knew them or not. Sort of a Forrest Gump philosophy: A stranger is just a friend you haven't met yet.

She didn't want to say that to Richard. She thought he might scoff at her. To him, strangers were strangers, and friends were friends.

But maybe he was starting to see things a bit differently after living here?

"Oh . . . something else about that Mr. Cyrus. We were in the living room, looking at the track I put down under the tree, and he saw the little Bible you found. It was out on the side table. He was really taken with it. He looked it over very carefully."

"Really? What did he say about it?"

Richard shrugged. "He asked where we found it and why it was in such good shape. I told him about the plastic wrapping. Then he asked if he could take it with him, to get an idea if it was worth anything."

"Oh. Did you give it to him?"

"I wondered at first if I should trust him. But he gave me a receipt, and if you take a look at that shop, I don't think he's going anyplace real soon." Richard stopped working and turned to gaze at her. "Do you think that was all right? I mean, it's your book. You found it. And you own this house and everything in it," he reminded her.

It wasn't only her house. His name was on the deed, too. But she didn't stop to remind him.

"I don't think we need to worry. How much could it be

worth—a hundred dollars or so? Even those editions he had in his case weren't worth very much. It's more of a family keepsake; that's why I like it. I want to research some of the names on the family tree when I have a chance. There's a historical society in town. I bet they have records about this house and the people who lived here."

Richard grinned, returning his attention to the train set. "I doubt it's worth anything, either. But don't worry, we'll get it back from him. If he doesn't get in touch in a few days, I'll go to the shop after Christmas and talk to him."

Regina felt better knowing Richard would handle the matter. She was so focused on Christmas, the little Bible wasn't high on her list of priorities. She wondered now if she would have even missed it.

"I was out on my lunch break today and found some great presents for Madeline," she told Richard. "A beautiful heart-shaped locket in the Bramble, and I drove up to Newburyport and found some suede boots on sale in a store Molly told me about. They have fringe down the front. That's what she wanted. I hope she likes them."

"I wouldn't worry. You usually pick out things she likes, a lot better than I can lately."

Richard gave a lot of thought to the gifts he chose for Madeline, but he was typically a few years behind her taste. Regina remembered the time he picked out a big pink sweatshirt with a teddy bear on it for her eleventh birthday, which was a gift she would have really liked when she was eight. There was something touching about these out-of-sync gifts. He always thought of Maddy as his little girl.

"I'll mark the packages from both of us," she added, just in case he didn't think she would.

"Okay. Thanks." He glanced at her a moment as he gathered up the train pieces and put everything away in a cardboard box. "I'll mark the trains from both of us, too."

"Everything is set then. I just need to wrap these last two boxes." Regina had been going over to the woodworking shop on her lunch hour and wrapping the boxes. All the gifts were ready to put under the tree. "I think we should spend a quiet night on Christmas Eve. I'll make a nice dinner and we can play games or attempt the gingerbread house again."

"That sounds good. When they go to sleep, I'll go into town and get everything." He paused, holding the carton to his chest. "I think we did a good job, Regina. I think the kids are going to have a great Christmas, a lot better than last year."

"I think so, too. I wasn't sure we would be able to do it," she said honestly. "But where there's a will, there's a way, right?"

"You mean, about buying all the gifts? You did most of that. You worked so hard. You deserve all the credit," he said sincerely.

Regina was surprised at his words. "Not all, but some," she agreed amicably. "I didn't even mean the gifts. They'll love the gifts, I'm sure. But I think they've really enjoyed the fact that we haven't been fighting," she said bluntly. "They enjoyed putting up the tree together and all the things we've done as a family. Peacefully. That's the best gift we've given them."

He nodded. "The clothes and toys will wear out and get put aside. Even the train set," he acknowledged. "But you can't wear out memories, especially good ones."

He sighed and looked down at her. She couldn't tell what he was thinking. Was he wistful about the good times they had shared in their life together, knowing it would soon come to an end? Or had this truce between them given him hope they could somehow find their way back and save their fragile, damaged marriage? She thought he was going to say something more, but instead he turned away, heading for the back door. "I'm going to put this out in the truck. I can finish fixing it tomorrow at the shop. You can go up if you want. I'll lock up down here and turn off the lights."

"All right. Good night, Richard," she said quietly. She turned and headed up to bed.

If Richard hoped for something to change, he wasn't ready to confide in her. Maybe she wasn't ready to hear it.

She had to be honest with herself. She had hopes but didn't want them. Hopes were painful when they failed to materialize. Still, she couldn't help it. You couldn't help who you loved, she once heard someone say. She believed that was true. Underneath all the hurt and disappointment, she still loved Richard. That had to count for something, didn't it?

RICHARD PACKED THE CARTON IN THE BACK OF THE TRUCK AND covered it with a plastic tarp to protect it from any snow or frost—and from Brian's curiosity in the morning, before he headed off for school.

He took a deep breath of the sharp, cold air and stared up at the night sky. It was the color of blue velvet, so dark and deep, and covered with a million stars, tiny pinpoints of light. This place was so remote, the night sky was amazing. He had never seen stars like this unless he was on a camping trip.

His gaze dropped to the old house, and he tallied the repairs he'd done and the ones left to do. He had managed to paint all the shutters and trim, despite the cold weather, and fix the porch steps, front and back. Little things, but they made a big difference, he thought.

The changes inside were coming along well, too. The new paint, refinished wooden doors, and the new molding helped a lot.

The house had good lines and some great detail inside, though much of it had been stripped away or hidden by what he liked to call "ruin-a-vation."

Regina had been right. The house had possibilities, more than he ever thought. By the spring, it could really be something. If he was still living here by then.

A light in an upstairs window went on. Regina was up in their bedroom, getting ready to go to sleep. He pictured her putting on her face cream, brushing out her hair.

The light glowed behind a lace curtain, and he felt a pang of longing. He wished they could go back in time, before all the trouble. Before everything between him and Regina had gotten so messed up and confused. They'd been getting along so well lately, it gave him hope. Until he remembered that they were just acting for the sake of the kids.

When he lost his job, his house, and everything he'd worked for, he'd thought he'd lost everything. But if his family broke up, too . . . that was what really mattered. Richard knew that now. He wished he could find the words to change her mind. But it never seemed to be the right time, and the right words just wouldn't come.

The light went out. He looked away, then headed back inside the dark house, feeling bleak and lonely.

WHEN ISABEL CALLED REVEREND BEN THURSDAY MORNING TO ask if she could see him, he sounded pleased but concerned. "Is everything all right, Isabel? You sound . . . distressed."

"I'm all right, but something has come up. A big decision for me. Tucker Tulley told me that the boards will recommend me to the congregation to be called as their full-time minister."

"Yes, I know. They asked my opinion on the matter. It goes without saying, I was totally in favor. I think this church would be very blessed to have you."

Isabel was overwhelmed by his generous words. It meant so much to hear that from Ben, who must feel some conflict about recommending a successor.

"I think any minister would be blessed to serve here. But . . . I'm not sure if it's right for me," she added.

"I understand. This is hard to talk about over the phone. Do you have any plans for Christmas Eve? Carolyn and I will be spending a quiet night at home. Why don't you come over and have supper with us?"

"I'd like that very much," Isabel answered. They set a time, and when Isabel hung up, she already felt a bit better.

ISABEL WAS BUSY ALL DAY THURSDAY PREPARING FOR THE CHRIST-mas service—proofreading the bulletin, writing her sermon, and watching over all the tiny details of a special service: the flowers and candles and music.

Last but not least, she walked into the sanctuary late in the afternoon. Carl and Max were there, putting the finishing touches on a huge display of red and white poinsettias right in front of the altar.

"That looks beautiful. What a terrific job you've done," she said sincerely.

"Same as we do every year," Carl replied in his low, laconic tone. "It's this nice metal rack that does all the work; sets them up all even."

"Whatever your trick, it looks perfect."

Max smiled and stepped back. She could see he was pleased with their accomplishment.

"The sanctuary is gleaming. No sign at all that it was recently a shambles," she added quietly, meeting Max's eye.

"Just keeping my side of the bargain," Max mumbled.

"Yeah, and you put your shoulder into it," Carl confirmed.

Isabel could see Carl's approval meant a lot to Max.

"My dad said I could keep working here . . . if you want me." The boy looked from Carl to Isabel, then back to the old man.

"What do you say, Carl?" Isabel asked. "Do you still need a helper?"

"If he's trained and minds me," Carl replied.

Isabel smiled at Max. "Looks like you're officially hired. I asked the trustees, and Mr. Oakes said the church can offer a small hourly wage." She named the figure and saw Max smile.

"That's great! I can't wait to get paid. I used almost all my savings on Christmas presents," he added.

"Oh, did you do some shopping this year?" So Max was thoughtful and mature enough to buy presents. That was good to know, especially when it seemed that his father might take little notice of Christmas.

"Sure, I did. I got stuff for my dad and my grandparents, and my aunt, uncle, and cousins. We'll be with them on Christmas Eve. I got something for you, too," he added quickly. "When can I bring it here?"

Isabel had gotten Max a gift, too. "How about tomorrow, on Christmas Eve?"

"I have to go out with my dad."

"Oh . . . well . . . maybe after Christmas then. That would be fine with me." She was about to ask if he would come to church on Christmas Day, then decided not to. He hadn't mentioned it, and it seemed pushy for her to make the suggestion.

"Sure. Whatever." He shook his head. She wasn't sure if he was embarrassed or felt a little miffed at her, thinking she didn't care that much about his present.

"You can bring it any time. I'll be around the church a lot the next few days."

"Sure. I know." He pulled his phone from his back pocket and checked the text. "My dad is waiting for me."

"Sure. See you soon. And if I don't see you before Saturday, Merry Christmas."

She smiled into his eyes, wishing she could give him a hug. But he slung his pack on his shoulder and shrunk away.

"Oh, yeah . . . Merry Christmas. Merry Christmas, Carl," he called to the sexton.

Carl stood in the doorway of the sacristy, on the hunt for more candles. "Merry Christmas, boy. See you in the new year."

Isabel hoped she would see the boy soon. Max waved as he headed out to meet his father.

She returned to her office to close her computer and gather her belongings. She was about to shut off her e-mail account when a new message caught her attention.

It was from a mission in Nicaragua, where she had applied months ago. Finally, an answer. She clicked it open with her eyes squeezed shut. She almost couldn't bear to see what it said.

The note was short and to the point. A post had opened matching her skills and experience. They would be happy to have her, and she could start immediately. Was she still available for the post? The head of the mission, Reverend Malcolm Buckley, had signed it himself.

Isabel's mouth hung open in astonishment. She stared at the note, unable to believe that now, of all times, she would receive this letter and be faced with such a difficult choice. As if her decision to stay or leave Cape Light wasn't confusing enough.

The Lord never gives you a heavier burden than you can carry, she reminded herself. *Though He does expect you to build a few new muscles as you tote it along.*

Chapter Fourteen

 ⌒◟

*S*NOW HAD JUST BEGUN TO FALL AS ISABEL DROVE ACROSS town to the parsonage. Isabel hoped that it wouldn't pile up too much and make it daunting for people to come out tomorrow to church. But a fresh coat was welcome, making the world clean and new again, quite in keeping with the real meaning of Christmas, she thought. A new life. A fresh start. A clean slate.

All in the form of a tiny baby.

She had been so rattled by the events of the week—first the offer to be the minister here, then the e-mail from Nicaragua— that she'd hardly worked on her Christmas sermon. She had a rough draft, of course, but she would definitely make this an early night and have some time later, when she got back to her room, for the editing and polishing.

The truth was, she felt too much static in her mind right now to think clearly and focus on her writing. A good talk with Ben should help clear that up.

The parsonage looked very charming, dusted with snow. A large wreath decorated the front door and the bay window glowed with the warm lights within, framing the family's Christmas tree.

"Isabel, so glad you came to see us tonight." Carolyn greeted her warmly at the front door and led her inside. Ben came out of the living room to welcome her, too. He looked very well, she thought. You would never guess he'd had open-heart surgery just a few weeks ago.

"Come right inside and warm up." He led her into the parlor to a seat near the hearth that was roaring with a large fire. A row of stockings hung across the mantel. Isabel saw Ben's and Carolyn's names, but also many others, which she assumed were the names of their children and grandchildren.

"Wow, Santa makes a lot of deliveries here, doesn't he?" She forced a smile, but the sight made her a little homesick.

"Oh yes, he does. I thought as I got older I wouldn't bother with stockings at all. But I was mistaken," Carolyn admitted with a smile. She had brought in a tray of cheese and crackers and a dip with vegetable sticks arranged around it on a plate. Now she handed Isabel a glass of red wine.

"Live and learn," Ben said. "We wouldn't have it any other way. It's the great pleasure of life, watching your children grow up and have children of their own."

"How about your family, Isabel? What do they do for Christmas?" Carolyn asked.

"They usually congregate at my parents' house. I have three older brothers, all married. One stayed in Minnesota, another is in North Dakota, and another is in Portland, but he comes back when he can. And there are loads of nieces of nephews," she added with a laugh. "I seem to be the only real wanderer, though I do get home for Christmas when I can."

"But not this year," Ben noted.

"No, not this year," she acknowledged.

"You must miss them." Carolyn passed her the tray and Isabel took a dab of goat cheese on a cracker.

"I do miss them," Isabel admitted. This was the hardest time of the year for her in that respect. She was otherwise usually very happy in her independent lifestyle. "We talk over the phone a lot and e-mail practically every day. And this year, we're going to have a video chat on our computers so I can join them for a little while at least."

"It is amazing, all these high-tech innovations," Ben said. "When I was young, we used to see predictions about telephones with TV screens and I thought, well, maybe someday, but probably not in my lifetime. Yet here it is. I can't keep up."

"I can hardly manage, either. But I have some good tech support. That boy Max, who's been helping Carl at church, helped me set up the Internet phone program. I couldn't have done it without him."

Carolyn nodded. "How is he doing? Is he still working at the church?"

"He just completed the time he promised. He did a good job, too. Even Carl said so."

"Carl did? Well, that's high praise indeed," Ben agreed.

"He wants to continue working after school as a helper. The trustees have agreed to give him a small wage. I think that was very good of them, considering how they felt when he broke into the church," she noted.

"They've really turned the other cheek," Carolyn said.

"Yes, they have. With a little coaching," Ben added, glancing at

Isabel. "Very admirable. You made the right call there. I think everyone can see that now."

Which brought the conversation back to her relationship with the congregation and the decision now set before her. But Isabel didn't think it was a good time to go into that matter. She could see that Carolyn was just about to serve supper.

"Everything's ready when you are," Carolyn said, walking into the dining room. Isabel saw her add a silver salt and pepper shaker set to the table, which suited the setting of china, crystal, and fine flatware. A beautiful centerpiece of white roses mixed with holly and pine branches decorated the center.

"Oh my goodness! You went to way too much trouble." Isabel followed Carolyn into the kitchen to see if she could help. "Ben said you were having a quiet supper tonight. No fuss."

"Nonsense. We've been wanting to have you over for dinner, and I'm so happy you could come tonight," Carolyn said graciously. "I just hope you like fish—I forgot to ask."

"Yes, I do. Any kind is fine with me. Whatever you made smells delicious," Isabel said honestly. Carolyn had prepared some sort of fish stew with tomatoes and peppers and what appeared to be loads of other vegetables in a fragrant, spicy sauce.

"Good. Because with Ben's heart problem, I really have to watch his diet. I'm specializing in heart-healthy recipes. No more steak and potatoes," she said in a low voice.

"I heard that," he called from the next room. "She's very tough, Isabel. You have no idea. I have fish and salad coming out of my ears . . . and dry popcorn. Totally dry. Lord, help me."

The two women laughed in surprise.

"The heart condition hasn't hurt his hearing any," Isabel observed.

"Not one bit. I think it's actually gotten sharper," Carolyn whispered back conspiratorially.

Isabel enjoyed a wonderful meal and more amusing, interesting conversation. Ben and Carolyn's company totally distracted her from the dilemma that had brought her there in the first place, and also from the pangs of missing her family and memories of her husband.

After coffee and dessert—a low-cholesterol meringue treat that was light and delicious—Isabel helped Carolyn clear the table. But once they reached the kitchen with the first load of dishes, Carolyn shooed her away.

"Thank you for your help. I can handle the rest. I think Ben is waiting to talk to you in his study," she said politely.

Isabel wasn't sure how the couple had communicated this plan, though they did seem so in tune with each other. She had no doubt that a little quirk of the eyebrow or a certain look she never noticed had passed between them at some point during dinner.

Isabel soon found Ben in his lair, a small, comfortable room with dark burgundy walls, many bookcases, and a large desk in one corner by a window. There was also a wood-framed couch, upholstered with a southwestern design. Ben sat in a leather chair. The lighting was subdued and conducive to talking, she noticed as she sat down on the sofa.

Most of all, she felt comfortable with Ben, who had quickly become a friend and someone whom she trusted.

"So," he began, "if you don't mind my curiosity, what are you thinking about becoming our new minister? Have you come to any conclusions?"

"No, not really," she admitted. "Partly because I've been so busy getting ready for tomorrow's service, I haven't had a quiet, still moment to figure out how I really feel about it."

"I understand. Sometimes my mind feels like a snow globe that someone has shaken up, with everything whirling around inside. I have to wait for it all to settle and become clear again. Then I can see what I need to see there."

"That's it exactly," Isabel said. "And now something else has been tossed into the murky mix. A while back, when I was recovering from the operation on my leg in Minnesota, I applied to a mission in Nicaragua. Their initial response was that there were no openings for someone with my skill set. But I just got an e-mail from the director. They have a spot for me now and have invited me to join them."

"Oh . . . I see. That does change the picture radically, doesn't it? Now it's not just a question of whether you want to accept the post as minister of this church." He sat back and was quiet for a moment before saying, "You know, there are some scientists who believe that we make up our minds about choices in a split second. Even life-altering choices like this one. The rest of the thinking-through process is just justifying that gut response," he added with a smile.

"Maybe that's true," Isabel replied. "About those scientists . . . Did they factor prayer into the experiments?"

Ben laughed. "I don't think so. Though that would be an even more interesting experiment in my opinion."

"I have prayed on this, Ben. I do believe God will make the right path clear to me. But in the meantime, I know I have to do some work, too. To sort this out as best I can. The past few weeks at this church have been a real learning experience for me. I think I came with certain expectations and quickly realized that I had made wrong assumptions about a lot of things."

"Really? For instance?" he asked curiously.

"For one thing, that a quiet little church in such a pretty town would be spiritually . . . complacent. The congregation here is anything but. They're extremely caring, so many truly seeking their connection with God. I've been impressed and humbled to see my expectation disproved."

"Your frankness is commendable, Isabel."

"Don't be silly. I don't deserve any credit for admitting that. But you deserve a lot of credit. Your influence all these years has shaped the spiritual nature of this congregation. I really wonder if I would be as strong a spiritual leader as you've been."

"Thank you, but I think you've already shown your mettle in that area. What other expectations did you have?"

"That it would be easier than working in a mission setting. It's more comfortable physically," she acknowledged. "I can take a shower anytime I like and drink clean water and eat nourishing food. I can sit and watch TV with Vera in her cozy living room," she joked.

Ben laughed but didn't interrupt.

"But a minister at a church like this wears so many hats," she continued. "And gives so much to so many. It's not just the sixty-minute service on Sunday. It's the other six days of the week, too. I've loved all that," she quickly added. "And I've really learned a lot these past weeks. In some ways, I think it would be good for me to stay here, to take on a role that challenges me in a different way and doesn't come easily. I know that any minister would be truly blessed to be called to serve this congregation. But I'm torn, because I love the other work, too, and I know I'm good at it."

"I see. That is a difficult choice," he agreed. "It's a choice between two positive paths, though, don't you think? Sometimes, Isabel, it seems to me that there is no perfectly right choice. There are always positives and negatives on any side of a question. But once we make a choice and start down that path in a committed way, we grow into the decision. It's a sort of synergy. The path changes us, and eventually it is the right choice, even though there might be some qualms along the way."

Isabel nodded. "I understand what you're saying. I think that's true. I wasn't that sure about going to Haiti when I left the Midwest," she admitted, "but it quickly became the right path. How about you, Ben? How did you decide to retire? Was it mainly because of your health?"

Ben couldn't answer right away. His mind seemed to be having a sudden attack of snow globe. This conversation with Isabel had brought up so many feelings about his own decision to leave the church, and now here she was, asking him that question directly.

"I guess it was a process," he said finally. "For the last few years, Carolyn and I would occasionally touch on the topic of my retiring, but we never really got around to deciding when that would be. I was feeling drained the last year or so, wondering if I was still up to this job, and thinking, well, maybe it's time. Then the heart attack brought everything to a head," he noted. "So . . . it all came together. I'm still getting used to the idea."

"Oh, I can understand that," she said. "You're still a big part of the church, even at a distance."

Ben felt gratified to hear that, even though he knew he really shouldn't.

"Do you have qualms, Ben? Do you have regrets?" she asked pointedly.

He didn't know what to say. "From time to time," he finally admitted. "But that's only natural since it's Christmas, and I really haven't been able to start down my new road yet," he quickly added. "It's still a big transition period for us. It will be, until I'm totally recuperated and we can travel and do some of the things we've talked about."

He tried to sound enthusiastic about those plans. But he was fairly sure he hadn't fooled her. Part of him still longed to be at the pulpit again, or in his office, fielding phone calls, working side by side with the congregation on their many outreach programs.

Isabel nodded. "You can't really enjoy your new life until you're healed and strong again."

"That's just it," Ben agreed. "But I'm getting stronger every day. And I'm hoping for a new fishing pole for Christmas," he joked. "More surf casting is at the very top of my retirement to-do list."

Isabel was silent and Ben wondered if she had her own to-do list, and if returning to mission work was part of it.

"I will tell you this," he went on in a more serious tone. "Whatever choice you make, you must follow your heart—and spirit. If you do decide to leave Cape Light, I know that this church will be missing out on a great minister. I think they all know that, too."

"That's kind of you to say, but if I decide not to take the post, I don't think the congregation will take it all that hard. Not in light of your leaving. You're someone they've practiced their faith with and known for years, who has shared their joy at baptisms and weddings, who has visited and prayed at their sickbeds and blessed their dead, who has been such an intimate part of their lives for so very long. I'm just a blip on the screen."

Ben blinked, feeling his eyes tear up at her poignant description. He quickly took out a handkerchief and pretended to cough. "Yes . . . well . . . I miss them all, too," he confided. "But it's time to make way for someone new. I, for one, will be sorry if you don't stay. But I'll be happy for you, no matter what you decide to do."

"I know you will, Ben," Isabel answered quietly. "Thanks for this talk. It's really helped me."

"I'm glad." *It's helped me, too,* Ben thought. *It's helped me see that I'm not nearly as settled about retiring as I thought. Perhaps I need to talk this through again with Reverend Boland after Christmas.*

Ben and Isabel joined Carolyn, who was sitting in the living room with a cup of tea. A book rested in her lap, but she wasn't reading, just gazing at the fire.

"This has been a wonderful Christmas Eve. Thank you both so much," Isabel said. "I'd better be going. Big day tomorrow."

"One of the biggest," Ben agreed.

"Thanks for coming, Isabel. This is one Christmas Eve that Ben has been able to relax and really enjoy, without worrying about the big service tomorrow," Carolyn said. "I guess we'll see you in church."

"Yes, see you in church," Ben added. *See you up behind the pulpit, where I used to be.* He knew that part would be hard tomorrow. But he would get used to this. What had he told Isabel? A person had to grow into their decision and then it would be the right one.

Ben hoped he could take his own good advice.

"FINALLY." REGINA CREPT DOWN THE STAIRS, CAREFUL TO AVOID the third step from the bottom that creaked loud enough to wake the neighbors. "They're both asleep," she reported to Richard with a sigh. "We can bring the boxes in."

Brian had gone up to bed at a decent hour, with only a few complaints. He was all excited about his gifts and the fresh snow falling outside, but went out like a light. Maddy went to bed later, of course; she usually stayed up reading or listening to her iPod. But when Regina had peeked in, the lights in her daughter's room were off and Maddy was curled on her side, deeply asleep.

"Okay, let's make Christmas," Richard said cheerfully. As Regina reached for her jacket, he stopped her with a hand on her shoulder. "The snow is getting heavier out there. No need for both of us to get wet and cold. I'll bring everything to the door, and you can put it under the tree."

"Oh, all right," Regina agreed. A relay did make sense, and she appreciated his considerate gesture.

The boxes were wrapped in big black trash bags, and also protected by a tarp over the back of the truck. Richard brought them to the door, and Regina removed the bags carefully, so she wouldn't tear the paper or bows or get anything wet with the random bits of snow that seemed to get inside despite their best efforts. By the time Richard carried in the last package, the carton with the train set, she had arranged everything under the tree and was already hanging up the new Christmas stockings she had bought for everyone.

"I wish we had our old stockings, but these aren't so bad." She hooked the loop on the last one and secured it to the mantel. "I found embroidered names for the kids. *Madeline* was not easy."

"They look fine. Very old-fashioned," Richard said. "The kids won't mind, as long as they find good surprises inside."

"Right, it's all about the presents," she agreed. "It will be the usual stuff—chocolates and candy canes, little trucks for Brian, fun socks and hair clips for Maddy . . . Oh, and a flatiron. She really wanted that."

"Is that for your hair?" Richard picked up the appliance and stared at it. "This looks dangerous."

"Not if you use it right." Regina smiled at him. "I'll help her. She'll be okay."

"I guess," he said doubtfully. "Oh, I have something for her stocking, too." He reached into his back pocket and pulled out a gift card. "I couldn't figure out what kind of clothes she likes. She exchanges everything I pick out now. This is for a store she talks about."

Regina smiled. "She'll like shopping for her own gift even better. Great idea."

Richard seemed pleased by her reply. He crouched down to get to work on the train set and gazed into the box with a sigh.

"Do you want some coffee or tea or something?" Regina asked.

"Maybe a little coffee . . . and some cookies? I could use a sugar-and-caffeine boost." He held up two pieces of train track, looking as if he'd never set eyes on them before. "This might take a while. I have a diagram here somewhere . . ."

Richard and his diagrams. Regina was sure he had made a whole stack of them for this project. It was going to be a long night.

"I'll be right back. Maybe I can help."

He glanced at her, surprised by the offer. "Would you? I really could use a hand. I don't want Brian to find me asleep in the middle of the rug and only half these trains set up."

"We won't let that happen," Regina promised. She left for the kitchen to make coffee, feeling uncommonly lighthearted and very much in the Christmas spirit.

The pile of gifts under the tree was a thrilling sight. One that she'd imagined and hoped for . . . but wasn't quite sure would really materialize. It was amazing what you could do if you put your heart into it and kept a positive attitude, she thought. This was something she had wanted so much. Now, here it was, just as she imagined, all coming true.

Except for one thing, she reminded herself as she filled the coffeepot. She and Richard had been united in this effort, but their future was still hazy and uncertain.

Lately they were getting along so much better. That was a miracle in its own right, she thought. Take tonight, for example. Their entire conversation and working together so easily would have been impossible just a few weeks ago. But they'd been able to put aside their grievances for the sake of their common goal: to give the kids a good holiday.

A holiday that would soon be over, and along with it, their truce. She would be sorry to see it go. Couldn't they get along like this all the time and rebuild their good feelings for each other—day by day, all the way into the new year? Was that even possible?

Regina set out some of the homemade Christmas cookies on a small plate. Well, it took two. She knew that much by now. She was willing, she realized. At one time, she really had given up. But here in Cape Light she'd had a change of heart without even realizing it. Did Richard have some glimmers of those same feelings?

If they could get that old toy train set up and running by tomorrow, didn't their marriage stand a chance of getting back on the right track again, too?

CHAPTER FIFTEEN

~

*I*SABEL HAD SERVED AT MANY CHRISTMAS DAY SERVICES, but never as the only minister and never in her own church. This could be her own church, she realized as she joined the robed choir just outside the sanctuary. A very wonderful church it was, too. As she had told Reverend Ben last night, any minister would be blessed to call this church their own.

The choir director marshaled the robed troops, lining them up in proper order. Worshippers were still wandering in, and ushers met them at the sanctuary entrance to help the latecomers find seats, which were very scarce despite the fact that Carl and Max had set up every folding chair in the building behind the standing rows of pews.

Isabel peered through the center doors. The church was packed, brightly lit, beautifully decorated. As the music rose from the organ for the entrance hymn, she could practically feel the Spirit filling her, giving her the energy and clarity of mind to bring God's word to these good people.

She would give a good service this morning, she decided. She would put her heart and soul into it. This wonderful congregation deserved no less.

The choir began to sing the opening hymn, "O Come, All Ye Faithful," and she took her place at the very end of the line, walking in decorously, singing the hymn along with them. They marched to the left side of the church and filed into the risers.

Isabel stood before the altar and picked up her Bible. While the choir sang the last few bars of music, she took a moment to scan the crowd—so many faces that were now familiar to her, so many encouraging smiles and warm gazes. She'd been here barely a month and felt as if she already knew so many of these people, each in a special way. She would be comfortable here, admired and respected, that was for sure. It wasn't one of those churches where the minister toils away, trying to win the congregation over and not always succeeding.

As the choir sang the final verse of the hymn, a certain familiar smile caught her eye. Seated in the last row, dead center, she saw Max, with Jacob beside him. Max looked fresh-faced and excited, his eyes gleaming. As if he were watching a particularly interesting sporting match, with one of his favorite players in the starting lineup.

That would be me, she realized.

He was excited to see her this morning in her role as minister. They'd come to know each other in a different way, more of a student-teacher relationship. More as friends, she hoped.

His enthusiasm was touching. When she met his eye and gently smiled, she almost thought he was about to wave. At the last minute, he nudged his father with his elbow, and then Jacob met her gaze as well. He slowly nodded, as if acknowledging that she had somehow won their argument—or at least an important round, getting him and Max into church on Christmas Day.

Isabel smiled to herself and looked away. The choral voices were hitting a high note, a crescendo at the close of the hymn. A lovely blending of voices . . . and then it was utterly silent.

"Merry Christmas, one and all," she began. "I want to welcome everyone to our service this morning, all the members of the congregation and all of our visitors, too. We'll dispense with the usual announcements today, which are printed in your bulletin.

"Let us quiet and clear our minds and hearts right now as we join together for worship. As if each one of us has been touched by the fresh coat of snow last night, making everything bright and new. So that we can truly hear God's word and celebrate the message and promise of the Christmas miracle."

THE CHURCH THAT REGINA AND HER FAMILY ATTENDED BACK IN Pennsylvania was a bit more conservative than this one. But Molly had persuaded her to bring the family here this morning, and Regina had to say that she had a good feeling. She felt it from the moment she had come through the doors. Everyone was so friendly and relaxed and welcoming. And she knew so many of the members, who were patients of Dr. Harding's or just familiar now from town.

She liked the woman minister, though she had heard that everyone just loved Reverend Ben, the minister who was retiring. He was here, too, she noticed, sitting a few rows away with his wife and family. Molly and Matt had saved seats for Regina's family, which was no small accomplishment. It was nice to sit with someone you knew the first time you came to a church. But Regina realized now that if her family had come in and sat anywhere, the odds were that she would have landed beside someone familiar.

Richard had not been that eager to attend, but he didn't argue with her. She could tell he thought it was good for the children to be reminded that the holiday was about something more than gifts under the tree and good things to eat and school vacation.

Regina thought she would like to join a church again, maybe this one. Even if she and Richard parted, she would bring the children. It would be more important than ever if there was a divorce.

But this morning she was here to give thanks. She had so much to be thankful for, her heart felt ready to burst. She had asked God time and again to help her family, and her prayers had truly been answered. In the few weeks since they had arrived here and moved into the old house, they had begun to recover, financially and emotionally. Regina knew there was a long road ahead, and knew it wouldn't be easy, but she could finally see a way out. She finally had hope again.

Only half-mindful of the prayers the minister was leading, Regina said her own, thanking God again for helping them and adding one for her marriage. *Thank you for a wonderful Christmas morning. Please help us throughout the day to show one another love and respect. And for the future, Lord, please show me and Richard the right thing to do. Help us to do what's best for our children and for ourselves. Please give us the strength and the kindness necessary, so that we don't lash out and hurt each other anymore.*

Richard touched her shoulder, a questioning look in his eyes. She thought for a moment he had read her thoughts, and she could feel herself blushing.

"Could you pass me that hymnal, Gina?" he asked quietly.

Gina nodded, returning from her solitary moment of prayer and handing it over to him. He took the book and opened it for

Brian, who had been sharing with Madeline but now wanted his own.

Regina took her own hymnal and quickly found the page. Everyone had started singing and she hurried to catch up.

REVEREND BEN KNEW ALL THE VERSES TO "O LITTLE TOWN OF Bethlehem" by heart. But he opened his hymnal anyway, just to blend in with the rest of the congregation. He was enjoying this service as a private citizen but in a way, was also feeling almost overwhelmed this morning with the realization that he'd lost his church.

An ordinary Sunday had been hard enough. But this was Christmas. And he was not standing at the front of the sanctuary, leading the worship and prayers, delivering a sermon. He was among the worshippers. There was a big difference between the two. One he'd never really stopped to consider all these long years, standing there, only ten yards or so away from where he now sat. But worlds apart, in another way.

A lifetime apart, he'd go so far as to say.

He swallowed hard, had to stop singing. His vision blurred a bit, and he took out a hanky and dabbed his eyes. Carolyn noticed and gave him a quizzical look. He shook his head, shaking off her concern. "I'm fine," he whispered. "I'm okay."

But he wasn't okay. Not entirely. He was facing something squarely that he had only been dancing around all these long weeks. Something that had jumped up and nipped him last night, when he was talking to Isabel about her decision. He could see that now.

The congregation was about to call Isabel to be their new minister. God bless her and bless her decision in that matter. But whether she stepped in or not—and Ben did believe she would step

THOMAS KINKADE AND KATHERINE SPENCER

in—the place he had left was going to be filled, one way or another. Sooner rather than later.

He had made his choice and life went on. No one was indispensable, no matter how people felt, no matter their loyalty. The church was more than one person. More than a mere minister, certainly. The church was the entire congregation, and they might miss him . . . but they didn't need him to survive. Hadn't he said exactly those words to Tucker a few weeks ago?

Oh, you sounded so humble and self-effacing, he chided himself. *You struck just the right modest note. But you didn't really believe that at the time, did you? You thought this place would actually fall down once you left the helm. You never thought anyone could come in and lead such a wonderful Christmas Day service, that's for sure. Be honest now.*

He nodded to himself just as the hymn was ending. Yes, it was true. He was not sure now if he should have retired after all. He felt one hundred and ten percent better, with more energy than he'd had in many years. He could have done wonders around here with all this fresh get-up-and-go. With his newfound gratitude and appreciation for merely being alive and cherishing every minute of every day. With the film washed from his eyes, he did see the world in a fresh, new way. He had an entirely new vision to share.

If only . . .

It was too late now. He'd made his choice and had to live with it. He only hoped that God, in His wisdom, would show him the right place to invest this newfound wellspring of energy and spirit if he couldn't use it here any longer.

Reverend Isabel had already started the second reading, and Ben turned his full attention to her. He was interested to see which one she'd chosen, though he loved all of the verses about Christmas morning. From today's lectionary, which were the choices of

Scripture assigned to each Sunday and church holiday, Isabel had chosen a reading from Luke 2, verses 1–20. By the time Ben tuned in, she had almost come to the end.

"'And it came to pass as the angels were gone away from them into heaven, the shepherds said to one another, Let us now go even unto Bethlehem, and see this which is come to pass, which the Lord hath made known unto us . . . And when they had seen it, they made known abroad the saying which was told them concerning this child. And all they that heard it wondered at those things which were told them by the shepherds.

"'But Mary kept all these things and pondered them in her heart. And the shepherds returned, glorifying and praising God for all the things that they had heard and seen, as it was told unto them.'"

Isabel closed the Bible and lifted her head. "This is the word of the Lord. Let us hold it in our hearts and in our minds." Then she set the Bible aside and looked out over the rows of expectant faces. Her sermon sat before her on neatly typed pages, though she never read it verbatim. She lightly straightened the sheets, just to ground herself, then took a deep breath and began.

"In this morning's Scripture, we hear about the revelation of the shepherds, who were guarding their flocks and visited by an angel. The angel told them, 'Fear not: for, behold, I bring you good tidings of great joy.' Your Savior is born, he's waiting for you, and you'll find him 'wrapped in swaddling clothes.'

"We all know that there were others who received a sign, a special message from heaven, that the long-awaited miracle, the birth of their Savior, had come to pass. Those others were the three wise men, or the Magi, as they are often called.

"Of all the familiar figures depicted in the crèche scene, these three visitors are perhaps the most well-known and the most fascinating. But who were these men, and why is the story of their revelation and journey an important part of this most important story?" she continued. "Why is their story relevant to us, even to this day?"

Isabel paused. A few of her listeners shifted in their seats; bulletins rustled and babies squirmed and whined. She could hear her own racing heart, beating beneath her cassock, and her face felt suddenly flushed. She still wasn't used to delivering a formal sermon, and knew it was an acquired skill.

Her gaze suddenly fell on Reverend Ben and his deeply interested expression and gentle smile, encouraging her to go on.

"There is not much known about these three men, and only one account in the Bible," she continued. "We find it in the Gospel according to Matthew, who doesn't even tell us specifically that there were *three* men, only that there were three *gifts*—gold, frankincense, and myrrh. In Matthew's account, the visitors are called 'wise men from the East' who came to worship the Christ. 'For we observed his star at its rising and have come to pay him homage,' they said.

"But how did they even know to look for a sign? Where did they come from, and who were they really? While different traditions have different names for them, in Western Christian churches they have commonly been known as Melchior, Caspar or Gaspar, and Balthasar.

"The phrase 'from the East' has been interpreted by most scholars to mean that they were from Babylon. Matthew's version states that the Magi found Jesus by following His star, which has become known as the Star of Bethlehem."

Isabel knew that this was a lot of information and wondered if she was losing her audience. But when she gazed around the sanctuary, most seemed involved in the story.

"Many early Christian writers studied and wrote on this subject," she told them. "But one work called *The Revelation of the Magi*, recently rediscovered by a contemporary Bible scholar, is said to be the firsthand testimony, written by the three wise men themselves. It describes in great detail their feelings and experiences upon sighting the star and their journey to Bethlehem.

"One can only imagine the difficulty of traveling in those days, even a short distance, much less undertaking a trip from one country to another. A biblical scholar at Duke University has worked this out, as well. The distance from Babylon—or Persia, as the area was also called—to Jerusalem was over five hundred miles. It's estimated that it would have taken twenty to fifty days to make that trip, with the travelers covering ten to twenty miles a day, depending on the weather and terrain, and the number in the caravan.

"That great distance would encompass desert and rough, uninhabited terrain—dry, barren stretches, unbearably hot during the day and frigid at night. A journey across mountains and rivers. Long stretches without water or respite at any inhabited place.

"The three wise men must have had a lot of practical concerns— worries about where they were actually going, how long it would take, how much food and water they would need, what sort of dangers would they meet on the way.

"But in a section of their narrative titled 'The Miraculous Journey,' they tell us they simply followed the star, which shone so brilliantly in the sky, they couldn't distinguish between day and night. In doing so, they traveled 'without distress or weariness.'

"Worries about running out of food and water were needless. They related that their provisions were continuously and mysteriously replenished and 'abundant.' When they crossed the dangerous places and faced wild animals, 'we trampled them.' Even the mountains, hills, and rugged places were smooth, and rivers were crossed 'by foot, without fear.'

"And so the Magi eventually found the Christ child in the manger, as their prophecy foretold, and presented their gifts on bended knees. Finally, we are told in the Bible that they were warned in a dream that King Herod intended to kill the child, so they decided to journey home by a different route, rather than return to him as commanded. And that is an important part of the story as well," she noted.

"What does this story mean to us today? How should we interpret and relate this vivid tale to our lives, to our own spiritual journeys?

"For me, the story holds an important message, one that is so central and essential to the miracle and message of Christmas. We're all given the opportunity to follow the star, to seek out God, to view and worship Him face-to-face, if we dare. The brilliant star, the sign that He is waiting for us, is there for all of us to see.

"But like the Magi, we need to take that heavenly sign to heart. To recognize it as a life-changing revelation and make its message a priority in our lives.

"When the wise men saw the star, their account says they rejoiced and 'gave unmeasured thanks to our Father of heavenly majesty that it appeared in our day. And we were thought worthy to see it.'

"Like the Magi, we must give thanks that we've been given this opportunity. We must drop everything in order to embark on this quest, a journey that can be fearful and dangerous. But if we commit to it with faith and trust, our fears and worries will be needless. We will be guided and protected each step of the way. We'll be provided for abundantly, and we will cross the rough roads, the deserts and mountains, and even rivers, without harm or effort."

Isabel stared down at her notes and took a settling breath. She wasn't quite sure how this was going over. Was she making her point clearly? Was her analogy here meaningful and reaching them?

"Lastly, like the Magi, we make the journey bearing gifts. Their hearts were filled with joy as they offered their treasures to the newborn infant. Isn't it true that God has blessed each one of us in some way, with some special gift? So that we can give that gift, the best that we have, back to the world, as an offering to our creator. As a way of giving thanks to our Savior for coming into this world and giving His life for us.

"Once we make that journey, like the Magi, we're forever altered and can never go back the same way," she concluded, emphasizing her words.

"Most of all, the story of the Magi urges us to seek out an intimate, one-on-one relationship with God, to make that a true goal and priority in our lives. And to offer our gifts—our talents, the best that we have inside—in the most meaningful way that we are able.

"In doing so, we all become wise men . . . and wise women. We all can claim a place in the scene at the manger. Each and every one of us steps into that familiar tableau"—she turned and motioned to the crèche that had been set up on the altar—"with a unique and important role in the Christmas miracle."

When Isabel finished, she felt a little as if she were waking up from a dream, or at least had not been fully conscious of the full sanctuary as she was delivering her final thoughts.

She looked around at her listeners. A few nodded and smiled at her. Some sat back with thoughtful expressions. Even Lillian Warwick, wearing a contemplative frown, seemed to have taken the sermon in and was giving it due consideration.

Isabel continued with the service, feeling relieved that she had jumped this very high hurdle. The rest would be easy, she thought. It would pass in the blink of an eye.

It was not quite a blink, but practically, Isabel thought a short time later. At the end of the closing hymn, Isabel stood in front of the communion table. She raised her hand over the congregation and gave the final blessing.

The choir sang a closing introit, a few bars of Handel's *Messiah*—the Hallelujah Chorus, of course. As those beautiful harmonies concluded, Isabel was supposed to walk down the center aisle of the church and wait in the narthex to greet the congregation members. But instead, she lingered at the front of the sanctuary. When the chorus was finished and the pews began to empty, she raised one hand, asking for attention.

"Before you all go, I have a few more words," she said.

There was a questioning murmur. Many were standing and putting on their coats, but they all soon found their seats again and looked up at her with curious expressions.

"I know this is very unusual. But I have a short announcement to make," she began. "It has been my great honor and privilege to serve at this church the last few weeks. I didn't know what to expect when I took the assignment. But whatever I did imagine this place and the members of this church would be like, I could have never imagined the wonderful spirit, warmth, and openhearted community that you have created here.

"Earlier this week Tucker Tulley told me that the congregation is considering calling me to be your full-time minister. When Tucker gave me this news I was . . . overwhelmed," she said honestly. "Any minister would be truly blessed to serve here and call this church their own. At the same time, I've also been offered a position in a mission in Nicaragua, continuing the service I was involved in before coming here. This was a spot that I applied for long before I'd ever heard of Cape Light. Now I wonder if I would have applied for it, had I first come here.

"But the Lord moves in mysterious ways and presented me with a difficult choice. A very difficult choice."

She paused. The sanctuary was utterly quiet, and faces stared back at her expectantly.

"Over the past few days, I've carefully considered this invitation and prayed for God's help and guidance. I've also sought counsel from a very wise man. Not one of the Magi," she quipped, "but very wise, nonetheless." She smiled at Reverend Ben, and he smiled back. Most everyone could guess whom she was talking about.

"I think I do have the answer and want to share it with you all now. At this time in my life, I don't think this church is the right place for me as a minister, despite the fact that I already feel a part of this place, as well as the many, many other reasons I would want to stay here.

"Like the three wise men, I've come to see that my personal journey must take me someplace else at this time. I feel that the best and most meaningful way to offer my gifts to the world—my abilities and experience as a minister—are in a different setting, in the type of mission work I was called to do five years ago. I feel I must go where I'm needed most, and where I can best serve.

"That's why I must respectfully—and gratefully—decline this wonderful invitation. I have been very torn by the choice, and it has been an extremely hard question to sort out. There's no question that part of me wishes I could stay here with all of you. I'll always remember the time I've spent in Cape Light and cherish the wonderful connections I've made here."

Isabel looked around. She didn't know what else to say. She

hadn't really planned her speech, but as the service ended, she felt it was the right time to tell everyone, while they were all in one place. It didn't seem fair to let the entire Christmas week go by with so many under the false impression she was considering the idea of staying.

Also, once she had truly decided, a large part of her just wanted to get it over with. She had made her decision late last night, after her visit to Reverend Ben and after a long talk with her oldest brother, who seemed to know her better than she knew herself sometimes.

Now that the hardest part was over, she really felt she had made the right choice. She would miss all these lovely people and this beautiful place. But she knew in her heart that she belonged elsewhere. She had to go where she was needed most.

Tucker was the first to respond. He stood up from his seat and smiled sadly at her. "I know it's not fair to say, but I feel as if we've lost two great ministers now. One right after the other."

Sam Morgan spoke next. "Reverend Isabel, I guess you've made up your mind. But we appreciate the time you've spent with us and all you've done for the congregation these past few weeks. When will you go?"

"I'm not sure," she said honestly. "They can use me there right away. But I promise to stay until you find a new temporary minister."

She could see that most in the congregation were not happy to hear that. They didn't want a temporary minister; they wanted a permanent one and were disappointed that it wouldn't be her.

While considering what else she could say to soothe them, her gaze fell on Reverend Ben. He was not looking at her, but down at his hands, which were clasped together near his knees. She couldn't tell if he was praying or not. But it did seem as if he was thinking very deeply about something. Something of great concern.

"'And we know that all things work together for good to them that love God, to them who are the called according to *His* purpose,'" Isabel said suddenly, quoting the book of Romans. She gazed around. "I know that's not part of the traditional Christmas Scripture readings, but it seems very appropriate to me at this moment." She couldn't hold back a smile. "I think I know of the perfect replacement for me. I think he's sitting right in this room."

She stared at Reverend Ben, waiting for him to look up at her. Finally, he did.

"Reverend Ben, would you be willing to come back from your retirement to help this congregation?" she asked quietly.

He looked shocked at first, but in the blink of an eye, very pleased. Isabel had guessed that he would be. While talking last night and even once or twice before that, she had gotten the sense that he was not entirely settled with his plan to retire and felt some regrets. Now the look on his face and the gleam in his eyes confirmed it.

He stood up and smoothed down his tie and jacket. "I'd be happy to step in, if the congregation wants me," he replied evenly. He looked around at all of them. As far as Isabel could tell, they were about to break out in cheers. Or at least some thundering applause.

"Reverend Ben, are you really able to come back so soon?" Grace Hegman asked.

"Yes. I could start part-time at first. But my doctor tells me I really am just about fully recovered."

At that, Sophie Potter did stand up and clap her hands. "What a wonderful solution—an answer to our prayers!"

Other voices joined hers with the same joyful note of approval.

"Reverend Ben, we appreciate your offer to fill the gap. But would you ever consider putting off your retirement and coming back for real?" Tucker asked hopefully.

Isabel saw the look of alarm on Carolyn's face and saw her tug on her husband's sleeve. Ben looked down at his wife a moment and patted her shoulder. Then he looked back at the head deacon and the rest of the congregation. Isabel thought you could hear a pin drop.

"To be perfectly honest, Tucker, I would indeed. Sitting here this morning, enjoying this wonderful service, I was asking myself, Ben, why did you ever decide to retreat from this church? There's so much good here . . . and much more work to do. And now you have all the energy, spirit, and passion to take another run at it. If only I could have a second chance, I said to myself . . . And now, by the grace of God, it seems I do."

Isabel was not surprised by his answer. She had seen his strength building week after week, and last night had wondered the same thing. He didn't seem at all a man who was ready or even resigned to retiring.

She also saw Carolyn listening attentively to her husband's reply. Then she sat back and shook her head. Her eyes looked a little watery, but she was smiling, too. She and Ben would have plenty to talk about over the next few days, Isabel was sure, but they were so close and loving, she was just as sure they would work it all out.

Everyone else seemed happily surprised at Reverend Ben's answer. There was no question that this congregation would reinstate him in a heartbeat.

Ben looked up at Isabel. "Reverend Isabel, you are clearly the answer to a prayer, arriving just in time to fill the breach when I fell ill, and also making me see that I am not quite ready to leave my post here, at least not as quickly as I thought."

Digger Hegman, the old fisherman, rose from his seat. "Now we all got the best surprise on Christmas morning we could ever have hoped for. Reverend Ben is our preacher again, and the good reverend has got his church back. If you ever doubt that the good Lord can work wonders, well, you sit back and remember this Christmas morning."

"Well said, Digger." Reverend Isabel had to smile at the old man's eloquence. "I'll always remember this Christmas morning as one filled with miracles. Merry Christmas to everyone! May God bless you and keep you safe from all harm!"

Isabel faced the congregation, happy and relieved. It had been difficult to turn down their invitation, but this last turn of events convinced her even more that she had made the right choice. God had a plan for everyone, and perhaps by following her own deep calling, she had helped Ben to recognize and follow his.

"Thank you, Digger. I do feel as if I've received a very unexpected gift this morning," Reverend Ben said. "A true treasure."

Ben's words were spoken from the heart, and as Carolyn reached up and squeezed his hand, he knew his wife fully understood the huge, impulsive U-turn he'd just made in both of their lives. Understood and accepted that this was what he needed to do right now. He could not have asked for a finer gift on Christmas than Carolyn's understanding and his returning to minister to this beloved congregation. Only now, he valued his place in the lives and hearts of these good people more than ever.

Closing his eyes a moment, he sent up a silent prayer. *Thank you, God, from the bottom of my heart and soul. You truly know what is best for all of us.*

The sanctuary soon emptied. Isabel took her post just past the big wooden doors to exchange a word or two with those who wished to speak to her and wish them a joyful Christmas.

Many of the church members she'd come to know best waited in line to greet her—Sophie Potter, Grace and Digger Hegman, her landlady, Vera Plante, the Tulleys, and Sam Morgan and his family. They all expressed regret that she was leaving Cape Light, but all wished her well and seemed to understand that her decision was the right one after all.

"Personally, I hope Reverend Ben stays here for another twenty years," Sam said. "But when he does decide to really retire, maybe you'll reconsider stepping in as our minister?"

"Oh, I certainly will," Isabel promised sincerely. "Please keep me posted."

"We'll all stay in touch with you, Reverend," Jessica Morgan promised. "We want to know everything you're doing, and I hope our church can support your new ministry in some way. Maybe the church school or the youth group can raise funds or collect supplies in the new year. We could partner with you in some way."

"What a wonderful thought. That would be terrific." The generous offer took Isabel by surprise. But then again, not from this group of generous souls. There were no hard feelings here, which was a great relief to her.

When Reverend Ben stepped up, he simply gave her a hug. "You surprised me this morning, Reverend. I was almost certain you would decide to stay."

"You surprised me, Reverend," she answered with a laugh. "But it seems like we were working together in some way, too."

"In some mysterious way, yes, it does," he agreed with a sparkle in his blue eyes. "Will we see you later at Rachel's?"

"I'm sorry, I'm still not sure," she said honestly. "But I'll decide before I leave church and let her know."

Ben and Carolyn had already invited Isabel to their family gathering at Rachel's house. She had so many invitations for the day, she wasn't sure yet where she would go. Perhaps she would just spend a quiet day on her own. Preparing for Christmas had been hard work, and with this big decision on top of it, she had hardly gotten any sleep. Having a quiet, restful day wouldn't be the worst thing, she thought.

"We understand. Whatever suits you. We'll be there all day, if you just want to drop in for dessert."

"I appreciate that, Ben. Merry Christmas," she said, hugging him again. Then she hugged Carolyn, who stood next in line, and exchanged more good wishes.

The line finally dwindled, and the sanctuary was practically empty. Isabel saw only a few deacons left, collecting discarded programs and extinguishing candles. She was about to head for her office to change out of her robes when she spotted Max and Jacob walking toward her. Max held a brightly wrapped package, and Jacob's offering was a wide, warm smile. Which was more than enough to remind her how much she liked him and how often his image had crossed her mind since their lunch together.

"Merry Christmas, Reverend Isabel," Jacob greeted her. "Max wanted to bring your Christmas gift—and see you lead a service."

"You picked a pretty good one," she said with a laugh. "Lots of unscripted moments. It's not always quite that entertaining."

"It was cool, seeing you up there in your robes and all," Max said sincerely. "Here, I got this for you. Merry Christmas."

"Thank you, Max. That was so thoughtful of you," she said sincerely. "But I won't open it yet. I have a gift for you, too."

"You do?" He seemed surprised but pleased.

"Of course I do. It's right in my office. We should open them together," she suggested.

Isabel had not counted on seeing Max this morning at the service. But she had hoped for it, she had to admit. She had left his gift at the church, just in case.

"Would you like to come to our house today?" Jacob asked. "You and Max can open your gifts by the tree, and you're very welcome to stay for dinner. Unless you already have plans," he quickly added.

Isabel was thrown off balance by the invitation. Even more so, since it had come from Jacob. Max looked surprised, too, but he quickly endorsed his father's offer.

"Yeah, come over to our house," he said. "My father made vegetable lasagna. Weird, right?"

"Vegetable lasagna . . . Gee, that sounds really good. I'd love to join you," she said. "What can I bring?"

"You don't need to bring a thing. We're just happy to have you," Jacob said.

Max nodded happily, bouncing on the balls of his feet. "Thanks. I'm honored to be invited," Isabel said honestly.

Of all the invitations she had received, she couldn't imagine a nicer way to spend the day.

AFTER ALL THE SHOPPING AND WRAPPING AND PREPARATION and anticipation, the day had gone by very quickly. That's the way Christmas was supposed to be, Regina reminded herself. The way it used to be in their family, before they'd had their setbacks.

They had started the day opening gifts. The kids had been delighted with all their presents; neither one had expected so many new things. Brian even got excited over his new ski jacket and waterproof gloves.

It had been doubtful for a while the night before, but Richard had finally gotten the train set up and running, including the steam engine that made a *toot-toot* sound as it rattled past the crossing. Brian had been shocked at first by the sight, then practically jumped on the couch with excitement.

"I guess that means you like it, right?" Richard asked sarcastically. But Regina could see that Brian's reaction made up for all the tedious repairs and lost hours of sleep. All that and more.

Church had been her idea, but the family didn't seem to mind once she managed to pull them away from their piles of presents. Madeline was happy for any excuse to wear her new boots.

Back at home, Regina served a big dinner in the afternoon, and spoke to her parents on the phone. Her parents had a lot of questions about the house and wanted to come visit New England once the weather improved. Regina had to put them off politely, because the future months still seemed unclear. But she was happy to report that the house was coming along and looked so much better now than when they had first moved in.

By the time the evening came, the kids were tired and ready to go upstairs earlier than usual. Brian claimed he had to rest up for tomorrow's skating. The Morgans had stopped them after church and invited them to their house for a skating party the day after Christmas. They had a big pond on their property and held a skating party every year. Apparently half the town would be there, and there would be a winter picnic and hot chocolate and a big bonfire. Of course, they accepted on the spot. Regina thought that even Richard seemed excited about the get-together. Regina had not been up on a pair of skates for decades, but knew she'd have a good time just standing on the sidelines with Jessica and Molly, watching everyone.

She was still cleaning up the kitchen and putting away leftovers when Richard walked in. He had been upstairs, settling Brian into bed. He brought in a platter from the dining room with a few telltale cookie crumbs left on the bottom.

"I hope we finished off the cookies today, Gina. I'm going to gain ten pounds if there are any more of those around the house."

"Just one more container. I'll bring them over to the Morgans' tomorrow," she offered.

"Good idea, though you might want to leave one or two for the kids. Let them down slowly," he advised. "They had a good Christmas," he added. "A great Christmas, I'd say."

"Yes, I think we all did," Regina agreed, turning to him.

He stared at her, his look suddenly intent. A million feelings seemed to flash across his face, yet she couldn't really say she knew what he was thinking.

"We did a good job, Gina. I didn't think we could pull it together. You know me; I get so doubtful sometimes. I get in my own way," he admitted.

She was surprised by this rare admission. "We all get that way sometimes," she said. "It's understandable, especially after the things you've been through."

"Not you. You just keep going down the track. The Little Engine That Could," he teased her.

She smiled and felt her cheeks get warm at the nickname.

"That's not entirely true, but thanks."

"Sure it's true. You never get discouraged. You never give up hope, no matter what. Sometimes I've thought you were just hopelessly naive or just not willing to face reality. But I can see now I was wrong. I never wanted to move here, I never thought it would work out," he said frankly. "I think I just went along to prove something—to finally hit bottom so I could give up and say, 'See, I tried. I went the limit.' And also because there didn't seem to be anything else to do," he admitted.

She sighed. "Yes, I know that."

"But I wasn't looking at things the right way, the way you were—trying to see just a little bit of possibility, a seed, to build on. You proved me wrong. And I'm glad you did," he added. "I'm sorry now for the way I acted, pulling in the opposite direction so much of the time when you were trying so hard to make things better. I know I made it even harder for you. But I was just so . . . so angry at the way things worked out. At the way I failed you and the kids. Angry at myself, really, though I know it didn't seem that way. It seemed like I was mad at you," he admitted. "I'm so, so sorry for that, Regina. Honestly."

For a long moment, Regina couldn't move, could barely breathe. She felt her own heart aching for his pain. She knew how much it had cost him to call himself a failure. Even after all the good things that had happened here, he was still tearing himself apart. At last, she walked over to her husband and rested her hand on his shoulder. But he wouldn't look at her.

"Listen to me," she said, her voice strong and sure. "You never failed us, Richard. I never once felt that way. It wasn't your fault at all. You tried as hard as you could to get us back on track. And you're still trying. I know that."

Finally, he met her gaze. "I did try. But . . . it didn't help very much. I feel as if I let you down, Regina. I didn't protect you and the kids. I didn't provide for you. I lost the house. I lost my job. I lost everything . . . I felt as if you didn't respect me anymore. I didn't deserve your respect, either," he added, "especially when we argued all the time. We both said a lot of hurtful things."

"I'm sorry for that, too. I know I said things that hurt you, things I didn't really mean," she admitted. "We were both disappointed at the way things were turning out for us. Nothing like we planned," she said wistfully. "We let the outside world pull us apart,

Richard. We should have stuck together more and not blamed each other. We both did that and that was really wrong. I'll never act that way again," she promised.

He looked at her curiously. "You mean . . . with me?"

She practically laughed at him. "Of course with you. Who else do you think I mean?" She looked around the kitchen quickly, as if checking to see if there were someone with them she hadn't noticed.

He took a breath and stared down at her. "I mean, are you saying, if we stayed together . . . would you try again, really?"

Regina paused, feeling her own heart racing. Richard was staring at her so intently, she had to look away for a moment.

"Yes, I would," she said finally. "I want to try. I think we could be happy again, I really do. I think these last few weeks have shown me that. We put aside our hurt feelings for the sake of the kids, to give them a good Christmas. But I think we gave each other a special gift, too. I think the past few weeks have shown me that . . . that I still love you and I don't want you to leave me. I don't want to break up our family."

Now Regina was afraid she might start crying. She felt her eyes brimming with tears about to spill over. But she'd said it. She'd had the guts to put it out there.

She tipped her head back to look up at his reaction. He looked completely stunned. His face was unreadable. Then his expression slowly softened and his eyes glowed with a warmth that she hadn't seen in months.

"Oh, Gina . . . I never wanted to go. Not really. I thought you didn't want to be with me anymore. I thought I was holding you back. I don't want to leave you. I don't want to break up our family, either."

Gina strained to hear his words, he was talking so softly. Her heart was suddenly filled to the brim, she felt such utter, unexpected joy.

Richard pulled her close, and they wrapped their arms around each other. "I love you, Gina," he whispered in her hair. "I never, ever stopped."

"I love you, too," she said quietly. "I don't think I ever really stopped, either. It just sort of got buried under a lot of other . . . stuff. Thank you for the best Christmas of my life, Richard. I'll never forget it."

"No, Gina. I'm the one who needs to thank you. Your wonderful loving heart saved me," he whispered. "You saved our family."

Then he turned his head and kissed her, as if it were their very first embrace. But it was actually ever so much better, Regina thought, kissing him back with all her heart and soul.

CHAPTER SIXTEEN

❦

$\mathcal{R}$EGINA FOUND THE MESSAGE ON THE ANSWERING
machine when they came in from the ice skating party
at the Morgans' house. It was only four o'clock, but the sun was
already low in the sky and the temperature had dropped along with
it. Everyone was cold and tired, but very cheerful from the get-
together.

"This is Sylvester Cyrus, from Chestnut Treasures in Hamilton. The toy train man?" he added for clarification. As if anyone
could forget that name, Regina thought.

"I have some information for you about that little Bible, Mr.
Rowan. We must meet right away. Please call me."

Regina exchanged a curious look with Richard. "'We must meet
right away'?" she said, echoing the shopkeeper's command. "What
do you think that's about?"

Richard shrugged and rolled his eyes. "Who knows? He seems a little eccentric. Or didn't you notice?"

"I noticed," Regina replied, smiling. "Why don't you call him? It's not late. Maybe he's still in the shop."

"I hope so. Now I'm curious," Richard admitted. He checked the number and called back.

The shopkeeper answered right away. Regina heard her husband saying, "So Mr. Cyrus, you said you had some information for us about the Bible?" She couldn't tell what the shopkeeper answered as Richard stood there, listening. "Oh . . . all right," her husband said finally. "If you really think that's necessary. Wait, let me check with my wife."

He covered the phone and turned to Regina. "He wants to come over and talk about it. He says it's hard to explain over the phone. We need to see the documentation or something? What should I tell him?"

Regina shrugged. "He can come over tonight if he wants to. We don't have any plans."

Richard nodded, then spoke to Mr. Cyrus again. "You can come this evening. Do you remember where our house is?"

When Richard hung up, she said, "What's the big mystery? Did he give you a clue?"

Richard turned to her. His expression was blank except for his eyes, which seemed to be very wide and startled. "He said that the Bible is a very rare edition. He sent it to an authority on rare books in Washington, DC. But it's too complicated to explain over the phone and he wants to return the book. He doesn't want to be . . . responsible for it."

It was the last part of her husband's reply that caught Regina's attention. "He doesn't?"

Richard shook his head. "Nope. He says it's much too valuable."

"Oh . . . my . . . When is he coming?"

Richard glanced at his watch. "He was about to close his shop and said he'd be here in about half an hour."

"Oh, Richard. Do you think it's really worth something?"

"It's hard to say. I don't want us to get our hopes up too high, but . . . we might as well hope for the best, right?" he added with an optimistic tone that was good to hear, if very unlike him.

"Yes, let's hope for the best," she agreed. Regina headed out to the living room to tidy up. The house was presentable, considering the chaos of Christmas. But she just needed something to do.

A short time later, the knocker sounded on the front door.

Richard opened the door. "Mr. Cyrus, come right in, please."

"Hello, Mr. Rowan, Mrs. Rowan. I closed the shop early and came right over."

"We appreciate that," Regina assured him. "Can I get you anything—coffee or tea?" she offered as she took his coat.

"Nothing at all, thank you. Let's get down to business. I want to tell you about your book. Your Bible."

"Yes, please do. Come right in, make yourself comfortable." Richard led the way into the living room and offered Mr. Cyrus the big armchair near the fireplace.

The old man sat down and started to unpack his briefcase, which held several large hardcover books and also a carefully wrapped packet, swathed in bubble wrap and rubber bands. Regina knew what that was.

"Ever since I made this discovery, I've been bursting to contact you. But I had to wait to have it verified. I didn't want to get everyone all excited over nothing. But, as I told your husband, now I know for sure. It's true. Highly improbable. But true."

"What was improbable, Mr. Cyrus?" Regina asked, with all the patience she could muster.

"Yes, what is it? What did you find out about the book?"

Mr. Cyrus leaned back and swept them with a glance. "The book, as you so casually call it, is an extremely—*extremely*—rare copy of one of the first editions of the Bible ever printed in English in Colonial America. This, sir"—he held out the wrapped packet—"is a first edition of an Aitken Bible, which was printed in a limited quantity primarily for the foot soldiers of the Continental Army to carry into battle. Hence the compact, pocket size," he added, turning the packet to and fro.

He set the packet down in the middle of the coffee table and let out a deep sigh. "Frankly, I hesitate to even touch it. The condition is . . . superb. Unparalleled. There are only two known copies of this edition. And you have discovered a third, in the best condition yet."

Regina and Richard sat together on the old couch, shoulder to shoulder. They turned to look at each other, both wide-eyed with shock.

"Wow . . . that's . . . unbelievable," Regina said. "We were just about to throw that book away. We had absolutely no idea—"

"I didn't even notice it," Richard admitted. "I didn't give it a thought. My wife found it out in the garage. With an old lace handkerchief and a shawl or something."

Mr. Cyrus smiled and nodded. "Some other family keepsakes, probably. You see that a lot in these old houses. The possessions of generations pile up, layer upon layer. Once you start digging, all kinds of things are unearthed."

Richard swallowed hard. "I'll say."

Regina sat back. "This is almost too much to take in at once," she admitted. "Who told you this Bible was that rare kind? What did you call it again?"

"An Aitken edition," Mr. Cyrus reminded her. "I suspected it and checked on the Internet. But I couldn't verify the authenticity myself, of course. I sent it to one of the most respected authorities in the country, at the Library of Congress in Washington, DC. He estimated the value at about two hundred thousand dollars, if you were to sell it to a museum or private collector. You could easily sell it at auction and perhaps get more."

"I'm sorry—did you say two thousand, or two *hundred* thousand?" Regina heard herself stuttering, but couldn't help it. She turned and stared at Richard. His complexion was pale as paper.

"Two *hundred* thousand," Mr. Cyrus said slowly as he smiled. "You see now why I didn't want to hold on to it a minute longer than necessary. You should put this in a safe-deposit box until you know what you want to do about it."

"Definitely," Richard agreed. "For tonight, I might have to put it under my pillow."

Regina picked up the packet that held the book and pressed it between her hands. "I think I heard somewhere that you should hide valuables in the freezer. The refrigerator is fireproof, too."

"Good point. Maybe just for tonight," Richard agreed. "We'll go straight to the bank tomorrow."

"Good plan," Mr. Cyrus said with a laugh. "I have all the information for you here, in this folder. You can contact these antiquarian book experts, and they will make up an official appraisal for you. You'll need that for the insurance. And there's another sheet with the names of museums and auction houses that would be interested. I could help you with that, if you'd like," he offered. "Don't hesitate to call me with any questions."

"We appreciate that, Mr. Cyrus. You've done too much already," Regina said.

"Nonsense. This is the find of a lifetime. I was thrilled to be involved. You can buy an awful lot of antique train sets with that money, Mr. Rowan."

"I can buy an antique train, if I really want to. A real one, I mean," Richard replied. He was still staring into space, blinking rapidly. *He's in shock,* Regina realized. She felt the same. It would take time to process this. To read the paperwork and decide what they should do next.

But the bottom line was, they had been saved by a gift from the blue. A found treasure. A godsend. Call it what you will. Regina thought it was clearly an answer to her prayers.

The funny thing was, money, or the lack of it, didn't seem nearly as important now as it had a few weeks ago. Now that she and Richard were together again. Money couldn't have solved that problem. But now that they had talked out their problems and decided to make their marriage work, this windfall would help them make a fresh start.

She didn't know about buying antique trains, large or small. She *did* know that amount of money would solve all of their financial problems. It was enough for Richard to go back to school for an advanced degree if he wanted, so he could find a new job.

They were free now to start over anywhere.

But Regina had a feeling that they would stay right here, in Cape Light. Where they had already made so many friends and connections. Where, slowly but surely, their lives had begun to move in the right direction.

EPILOGUE

~

*B*EN PULLED BACK THE BEDROOM CURTAIN SUNDAY
morning and blinked at the bright sun. The sky was a
clear, vivid blue with only a few high clouds, and the air outside
already felt warm. It was going to be a perfect day, he thought. A
good one for gardening if he got out there before the heat of the
day, and if Carolyn didn't make too much of a fuss. Even if he
didn't mow the lawn, he could pull a few weeds and clip things
back. The shrub roses and daylilies were already in bloom, the
hydrangea and daisies on their way. All they needed was a little
encouragement.

He had big plans for his garden this year, thinning out the tiger
lily patch and putting in some fresh new perennials and an herb
garden by the back door. He could picture it all in place and how
good it would look by midsummer.

Ben quickly showered and dressed, then headed for the church.

With such fine weather, there would be sparse attendance today. The children had soccer and baseball games, and there were weekend trips for families. But that did not stop Ben from preparing an interesting sermon, whether he was preaching to one congregant or one hundred.

He donned his white cassock and arranged the stole over his shoulders. It was green this time of year, Ordinary Time in the church calendar, for the color of life and new growth. Ben smoothed down the edges of the fabric, feeling as if it was a flag of his spirit. Ever since he had returned from his heart surgery, he'd felt the rush of new energy in his work here. New life, new growth, and he was very thankful for it.

After saying a short prayer, Ben gathered the notes for his sermon and this morning's announcements, with a very special message to the congregation right on top, and headed for the sanctuary.

As he'd guessed, the pews were partly empty this morning, but everyone in attendance seemed cheerful and bright. The sanctuary doors and the doors to the outside had been left open to let in the fresh air and sunlight. As the choir concluded their opening hymn, he took his place at the pulpit and stood quietly for a moment.

Then he smiled at the congregation and said, "I want to welcome everyone who has come to worship on this beautiful Sunday morning. Before we begin the service, I have a few announcements. But before that, I want to share a special message I received, just last night, from Reverend Isabel Lawrence."

"As most of you know, she has been working in a mission down in Nicaragua for the last six months, since leaving Cape Light."

Ben noticed the reactions of the church members, their murmurs and pleased expressions as they sat up to listen.

"Here's what she says: 'Dear Ben, First I'm writing to let the congregation know that we've just received their donations and all the supplies. Wow . . . what an amazing gift! We are so thankful to all of you for making the effort to help us this way.

"'The priority right now is fresh water, and these funds will go a very long way to building a water system in this village.

"'The school supplies are also greatly needed, and the children here are thrilled with every last pencil. They'll write their own thank-you notes soon to the children of the church school. We love the idea of having pen pals up in Cape Light, so please thank Jessica Morgan for that wonderful invitation.'"

Jessica was in church today, and Ben caught her eye. Inviting the children in Isabel's village to be pen friends with the church school students had been an inspiration. He thought of how much both groups of children would learn, and how it would go far toward building a relationship between the church and the village, something he planned to work on, too. Sometime in the near future, he hoped to take a group from the church there for a work visit. An adventure he'd planned for his retirement, he recalled with a secret smile. But why wait?

"'What can I tell you about my life down here?'" he continued from Isabel's letter. "'I suppose most people would say it's hard work, but I honestly don't see it that way. I'm helping in the village, both with the building and in the school. I do feel tired at times, but in a satisfied way. Which makes all the difference in life, I guess.

"'We can see that we're making a great difference in the lives of these families every day, especially the children, who are now growing up with better health and education and a more hopeful future.

"'Please tell the congregation that I miss all my friends there and think of them often. It was very hard to leave Cape Light, but the fact that you were able to return to your church—and I have and will always think of it as yours, Ben—made everything so clear to me.

"'I appreciate your offer to hold another fund drive for us. The church can send the donations from that collection with Jacob and Max Ferguson, who plan to visit in July or August.'"

Ben checked the pews and found Max and his father and smiled at them in acknowledgment. The two had been fairly regularly in attendance ever since Christmas, and Ben knew that they'd kept in close touch with Isabel. He was pleased to see that relationship thriving this summer, too.

"'I'm not sure when I'll be back in the States,'" her note continued, "'but when I do return, I'll be sure to visit all of you. May God watch over you and the entire congregation, and bless all that you do. Much love, Isabel.'"

Ben smiled gently at her closing words, then paused a moment and looked out at the familiar faces. Through the open doors of the sanctuary, he could hear the sounds of birds chirping and children playing on the village green. The sounds of life, in all its richness and fullness.

He felt a sudden rush of gratitude to be here on this summer morning, feeling strong and full of spirit and about to lead worship at the old stone church on the green in Cape Light.

As Isabel had called it, *his* church.

READERS GUIDE FOR

∾

Christmas Treasures

BY THOMAS KINKADE & KATHERINE SPENCER

DISCUSSION QUESTIONS

Please note that some of the questions reveal important plot points. Readers who have not finished the novel may want to stop at this point and return afterward.

1. Do you think being a woman influences the way Isabel ministers to the church? Why do you think the congregation was able to accept Isabel so easily and with so little controversy?
2. Did you sympathize with Richard despite his negative attitude and unwillingness to accept help?
3. When Max gets caught vandalizing the church, he refuses to give his friends' names to Tucker. Do you think Isabel was right not to pressure him on this?
4. Why do you think Carl and Max form such an unlikely bond while working on the church repairs?
5. Max's time at the church begins as a form of punishment, but Jacob eventually starts using it as an incentive for his troubled son. Why does this turn out to be such a positive experience for Max?

6. It is certainly true that the heart attack influenced Ben's decision to retire. What other reasons do you think were as important? Was any other reason more important?

7. Do you think Richard and Regina ever really gave up on each other? Was one more hopeful than the other?

8. How do you think Carolyn really felt about Ben's final decision not to retire? Do you think he was right to make that decision without talking to her first?

9. Why does Isabel find more meaning in mission work than in a church ministry?

10. Do you think Isabel and Jacob's relationship will continue to grow despite Isabel's move to Nicaragua and their differences?

11. On Christmas Day, Isabel delivered a sermon about the three wise men and their journey to see the Christ baby. She tells the congregation that by following "the star, that shone so brilliantly in the sky, [the Magi] couldn't distinguish between day and night. In doing so, they traveled 'without distress or weariness.'" How does this message perfectly embody the spirit of Cape Light and the people who live there?

12. The Bible Regina discovered certainly turned out to be a very valuable "Christmas treasure." What other treasures were discovered throughout the story?

NOTES

NOTES

NOTES

NOTES